ONE WICKED NIGHT

Shayla Black
writing
as
Shelley Bradley

One Wicked Night   Shayla Black

One Wicked Night   Shayla Black

ONE WICKED NIGHT

Shayla Black
writing as
Shelley Bradley

Published by Shelley Bradley
Copyright 2000 Shelley Bradley LLC
Edited by Amy Garvey and Christie Von Ditter

Also from Shayla Black/Shelley Bradley:

EROTIC ROMANCE

The Wicked Lovers Series

Available now:

WICKED TIES

DECADENT

DELICIOUS

SURRENDER TO ME

Coming soon:

BELONG TO ME

"Wicked to Love" novella

MINE TO HOLD

BOUND TO YOU

Sexy Capers Series

Available now:

BOUND AND DETERMINED

STRIP SEARCH

Coming soon:

XXX – HOT IN HANDCUFFS Anthology

NAUGHTY LITTLE SECRET (as Shelley Bradley)

"Watch Me" – SNEAK PEEK Anthology (as Shelley Bradley)

DANGEROUS BOYS AND THEIR TOY

"Her Fantasy Men" – FOUR PLAY Anthology

THEIR VIRGIN CAPTIVE

PARANORMAL ROMANCE

The Doomsday Brethren Series

Available now:

TEMPT ME WITH DARKNESS

"Fated" novella

SEDUCE ME IN SHADOW

POSSESS ME AT MIDNIGHT

"Mated" – HAUNTED BY YOUR TOUCH anthology

ENTICE ME AT TWILIGHT

Coming Soon:

EMBRACE ME AT DAWN

HISTORICAL ROMANCE (as Shelley Bradley)

Available now:

THE LADY AND THE DRAGON

ONE WICKED NIGHT

Coming Soon:

STRICTLY SEDUCTION

STRICTLY FORBIDDEN

CONTEMPORARY ROMANCE (as Shelley Bradley)

Available now:

A PERFECT MATCH

One Wicked Night   Shayla Black

CHAPTER ONE

June, 1816

An air of defeat hung about Serena's husband like a cloak as he rose from her bed. She felt her dream of motherhood die with his sigh of finality.

"Cyrus?" she called, pushing a stray lock of blond hair behind her shoulder with trembling fingers.

He didn't face her, didn't reply, but answered with a tight shake of his head, not breaking the heavy silence between them.

Serena righted her dressing gown about her legs to ward off a sudden chill. What had gone wrong tonight, when he had seemed assured for the first time in months?

Despair clutched at Serena like a tight fist, strangling all hope from her heart as Cyrus retrieved his robe and covered his sagging shoulders.

"Is it my fault? Have I done something to displease you?"

With a diplomat's precision, Cyrus knotted the blue velvet tie around his soft middle and cleared his throat. "The fault lies with me, my dear. I should not have embarrassed either of us again."

Without a backward glance, Cyrus crossed the Aubusson carpet for the door.

Serena leapt from the bed and closed the distance between them. Tentatively, she reached for his hand. "Please, Cyrus. Do not leave. Truly," she placated him, "you did not embarrass me. Come. Let us...try again."

"No." He withdrew from her touch. "It's ludicrous to continue hoping our union will bear fruit. We have been married these three years past, and I have been without the ability since we wed." He looked away in disgust. "Bloody fever."

"It will happen...someday," she insisted, hearing his self-directed rage and mortification. "We must simply be patient."

"My patience is thin. Alastair is behaving as though I've got one foot in the grave, supporting deplorable habits with money he has not yet inherited. I can feel him waiting for rich Uncle Cyrus to die," he sneered.

Serena's troubled gaze touched the furrow on her husband's lined brow, ran over the down-turned mouth which served him so well in his brilliant career in the House of Lords. He was a true statesman, able to smooth out peace between law-making men and ease warring countries toward a truce. She admired him greatly. Why couldn't their comfortable marriage have been blessed with children, as well?

"Alastair is young yet," she offered. "Perhaps he will mature."

"Perhaps, thought I suspect George the Third will regain his sanity first," Cyrus spat. "Alastair is thirty-five. What has he ever accomplished above producing illegitimate children? He has no wife, nor would any suitable woman have him. Responsibility is not a word that haunts his foul vocabulary. How will he manage an estate this size and assume the duties of a dukedom?"

Serena floundered for an answer, her heart aching for him. Alastair *was* interested only in what would please or benefit himself. He would take everything Cyrus had nurtured during the fifty-four years of his life and destroy it with his reckless disregard.

Her husband sighed tiredly. "If only I had someone, even a distant cousin, I could adopt as my heir. But short of selecting someone off the street, I know of no one."

"Cyrus, you mustn't worry so. Your...ability may return. Please, until then, do not dwell on it."

Incredulity sharpened his gaze. "Serena, I have never been incapable of anything in my life. Now that I have a beautiful young wife and have need of an heir…How can I think of anything else?"

Serena felt the need for a child as keenly as Cyrus. As much as she ached to hold a sweet child in her arms, she knew Cyrus needed such a child to protect his heritage. The *ton's* latest scandals often included Alastair. He was an embarrassment to the family. She had no doubt Cyrus's inability to perform his husbandly duty was killing him.

Serena tugged on his hand, urging him to sit beside her on the pale, multi-hued coverlet. Her heart twisted at his defeated expression. "Everything will right itself. You'll see."

Shaking his head, Cyrus raised a spotted hand to stroke her cheek. "You always try to lift my spirits, my dear. It's one of the qualities I adore about you. You deserve so much more from a husband."

"Cyrus, you mustn't say such a thing! You have been a devoted husband, and I care for you very much."

"As you would a favored uncle," he pointed out.

Serena wanted to deny his words, but could not. "Stop this talk. We have tomorrow and every day after."

"This was the last time. You and I both know this consummation will never come to pass. The fever and my gout have seen to that."

Serena bit her lip and looked away, hoping to hide her disappointment. But Cyrus knew her dreams. In the early weeks of their marriage, they had often discussed her impatience for motherhood. Now Serena wished he knew nothing of her longings. He would only use them to torture himself.

He sighed heavily. "You're thinking of children again, are you not?"

Her eyes welled up with moisture as a thick lump of despair stuck in her throat. One traitorous tear, followed by another, slid down her cool cheek. She tried to swipe the drops away before Cyrus saw. Instead, he took her hand in his, then dabbed her tears with the linen sheet.

"I am sorry, more sorry than I can say." His voice cracked with regret. "I know the pressure your grandmother has put on you. I realize how difficult it was to attend your sister's lying-in."

"Grandy only wishes for my happiness, and Catherine's confinement was a joy."

Cyrus frowned. "So you tell me. Caffey informs me you cried all afternoon when you arrived home."

Serena rose, presenting her back to Cyrus. She clenched her teeth, making a mental note to chastise her maid later. "Caffey talks too much."

"But she speaks the truth, my dear, and we both know it." He rose and moved to her side. "Serena, I have debated this issue thoroughly. You know I am a man of logic. And I have come to the conclusion we have only one suitable option."

With an uncertain nibble on her lip, Serena turned to her husband. "What is that?"

The dark eyes usually filled with affection now flashed with conviction as he sent her a grave stare. Prickles of alarm dashed up her spine.

"You must take a lover," he instructed. "Stay with him until you conceive a child."

Incredulity erupted within her, followed closely by a sense of betrayal. Dear God, did Cyrus understand the significance of his request?

Mouth gaping open, she demanded, "How can you suggest such a thing? I—it's adultery!"

He grabbed her shoulders. "Serena, listen to me. It isn't, not exactly," he argued. "I am giving you leave to fulfill your dream of motherhood. Understand that, please."

She wrenched from his embrace, staring at his familiar face in shock. "I stood before an altar in the house of God and vowed to be faithful as long as we both should live, not as long as you wished me to be."

"I would not ask you to take a lover if I doubted this decision was the right one. I need an heir to protect a title and fortune over four hundred years old. And you, my dear, desire a child. At twenty-two, most married ladies have at least one. I alone must bear the blame for that lack."

"Cyrus, you could not have known—"

"I did know," he interrupted. Pinching the bridge of his nose between thumb and finger, Cyrus winced. "Serena, I married you almost certain that I could not...perform. But for some bloody reason, I had convinced myself that a young wife would bring my ability back. It's because of that selfishness you're not a mother. Had you married any other man, you would be bouncing a babe on your knee now, perhaps two."

He had known of this deficiency, yet married her anyway? Serena raised a shaking hand to her gaping mouth, anger beginning to wash over her shock in an icy cascade.

Cyrus eased her hand from her face and into his, then knelt before her. His dark eyes scanned her face with concern. "You must see, I've wasted three years of your life that I cannot give back. All I can do is give you leave to conceive where you may."

The bleak gray of Cyrus's eyes matched the resignation in his stance. Serena's ire dissolved as compassion overtook her heart. After all, Cyrus had more at stake than a dream. Centuries of family pride rested in his hands.

"Our marriage has not been fruitless," she argued. "You've taught me so much about life, people, politics—"

"Yes, yes. But all that aside, you desire a child; I cannot give you one."

His hard-edged tone rattled the tight control governing her emotions. Tears prickled the back of her eyes again. "Think of what you ask me."

"I have, Serena." He nodded, his face austere. "I understand very well what this means."

"Then you know I cannot. You're asking me to compromise myself." She lifted a trembling hand to her throat. "To behave like..." She sighed, then whispered, "My mother."

"Never that," he insisted. "I am asking you to find a man, just one, who can fulfill your dream—and give me an heir."

Shaking her head, she looked at her husband through a blur of tears. "We must trust God. He has a reason for our chastity, and when He deems it appropriate, all will be right between us."

"God has done nothing for us," Cyrus ground out. "By the time He deems our consummation appropriate, I will surely be on the far side of the grave." He grabbed her shoulders and shook gently. "We must take matters into our own hands."

"Cyrus, no. I cannot…"

"Take a lover. You can," he vowed. "You must."

"I-I wouldn't know how."

A smile broke the severity of his scowl. "My dear, you won't have to do anything but acquiesce. If you but give men the slightest encouragement, instead of rebuffing them, they will do everything possible to charm you. You will scarcely need to bat an eyelash to get their attention." He smiled. "Believe me."

Unbelievable. Heady. Scary. "Please don't ask this of me. You know such fast behavior goes against everything I believe. I could not bear to be labeled my mother's daughter in every sense."

"Serena, I understand your fear, but sometimes we must do things we would rather not to further an important cause. You know how I deplore battle, yet I advocated the Peninsular War because I believed in my country and our cause."

"But you weren't asked to shoot the French, just to negotiate peace," she argued.

"I also had to vote for a declaration of war, knowing I would send England into submission or thousands of young men to die. The decision was practical, not emotional."

Serena hung her head, feeling inexplicably betrayed by his request, as if Cyrus were telling her he had a lover instead of asking her to take one herself.

"People would know the child was another man's," she argued.

He stared at her, his eyes reflecting patience. "Not if you were discreet. Women in the *ton* engage in other liaisons frequently, many you've met."

"Who?" she asked, scarcely able to imagine any of her acquaintances indulging in illicit liaisons. She had purposely avoided women like her mother.

"Who is of no consequence. The point is, the practice is not an uncommon one."

"Mimicking others with low morality hardly makes the thing right. To lie in another man's bed and..." She hung her head, disturbed by visions of acts she did not understand. "I doubt I could."

Cyrus took her hand in his. "Darling, you have yet to try. Sometimes a spark will occur between a man and a woman that compels them together. Once you feel that, your fears and resistance will melt away, I vow."

Unlikely. The thought of consummating the unknown acts of the marriage bed even with Cyrus felt tantamount to jumping off a cliff. But to share something so intimate with a stranger and not be anxious or worry people would brand her wanton...Highly unlikely, indeed.

"What of the child's natural father? Certainly he would know who sired your heir."

"You're so wonderfully naive." Cyrus smiled. "It is common for men of the *ton* to have children scattered about. One more should hardly lift a gentleman's brow."

Serena absorbed that unfeeling view with a gasp. One more reason she had held society and its doings at arm's length these years.

Still, the need to have her own child churned within her. More than anything, she wanted to hold her babe, touch its downy head, sing it lullabies each night, feed it milk from her breast...give it her love. And Cyrus needed an heir. The plain truth was, she could not conceive without a healthy man.

She swallowed, wondering if, as with most things, Cyrus was right. "I will consider it."

"My dear, you will not be sorry," he vowed, rising from the floor with a smile. "Get a good night's rest. We leave for town in two days."

"We? You're taking me with you to London?"

"For the rest of the season," he confirmed. "This small corner of Sussex is hardly big enough for you to carry on a discreet affair."

*****

Lucien Clayborne, the fifth Marquess of Daneridge, stood at the edge of the cold grave. He closed his eyes and bunched his fist around a bouquet of spring flowers. The smell of the blossoms and freshly cut grass blended with his grief to swirl a guilty nausea through him. He relished the pain, along with the discomfort of the morning drizzle.

Chelsea had been dead three months, and he had no one to blame but himself. He cursed into the biting wind. Why couldn't he have breathed twenty years of his own worthless life into her precious little body?

Flooded with grief, he sank to his knees, not giving a damn that mud fouled his gray wool trousers. Carefully, he placed the flowers over her grave, next to the others he had brought the day before. Chelsea would have accepted them with one of her bright, guileless smiles.

Lucien cursed heavenward, glad he was insulting the God who had taken Chelsea from him. He wanted that God to feel his anguish. He wanted that God to understand he no longer believed in Him.

Hot tears scalded the back of his eyes. He swallowed back the unmanly show of emotion.

For the thousandth time, he asked himself: Why Chelsea? As usual, no answer came.

His body ached from lack of sleep as he rose. How long before he could pass a whole hour without thinking about her and the knowledge that he had failed her? How much longer would regrets and recriminations taunt him, keeping him awake through the night?

Those torments were no more than he deserved — for the rest of his life. After all, he had been immersed in his much too public divorce and escaping its unpleasantness to notice Chelsea. Consumed with rage and bruised pride, he had spent all his energy shedding Ravenna legally and emotionally, while trying to ignore her indiscreet tryst with Lord Wayland and their flight to Italy.

He had failed to notice his own daughter's confusion or need for affection until it was too late.

Lucien turned away from the grave. As his lonely black carriage traveled up South Audley Street, he watched St. George's burial ground slowly slip from his sight. He made himself a vow: If he ever had another child, he would be a *much* different father.

****

"My dear, Serena! It *is* you," her grandmother said with surprise, rising from the damask-covered Grecian couch. She grasped Serena's hands with her own frail ones. "You look lovely. Why didn't you write to tell me you were planning a trip to London?"

"Grandy, I had no time, and I did not want to come. Cyrus insisted," she explained. "I realize it's early. Have I come at a bad time?"

"Oh, no. Now, you must sit and tell me everything." Her grandmother's face lit up in a beaming smile. "Have you come to town early to prepare for your confinement?"

Serena sighed, bracing herself for her grandmother's disappointment. "No, Grandy."

"Are you doing something to prevent conception?"

Serena stared at her grandmother in astonishment. "Grandy! Of course not. I would hardly know how."

Speculative blue eyes assessed Serena. "Then why aren't you in the family way yet? Your health is not failing, I hope."

Embarrassed by the turn of the conversation, Serena cast her gaze down. "No, things simply have not worked out as Cyrus and I had hoped."

"But you are still trying?"

"Grandy, could we please discuss something else?"

The older woman sighed. "Talk to me, lamb. Your husband is a duke. He needs an heir other than that worthless nephew of his. And I want a great-grandchild from you."

"I am ever aware of that, Grandy," Serena answered patiently.

"When I was your age, I had two children and one on the way. I only stopped conceiving when I started refusing Aldus." Her grandmother's blue eyes narrowed. "Is that your game?"

Serena felt her cheeks heat up. "Grandy! Such indelicate talk is—"

"Warranted in this situation," she interrupted. "Are you barring your door against him?"

"Of course not. I try to be a dutiful wife in all respects."

"You try? Is something wrong between you?"

She looked away, shifting uneasily. "Grandy, this is something Cyrus and I must work out."

"You look unhappy. Are you quarreling?"

Serena shook her head. "No, nothing like that."

Grandy took her hand. "Oh child, you must tell me it's not true."

"What?" Serena whispered, feeling an ominous sweep across her heart.

Her grandmother frowned, her eyes full of displeasure. "The gossip before you two wed was that he had cast aside his mistress of many years because he was no longer...capable."

Cyrus had kept a mistress? Serena shouldn't be surprised, as nearly all men of wealth did. "Capable?"

Her grandmother nodded. "That he is impotent. And I would say Madame Maria ought to know. She bore your husband three daughters."

Serena's mouth fell open in shock as a hot bolt of envy pierced her. Another woman had borne Cyrus's girls, and she, his wife, would never conceive. How unfair!

"Serena, is this true?"

Numbly, she nodded. Here was a whole part of Cyrus's life she knew nothing of. She had never heard of Madame Maria or her children. A thousand questions, along with a well of pain, rose up within her, leaving her raw and aching.

"I knew I should have protested the marriage, but he claimed he was marrying to beget an heir. So, I assumed the rumors were false."

Serena barely heard.

Grandy shook her shoulder, regaining her attention. "Does this have anything to do with your sudden trip to London?"

"Yes." Serena felt a new onslaught of tears and fumbled to produce a handkerchief from her sleeve. She twisted it in her hands. "Cyrus has asked me to take a lover."

Her grandmother quirked one silver brow in disdain. "This is how he intends to get an heir?"

"Yes, and I cannot do it." She paused, fists bunching. "He's asking me to commit adultery."

"Oh, phoo! I could kick your Aunt Constance, rest her soul, for feeding you too much moral rubbish. All those prayer meetings affected your thinking."

"It *is* adultery, even if Cyrus condones it."

"Really, lamb. Don't be so provincial. Such affairs are quite common among the *ton*. Look at my good friend Lady Bessborough. It's quite known she had children by men other than her husband. She has not been ruined at all."

"But I cannot picture myself engaging in—in the same illicit acts that brought Mama such shame."

"Your situations are hardly alike. Having one discreet affair for the sake of conception hardly compares to taking as many lovers as suits your whim and flaunting them."

"But one lover or a hundred, the number should not signify," Serena argued. "It is immoral."

"I agree with your husband; it's also necessary. You can and you must take a lover. It will be good for you to find someone devilishly handsome and let him seduce you."

"But Grandy, to behave as if I've no morals--"

"Let your overstarched morals retire in peace, along with your Aunt Constance. You're too young to bury yourself with her and that old stuffed shirt you call husband. Here in Town, very few people note the doings of a married lady, as long as you're discreet. Besides, I think it's time you followed your heart."

CHAPTER TWO

Gold, red and white oil lanterns burned brightly around Vauxhall Gardens, stinging Serena's eyes beneath her silk mask. A passing couple elbowed her as they jostled past. Another man's braying laugh prompted a staccato pounding in her head.

She didn't want to be at these public gardens. Large gatherings, like the ones she had attended nearly every evening for a week, all seemed so lavish and pointless. Vicious gossip proved their attendees awaited the next scandal with the same anticipation a mongrel stalks its prey. That, coupled with her mother's scandalous reputation, had motivated Serena to accept Cyrus's suit three years ago, just days after her come-out. Marrying quietly had appealed much more than this social ordeal.

But tonight, she had promised Cyrus she would "socialize" with the widowed daughter of a friend. So she turned her concentration to the impending fireworks and ignored her uneasiness, as well as the threat of rain.

A throng of people swirled through the gardens. From the lowliest tradesman to the most respected member of the *ton*, she noted all were dressed for the gala masquerade.

"What do you think of him?" her companion Melanie asked above the strains of a violin, gesturing across the Grove.

Serena looked at the very dull Lord Highbridge, their escort, to see if he had heard Melanie's question. He appeared intent on the orchestra, so she shifted her gaze to the young blond man in question. He looked fashionably bored, as did all the others. She turned to her friend with an indifferent shrug.

"Not that one either? I thought he was quite handsome."

"You think each one is handsome," Serena pointed out.

Melanie shrugged. "I fear I've been by myself too long."

"Are you husband hunting?"

"Perhaps." She cast Serena a sideways glance. "Or perhaps something less permanent."

"A lover?" Serena asked, brow raised in surprise.

With a cryptic lift of her shoulder, Melanie turned away, leaving Serena to wonder if everyone she knew had lost their sensibilities. Or was she, as Grandy had suggested, living to avoid Mama's mistakes by clinging to Aunt Constance's values?

The orchestra stopped playing. With the announcement that Madame Saqui, the French rope dancer, was about to begin her performance, the mass of people around Serena rushed for the fireworks platform. They bumped and shoved, until she found herself crushed against the wall of the Roman amphitheater.

People in the boxes nearby called out bawdy encouragements as a stocky woman dressed in spangles and feathers materialized on the rope. Around her, blue flames burned, giving her a ghostly appearance.

Serena watched, spellbound, as the woman twirled on the suspended rope. Holding her breath, Serena prayed silently for the fearless, leaping woman. The dancer hopped and turned, never losing her balance, never looking down.

Transfixed, Serena never sensed danger until a steel-gripped hand clamped around her wrist and pulled viciously. Pain twisted through her fingertips as she felt a vice-like hand wrap about her elbow and drag her into the bushes.

She screamed. The crowd's gasps of astonishment at the rope dancer's performance overshadowed her cry. Though she bucked and writhed in an attempt to escape, her unseen attacker pushed her to the ground. Her backside met the hard dirt and spindly branches. The abused flesh throbbed in protest. Fear poured over her in an icy stream.

She looked up at her attacker, staring at the dark, masked figure. Light behind him cast the shadow of his menacing stance over her.

She screamed again.

"Shut up," his harsh voice ordered.

To lend backing to his command, he produced a knife from a well-worn black boot. Serena followed the blade's progress from his feet upward, as it sliced toward her. Her assailant thrust the weapon above her left breast, resting its tip against her bare skin. Shock and confusion cut through Serena, terrifying her with a cold stab of dread.

"Please," she begged. "Do not hurt me."

With a grunt, her attacker shoved her to her back and straddled her. Cast in near darkness by the shrubbery, Serena discerned little except that he was large, masked, and dangerous. Her virginal, childless life flashed through her mind's eye.

She pummeled her fists against his chest, twisting for escape. As he increased the pressure of the blade against her skin, her heart beat against her ribs in a frantic rhythm.

The man inched the tip of the knife lower, until it sunk beneath the fabric of her bodice. He cut a small hole in her dress in silent threat. Serena prayed as she never had, even as fear covered her with a sheen of cold sweat.

Outside the bushes, away from her plant-walled horror, the audience gasped then clapped wildly, signaling the end of the rope dancer's performance. Serena screamed again for help.

With his free hand, her assailant clapped his clammy hand over her mouth. "Shut up, or I will kill you."

He pricked her again with his blade in warning, closer to her throat. A drop of hot blood rolled across her skin. Her heart chugged madly. When he lifted his tense hand from her mouth, Serena wanted to scream again, but terror closed her throat.

With a grunt, the man opened her reticule and pocketed her money. He ripped the pearls from her ears and throat before he fit his blade beneath her left glove and sliced upward, leaving a thin, red cut marring the center of her palm.

Again, Serena struggled, kicking, pushing against the man. He shoved her back to the ground.

"Stop it!" he demanded, whipping the blade up to her neck.

Nodding stiffly, Serena watched his fingers close about her wedding ring. Ignoring her cry of distress, he yanked the band past her knuckle, and pocketed the jewelry into a dark waistcoat.

The leaves around them rustled with intrusion and her assailant jerked his gaze up to the sound. Serena held her breath as another man crashed into the clearing. Her attacker rose and whirled to meet the threat of the larger man.

"Did someone scream?" the newcomer mumbled.

The thief raised his knife above his shoulder, the point of the blade aimed menacingly at the second man's chest.

Cursing, the stranger lunged for her armed assailant.

Serena reacted, pushing at the thief's legs with every ounce of her strength. He tripped, sprawling to his knees at her rescuer's feet. The knife dropped to the ground.

The thug scrambled upright and jabbed the second man in the ribs with a vicious elbow, then darted away through the shrubbery. With a grunt, her rescuer fell, clutching his side.

At her assailant's abrupt departure, Serena drew in a deep, jagged breath as relief crashed through her. Incredibly, her ordeal had ended as abruptly as it had begun, thanks to the stranger.

He turned to face her and clasped large, solid hands about her shoulders, eyeing the trail of blood across her collarbone. "How badly did he hurt you?"

Serena's hand automatically lifted to the small cut where her attacker might have ripped out her heart had the whim suited him. The gravity of the attack and the magnitude of what might have happened slammed into her.

No words came forth. Serena opened her mouth as she knelt near the stranger. He eased his arms around her. Breath hitching in her chest as she held back tears, she accepted his solace. Security enveloped her at the feel of his strong arms about her. She pressed her face against his hard chest and let loose a broken sob of relief and latent fright.

"Shhh," her rescuer soothed, hands gliding lightly down her back. "You're safe now."

Serena lifted her head, lifted it a long way, before her grateful eyes found his face. Black velvet masked the upper half of his face, accentuating a strong, square jaw and black, collar-length hair. He, too, looked dangerous, dressed like a highwayman for the masquerade. The imposing width of his shoulders lay barely concealed beneath a dark cape and blocked out all light save that from the full moon. His eyes glittered with danger, their color indiscernible in the near-dark as he probed her face intently. She didn't understand why his stare made her shivery and hot.

Yes, this man was definitely dangerous, in a different sort of manner than the first. She leaned away.

"Come now. I've no wish to hurt you," he murmured.

He lifted his fingers from her back, touching his way up her bare shoulder. A warm flush suffused her skin at his touch.

"Tell me what happened." He helped her to her feet with a steadying arm, until he staggered a moment himself.

Finding her courage and her voice, Serena answered, "I was watching the dancer and he--he pulled me into the bushes. He took my money and jewelry."

"Did you see him well enough to describe him?"

Serena's brow furrowed as she tried to recall. "He seemed taller than average. Ah..." She sighed. "Of average build."

"Did you see the color of his hair or eyes? Notice what he wore?" His voice became crisper with each word.

She shook her head. "He wore a hat. Other than a black waistcoat and breeches, I could see nothing."

"Did you perhaps notice anything odd about him?" he pressed. "Anything about his voice or speech."

Serena looked sightlessly into the night, scanning her memory. Something there tugged and pulled, but she could pinpoint nothing specific. "I'm not certain." She sighed in frustration. "It...I was too frightened."

"Think on it," he suggested. "Perhaps it will come to you."

Her rescuer put a gentle hand beneath her elbow and eased her against his side. Again, she became aware of his height as he towered above her, of his breadth beside her. He could easily protect or harm her, as his mood allowed.

He pushed the shrubbery aside, and they exited. No one around them noticed except a young man in worn workmen's clothing. A sly smile crept across the boy's pale face. Clearly, he thought they had engaged in something illicit. Had the stranger seen the young man's expression, read his thoughts? Serena risked a sideways glance at her rescuer.

He looked down. Met her stare. Catching her first glimpse of him in full light, Serena was ill-prepared for such utter male magnificence. Her breath caught in her throat.

Green. His eyes were green—deep as an ancient forest, as expressive as poetry, as seductive as sin—set deep in a face of hard, classic angles. Serena felt frozen, unable to look away.

His eyes crinkled up at the corners with a smile. "That chap has some interesting ideas about us, it seems."

Blood heated her cheeks—and oddly, her belly. She cleared her throat. "Indeed."

"Let's see if we can find a constable and put an end to this frightful business, shall we?" he suggested.

Serena shook her head, wanting nothing more than the familiar surroundings of home. "'Twould hardly come to any good now. The thief has more than likely fled."

He nodded. "There is that chance, I fear."

Serena gazed down at her shaking hands, at the blood running in rivulets down the fingers of her left one.

Her rescuer peeled away the remnants of her tattered glove and produced a snowy handkerchief from his waistcoat pocket. He pressed the cloth, along with his palm, against hers.

"Are you here with someone?" At her slow nod, his gaze asked what his lips did not: Who?

"I came with friends," she answered. Odd, the way her pulse hammered in her chest the longer she looked at him. Nervously, she smiled. "I shall have to find them."

"I'll help. Clearly, you're not safe alone."

Was she safe with him? Moments ago, she had thought so, but something about him, his powerful, thoroughly male presence, made her unsure. With his hand enveloping hers, security had given way beneath the depth of his green stare to an inexplicable disquiet.

She freed her hand from his grasp and gazed through the crowd, toward the platform where Madame Saqui had taken her last leap. She gazed about frantically for Melanie and Lord Highbridge. They were nowhere in sight.

"Melanie," she called futilely among the crowd. "Melanie!"

Her rescuer whispered beside her, "It's not likely you'll find her among fifteen thousand people, especially if your Melanie is kissing a beau beneath this full moon."

"Kissing?" The startling word struck a warm chord within her.

The corners of her rescuer's full mouth turned up in a slow, smile, showing a flash of white teeth. "You know? Lips pressed against soft lips, exchanging breaths in a sigh. It's a pleasant pastime." He leaned closer. "Do you not agree?"

His tone hinted that he was no longer referring to Melanie. Instead, his voice intimated something more personal. With sudden, shocking clarity, she pictured her rescuer bending to her slowly to cup her cheek in his palm. She imagined his intense stare fixed on her as he drew closer...before brushing her lips tenderly with his own.

She shook her head to clear the improper image. What was wrong with her, indeed with everyone, tonight? She should not be talking to this stranger. True, he had saved her, but what did she really know of him? They had not been properly introduced.

"My thoughts do not dwell on kissing." The crisp comeback she intended sounded more like a whisper. "Thank you for your assistance. Now, excuse me. I must find my friend."

Before she could turn away, he responded with a devilish grin that charged her stomach with heat. "Hmm. Why have you not thought of kissing? Has no man inspired you?"

Until he had crashed through the bushes and flashed those eyes of green fire, no. Such inspiration could only lead to immorality. Yet she felt swept up in his stare.

"No." Uncomfortable with such a realization, she strode toward the Prince's Pavilion in search of Melanie and quick escape. The stranger reached inside her domino and gripped her arm. A shiver snaked up her spine at his touch. A flurry of tingles shot up her arm at the warmth of his fingers.

"I daresay I could only hope to inspire you, lovely lady, half as much as you've inspired me."

His words filled her body with a foreign heat her mind recognized as dangerous. She needed to escape, but turning her back on him seemed impossible.

"I've no wish to be inspired," she said, even as she wondered if this was how her mother had fallen prey to sin. "Thank you again for saving me, sir. I greatly appreciate it, but I must be on my way. Good evening."

Discreetly, she tried to free her arm. He did not release her, but instead leaned closer, until he loomed above her. His glittering gaze held her mesmerized.

"I would rather hear 'good morning' from your sweet lips."

The smell of alcohol, faint and sweet, carried on his breath. She stepped away as much as his firm grip allowed. "You've been consuming spirits."

His raucous laugh resounded. "No, I've been drinking, and I'm well on my way to drunk. Which is a great relief. For the first time in eighty-nine days, I feel nothing." He shrugged, wearing a suggestive smile. "Well, next to nothing."

She frowned. "Why would you want to deny your sentiments?"

His smile faded. "Ever endured the death of a loved one?"

Understanding dawned. Sympathy stirred within her, and though unwanted, her heart ached for her dark, unlikely hero. "I lost my aunt two years ago, and my parents before that."

"Then you know death is a living hell." He tipped his head forward. "My condolences."

Serena closed her eyes, remembering the inconsolable grief she had experienced at Aunt Constance's passing. Only Cyrus's strength and patience had made the time bearable.

"I'm sorry for your loss, as well," she answered. "I remember that bleak time well."

"I shall never forget it."

Serena could think of nothing more to say, not even the traditional platitudes strangers muttered awkwardly in sympathy.

Through the uncomfortable silence, she felt the splatter of a water drop on her face, then another on her arm. She watched several fall on the man's mask before the sky opened wider and rain poured through.

The stranger grabbed her hand and darted for shelter, tugging her along. Together, they hurried to the Prince's Pavilion and found a dry spot inside. Unfortunately, hundreds of other patrons sought the same protection. Serena soon found herself and her uncomfortably wet clothing crushed against the stranger's broad chest.

She met his gaze. Her heart all but stopped at the heat on his masculine face.

"If I had known this would happen, I would have prayed for rain sooner," he whispered, his hot breath caressing her temple.

Ignoring the illogical thrill his words incited, she said, "Step back, if you please."

"Actually, it wouldn't please me. I like where I am."

His voice, like his mask, was velvet—smooth as it glided over her senses. She swallowed hard. "Truly, sir. I cannot breathe."

He inched back. "Better?"

"Very much. Thank you," she answered in her primmest tone.

"You're quite welcome." That naughty grin spread across his face again. "If I can do anything else to please you, pray do not hesitate to let me know."

Another suggestion cloaked in polite chatter. Serena knew she should be offended or afraid. She wasn't for some unknown reason, and that fact confused her.

"I—I truly should go now. It's been a harrowing evening." She risked a peek up at him. The gleam in his eyes sent her breathing into a faster rhythm. "Thank you again, sir, for saving me." Before he could object, she spun away, trying to find a path through the thick crowd.

Immediately, Serena encountered a pair of unkempt sailors. One red-faced, foul-breathed man wrapped his arm about her waist. With a lift of her chin, she stepped back—only to meet her rescuer's chest. He put a possessive hand about her waist, fingers splayed across her abdomen. With a curse, the sailors turned away. The stranger's hand lingered before dropping to his side.

She turned to face him, appreciation for a second, more subtle rescue ready on her tongue. But a flurry of tingles raced over her skin where his hand had been. Without doubt, such a reaction, one that brought back a picture of their imagined kiss so forcefully, was wicked.

Her gratitude caught in her throat as she glimpsed his full mouth tip up in a roguish smile, displaying dimples once again.

"It would seem you're not safe tonight anywhere, except with me." He paused and gazed at her, an expression in those exotic eyes she could only term hungry. "My God, do you realize how beautiful you are?"

His voice caressed her as the stark black of his cape made her doubly cognizant of his captivating eyes. Serena did not know how to respond. The man was somewhat less than a true gentleman, and she really should not talk to him. But she was. She should be frightened of strangers, particularly one with questionable intentions. Without knowing why, she wasn't.

How would it feel to have him for a lover?

The vision of his imaginary kiss lingered. She shoved it to the corners of her mind. She was not her mother and would not engage in illicit thoughts.

"Sir, you should not say such things. I do not know you."

"You may call me Lucien. And you are...?"

"I will not use the Christian name of a man I hardly know. It's most improper."

"I'll make certain you come to know me very well then," he murmured, his eyes lighting up with hot suggestions.

"Perhaps after we've had a proper introduction." Serena backed away anxiously. "For now, I think I should go."

"Not yet." His gaze, silent, imploring, rooted her in place as forcefully as a restraining hand. "Not by half." A frown overtook his features, slashing dark brows downward. "What if your thief is waiting for another moment alone with you? Let me at least help you to find your friends."

His request was simple, one she could have denied. But his point was well taken. She had no wish to suffer another attack.

"P-perhaps you are right. Thank you."

Lucien nodded, his face suddenly relaxed.

In the odd pause that followed, he produced a silver flask, ornately engraved and bejeweled. He unscrewed the cap then drew in a long swallow. Serena stared, wondering why she found this sinner so intriguing.

When he finished, he let out a purely male sigh of pleasure that sent her thoughts—and her pulse—into turmoil. "Drink?"

"You shouldn't consume strong spirits. God will damn those who do," Serena said solemnly.

His deep laughter roared in her ears. "Sweetheart, He's already damned me. A little nip here and there will hardly signify. But thank you for your concern, even if the sentiment is provincial."

There was that word, provincial. She couldn't fathom why everyone insisted on calling her that.

"I am not provincial," she insisted, "merely concerned for my moral health."

"Which means provincial, more or less. Don't be offended," he rushed to say at her frown. "Think of it as a compliment. You're not jaded, and you haven't succumbed to the temptation to cut that gorgeous golden hair."

He reached toward her, fingers outstretched. Her breathing tripped. Serena knew she should stop him, but she remained immobile, transfixed by the rush and tumble of feeling he aroused within her. A strange coil of anticipation built in her belly.

He caught tendrils of her wispy, damp tresses between his fingers. Their gazes collided. Serena felt herself drawn her into the mysterious realm of his stare.

His eyes spoke in carnal whispers, promising pleasure. Overwhelmed by his magnetism, his presence, she stood motionless. She felt so...breathless, so drawn to this rake. He wasn't like the *ton's* other gents she had met and danced with; he was no strutting peacock. This broad-shouldered, narrow-hipped man demanded attention, and not just for his direct speech.

Was God testing her, throwing temptation her way? If so, Serena feared she was failing—just like her mother.

He drew a finger across her cheek. "I would give every cent in my pockets to know the thoughts behind those troubled eyes."

Fearing he could indeed read them, Serena gathered her strength and looked away. She spotted Melanie's purple-turbaned head. But her friend wasn't alone, nor was she with Lord Highbridge. She was with a stranger, and they were kissing, their mouths clinging desperately. She watched Melanie throw her arms around the man's neck, then saw him deepen the kiss. Around them, few people appeared to notice.

"Melanie," she gasped.

Lucien turned and followed her gaze. "Your friend?"

Serena nodded slowly, numbed by shock. Clearly, something had overcome everyone tonight. Even she felt affected.

"She seems to have the idea of it."

Serena turned to him, mouth agape. "They look indecent!"

He grinned. "I'll admit it's not the kind of thing I do in public, but in private...it can be most entertaining."

Wide-eyed, she stared at him. That imaginary kiss arose again in her mind, his fingers touching her cheek, his lips covering hers. If he kissed her as the man was kissing Melanie, she had little doubt she would enjoy it, too much. His shoulders would feel solid and warm beneath her palms. His hands touching her back and shoulders would bring pleasure. Merely imagining it stoked a fire in her belly and snatched a breath from her lungs.

By the saints, she needed to collect her thoughts, which hardly resembled those of the morally upright woman she'd been this morning. But for some reason, after the threat on her life, after meeting Lucien, she felt too off balance to be that woman.

Stung by her body's reactions, she whipped her gaze from his much too handsome face back to Melanie—and was stunned to find both her and her newfound escort heading for the exit.

"Melanie!" Serena shouted above the din of conversation. Instead of turning around, Melanie laughed and tossed her head coquettishly at something her companion said.

"Melanie!" she shouted once more in vain. Seconds later, Melanie, her purple turban, and her mysterious new lover were gone. In disbelief, Serena shook her head. Her head hurt, the rain fell in sheets, and her ride home had departed without her.

The rake stepped in front of her, shaking his head. "What will you do now?"

Serena lifted her gaze, and immediately wanted to wipe the smug grin from his face. "Do? I shall go home."

"How? Did you come in your own carriage?"

"Of course not. I'll hire a sedan chair."

Lucien shook his head. "Not likely."

His language raised her ire. "Why do you say that?"

"Sweetheart, everyone here wishes themselves at home. You cannot imagine you're the only one in need of a ride."

Splendid. Naturally, he had to be right.

"Besides," he added, "it is not likely a driver will stop for a woman alone, because that suggests you are either you a lightskirt or a woman without money." He shrugged casually. "Whatever the case, the driver isn't likely to receive a farthing for his trouble."

Again, he was completely correct, curse him. Serena sighed in frustration.

"Let me take you home," he suggested, his rasp compelling.

She shook her head, scandalized by how a cozy carriage ride with him appealed. "I could not impose. Besides, it's much too improper."

"The only other alternative is to walk."

Alone? At night? Across town?

"Better improper than dangerous, wouldn't you say?" he prompted.

"But—but I—" she stammered. She was too drawn to him by half to be rational in his presence.

"Have you a choice?" He raised a brow lazily in inquiry.

"No." *Drat him.*

He proffered his elbow to her. "Your carriage awaits, my lady."

Serena chewed her lip with worry, quaking inside, before reluctantly accepting his arm.

****

Under the dry protection of Vauxhall's entrance, Lucien waved the emerald-and gold-clad footman away, then handed Serena into a sleek, narrow vehicle. She caught sight of a lozenge on the door, which, like the rest of the carriage, was painted a dark hue that gleamed a glossy black in the cloud-enshrouded moonlight. She peered at the diamond-shaped crest, tried to decipher it, but her dubiously benevolent rescuer touched a hot hand to the small of her back, spurring her into the coach.

He mumbled something to the coachman she did not quite hear. The servant replied with a crisp, "Very good, my lord."

He was a member of the *ton*? Apparently. She shouldn't be terribly surprised. The man had enough bravery—and charm—for a dozen lords. Was he *haut ton*? Or a part of the fast set that overindulged with the Prince Regent at Brighton with revolting regularity?

He settled against the plush wine-dark seat beside her and, after removing his mask, thrust aside his cape and a carved walking cane she had not previously noticed. As he leaned closer and stared, the small coach suddenly felt very small.

He emanated heat, smelled of rain and sultry night air. His bold gaze held hers prisoner. His eyes glittered with forbidden promises of unknown pleasure from which she knew she should turn away. A virtuous woman would do no less.

Her erratic pulse thudded as her breasts tightened beneath the edges of her muslin chemise. A damp heat, an ache, gathered in her nether regions, the cause of which she didn't even want to consider.

The coach jolted forward. She sent a quick prayer upward.

The clippity-clop of the horses' hooves seemed a distant rumble in comparison to his quiet breaths inches away. Tearing her gaze from his, she concentrated on restraining her trembling fingers. She could not fathom what it was about this man that disturbed her so. Or comprehend this foreign reaction that continually brought to mind sinful possibilities.

Out of the corner of her eye, she saw him quirk one dark brow in speculation. She scooted closer to the carriage's side, away from him.

Casually, he draped his arm behind her shoulders, his fingertips toying with the exposed skin at her nape. "How is your hand feeling?"

The warmth of his touch settled across her shoulders, drifted over the back of her sensitive neck, cascaded down her décolletage. She swallowed hard, closing her eyes against the rush of tingles. "The bleeding has stopped."

The corners of his mouth lifted in a warm tilt, his sensual lips surrounded by beguiling dimples. His green eyes gleamed in the near-dark, drawing her in without mercy. "Good news."

Digging her nails into her palms, she struggled to keep the anxiety from her face. She prayed he couldn't hear the *thump* of her beating heart or the churn of thoughts in her head. "Sir, really, you should not...touch me so familiarly."

His dark brows drew together in a frown as he scanned her expression. Her gaze climbed to his with reluctance. Abruptly, he withdrew his touch.

The air's chill surrounded her like a Highland snowstorm. Huddling within the folds of her domino, she told herself it was merely the chilly summer rain.

"I apologize," he said, pulling out his flask once again. "I guess my gentlemanly manners aren't quite the thing."

She watched him take a long, sinful swallow of the liquor. "So I see."

He shrugged. "At least I know how to enjoy life. Can you say the same?"

She had her gardening, her reading, various charities, and Cyrus, who indulged her in all areas of education, even in mathematics and the sciences. "Of course I enjoy life."

"But does it excite you? You hardly seem like a woman who's ever thrown her bonnet over the windmill." His gaze mirrored the challenge in his voice.

He made it sound as if safety was something to be avoided. "Such actions ruin reputations. I prefer knowing I will be received wherever I call."

He laughed at her. The harsh, cynical sound mixed with the vehicle's musty smell to choke her.

"Sweetheart, life can end. Anytime. In an instant—" he snapped his fingers, the sound bursting through the small space like the crack of a whip "—your life can come to an unexpected halt. Did tonight not teach you that?"

In the silence, she realized he spoke the truth.

"If you had died tonight, could you say you did everything you wanted? Or anything so exciting its remembrance would have brought you a smile?" he challenged, leaning closer. "I'll bet you're too busy being cautious, too worried about what the *ton* will think of you."

Serena glanced out the window, noting the rain had dwindled to a drizzling mist. Hadn't she had thoughts of her unfulfilled dream of motherhood a mere hour ago? If she had died tonight, she would have left this earth with regrets. Not for marrying Cyrus. He had been kind and indulgent beyond hope. But oh, how she would regret dying a childless maiden.

She turned back to Lucien. "And what, sir, are you suggesting I do to make my life more interesting?"

"Nothing," he said. His voice dropped to a smooth whisper that caressed her skin like silk. "Except allow me to kiss you."

Coming from anyone else, the suggestion would have stunned her. But not from him. From Lucien, she was rapidly coming to expect the unexpected. So far, nothing about this man had fallen in the realm of her experience. He was brave, implacable, outrageous...and fascinating. She bit her lip, torn between intrigue and indecision.

"And if I allow you to kiss me, that will prove I am capable of leading an exciting life?"

He flashed a pirate's smile, predatory in its pleasantness. "Something like that."

Her heart thudded. "Why should I allow *you* to kiss me, and not someone else?"

His strong hand closed around her fingers. The contact jolted her with tingling energy. Then he turned her hand over, and those same fingers whispered across her damp, sensitive palm. Shivers ran up her arm and down her spine.

"You want me to kiss you," he said quietly.

She shook her head, but couldn't make herself speak the lie.

Then she heard the rustle of his dark evening clothes, the squeak of the carriage seat, as he leaned closer.

With the dim light from the carriage's outside lanterns, she focused on the black ring encircling his unusual green eyes. Sitting this close, she could nearly feel the dark stubble on his square chin and firm jaw. His snowy cravat sat askew after their mad dash to the carriage, exposing the strong column of his neck. She knew an insane urge to press her lips there. His mouth, so full and curved, was one she would have expected on a French courtesan, not an English lord.

Serena felt lightheaded. A desire to touch him that she could not explain rushed through her in a hot, dangerous surge. She had never reacted like this to any man. Why him? She was acting as if her common sense had deserted her.

He trailed a finger from her temple to the corner of her mouth, then paused. Breath suspended, she waited, watching his Adam's apple bob in his throat. Nervously, she swallowed too.

His thumb skimmed her lower lip as he leaned closer still, until their lips lay a breath apart. "You have a beautiful mouth," he whispered. "May I?"

Assuring herself one kiss couldn't be a grievous sin, she nodded.

His mouth descended on hers. At his first touch, heat suffused her. A tingling shock found its way to her mind next, suspending all thought.

His tongue touched her bottom lip, its foreign texture and silky invitation stirring her from immobility. She leaned forward and opened slightly, hesitantly returning the kiss.

Instantly, he leaned into her, on top of her, his palm at the small of her back urging her closer. His mouth opened, parting her lips widely beneath his. Tasting of sweet liquor and heady sensuality, his tongue swept through her mouth boldly. The heat in her belly exploded through the rest of her body. His kiss brought her level of intoxication as high as the alcohol had surely raised his.

He wrapped his other arm around her waist, drawing her closer still. At that moment, she had her first awareness of full male arousal. He pressed the hard length intimately against the mound of her female flesh. She gasped into his kiss. He merely probed deeper, his tongue seductive and determined, encouraging her response.

Curling one of his hands behind her neck, he held her yet closer, giving no quarter. Their kiss deepened, turned urgent. Desire for something she could not understand ripped through her body like liquid fire.

He toyed with the tresses lying against the back of her neck. Wrapping his fingers around them, his palm cradled her head as he continued his thrilling exploration inside her mouth for a long moment. Then he pulled away.

Denial and regret slammed her hard. What must he think? But instead of retreating to the other side of the carriage, he edged closer, nipped at her bottom lip, taking it into his mouth. He sucked on it, returned it, then drew it in once more. With a small moan from her throat, Serena melted into heaven.

Again, he plunged into her mouth, coaxing hers to mate with his. And she discovered rapidly that she liked it. A great deal, in fact. She moaned again.

Suddenly, he returned her moan with one of his own, its low-pitched sounds resonating through her body, causing her breasts to tighten, tingle. A sudden ache to be touched, slowly, thoroughly, by him and his hot, capable hands assailed her.

As if he heard her inner thoughts, he curled his hands around her shoulders, caressed her collarbones...then cupped her breasts.

She gasped at the heat of his touch as his mouth captured hers again. Through the rose silk of her gown, his thumbs swept across the aching nipples, molding her flesh within his grasp.

He lifted his mouth a fraction, panting. "Another kiss?"

Without thought or hesitation, she gasped, "Yes."

Serena met him as their lips collided again. As she had hoped, his tongue scorched back into her mouth. Lucien gripped her sides, his hands sliding down her waist. A moment later, after hearing the rustle of silk, she felt a draft of cool summer air under her skirt—and his hand on her thigh.

She halted, frozen, awash in emotion and uncertainty, even as she realized this was the very thing Cyrus wanted her to do—allow a stranger to seduce her. Yet such an act countered all her beliefs.

But God help her, she wanted this man.

The rough pads of his fingers skimmed deliciously across her knee. His palm drifted up beneath her chemise to cradle her hip. He held her closely, his fingers caressing from her waist, down to her female mound. He caught her response, something between a whimper and a moan, with his mouth.

He worked magic with his touch. Any thoughts she might have had, he burned away with the heat of his onslaught. She clung tighter, her fingers beginning a tentative journey up the surprisingly hard ridges of his chest, to the top of his shoulders, finally to sink into the luxurious thickness of his inky hair.

"That's the way, sweetheart," he whispered, nuzzling her neck, leaving a hot path of tingles where his warm breath caressed her skin.

His voice, foreign and suggestive, dashed her back to reality. Mercy, she was allowing a stranger to touch her in the most familiar ways. His kisses, his touch, were a dark temptation that would lead her down her mother's path to pure sin.

She pushed at his chest. "I hardly think—"

"Do not think, love. Feel," he encouraged, his lips looming closer.

"You said just one kiss," she reminded him.

"Why stop now?"

"I should not be here, not like this."

He clutched her arms. His green eyes, powerful when filled with desire, were doubly potent when filled with desperation. "I need you. You help me to forget. Please," his ragged whisper entreated. "Do not push me away."

His jagged plea stilled her tongue. How many times had she needed a human touch during her times of grief? Too many to count.

On the wings of her silence, his lips blanketed hers again, his tongue penetrating. In seconds, he caught her up in the cyclone of returning desire, whirling her up in its vortex.

His hand returned to her thigh. This time he did not linger to caress the flesh, but parted her legs with a gentle nudge, then sought the core of her femininity.

Cyrus had touched her there once or twice and had roused only embarrassment. Lucien's touch awakened an entirely different emotion. His hands were skilled and determined. Her insides melted.

His fingers whispered across her innermost thighs, his palm cradling her mound, rubbing the sensitive center of her desire. She writhed with an instant, blinding burst of heat.

Slowly, torturously, he pressed his fingers inside her. Without thought of restraint, she gasped, tilting her pelvis up to his hand.

"Oh, yes, you are so sweetly wet," he whispered, his lips an inch from hers, his breath coming hard and fast. "God, I want you."

His mouth covered hers again. His thumb massaged the very bud of her need, his fingers still withdrawing and entering.

Desire poured in from all regions of her body; her head fell back. He held her neck with one palm, arching it up for his mouth.

The ache within her grew to something intense, excruciating, coursing through her like a heated flash flood. It built inside her, eradicating all thoughts, making her feel as if the only living part of her body lay below her waist and above her knees. She heard the soft, mewling sounds coming from her throat, but could not stop them. Mindless to all but his rousing fingers within her, Serena arched against his hand.

The coach jerked to a stop. Vaguely, she heard the footman step down, toward the door enclosing them in privacy. With a curse that burned Serena's ears, Lucien withdrew his pleasure-giving hands and smoothed her skirts in place.

Still aching and disoriented, she hung back.

The footman opened the door, illuminating their intimate cocoon with silvery moonlight. Lucien stepped down and faced her. A roguish smile that held a measure of unexpected tenderness curled his lips upward. "Come inside my house, sweetheart. It will be heaven. I promise."

He held his hand out to her. Serena stared at his palm, broad and warm. Accepting his invitation would lead her down the path to adultery and sin. Rejecting it meant missing the fulfillment her body craved—and more importantly, the child she wanted and the heir Cyrus needed.

Given those choices, and her fever-high need, Serena touched his fingers, then placed her trembling hand in his.

CHAPTER THREE

Serena emerged from the carriage before the gray stone structure of an elegant Hanover Square town house. The rain had all but faded to a haze of wet fog.

Her gaze climbed up Lucien's dark sleeve, past his wide shoulder, to his profile. She studied his straight nose and the inky sideburns hugging his ears. An implacable jaw sat beneath the sculpted splendor of his lips, she noted as her feet carried her closer to his front door. Her body, both inside and out, shook with anxiety, but more with the desire he had aroused, with the craving to know more of his drugging touch.

A moment later, the coach and the footman disappeared. She and the stranger stood alone in the courtyard. Her ears detected his breathing, in harmony with the night's sounds.

She glanced at the town house's towering wall before her. Irrationally, she wished the stranger would guide her there, put her back to that wall, and gift her with more of the hot, wondrous kisses he had given her in the coach. Instead, he led her forward, holding her hand, twining their fingers in a gesture of further intimacy that warmed her.

The door opened before them. A tall, portly servant greeted his master politely. "Good evening, my lord."

"I assume the others have sought the comfort of their beds?"

"Indeed."

"Good. Do the same, Holford, and send my valet on as well. I'll manage out of my own clothes this evening." His voice held a repressed smile.

Holford's eyes never strayed Serena's way, but she knew he noticed her all the same. Heat rushed to her cheeks.

"Would you care for refreshments before you retire?" Holford's voice was both formal and polite.

"Nothing, thank you."

Holford inclined his head forward. "Very good, my lord."

As the butler left, Lucien escorted her into the entrance hall. The contrasting dark and light ceramic tiles of the floor were exceeded in beauty only by a towering white domed entry. Boot heels clicking on the hand-painted tile, Lucien led her past a marble table of obvious Chinese origin.

At the room's rear, through an archway, they mounted a curved staircase. Covered by a resplendent red carpet, it led up to the first floor. Lucien mounted the first step.

Serena hesitated. He looked back at her, saying nothing. His green eyes held a promise of pleasure she found more persuasive than words.

With her decision firmly in mind, she followed.

Lucien ascended with a stiff-kneed gait, leaning on the carved walking stick in his grip with every other step. What had happened that he needed a cane?

"Is your knee well?" she asked him hesitantly.

"As well as this weather allows," he responded without facing her.

"Can I help?"

He turned slowly to face her, his expression stiff. "Does my limp bother you?"

Serena swallowed, certain she had touched upon a sensitive subject. "No, I was merely concerned."

He raised a dark brow. "Thank you, but my injury was a departing gift from the war. There is nothing you can do."

"You served?"

He paused. "Three years in Portugal."

Her gaze roamed his tense profile, taking in his strength. He hadn't shirked his duty to his country or paid another to take his place. He'd been brave and responsible, even though his service had cost him dearly. A new respect dawned within her.

He turned away and began mounting the stairs again. Down a long hall, past a French Rococo pier glass and table, he escorted her to the library. The silence within the small room was complete, seeming to echo off the mahogany bookcases lining the walls on her left and right.

Without a word, he led her to a plush ivory-colored sofa beside the fireplace. On a waist-high marble table rested several decanters. Lucien chose one, poured two glasses of the liquid, and crossed the room to her.

He sat beside her on the sofa, hip to hip, and handed her one of the glasses.

Trembling, Serena raised it to her nose and sniffed alcohol.

"You need a good drink. Go on," he said.

Serena hesitated, watching as Lucien brought his glass to his mouth. He drank, his lips caressing the glass as he drained the liquid in long gulps. When he finished, Lucien set his glass on the table beside him.

His unnerving gaze landed on her. Serena transferred her glass from one hand to the other before lifting it to her lips. Anything to avoid his stare.

She recognized the drink as a light, dry wine; it was the kind of thing Aunt Constance had approved of upon certain occasions. Perhaps this circumstance qualified.

Lucien rose to pour himself another. To calm her reawakening anxiety, Serena took another sip.

She cast her eyes around the library, studying the globe in the floor stand, the ceramic busts within the bookshelves, and the Oriental rug of rust, ivory, and various green hues. All shouted wealth and power, the kind which she had been born and married to. Might this stranger know Cyrus? If so, and she conceived, would Lucien confront Cyrus or, God forbid, the *ton*, about the Warrington "heir's" true sire?

With that alarming thought, she set her glass on the table beside the sofa and rose. "It's getting rather late. Would it be possible for you to see me home now?"

Surprise registered with the lift of his brows. "If that's your wish."

Lucien crossed the floor to stand beside her, leaning on his walking stick with every other step. "I don't mind telling you I'm disappointed. The way you returned my kiss, I thought..." He sighed. "You seemed to want me, too. Was I wrong?"

He certainly believed in direct speech. Serena withdrew her handkerchief and pressed it to her trembling mouth. "W-want you? To do what?"

She could tell by his expression he was suppressing a smile. "To make love to you. What else?" He reached for her hand. "I wanted you the instant you turned those blue eyes on me, sweetheart."

"Oh," she said, clutching the little linen square. What was she supposed to say?

Lucien took a long swallow from his glass before setting it on a cherry secretary. "Your eyes said, 'Touch me—now.' When I did, you ignited."

Serena felt color suffusing her cheeks. "I never intended that. I—it just...happened."

He shook his head. "It happened because we need each other. I think you're as lonely as am I." He wrapped hard, desperate fingers around her shoulders. "Together we can forget, celebrate life."

He wanted to celebrate life. She had followed him here to create it. She still wanted that, but she also wanted him— and knew that she should not. If she stayed, she would commit the sins of the flesh that had gained her mother such notoriety.

"I should go. Besides, I would be ruined if anyone were to—"

"Find out?" he finished for her. "No one need know that you comforted a grieving man, if that's your wish."

He leaned closer, closer, until his lips touched hers. Serena inhaled a ragged breath and tried to remain stiff against his gentle possession. Yet she could find no will to resist. She wanted to know Lucien and his touch, and she craved the results their union could bring. Serena followed him into another intimate kiss that had her toes curling and her breath sawing out of her chest as she melted against him.

"Stay," he whispered as he wrapped his arms about her waist, molding her against the hard wall of his chest. "Please."

Serena's insides turned heavy, fine-tuned by a throb winding its way through her to the intimate center of her body. His hand, with its seeking thumb, sought the sensitive tip of her breast. He rubbed it, creating a delicious friction against her areola, reviving the ache he had produced earlier. Instantly, her nipple hardened for him.

He continued to kiss her, his mouth both clinging and demanding, while massaging the tight bud of her breast between his fingers. And those fingers were pure magic, casting a spell on her ability to reason, melting both muscle and mind into clay to shape as he pleased.

His tongue scorched its way through her mouth like a hot blade, urging her to respond—and not giving up until she did. Hesitantly at first, then more boldly, her tongue soon met his in a wild, abandoned foray.

Lucien left no part of her mouth neglected. He nibbled again on her lower lip, in the manner that had turned her insides to jelly in the carriage. And his hands.... Sweet mercy, those hands seemed to detect her aches, then intensify them. Even now, his palm brushed the juncture of her thighs. Her handkerchief slipped from her grasp to the floor. Before she could stop the sound, Serena moaned.

He lifted his head, breathing ragged, pupils dilated. The need in his eyes, the desire branded on his face, singed her with another wave of want.

Breath unsteady, he cupped her chin. "Stay. Tell me you want me as much as I need you."

What could she say that her traitorous body had not? Between short inhalations, she said, "Certainly you can see..."

"I need to hear that you want to stay," he said. "You're the first person who has touched me at all, in months."

That admission hit like a blow to the stomach. Nobody had touched him for months? Cyrus was very affectionate, despite the fact that their relationship was not physically intimate. Rare was the occasion they met one another in a room and did not share a passing touch or glance. She couldn't imagine Lucien's isolation in having no one.

"Why? You're very handsome." She cast a shy glance to the floor. "Certainly any woman you desire would fall into your arms."

She looked up to see a raw desperation in his green eyes that displayed the depth of his pain. One that tugged on her heartstrings.

With an anguished frown, he shook his head. "No. But please say you're falling into mine, sweetheart. Do not make me release you. Not yet."

Her heart flip-flopped. Everything within her wanted to comfort and reassure him; she was simply that type of person. She knew this situation, indeed this man, was dangerous. But he clearly needed her, and she realized how much she craved that.

To soothe him, she placed her hand against his cheek. He turned his face a fraction to kiss her tender palm.

Sending him a shaky smile, she whispered, "I...I'll stay."

He pulled her forward, clutching her against his chest, his arms wrapped tightly about her. For long moments, he did not move, but simply held her. Moved by his unexpected show of emotion, she cautiously wound her arms about his neck.

She fingered the dark hair that had grown over his collar. At her touch, he arched his neck, sending her fingers through the soft mass of his hair and a whirl of awareness through her body.

"Are you as beautiful inside as you are outside?" His voice was a whisper, but Serena heard it.

Serena swallowed. "I'm human, like everyone. I have faults."

Lucien stroked her cheek, his eyes so bleak and unshielded, Serena swore she could see into his soul. And what a sad soul it was. "Not to me. Not tonight."

He claimed her mouth in another kiss, this one more tender—and desperate—than the others had been. The thorough, gentle contact, accompanied by the caress of his fingers down her spine, made her soften against him in acquiescence.

After the kiss, he reached for her hand, then he led her out of the library, down the shadowy hall. At the end of the corridor, he pushed open the last portal and stepped aside. She brushed him as she passed. The light contact tantalized her as she entered his fire-lit bedroom.

The large, high-ceilinged room had wide floor-to-ceiling windows. The room's sparse but striking decor was done in rich hues of burgundy, deep blue, and cream, but seemed inconsequential surrounding his bed. The gleaming old piece was giant, covered with intricate hand carvings up its massive, cylindrical posters. A powerful mahogany tester, also exquisite in its etching, lay like a ceiling atop those posters.

"It's beautiful," she breathed, staring at his bed.

"It was my parents'. They collected antiquities. This was constructed around 1580 and brought from a castle in Shropshire."

Unable to resist, Serena wrapped her palm around one of the posters, her fingers stroking its carvings.

Lucien walked to an adjoining sitting room and poured liquid into a glass. He returned with a measure of the same wine they had sipped in the library and dipped one finger into the alcoholic liquid before skimming it across her lip. A drop beaded, threatening to run down her chin. Reflexively, her tongue peeked out to catch it. She tasted the wine as it mixed with the intimate tang of his skin. Another ribbon of desire wound through her.

Her gaze caught his an instant before he bent to devour her mouth again. As his tongue penetrated and engaged hers in an impossible-to-resist dance, her emotions whirled within her like autumn leaves on a windy day. Her breath caught in her throat. She clutched his shoulders, hanging on so that her weak knees did not sink to the carpet.

He bent down, his arm reaching behind her legs. In a single sweep, he lifted her and turned, then set her on the massive bed. She felt the soft coverlet beneath her fingertips—and incredulity rushing throughout her. Sweet mercy, whatever he was doing to her, the sensations he roused felt heavenly.

Her resistance to stop him dissolved.

With expectant eyes, she watched him remove her shoes one at a time, kissing each instep as he exposed it. She shivered as he caressed her ankles, fingertips teasing her calves. Up the length of her stockinged leg, his mouth followed his hands. Closing her eyes, Serena opened herself to the tingling sensations he aroused.

"How perfect," he whispered. "The blush of your stockings matches the blush on your cheeks."

Perhaps the wine had made her bold. After all, she had consumed the whole glass in minutes. But she didn't care. This stranger, her rescuer with devilish good looks, seemed straight out of a young girl's dreams, dreams she had put away when she married Cyrus.

Yet more than his appearance drew her. He possessed magnetism and need, a combination that made him nearly impossible to turn away. As his fingertips toyed with the sensitive skin behind her knee, arcing pleasure up her thighs, she acknowledged part of her attraction to him might be the wondrous new desire he had roused within her from the first moment in his arms.

"You are incorrigible." The chastising tone she had planned manifested as a husky whisper instead.

His head snapped up, his gaze zeroing in on her face. "Is that your polite way of saying I'm a cad?"

Serena was charting unfamiliar territory, flirting with a man, playing games that involved both mind and body. She bit her lip, uncertain if the situation called for honesty.

"Would you admit it if I said yes?" she asked uncertainly.

Again, his palms climbed higher, like twin fires scorching their way up the sides of her thighs to cradle her hips. With a single movement, he unplucked one tie securing her stockings.

"I couldn't possibly admit to being a cad. A little difficult, perhaps, and very stubborn. But I have never brought a...new female acquaintance to my home. I don't make a habit of seducing strangers."

Lucien could be lying. But as another of the ties holding her stockings gave way beneath his knowing hands, she refused to believe his words were anything but the truth for the sake of her sanity.

"Why, then, did you make an exception for me?" She swallowed hard as his fingers drifted across her leg, closer to the ache that was becoming impossible to ignore.

A roguish smile lifted the corners of his mouth. "Now that question is an easy one to answer," he replied, slowly rolling one stocking down her thigh. When it came free, he held it up before her gaze then let it drift to the floor. "I only intended to overindulge in strong drink and music tonight," he confided, his speech a bit slurred again. "But when I heard your screams, saw the terror on your face...all I could think of was protecting you. You should not have been alone, prey to criminals like that."

His hands ceased exploring her thighs. Serena's breath quickened as Lucien leaned closer, his mouth nearly brushing hers.

"You shouldn't be alone at all. Ever. I know what being alone is like." His usually smooth voice turned raspy. "It's damned awful."

He kissed her, his hand winding around to her nape, caressing the sensitive curve before his palm smoothed down her back to the first hook of her dress. Between his dexterous fingers, it came undone, as did several others below.

He pushed the sleeve of her gown down, baring the curve of her shoulder. His fingertips whispered down the joining of her neck and shoulder, and a flurry of tingles tumbled over her flesh. "My God, you have beautiful skin."

His voice held something akin to worship. Serena melted into his embrace, his words making her certain, for once, that she was indeed desirable. "Th-thank you."

"You mustn't thank me. I had nothing to do with it. I was merely observing the fact your skin is soft and perfect, so fair, but with a hint of honey that tells me it will taste delicious."

As if to make his point, he planted kisses across her collarbone and drifted across to the top swells of her breasts. He moaned, a deep guttural sound, as his tongue laved her skin.

Serena gasped, thinking his kisses were more intoxicating than the wine she had consumed. Throwing her arms about his neck, she pressed her lips to his, knowing the move was a bold one—and no longer caring. She felt so feminine, so desired, surrounded by Lucien's broad chest and steely arms.

He responded to her kiss with frenzy, his fingers working the remaining fastenings at the back of her gown. Within seconds, he opened them all and wasted no time in freeing her arms from the sleeves. With impatient hands, he pushed her silk bodice around her waist and fixed his gaze below her neck.

Serena followed his stare, and discovered the swells of her breasts, pushed up by the boning of her stays, barely within the confines of her chemise. Did he find such a display vulgar? She wiggled self-consciously, crossing her arms across her chest.

"Oh, sweetheart." His voice was hoarse as he grasped her wrists and drew her stiff arms from her body. "Never hide. You are far too beautiful for that."

He lifted her to her feet. Bending before her, he grasped the hem of her dress and lifted it above her, his hands making tingling contact at her hips, her waist, then a lingering touch on her breasts. He tossed the dress on the floor.

One by one, Lucien tugged on the waist-ties of her petticoats. She trembled as the garments caressed her legs on their way down, before puddling about her feet.

Lucien held out his hand. Serena watched him, his face tense and needy. He clenched his jaw tightly, as if willing self-control. Those green eyes of his, and every emotion within them, were open to her and melted the last of her resistance. They conveyed the hunger of a man too long without sustenance, both physical and emotional.

As she returned his stare, his breathing turned ragged. She swallowed when he reached for her hand, enveloping her palm within his warm, commanding one and urged her to step from the circle of her petticoats.

Silently, he turned her away, and set his fingers to the lacings of her corset. Within seconds, he tossed the stiff-boned garment from her body.

His hands smoothed the wrinkled linen of her chemise, stroking the curve of her waist. The heat of his palms penetrated the thin material, and the pulsating ache thrumming between her thighs throbbed faster, demanding his attention.

As his hand rose to her shoulder, their gazes locked. His hot fingers on her skin flooded her insides with a rush of warmth and anticipation. Using one forefinger, he slid the sleeve of her chemise down to her elbow. Still holding her gaze captive, he did the same with the other.

Serena felt her undergarment cling to the tops of her breasts in a valiant effort to cover them. Lucien hooked his thumb on the tautly-stretched fabric. The chemise fell to her waist, baring her breasts, tight nipples and all, to his rapt gaze.

He swallowed hard as he reached out to caress her. When he took her breast gently in hand, his thumb brushing its beaded center, she closed her eyes for a brief moment and reveled in the cascade of warm pleasure.

Lucien covered her mouth in a hot, urgent kiss. Serena found her arms still pinned to her sides by the sleeves of her chemise. Denied the luxury of clasping her hands around his powerful shoulders and bringing him closer, she returned the kiss with her mouth, using it to communicate the depth of her need.

He pushed her chemise over her hips, down to the floor. Naked, she stood before him, he still fully clothed. She watched his gaze sweep across her breasts, over her abdomen. His eyes stopped at the golden triangle of hair covering her femininity. She shivered. The appreciation in his eyes dissipated her misgiving, replacing it with anticipation that burned like a flame.

She stepped forward, against him. His arms tightened around her, bringing her against the hard crush of his body. At the abrasion of his clothing against her flushed, tingling skin, she shifted restlessly in his arms, seeking some form of relief from the ache he had created.

"Soon, sweetheart," he promised, then captured her mouth in a blistering kiss. When she responded in kind, his palm cupped the center of her desire, fingers probing within the moist folds.

She felt hot and boneless, like a candle that had melted into a puddle of burning wax. A tiny moan escaped her mouth, and she clutched him for support.

"Take my cape off, sweetheart," he whispered, coaxing her legs further apart.

With shaking fingers, she unhooked the garment and watched it ripple to his feet, even as his fingers probed her femininity more intimately, testing the swollen bud of her desire. While she gasped at the kaleidoscope of sensation, he tore his cravat away and freed the buttons of his waistcoat with his other hand. With a soft curse of impatience, he turned the attention of both hands to his clothing to strip off his shoes and shirt.

He stood clad only in trousers, the firelight playing over his flesh, creating a vision of shadows and strength. The only naked male body she had ever seen was Cyrus's, and she was awed by the differences in Lucien's.

Chest bare, he stood more powerful, more inspiring, than Michelangelo's *David*. His flesh was smooth and carved with muscle, his abdomen ribbed. A fine, soft sprinkling of hair extended across the breadth of his chest, ending at the ridge of his muscles. The downy dark hair picked up again just above his waistband, and formed a thin, intriguing line that disappeared into his pants.

Sweet heaven, Lucien was gorgeous. He was a beautifully rugged male, clearly virile enough to satisfy any woman in his bed. She had experienced the touch of his fulfilling hands and would soon know the ecstasy of his lovemaking. She bit her bottom lip nervously.

He reached for her. His palms, warm and reassuring, rested on the top curve of her hips. "Don't bite your lip. Bring it to me so I can kiss it."

She swallowed. Did he have any concept of the havoc he was playing with both her logic and emotions?

He closed the distance between their mouths, claiming hers in a soft, searching kiss.

"You feel wonderful," he whispered against her skin.

She closed her eyes against the pleasure of his voice washing over her. The feel of his flesh, hard where hers was soft, aroused her. "You do, too," she said hesitantly.

"God, sweetheart, you don't know how much I needed to know that."

Serena never had the opportunity to reply. Instead, Lucien lifted her onto the sheets. He didn't wait an instant before bending to worship her breast with his tongue.

Stunned by the unexpected sensation, she grasped his shoulders. She withheld a groan, the admission of her pleasure, until his lips caressed her nipple to an aching point while his tongue paid it swirling homage.

He lifted his head and smiled at her pleasure, not the cocky smile she would have expected, but a smile of sharing. Gently, he reached up and pulled the remaining pins from her hair. The mass cascaded around her face and across her shoulders, faintly golden against the crisp white linen. She knew it was a wet, tangled mess. But Lucien's expression said otherwise. His fingers slid through the strands with reverence.

"You are...beautiful," he breathed. "That word seems so inadequate. I have never seen hair your color. At first, in the dark and the rain, I thought it merely blond. But it I see now it is more like white gold."

She shrugged shyly. Cyrus had never said a word about her hair color, good or otherwise. "Nothing so spectacular as that. It is simply what I was born with."

"I think it is spectacular, and on you it is perfect."

Casting her gaze away, she smiled. "Thank you."

Shaking his head, he lay on the bed and urged her to lie beside him, face to face. Wrapping his arms around her, his hands swept down her back and took her buttocks in his palms. He squeezed her, shifting closer, before drawing her leg over his hip. He caressed her thigh, while his lips conducted a leisurely sweep up her neck, then across her jawline and cheeks. When his mouth finally touched hers, a welcome succor pervaded her, mixing with a charge of desire.

He slowly ravished her with his kiss. As he did, he exposed emotions and passions trapped under the daily facade of logic. Thoughts no longer ruled her actions. Instead, when Lucien rolled her to her back, fitting his hips intimately between hers, she welcomed him with a soft gasp of pleasure. He pressed against her, the silk of his trousers rubbing her neediest spot to higher arousal. Instinctively, she lifted her hips to him.

Wordlessly, he rose. Serena watched through heavy lids as Lucien removed his trousers and drawers. Firelight played over him. The natural tone of his skin was many shades darker than her own. And Serena's curious eyes followed that trail of dark hair she had noticed earlier. As she had suspected, the line continued downward, over his navel and lower, spreading around his stiff sex to frame it.

Her first sight of the aroused male body appeared to be what Cyrus had told her to expect, only different. This male specimen was more compelling, not only because the man himself was exceedingly well formed, but because he *wanted* her—and made no attempt to hide that fact.

"You're staring," he commented almost curiously.

With a blush Serena felt from head to toe, she said, "You're...beautiful."

Walking back toward her, he smiled. "No, only the company I'm keeping is, sweetheart."

The mattress creaked, then sagged beneath his weight once again. Before she could breathe or speak, he kissed her once more, positioning himself on top of her. Of their own will, her legs opened for him, and with a groan, he accepted her invitation.

Awareness flooded her with pleasure. The heat of his hard chest against the softness of her breasts; the rasp of the downy hair on his legs teasing her tender inner thighs; the cadence of his breath against her neck.

Briefly, she felt his hard shaft probing the folds of her femininity. He found his mark and surged forward in one powerful thrust.

Serena gasped as a jagged bolt of pain tore through her. Gasping, she tensed as he sank deeper into her body. She cried out as the sharp pain cut her again.

A frown blazed across his face, dark with suspicion. Then he lowered his mouth and swept the inside of hers with his tongue. Invaded by heat and the enticing taste of man and wine, Serena returned the kiss, recreating the delicious desire he had given her previously.

When the kiss ended, he lifted his head, still wearing a slightly puzzled expression. Suddenly he shook away the question on his face. "I'm sorry, sweetheart. I shall be more careful."

To prove his point, Lucien withdrew almost gingerly. This time, he prolonged his entry, each inch of his flesh lingering at her entrance before sinking in like molasses. Another pinpoint of pain speared, but it dissipated quickly, replaced by a pleasurable fullness. Blazing heat radiated through her moistness and penetrated her body deep within her core. It felt like heaven.

"God, you're tight," he rasped in her ear.

Not really certain what he meant, or if that condition were good or bad, she simply nodded.

With the next lunge of his hips, that ceased to be an issue. His stiff flesh stayed within her only an instant before withdrawing. A split second later, he returned with a firm thrust. Again and again, his shaft penetrated and retreated, creating the delicious agony his hands had begun in the carriage, and his body promised to finish here in his huge bed.

As he plunged again within her, she arched her back in bliss, meeting him.

"Yes. That's it," he chanted, fitting his hands beneath her hips and tilting her up to further feast on her response.

That position lent her a new degree of sensitivity. Her body bucked beneath his, instinctively reaching for fulfillment. His plunges inside her increased, deep and controlled and ruthless. Jolts of pleasure dashed from her most forbidden flesh, where Lucien made his welcome invasion into her, all through her body.

The sensations rushed upon her, stealing her breath. The sudden vortex of pleasure was both towering and swirling within her. It frightened her as it threatened to rob her sanity and consume her.

Pushing on his shoulders, she wriggled beneath him, trying to break free before the tidal wave of need crashed over her body and swallowed her whole.

"Relax, sweetheart."

"But I—"

"Trust me." His voice was gravelly and rough. "Take me."

Finally, as he thrust into her once more, what she'd feared most became what she needed most. Ripples of release stormed throughout her, pulsing, vibrating, until the explosion inside her culminated with a blinding burst of satisfaction and a loud, staccato cry.

An instant later, he buried his face in her neck. His fingers tightened around her hips, grasping her, tilting her up with need. His whole body tense, he groaned, flooded her with something hot and thrilling, then fell against her, spent.

Serena lay beneath him, torn between wonder and the fervent wish he would say something. As he drew in long breaths, she felt the slick perspiration between their bodies and the heat of his skin touching her everywhere.

When his breathing slowed, he stroked her hair away from her forehead. His eyes, an even darker green by the mesmerizing firelight, lay open to her, stripped of all artifice. She saw the emotion churning within him, compelling him to speak.

"You are...unbelievable."

The awe in his voice, coupled with the raw emotion in his eyes, opened a path to her heart, connecting her to him on a level that went beyond mere physical joining. Something profound and elemental moved inside her, misting her eyes with tears. Quickly, she averted her gaze, praying he would not see her reaction or guess that, until tonight, she had known neither completion nor ecstasy.

His arms winding around her shoulders, Lucien held her close. Further touched by his intimate gesture, Serena fought a new onslaught of tears.

Wordlessly, he held her against his chest, sheltering her in the solace of his embrace. He dusted her face with soft kisses while she listened to his breathing, felt his heartbeat against hers. Closing her eyes, she sighed, feeling the tension ebb from her body. Lucien's fingers feathered up and down the naked length of her back. And soon, she slept.

****

Lucien rolled away from the slumbering beauty in his arms and tucked the covers around her. As he rose and donned his pants, he marveled at her placid expression. Hell, he was still shaking from a climax so stunning, it surpassed anything in memory, recent or otherwise.

Kneeling, he brought his face level with hers. Her hair was by far her most magnificent feature. The white-gold length streamed about her in a straight, silken cloud. But that wasn't what fascinated him. It was her face.

Both oval and angelic, it showcased her honey skin and raspberry red mouth to perfection. His eyes traced the firm, sloping line of her jaw and her round, stubborn chin. Next to one platinum brow lay a tiny mole, but rather than detracting from her striking beauty, it enhanced. With her as temptation, how could he resist?

Lucien smoothed a curl from her cheek, rosy from the rub of his whiskers, and turned away. Despite the relaxation curling through his body, his mind was in turmoil.

The last time he'd had a woman in his bed was three months ago. That night, he had left his daughter in the care of servants, writing off her tears as a child's antics for attention. He had spent the evening with his former mistress, indulging in mindless, emotionless sex. When he had arrived home in the wee morning hours, Chelsea was dead.

Closing his eyes with a pained grimace, Lucien reached past the decanter of wine he had poured from only an hour ago, and instead grabbed the Irish whiskey. He drew it to his lips, gulping in long swallows. As the liquor scorched its way down his throat, he felt satisfaction and a certain safety that, if he consumed enough, he could eventually drown his guilt.

But the images haunted him: her tiny body trampled by the carriage, the white nightgown reddened by her blood. That next morning had been a shock of disbelief and questions—and astonishment to learn that Chelsea had left the house determined to find her mummy and bring her back home to her daddy so they could all be happy.

He brought the bottle to his mouth once more for a long swallow. *Bloody hell.* His self-induced celibacy had been torture, but he had not weakened from his penance—until tonight. He should never have listened to Niles. True, the man was his only friend at the moment, but the pup was wrong. All his aloneness was not unhealthy; it was deserved. But no, Niles had insisted just this morning that he accept his life without Chelsea and carry on. Lucien shook his head in self-disgust. Like a fool, he had listened.

His gaze again rested on the fair-haired goddess in his bed. *So much for penance and celibacy.* Instead of coming back to life a nibble at a time, he had started with a feast of honeyed skin and welcoming arms. He had known the first moment he really looked at her, terrified and alone, that he had no business pursuing her. But something about her, the need and loneliness on her face, had called to him. And God, after touching her, she had felt too good to even consider releasing.

But in the morning, he would do just that and resume his self-induced punishment. Despite the fact he wanted to keep her with him, learn about her and laugh with her, he could not. When she woke, he would find out what sort of reward she wanted for leaving him permanently, then set her free.

Tipping the bottle to his mouth again, Lucien emptied its contents. He set the bottle on the bedside table quietly. Then, seething with self-loathing, he crawled into his bed beside the sleeping woman and closed his eyes.

CHAPTER FOUR

The sounds of faint male snoring awakened Serena, along with the feel of hot flesh and a blast of body heat. She rolled to her side and opened her eyes.

Her gaze tripped over the dark stranger—her lover now, she amended—both perfectly handsome and perfectly naked as he lay on his stomach. The sight of his rippling shoulders, taut backside, and long legs brought her fully awake. Biting her lip to hold in a gasp, she rolled from the bed as noiselessly as possible. The darkness outside the windows was an unexpected blessing.

Sending a silent thanks upward that the fire had not died altogether, she gathered her clothes from around the room, trying to stifle both her panic and her tears.

Dear God, what had she done? *You allowed a perfect stranger to seduce you.*

Reality sunk into her like a stone through water. She had surrendered to the temptation of the flesh, allowed her logic to be swayed by pretty words and her body to be wooed by heated kisses. She had compromised her Christian values with little thought for anything but the pleasure the man was obviously accustomed to giving, and offered her maidenhood as easily as a light-skirt offers herself nightly.

Fortunately, she did not think he had realized her innocence. If he had, he'd made no mention of it. But perhaps he made a habit of divesting women of their virginity. That possibility flooded her eyes with tears, along with the realization that she knew next to nothing about him.

Heartless rake or not, she had to leave before he woke up, before he started asking questions. Before he learned her name.

The possibility that he knew Cyrus quickened her tears. Not only had she shamed herself with her behavior, but her husband as well. And what if a child resulted? She had hoped for one last night. But how could she cheat this lonely man of his babe and deliver her husband a bastard? True, Cyrus professed to want such an occurrence, but if faced with the reality...would he feel the same?

Think! Serena demanded of herself, only to find that fulfilling the request was impossible. Her mind swirling, she shoved her stockings into her reticule, then donned her chemise and dress as best she could. She knew gaping holes existed where her hands could not reach the hooks and left her chemise-clad back exposed.

Eyes darting around the room, she spotted the wardrobe. Snatching it open, she withdrew a dark cloak and threw it about her shoulders. She tucked her stiff-boned corset into one of the inner pockets.

With shaking fingers, she tied her slippers. Her gaze, pulled by some nameless force, made its way back to the stranger. To Lucien, she corrected herself. After all, now that he knew her in the biblical sense, a pretense of formality was pointless.

The hours in his arms and in his bed had been a sinful slice of heaven. But she would not allow herself to think about it or him anymore. He was the weakness Satan had presented her with. And she had made her choice. With desire-induced logic, she had failed her husband and God. She had become more like her mother's daughter than anyone, including herself, had suspected. Whatever the case, she was not going to fail further by dwelling on the warmth of Lucien's words or kisses, or thinking of the gratification he delivered with such ease.

Fighting unshed tears, her gaze wandered over the taut, muscled breadth of his back, his slim hips, and the length of his powerful legs, which had kicked away the covers. She studied his profile one last time. He was handsome, devastating...dangerous to her sanity. She turned away.

She must never seek him out, never entice herself with his brand of temptation again. She was afraid her Christian will would crumble beneath the hammer of desire he created. Afraid that she could not resist.

She could never see him again.

Something about that reality she did not want to examine too closely made her eyes well with tears once more. Before her sobs awakened Lucien, she crept out of the room, down the stairs, and fled into the London night.

****

"Get up, old man."

Lucien heard the familiar voice nagging him. Something poked him in the ribs, and he squirmed to dodge the discomfort. When he felt the prod again, he groaned loudly in protest.

"Come on. You promised me an afternoon at Gentleman Jackson's. It's my turn to beat the hell out of you."

Niles, Lucien's cloudy brain realized despite the vestiges of sleep and the bang of his headache. The man was the most persistent nuisance...and the best friend.

Lucien groaned. "Go away. I don't want to box. I've already been beaten." At least his head felt that way.

"And who did the beating? Was it the 'lady' Holford tells me you brought here last night?" Niles asked, his voice laughing.

With that reminder, Lucien's memory flashed him a vision of white-blond hair and smoky blue eyes provocatively half-closed in pleasure. Instantly, he remembered the intimate feel of her body pulsing around him in blazing climax.

He sat up and scanned the room. "Where is she?"

"Haven't seen her. I assumed you paid her and sent her on her way."

"No. I laid down beside her. She was asleep." He looked at his friend, trying to puzzle it together. "That's the last thing I remember."

Niles laughed, tossing Lucien his cape. "Check your pockets, my friend. She probably ran off with everything in them."

"No. She wasn't a whore."

Niles brows rose dubiously. "The best don't let on they are, at first. Where did you find her?"

"Vauxhall," Lucien replied.

He shrugged. "That ties it. She was just better than most."

Lucien emptied the contents of his pockets and found everything present. "It's all here, exactly where I left it."

Niles expression finally melted from cynicism to puzzlement. "Who was she, Clayborne?"

Lucien shook his head, rubbing his aching forehead with his palm, trying to remember. "I couldn't say. We met after I saved her from a thief, so we were not formally introduced."

"You never learned her name?"

"No. The robbery shook her and she started to cry. After that, the subject never arose," he admitted.

"You have no idea who she is?" Niles pressed.

"None. But she was the most beautiful woman I've ever seen. She had the fair hair of an angel and the honey skin of a temptress. The way she made me feel... Lucien closed his eyes in remembrance, feeling a surge of arousal.

"She's exactly what you need. And you let her get away?"

"She must have bolted during the night. But damn it, why?"

"This might give you a clue to her identity. Holford found it in the library."

Niles dropped a soft white handkerchief in his lap. Lucien fingered it, smelled her faint sultry scent, something reminiscent of gardenias, then turned it over. The initials SB had been embroidered into the linen square with fine pink thread.

"No, it doesn't help. She's still a mystery."

"What are you going to do now? Find her, I hope."

Visions of Chelsea brought back his onslaught of guilt. "No. It was one night, nothing more."

Niles crossed his arms over a silk, striped waistcoat. "Ah, so you're going to resume punishing yourself for an accident you could not prevent."

Grinding his teeth, Lucien replied, "At least I *might* have prevented her death, had I been home, where she needed me."

"That's bloody nonsense! When are you going to face that?"

He gestured to the door. "If you dislike my attitude, Holford can show you out."

"For an old man, you lack all common sense."

"I only have two years on you, and I have a sense of *honor*, damn it."

Niles nodded. "Yes, but the truth is you don't want to gamble with love again. Ravenna burned you too badly."

Throwing the covers aside, Lucien leapt out of bed and donned his breeches. "That's over."

"Is it? I've no doubt you wonder every day what would have prevented her from trysting with Wayland. Nothing, I'll tell you. The woman was no good."

"You meddle too much in others' lives," Lucien ground out, crossing the room to his wardrobe.

"Clayborne, did you cut yourself?"

The inquisitive tone in Niles's voice gave Lucien pause. He turned to his friend. "No. Why?"

Niles emitted a low whistle and gestured to the bed. "My friend, you may have another problem on your hands. A big one."

Lucien followed the direction of his friend's gaze and spotted the dark crimson spots on his stark white sheets. Disbelieving the proof his eyes presented him, he walked half-dazed toward the bed and peered closer.

"Any chance your whore was a virgin?" Niles asked.

A wave of hot confusion and disbelief swept over Lucien. "I thought...That is to say she felt like...Damn!" He raked tense fingers through his hair and loosed a long sigh. "Last night, I swore I felt her tear. But she didn't say anything. She never indicated it was her first time."

"Not a word?" Niles looked confused now as well.

"Just a gasp, so I thought I was mistaken or too much in my cups. No innocent miss I've ever seen could undress a man with her eyes as this one could. Surely a virgin wouldn't come home with a complete stranger and offer him her virtue?"

"It seems she did just that."

"Oh, Christ," he breathed, shock permeating every nerve.

"Who do you think she was?"

Lucien shrugged. "I don't know. She wasn't a whore. But I practically took her in my coach, and she offered only a small protest. Given that, and the fact she wasn't with a proper escort, I assumed she was someone's mistress. I even wondered if she was a young war widow."

"It appears to me she is someone's daughter," Niles said.

"Ruined daughter now." Lucien scrubbed a hand down his face. "Damnation!"

"Any chance her father is a member of the *ton*?"

"Her parents are dead." Lucien reflected on the grief he had seen on her face. That and her compassion had been two of the qualities that had drawn him. "But she was dressed well, no mistake. It's entirely likely she's well-born, but she didn't appear just out of the schoolroom. She was perhaps twenty."

"All right, so she's a spinster."

Lucien shook his head with disbelief. "I suppose, but I can hardly credit that. I've never seen a spinster that looked as good as her. She was all moonlight and temptation."

"Regardless, that is the probability. Mayhap she has no dowry. The question is what will you do about her now?"

Niles's question wasn't unexpected; he always thought something had to be done. Only this time the man was right, and one answer loomed, threatening to eat away at Lucien's freedom and peace of mind.

"You know the obvious answer," Lucien finally answered. "I'll have to marry her."

Niles laughed harshly. "You've really tangled yourself a pretty coil."

"You're right. And just what do you suppose her guardian will say when he learns a divorced man has ruined his charge?"

"Before or after he calls you out?"

Lucien sighed grimly. "Exactly, but I must find her first."

A strange sense of anticipation sluiced through Lucien at the thought of seeing her, of making love to her again. He pushed the ugly reality of Holy Matrimony from his mind as he strode to his wardrobe and shouted for his valet.

"I'll help you search." Niles grinned wryly. "Does this mean I'll get to stand up with you at your wedding?"

Despite the bleak situation, Lucien laughed. "Bugger off."

"I expected you to say as much."

Impatient, Lucien began pulling the day's garments from his wardrobe as he formed a retort. He noticed then his favorite gray cloak was absent.

"There's a bloody surprise," he muttered. "She took my cloak." He turned to his friend. "It was here last night, gone this morning."

"You have something of hers, too." With a smile, Niles gestured to the scented handkerchief in Lucien's hand.

He toyed with the scrap of linen. "This should make for an interesting trade indeed."

****

With a sigh of utter relief, Serena slipped into her bedroom. Closing the door behind her, she leaned against it for support. She had run through the predawn gray from Lucien's Hanover Square home, down Brook Street, to her own Grosvenor Square residence. Panting with exertion and fatigue, she closed her eyes.

Mercy, it was good to be in her own room—alone. She needed to sort through her thoughts, to think of what she would tell Cyrus about her deplorable behavior, and find a way to forget the rogue who had held her in his arms last night. Maybe then she could forgive herself and reconcile with her sin. Maybe God would forgive her.

"Where've ye been, milady? I've been waitin' up all night for ye. And ye come trouncin' in just before the sunlight, lookin' like you've been fightin' with a pack o' cats."

Serena opened her eyes and gave her Irish maid her sternest look. "Not now, Caffey. I am not in the mood."

Gesturing aside her mistress's foul mood, Caffey hurried across the room and lifted the heavy cloak from Serena's shoulders.

The maid gasped in shock. "Faith, milady, who hooked your dress?"

"I did."

Caffey lifted a flame-hued brow. "Who unhooked it?"

Serena tried fixing Caffey with another icy stare. The problem was, Serena realized, they had been more than mistress and servant since their childhoods; Caffey knew when she was bluffing.

"Stop. I've had a rough night."

"Aye, from the looks of ye, I'd say so."

Serena felt her patience rapidly giving way to frustrated anger and the urge to cry. "I would like a bath, if you please."

Caffey pinched her dainty little mouth and lifted her chin. Serena knew her maid wasn't disapproving, only hurt Serena wouldn't share her secret.

Caffey positioned herself behind Serena and began working at the few fastened hooks down the back of her dress. Once they came free, Serena peeled the dress from her torso and let it fall to the floor. She noticed then her chemise was on inside out.

"Where's your corset, milady?" Caffey's tone sounded smooth, even halfway obedient.

Serena felt the color rising up her face. "Inside the cloak."

"Who shall I be returnin' this to?" Caffey asked as she held the dark, masculine garment.

Serena couldn't answer that question. She closed her eyes, feeling the rush of new tears. Sweet heaven, what had she done? "Please don't ask me."

"All right, milady. If ye be wantin' an ear, I'll listen."

Serena clasped Caffey's hands. "I know. Thank you."

Caffey nodded and went about her work. She had the tub and water brought in and quickly set about preparing a bath.

Serena looked at the water gratefully. She felt changed, both inside and out, and wondered if she could ever feel again as she had before Lucien entered her life. She prayed she would, but when she lifted her chemise from her body, she inhaled Lucien's scent, bringing her both weak-kneed remembrance and doubt. Then she heard Caffey gasp.

"Oh, dear Lord! What did that man do to ye?"

Serena looked at herself in the glass and understood Caffey's horror. Her breasts were rosy from the stubble on Lucien's chin. Little love bites dotted her neck, abdomen, and thighs. She looked away in mortification, wishing she could go back in time, wishing she had damned her foolish feelings and refused the handsome devil who had wrought both temporary and permanent changes to her person.

"Please, go now. I'll bathe myself."

"And if His Grace inquires after ye?"

Serena bit her lip, swallowing hard as another blast of shame and guilt pummeled her. "Tell him I'm sleeping."

"As ye wish," Caffey replied, then closed the door behind her.

Serena immediately sank into the hot water of her bath and scrubbed herself red. And cried.

ᴀᴀᴀᴀ

Serena felt her fragile expression collapse the instant the butler showed her into her grandmother's drawing room and closed the door behind him. The few tears she hadn't spent during her hour in the tub surfaced now.

Concern transformed her grandmother's expression as she hurried across the room to wrap Serena in her embrace.

The feel of her reassuring arms, the croon of her soft voice, brought another burst of tears.

"Serena, what on earth has happened? Has this anything to do with your husband's...problem?"

"No." Serena hiccupped. "Yes."

Grandy patted her back. "Child, you'll have to be clearer about the problem if you want my help. I cannot read your mind."

Serena nodded miserably, then sobbed, "I did it."

"Did what?"

Sniffing, she answered, "What Cyrus asked of me."

Her grandmother released her from her embrace and led her to the sofa. Clasping her hands, the older woman asked, "You took a lover?"

Closing her eyes, hoping to close out the shame, Serena nodded.

"How delightful. Why, then, are you upset?" Her grandmother cocked her head to one side. "Did he hurt you, lamb?"

Adamantly, Serena shook her head. "It was wonderful and breathtaking. Everything I never imagined."

"Splendid," Grandy declared. "What could possibly be wrong?"

"I-I wanted him so much, I convinced myself that lying with him was the right thing to do." Misery wrenched the words from her throat. "Like Mama, I gave myself so easily."

"I commend the man. He must be quite special."

"Grandy, don't you understand? I've sinned terribly. How will I ever look at Cyrus again? What shall I say when he tells me he loves me? I cannot be worthy after the way I behaved."

Her grandmother loosed a long sigh. "You silly child. Cyrus himself suggested you take a lover. You simply fulfilled his request."

Serena shook her head violently. "I had no intention of doing so. But then Lucien touched me and...I didn't want him to stop."

"Lucien? Does he have a last name?"

Serena felt her face color to a painful red. "I do not know it."

Her grandmother paused, obviously scanning her memory. "Your Lucien wouldn't happen to be a tall gentleman with very dark hair and exquisite green eyes, would he?"

Serena's breath rushed out in surprise. "Yes. You know him?"

Her grandmother smiled. "We are acquainted. His name is Lucien Clayborne. He is the current Marquess of Daneridge. He's a somber sort, from what I can tell." Grandy paused, as if weighing her words, then said, "He's divorced."

Serena raised a trembling hand to her gaping mouth. "Oh, mercy! Not only did I break my marriage vows, I lay with a divorced stranger. Grandy, this is awful."

Her grandmother embraced her once again, patting her back in a soothing rhythm. "Now, lamb. I would hardly term your tangle the end of the world. From what I understand, Lord Daneridge is a good man; he simply had the misfortune of choosing a trollop for a wife."

"Regardless, marriage is forever. It should sustain you through your life. He ended his. And I've ruined mine."

Grandy sighed. "Serena, someday you will understand that not everything falls into your neat little categories of good and bad. Upon occasion, things fall in between. You must learn to forgive your mother, and yourself. You cannot continue to put yourself through this torrent of guilt."

"But what I've done is unforgivable. What if I...conceive?"

"You will have a baby," her grandmother answered succinctly. "And you will love it, boy or girl. Cyrus and I will be thrilled. You know, you must dote on your elders."

Her grandmother's proclamation made Serena laugh through her tears.

"That's better. Lamb, try not to judge yourself by those silly evangelical standards your goose-headed Aunt Constance preached. You have too much life within you to be suppressing all your desire, especially for the love of a healthy man."

"But—"

"You did as your husband bid. You have no cause to reproach yourself. And that"—she rose—"is that."

****

Later that evening, Serena tried to take her grandmother's advice, indeed yearned to believe no reason for her guilt existed. She wanted to tell Cyrus what happened last night and vowed to try.

As she entered the dining room, she spotted her husband. As usual, his evening black trousers and dark superfine coat enhanced his intelligent, well-bred air.

Half of her wanted to fling herself into his comforting arms and beg forgiveness. The confession of her perfidy stuck to her tongue. How could she possibly disillusion him? Her other half wanted to seek the solace of her room and hide until assured Lucien Clayborne and their night together was naught but a dream.

"Hello, darling." Cyrus rubbed her arm with affection and paused to study her face. "Are you feeling well? You look tired."

His concern nearly started her tears again. She could feel the rush of mortified color creeping up her face as she looked for the words to explain her weariness.

"I'm well," she lied. "How are you feeling today?"

"This bloody back of mine. I'm sorry it has caused you to miss so much of the social whirl since we arrived."

"I quite prefer staying here, Cyrus," she assured. "You know I am not one for large gatherings."

"Still, I want you to enjoy your time in London, meet people your age."

Meet men; that's what he really means, Serena thought angrily. "You mustn't fuss over me. Worry about yourself."

He smiled. "We've been invited to a rout in a few weeks by Lord and Lady Raddington. I'm endeavoring to win Lord Raddington's support on a new bill up for vote. If my back permits, will you accompany me?"

More than anything, Serena wanted to refuse him so she could remain here within these safe walls, where she would never have to fear encountering Lucien again. But, as she always accompanied him to these functions on the rare occasions he requested it, she knew she could not cry off without arousing suspicion.

"Indeed. Just let Caffey know when," she answered.

"I'll make a point of it."

As she sat to her husband's right at the dinner table, he said, "I spoke with Caffey this afternoon."

Serena's heart leapt into her throat. She concentrated on her plate, though the food made her slightly nauseous, and prayed Caffey had kept her secret. "Oh?"

"She said you had gone to visit your grandmother. How is she? Well, I hope."

"Yes. She is as healthy as ever." Serena pushed her fish about on her plate then nibbled on a few peas for effect.

"Glad to hear it." He reached for her hand. "I know you worry about her."

"She is very dear to..." Serena trailed off when she noticed Cyrus staring at her hand, wearing a frown.

"Wherever did you get this awful scrape on your finger?" he asked, glancing at her with concern. "Is it the reason you aren't wearing your wedding ring?"

Serena paused. Here was the perfect opportunity to tell Cyrus everything about last night. "I went to Vauxhall with Melanie to see that rope dancer everyone is so awed by and...and I was set upon by a thief. He...he took my money and jewelry."

Cyrus stood, eyes wide. "Darling, did he hurt you? How did you escape?"

"A...a stranger saved me before the cur could harm me."

"Who? I should like to personally thank the man for his courage."

Serena paused. With a simple sentence she could relieve the burden of her guilty silence. She could tell Cyrus he might have his heir nine months hence.

Cyrus's gaze moved over her with such concern and caring. Serena feared her confession would transform his expression to loathing, perhaps even prompt a slur that she possessed her mother's propensities after all.

"I haven't a...a clue," she lied. "The incident happened so quickly, and then ...well, the rain separated my rescuer from me. I never...ah, had the opportunity to ask his name."

He brought her into the comfort of his arms. "No wonder you're so shaken. You must retire immediately and rest."

She nodded and rose, guilt whipping her like a wet rope. "I am certain that would be best."

Cyrus clasped her hands before she could leave the room. "Why didn't you wake me with the news last night?"

"You know how I hate to worry you." She pasted on a smile, though another gash of guilt twisted within her for telling such an outright lie. "Besides, it's all over now. I feel certain such thieving will not happen again."

His frown told Serena her answer hardly satisfied him, but he let the matter drop. With obvious reluctance, Cyrus released her arm. "Sleep well."

Serena fled the room, wondering if she would ever find enough peace with herself to do as Cyrus had bid.

CHAPTER FIVE

"Clayborne, I'm beginning to question your sanity," Niles said, interrupting Lucien's thoughts.

When he made no remark, Niles continued, "Really, old man, we've looked everywhere for the girl. She knows where you live. If she felt you owed her the honor of your name, surely she would have sought you out these last three weeks."

Lucien answered his friend with a shrug, but his thoughts echoed Niles's words.

Yet he couldn't give up. Quite simply, the woman haunted him. He found himself daydreaming, of all things, like a boy in calf love. At night, dreams of her sweet body soothed him when the visions of Chelsea's agony beneath the carriage wheels ripped through his sleep. Where the hell was she?

"You have no idea who this woman is," came Niles again.

"Clearly," Lucien admitted, keeping his gaze fixed on London's streets through his carriage window.

Several weeks ago, with high hopes, he had queried his Aunt Elizabeth about a person of his mystery woman's description. Aunt Elizabeth knew everybody, or so Lucien had thought. She hadn't known his fair-haired virgin from Vauxhall.

At times, Lucien wondered if that entire night had been a drink-induced illusion, spurred on by his lonely imagination. But he had only to look at her handkerchief and recall his scarlet-stained sheet to know otherwise.

"Three weeks is a long time to search," Niles complained. "I'm supposed to be attending to my personal matters."

"So attend to them." Lucien shrugged.

"And let you bury yourself in that tomb of a town house to brood until the second coming of Christ? It's unthinkable."

"Hmmm," Lucien replied noncommittally. "What is your urgent personal matter? Do you have a new mistress?" Lucien inquired, wanting to change the subject. He didn't need to hear that his odds of finding his innocent from Vauxhall were unfavorable. He was all too aware of that fact.

"Now you sound like my father. Next you, too, will be commanding me to take a bride."

"Not me," Lucien returned. "I'm much too familiar with matrimonial bliss."

Niles sighed in exasperation. "Not all women are like Ravenna."

Lucien turned his gaze from London's pedestrians to face his friend. "No, only three quarters of the *ton* cuckold their husbands. The other quarter is either too old or with child."

"Do you think your mystery woman would join that first three quarters?"

Lucien shrugged, but acknowledged he did not want to believe that she fit into that devious category. Certainly, she was different. At the worst time in his life, she had appeared, sharing herself with beautiful abandon and soothing his raw grief with her touch. Maybe that explained why he couldn't stop searching; he had faith in the healing touch of her honey skin, in her. Then again, perhaps it was guilt for having ruined her. He didn't know.

"We've been to every rout, soiree, tea, and waltzing party since she disappeared, and we haven't caught the slightest glimpse of her. I'm getting damned tired of all that polite company," Niles mumbled. "I miss a good evening at my club."

"Then go. The gents at White's surely miss fleecing your pockets."

"That's hardly funny." Niles shifted his stubborn gaze out the carriage window.

"Did I laugh?" Lucien inquired, suppressing a grin.

The carriage rolled down Ludgate Hill and halted at Number 32, Rundell and Bridge's jewelers. As they entered the shop, Lucien found himself impatient to find Niles's trinket and be on with their search for his beautiful angel.

"Where is this snuff box you're so enamored of?" he asked.

Niles pointed, and over the next fifteen minutes, the shopkeeper showed them a variety of snuff boxes, each more elaborate and expensive than the last.

Finally, Niles threw his hands up. "I can't decide. Help me, will you, old man?"

Lucien studied each, finding them all too ornate for his taste. But then Niles was much more flamboyant, as evidenced this morning by his scarlet and gold waistcoat of Chinese silk.

"Dear God. She's beautiful," Niles gasped, his whisper awe-filled.

Accustomed to Niles's penchant for finding the lovelies in any room, Lucien's gaze wound slowly around the shop before coming to rest on a lone figure.

His heart jumped, lurching against his ribs, then began chugging a double-time rhythm.

The afternoon sun slanted through the door behind her, making it impossible to see her face. But nature's light illuminated her white-gold hair with the brilliance of a hundred candles. He watched the way she moved, the manner in which she walked, the tilt of her head, the almost otherworldly halo around her. He'd found her. Finally. That certainty washed over him, along with a surge of desire that slammed into his gut, robbing him of breath.

She paused, turning to say something to a flame-haired woman trailing behind her. The words were unintelligible, but her voice, a little huskier than most women's, played the kindling to an already ignited flame.

"Who is she?" Niles whispered, his voice reverent.

"Mine." Lucien stalked toward her, not certain if he planned to merely speak to her as he should, or do as he wanted and brand her with a fierce, possessive kiss before God and the shopkeeper of Rundell and Bridge.

At his approach, she turned. The smile on her face died, replaced by instant panic in her smoky eyes as she retreated a step. Clearly, she hadn't expected to set eyes—or anything else—on him again.

"I see you remember me," he growled.

She opened her mouth, only to close it in uncertainty. Biting her lip, she looked about, as if wishing for help.

"Excuse me, my lord." She tried to step around him.

He stepped in her path. "'My lord,' is it? I thought surely we had graduated to something more ...intimate."

Lucien watched the becoming rose of her blush creep up her cheeks, but she said nothing. Somehow that infuriated him more. "Surely you have some spark of recall for the man who took your maidenhood. Or did your memory desert you when you left my bedroom?"

She swallowed hard, her face a tense mask. "Leave us, Caffey."

"Are ye sure, milady?" the Irish girl asked.

His mystery woman gave a shaky nod, then hesitantly lifted her eyes to his. "People are staring."

"Bloody well let them. You owe me an explanation."

She wrung her hands nervously. "I owe you nothing, my lord. Can you tell me you did not receive what you expected from the encounter?"

"Oh, yes," he whispered. "I received everything I expected, and more. Damn it! Why didn't you tell me you were innocent?"

"Stop swearing at me," she hissed. "What makes you think I was?"

"Well, *my lady*," he mocked, "I felt it. I saw the blood. Who are you?"

She blanched white at the question. "No one important. Now, I must leave."

Realizing he'd charged at her like an enraged bull, he softened. After all, she was little more than a girl in her dealings with men. "Why, sweetheart? Why did you not tell me? Why didn't you push me away or say no? God, if I had known ..."

"Exactly. Now, excuse me."

"What does that mean?"

When she tried to step around him without responding, he grabbed her arm.

"Everyone is watching," she said in panic.

"I want answers," he grated out, then drew in a deep breath. "I've ruined you and I'm sorry for the manner in which it happened. An innocent should have a wedding night and a gentle husband—"

"It's of no consequence."

He watched her hands tremble. Her gaze met anything but his, and his eyes narrowed with confused suspicion. "Of course it is, and I'm aware of my responsibility. Tell me who your guardian is so I can settle with him. We can be married within the week by special license."

She put her hand over her mouth to stifle a gasp. Pure alarm entered her eyes, both confusing and infuriating Lucien. He noticed tears gathering in her eyes. What kind of unmarried girl who was no longer innocent did not seek a marriage?

"Trapping you into matrimony was not my intent. You need not worry about settlements. Marriage will not be required," she assured, her husky voice shaking.

Had she lost all sanity? Or was it possible she did not understand the possible consequences? "You may be carrying my child even now. Have you considered that?"

Her face turned whiter still. She jerked away. "Please leave me be."

Again, Lucien tried to clasp her arm and hold her by his side. This time, she moved too quickly. He watched her exit the jeweler's and inhaled the sultry scent of gardenias in her wake.

"What did she say, old man? She looked frightened beyond bearing."

He cursed, a sound both soft and bitter. "She was, even as she said that marrying her was not necessary."

"Not necessary?" Niles said, astounded.

"Exactly my thoughts. Go ask the shopkeeper if he knows who she is. I'm going to follow her."

Each man raced to his chore. Niles frowned when the shopkeeper informed him that particular lady had never been to Rundell and Bridge. Lucien swore when he discovered no carriage parked in front of the shop but his own and his mystery woman nowhere in sight.

****

Her hands trembled, and Serena hoped the rocking of the coach disguised it, at least a little. Well aware of Caffey's probing eyes, Serena clasped her fingers together tightly in her lap and looked straight ahead.

"He's a handsome devil, milady."

Nothing could be truer. Those green eyes glittered even more beautifully in daylight. But the intimate knowledge his stare held, her remembrance of his wide shoulders looming above her during their lovemaking, singed her with forbidden heat. His scent, something very musky, very manly, stayed with her, causing a trembling deep in her stomach.

She had tried to forget the masculine angles of his chiseled face, but one look this afternoon had brought it all back, complete with the memory of his wide mouth spreading heated kisses over her.

"I would prefer not to discuss it." She hoped her voice sounded authoritative.

"Me mum always said keepin' secrets inside was bad, that they'd get bigger and bigger until they ate ye up, heart and all."

That perfectly described how she had been feeling these last three weeks, Serena thought. She had approached Cyrus several times, certain that prayer had given her the strength to confess her sin. Each time, she would look at his kind face and see the concern in his eyes. She would turn away, guilt unspoken. And it was eating her alive.

"What did he want, milady?"

"Something impossible."

****

Through bleary, whisky-blurred eyes, Alastair Boyce surveyed the gaming hell's roulette wheel. Actually, he saw three of them, but was fairly certain he knew which one truly existed, displaying the ball resting in the pocket of the black ten instead of the red twenty-one.

He'd had lousy luck, a long streak of it, and he had lost the money from the sale of "Aunt" Serena's jewelry he'd pilfered at Vauxhall. He would have stolen a quick tumble and ended her cursed life, too, had that damned stranger not saved her.

"Care to try again?" the dealer asked.

"No. Get me a woman."

The dealer motioned to a gaudily clad blond woman against the wall. Looking haggard and unenthusiastic, she came forward.

"You want somethin', guv?"

She looked enough like Uncle Cyrus's self-righteous wife Serena, the beautiful bitch. But her indifferent voice would never do. He wanted to hear her scream as Serena had at Vauxhall; he wanted to see the fear he incited in her eyes once again. He grabbed her arm, squeezing until he had the satisfaction of witnessing pain cross her face.

She tried to twist away discreetly. Alastair smiled coldly as he exerted more pressure.

"Yes, I want somethin'. I want your skirt raised around your neck so I can fuck you hard." He pulled her toward the stairs.

"My lord?" a voice behind him queried.

Was the voice talking to him? Alastair wasn't sure. Slowly, so he wouldn't lose his balance, he turned toward the sound. He tried to focus the three images of the club manager into one.

"You lost quite a bit of blunt tonight."

"I did? Oh, yes. Your point?" Alastair slurred.

"And you're overdue on your other losses. It's time we made arrangements."

"See my secretary. Milton's his name."

Even through his stupor, Alastair saw the ruthless edge carve its way across the man's face. "When you lose money, I deal with you."

"Bloody leech," Alastair mumbled.

"You owe this establishment three thousand pounds. I expect you'll pay it by Friday next."

"I'll see to it. Now get out of my way. You're interferin' with my pleasure," he slurred.

Alastair only made it halfway up the stairs before he tired of waiting. Impatiently, he pushed the whore down and hiked up her skirt. The moment he entered the woman, he closed his eyes. Serena. Yes...But her bored expression would never do. He beat it from her face with his fist. As she gasped in pain, Alastair plunged into her body ruthlessly, then climaxed in pleasure.

He focused the woman below him into one image. Damn it, she wasn't Serena. Not at all. He smacked her again, then stood and jerked up his breeches with a curse.

If he had truly bedded Uncle Cyrus's holier-than-thou wife, she would have begged and screamed and cried for mercy, as she had when he'd held the knife to her throat. The thought made him hard again. But the haggard whore would no longer suffice. Her hair wasn't that brilliant pale color. Her skin betrayed her advancing age. Her manner was too forward. He shoved her away.

He sat on the stairs, his clothes smelling like whiskey, and thought. Three thousand pounds. Where would he come up with it? His property was already mortgaged. He owed his friends too much money to ask for more. No one was allowing him to borrow on his expectations of inheriting the dukedom any longer, now that dear Uncle Cyrus had taken a young wife. And Uncle Cyrus had made it clear no more money would be forthcoming until his death.

Ah, death; now there was an idea. He was heir to a vast dukedom. Uncle Cyrus had held it far too long. Certainly, Alastair deserved a turn at all that money lying around in bank accounts, gathering dust. Of course he had no need for Uncle Cyrus's businesses or his seat in the Lords. Just the money.

And Uncle Cyrus's widow would need hours of comforting—with her legs spread. He rose and exited the gaming hell, whistling a chipper tune.

CHAPTER SIX

Lucien walked among the throng of people attending the Raddingtons' rout and surveyed the ever-thickening crowd, but found no sign of his mystery lady.

Niles turned to him with a sigh. "I do not see her."

Lucien scanned the room, his eyes still seeking a luxurious head of white-gold hair. "Neither do I. Keep looking. She will certainly show her face in public again someday."

"Perhaps," Niles hedged. "But clearly she's done very little of that in the past."

The woman, *his* woman, weighed heavily upon Lucien's mind as the days passed, and tonight in particular. Was she well? Did she ever think of him, too?

"Hello, Lord Daneridge. Did my brother drag you here to help him endure my soirée?" a feminine voice asked from behind, turning both men in her direction.

Wearing a faint smile, Lucien glanced at Niles before gazing back to his friend's sister. "Actually, no. I enjoy your parties, Lady Raddington. I consider it a privilege to be on your guest list."

"La, how you flatter. Is that a nasty habit you acquired from Devon?"

"Not me, little sister," Niles interjected. "I'm all manners, don't you know?"

"Yes, I know all too well." Anne laughed, then drifted off to greet another guest.

Niles took a sip of champagne. "So what will you say if you find this woman again?"

Lucien shrugged, not certain himself. Would he scream, implore her to see reason, or simply succumb to his urge to kiss her?

The smell of gardenias lingered in the air. Every time he breathed that pungent scent, he half expected her to precede it. He could almost feel her here. Something in the air made his spine tingle. He scanned the room for her again.

And saw her.

Dressed in a low-cut creation of the most tantalizing shade of sapphire, she shimmered around the dance floor in the arms of an elderly, portly gentleman. Her cloud of white-gold hair was piled exotically on her head, a trail of curls caressing her neck. Her flawless honey skin held a hint of becoming rose tonight, he noted, studying her delicate profile. As before, raw desire slammed into him, stealing his breath, leaving him shaking and hungry.

"There! Do you see her, Clayborne?" Niles asked beside him.

Eyes never leaving her, Lucien nodded.

"Who is the old gent with her? Looks like the Duke of Warrington. Her guardian, you suppose?"

"That would be my guess. He's old enough to be one of her father's or grandfather's cronies."

With a low whistle, Niles commented, "Powerful guardian, old man."

Lucien nodded, a determined tightening in his jaw. "Quite so. But I will convince His Grace I am the appropriate suitor for his charge."

"Will you tell him the truth?"

Lucien paused. "Only if he forces the issue."

Anne, wearing a harried smile, strode by then. Niles grabbed her arm, halting her progress.

"Dear sister, who is the lovely blond creature over there?" Niles pointed discreetly.

"Falling in love, Devon? If so, she should definitely be off your list of eligible ladies."

"Why?" Lucien snapped.

Looking confused at his tone, Anne replied, "She's the Duchess of Warrington."

Lucien felt his stomach execute a painful plunge before it crashed to the ground. A simultaneous wave of dizziness and nausea spiked through him. The blood left his face.

Married. And a virgin? What the hell had he done? What had she let him do?

Lucien was vaguely aware of Niles's stunned stare, but could not return it.

"How on earth did she ...was she ...?" Niles trailed off in confusion.

"I don't know," was all Lucien could answer.

"What are you two talking about?" Anne demanded to know. "Have you met the duchess, Lord Daneridge?

Met her? Oh, yes. He was thoroughly acquainted with *Her Grace*, the cuckolding bitch.

What was her game? The man had obviously never bedded his wife. Was she seeking to gain an indifferent husband's attention with coy schemes of jealousy? Or perhaps she had never wanted to marry an older man and decided to cuckold him with younger amusement for spite. For a moment, he wished he listened to the *ton's* gossip more often; it would likely answer his questions.

Whatever the answers, she was no different from Ravenna.

For Anne's benefit, he fabricated a tale. "We ran into each other, quite literally, at Rundell and Bridge, Lady Raddington. I'm afraid I did not catch her name, but she did drop this." Lucien retrieved the duchess's handkerchief from his waistcoat.

"I will be certain she gets it." Anne reached for the square of linen.

Lucien held it away. "Actually, I think I would like to give it to her myself, as a surprise, you understand."

"What do you mean, my lord?"

Lucien flashed a sudden, charming smile. "Would you be so kind as to send her a note telling her a surprise awaits her in the library?"

"Lord Daneridge, that would be highly improper, considering you've never been formally introduced. What is going on here?"

"Suffice it to say, dear sister, that propriety is no longer an issue between Her Grace and Lord Daneridge."

Lucien whirled on his friend. "Niles, shut up."

Anne gasped. "The Duchess of Warrington? She's a noted evangelical, quite devoted to her cause. Are you saying you—"

"I am saying nothing except that I would like a few words alone with Her Grace." He enunciated the last words bitterly.

"Is the handkerchief really hers?" Anne asked.

Lucien only replied with a terse, "What does 'SB' stand for?"

Anne clearly wanted to know how he could bed a woman and not know her name, but wisely refrained from asking. "It stands for Serena Boyce."

Gaze riveted on her dancing figure, her stunning smile, he nodded. "Will you please send her that note, without mentioning I will be awaiting her."

"Is it necessary?" Anne asked with an apprehensive glance.

He nodded. "I promise the discussion will be quick, and I will do nothing to cause scandal in your house."

Anne looked undecided. Niles prompted her with a nod.

"It is against my better judgment, but I will do so. The library in twenty minutes?"

Lucien glanced at his watch and nodded. And waited.

****

Serena stared at the cryptic note in her hands, delivered only moments ago by a passing servant. A surprise? What manner of surprise? *Go find out, silly,* she told herself. It might even be fun. After all, Lady Raddington had signed the note, and she would never sponsor anything devious. Nonetheless, it made Serena uneasy. She did not know Lady Raddington well, and could not imagine what this impromptu meeting could possibly be about.

"What is it, darling?" Cyrus asked from his chair.

"Nothing at all," she answered, quickly tucking the note away. She placed a concerned hand over his. "How is your back feeling?"

"Not well. I'm going to have one last word with Lord Raddington to thank him for his support, then we will depart. All right?"

"Of course. I'm going to the library to speak with Lady Raddington myself. Fetch me at the library in half an hour?" Serena proposed.

"Splendid."

Serena watched her husband rise and leave the room. With a mixture of curiosity and spine-prickling intuition about her upcoming appointment, she also exited the ballroom.

Much further down the hall, away from the revelry of the rout, Serena found the library. She paused outside the door, listening for her "surprise." It was eerily quiet.

Cautiously, she pushed the door open with her fingertips and cast her eyes about the room. No one awaited her behind the giant cherrywood desk, nor did anyone sit on the massive green brocade sofa at the back of the room. Something in the air, something different, something that disturbed her, lifted the hair at the back of her neck, making her shiver. She paused in the threshold.

Oh, you silly ninny. Lady Raddington will be along in a few moments. She had probably been waylaid in her hostessing duties.

With that thought, Serena stepped further into the long, narrow room. Massive bookshelves lined the walls to both the left and right, reminding her of a library she had visited a month ago—the night she had allowed an unforgettable rake to seduce her.

As she passed through the door, it shut behind her with quiet menace. Startled, she whirled toward the door—and gasped.

Lucien Clayborne. He stood tall, his broad shoulders square and taut within his stark black coat. Her eyes flew to his in question. It was a mistake. The flaring censure, the blazing damnation in those emerald depths filled her with trepidation.

"Hello, sweetheart." The endearment, once spoken like a caress, he now wielded like a knife, sharp and cutting, stabbing her with alarm.

He stepped toward her. Reflexively, she stepped back.

"Or should I properly address you as Your Grace?"

Dear God, he knew. A crash of apprehension roared in her head. Perspiration broke out in fine beads on her palms. She rubbed them together nervously.

"How did you find out?" she asked, her voice trembling.

"Does it matter?" Fury raced across his face, resounded in his deep voice. His eyes glittered dangerously with it, holding the look of a man betrayed, the expression that had been permanently etched on her father's face.

She swallowed. "I...suppose not."

Before she could move, he took the final steps toward her. He grabbed her arms and pulled her forward. His sensual mouth, the one that had taught her such ecstasy, then condemned her.

"What kind of games are you playing?"

She recoiled from his hard-edged rage. "It wasn't a game. I allowed it to happen." She swallowed. "And I should not have."

He paused, and Serena held her breath, praying her honesty had diffused some of his rage.

Instead, her words had the opposite effect.

He clutched her more tightly, his cheeks and mouth tight with fury, his scowl fierce. "Oh, no. You could have backed out anytime. Hell, all you had to do was say no, or better yet, inform me of your married state. Believe me, I would have taken my hands off you in an instant," he snarled. "So what was it you wanted? To make your husband jealous? He's obviously never taken the time to bed you himself." His mouth turned down in open contempt. "Or was that the problem? Were you bored and hot for a man between your legs? Did it feel good to use me?"

She flinched. "Tell me you did not intend to use me, Lord Daneridge," she retorted sharply. "Did you not intend to find a way under my skirt? You intoxicated me with liquor and compliments and kisses, and got what you wanted."

"I'm guilty on all those counts, but I had no knowledge of your virginity or marital status."

Serena looked away from the brutal contempt in his eyes. "I'm sorry. I had no idea it would matter to you."

His voice rose to new levels. "You didn't think it would matter? What happened between us was like *nothing* I've ever felt. Then I woke up to discover you missing and my sheets stained with your virgin's blood. Damnation, how could that not matter to me?"

"It's not something most men would give a second thought," she retorted, remembering the parade of Mama's lovers.

The scowl on his face deepened at that truth. "We are not discussing anyone but you and me. To me, it mattered a hell of a lot."

Serena swallowed a lump of guilt. Not only had she broken her vows to Cyrus and God, but also disillusioned the rogue who had given her such tender pleasure. "Again, I apologize."

"I've no wish to hear another apology, damn it. I want to know why you let me bed you."

She looked down at her hands wringing one another in a nervous, white-knuckled grip. Her voice shook. "I did not intend that at all. Once you rescued me, and then when you...touched me, I simply could not resist."

With a fierce grip on her chin, he forced her gaze upward. "Is that your attempt to flatter me out of my anger, Your Grace?"

"No, I—"

He released her abruptly. "Save the denials. I've no wish to hear them."

"But I am telling you the truth!"

"A woman always is." The biting edge of his sarcasm told her she had confessed her greatest sin in vain.

He paused, sliding spread fingers through his hair. Stray locks fanned out across his forehead rakishly. The implacable line of his jaw made her too aware of him as a man, and she damned herself for thinking carnal thoughts in the face of her guilt and his rage. But damning did not help. Her eyes strayed to his mouth, firm and oh so capable. Her knees melted in remembrance. She felt every inch like her mother.

"I already divorced a traitorous witch like you," he continued. "I have no desire to consort with another who practices deceit as easily as she breathes. And you, sweetheart, fall into that category. *Never* come near me again."

He whirled for the door.

"Listen, please!" She raced after him. "I did not mean to deceive you."

Lucien didn't even pause. He exited the library—and her life—with a slam of the door.

CHAPTER SEVEN

Serena dreamed of him in color.

Lucien kissed her face, his mouth making a teasing foray around her lips. She clasped her arms about his neck and pulled his mouth down to hers. The strains of an orchestra played deep in the background, as the gentle splatter of warm rain on her body saturated her sheer chemise. Then came the hot caress of Lucien's tongue against her own, swirling, entreating—utterly arousing.

Gently, he laid her back in the summertime grass. Its damp, earthy scent, along with the soft blades against her bare back, roused her as he lifted the soft chemise from her body.

Flowers stood high all around them, sequestering them in privacy. He reached for one, a spectacular white orchid just opening its petals to the world. Plucking it between his fingers, he circled her nipple with the bud. Under the guidance of his fingers, the delicate flower drifted downward, touching the sensitive skin of her abdomen. His mouth followed, bestowing one pleasurable kiss after another upon her flesh.

He parted her legs, and she felt the whisper-soft touch of the flower there, where she was most sensitive. When his fingers followed, teasing, tormenting, titillating, she gasped.

"Please," she gasped. "Now."

He chuckled and rose above her, now looming. She noticed then he was still fully clothed, despite her nakedness.

"Please?" he repeated, as if testing the word.

The smile on his mouth died. He grabbed her shoulders and wrenched her from the grass.

"Please what?" he growled. "Bed you again so you can cuckold your husband? So you can use me once more?"

No, she answered silently. Yet, she felt his hands on her body, remembered their pleasure-giving abilities. She yearned for another kiss, like the kiss they shared moments ago. Yes...She did want him, couldn't stop wanting him—

The abrupt, all too realistic slam of a door rent her dream.

Serena gasped, opening her sleepy eyes in disorientation. Cognizant of the perspiration moistening her nightgown—and the damp ache in her body—she looked about her semi-dark bedroom. Light streamed in from behind the blue velvet of her curtains.

No rain, no flowers...no Lucien. She closed her eyes, trying desperately to banish the vision, to understand why the dream haunted her with frightening regularity. Was this how Mama had felt with a new lover?

"Here we go, milady," Caffey piped suddenly from across the room. "Your mornin' chocolate. I brought ye a muffin, too."

Food? Even the thought of it made her stomach protest. "Take it away, Caffey, please."

"Milady, ye must eat. Ye didn't eat yesterday mornin' either. Is somethin' wrong?"

Besides her gnawing guilt? "I've simply no time this morning. Is my husband breakfasting?"

"Aye, milady. Just sat down a few minutes ago."

"Good. Help me dress."

Within half an hour, Serena descended the stairs in search of Cyrus. Today, she decided firmly, she would tell him everything. Perhaps then the dreams would stop. Maybe she would no longer hear the echo of Lucien's contemptuous voice in her head as she had for the last week. *What games are you playing, you little witch?*

Serena reached the dining room, but found it empty.

With an urgent stride, she ventured to Cyrus's office. Knocking discreetly on the closed door, she sighed with relief when he bade her to enter a moment later.

Biting her lip nervously, she stepped into the familiar room and found her husband seated behind his corner desk. His secretary, a middle-aged, bespectacled man, sat on a chair beside him.

"I've no wish to interrupt. Forgive me," she said softly. "I shall come back later."

"Actually, darling, we were just finishing. Good work, Clemson," Cyrus said to his secretary. "If you learn anything else, let me know."

"Of course, Your Grace," the man replied. He cast Serena a contemplative glance that baffled her, then left the room.

"Did you need something, my dear?" Cyrus inquired.

He stared at her, his expression unfamiliar, a look both speculative and knowing. A chill of foreboding crept through her.

She retreated a step. "No. I just came to say good morning. I will see you later this evening."

"Serena, I want to speak with you before you go."

What if he knew? *Oh mercy, what do I say? How do I explain my sinful behavior?*

"About what?" She forced a casual note into her voice.

"The night of June eighteenth, my dear. Would you like to tell me where you were?"

The night she had spent with Lucien. His words ripped the breath from her lungs, tripling the dread and nausea in her stomach.

She looked down, trying to concentrate on the bronze and black design in the carpet. "Melanie and I went to Vauxhall."

"Yes. I remember the two of you leaving here when Lord Highbridge arrived. What happened after that?"

"During the rope dancer's performance, we became separated." She paused to moisten her suddenly dry lips. "As I told you, a man robbed me of my jewelry. A-a stranger saved me."

"I see," he replied, rising to his feet. "And Lord Daneridge was that stranger?"

She swallowed, not daring to take her gaze from the carpet. "Yes."

Cyrus cupped his hands about her shoulders. "My dear, I ask you, not so you can feel guiltier than I know you have been, but to be certain my information is correct."

In surprise, she lifted her gaze to Cyrus's. "Information?"

"Yes. I had Lord Daneridge's situation looked into after I overheard you two talking at the Raddingtons' last week."

Her heart pounded into her throat. "You've known all this time and didn't tell me?"

"I wanted to investigate him before I spoke with you. Quite frankly, I knew very little about the man. And this kind of tryst is so frequent, I could not understand his anger over your marital status."

"He felt that I deceived him purposefully." Her words shook as much as her fingers.

"Yes. I received the report from the investigator this morning. In fact, Clemson was briefing me on it when you knocked."

Serena closed her eyes to endure the jolt of shock and guilt. The hired help knew. Dear Lord, how long before the rumor was all over town? How long before Cyrus was ashamed to call her his wife?

"Oh," she managed the half-whisper.

"The report is quite interesting." Cyrus went on easily, as if discussing nothing odder than the weather. "It explains his behavior at the Raddingtons' thoroughly."

She shook her head. "Cyrus, he won't speak to me again, ever. I cannot see the point in listening—"

"Because someday, perhaps soon, I'm going to die. I will not have you left alone. I've stolen years of your youth. I've told you I realize how selfish I was to seek this marriage. I'm terribly sorry my...condition has led you to this." He patted her back. "I know your tryst with Daneridge never would have happened had I been a healthy man. And when I am gone, I will rest easier if I know you are happily remarried to a man capable of giving you children."

She raised imploring hands. Remarried? "You're healthy, Cyrus. You will not die soon. Do not even say that."

"I am fifty-four and I have gout. I cannot live forever."

Wringing her hands, Serena sat silently, absorbing the truth of his words.

"I investigated Lord Daneridge because, in light of your association, I thought he might be the most suitable choice of a husband."

"Now that we know he is not, must we discuss this?"

"On the contrary. He's of impeccable family. He is wealthy, well-educated, respected by his peers. His divorce is hardly the latest scandal anymore. I think he is an excellent choice."

She couldn't understand why Cyrus was intent on pushing her toward a man who despised her. Or why was he behaving as though he were already in his grave.

"This is lunacy!" Serena insisted. "He is not at all right for me."

"Once you hear what's in this report, I think you will see the matter differently."

She gaped at her husband. "How could I? Cyrus, the man drinks and swears. He is divorced—"

"I am aware of all that. In fact, his divorce is the heart of the issue."

Unwillingly curious, Serena asked, "What do you mean?"

Cyrus rose and began to pace, an action he usually reserved for the delivery of his most persuasive arguments to the Lords. Serena felt a distinct prickle of alarm.

"He married a beautiful girl, Ravenna Stansworth, during her first season," Cyrus began. "Clayborne himself was about twenty-five. Several years later, rumors about town indicated Lady Daneridge was indulging in frequent trysts with several of her footmen. Of course, those were rumors, but one member of the marquess's household staff verified it. He also told the investigator that Clayborne himself discovered his wife with one of the servants."

Understanding dawned with vulgar clarity, painting a warped picture of the woman Lucien must imagine her to be. "Oh, Cyrus. He must think I'm exactly like his former wife."

"Precisely," Cyrus said. "Even worse, Lady Daneridge began a liaison with one of Clayborne's best friends, Lord Wayland. It was an affair of the most embarrassing magnitude. In fact, I recall snatches of the gossip, and you know I rarely listen to much of it. Lady Daneridge wrote Wayland daily. Her pages hounded the man constantly. She followed him at any social gathering where they chanced to meet, and indulged in the most indecent theatrics."

Serena shook her head. Ravenna Clayborne and Mama had been made from the same mold. "Oh, no."

"Yes. And according to the people my investigator spoke with, Clayborne picked Lady Ravenna, and her father agreed to the match. Clayborne wasn't Lady Ravenna's choice of a mate, though, and I suspect she wanted to make Clayborne regret his choice.

"Then," Cyrus continued, "Lord Daneridge received the final insult just over a year ago. He had finally called Wayland out. They had appointed their seconds, who arranged the time and place. Wayland never put in an appearance. Instead, he and Lady Daneridge fled to Italy. Rumor had it she was *enceinte*. The following week, Clayborne began divorce proceedings."

Nausea rolled in her stomach. What kind of a depraved woman would lay with her footmen or allow herself to be seduced by her husband's friend? And what kind of wife with a husband as capable as Lucien would want another man's bastard?

She hung her head. What kind of woman allowed a stranger the liberties her caring husband could not partake of? The possibility that she shared her mother's wantonness grew stronger each day, eating at her.

She did not have to wonder what Lucien thought of her; she knew he believed she and Ravenna Stansworth to be cut from the same cloth.

"Cyrus, I've hurt him terribly. I see now why he is so angry."

"I thought you might. I've also learned something of his upbringing, his education, and his military service. Clayborne is a decorated soldier, and even spent some time in Portugal as a spy until he sustained a leg injury."

"Yes," she whispered absently. "His left knee."

"I believe you're right," Cyrus answered. "He has also suffered a terrible loss recently."

"Yes. We've spoken of it," Serena said numbly, mind whirling.

"I see. Well, you do understand, then."

Yes, she understood grief, that strong, needful emotion that had drawn her tender heart to him and his sad eyes — and led ultimately to her moral downfall.

Yet now that she understood even more, could she continue to let Lucien hurt because of her behavior? No. But neither could she face him in person, to see the scorn on his face. The situation required an apology, no doubt. She hoped he would accept a written one, and prayed it would ease both the pain she had caused, as well as her guilty conscience.

****

"I'm bored," Niles pouted. "It's shocking to admit, but your season is more amusing than mine."

Lucien glanced up from the morning's edition of the *Times*, which told of a conspiracy of police officers that framed young boys to collect reward money. "I feel certain that won't stop you from finding trouble soon."

"Of course not. Such tame living would destroy my reputation." He paused, as if in consideration. "Until then, however, I must live vicariously. Tell me what you plan to do about your virgin duchess."

Lucien set aside the *Times*. "She is *not* mine. We all know that."

"In a way, my friend, she is." Niles seated himself at the end of the sofa. "Can you let her go so easily? Are you not tempted in the least to seek her out again?"

"Knowing now what kind of woman she is, I am certainly better off without her."

Now Niles returned the arched brow. "So that is the excuse you use to console yourself."

In an agitated lunge, Lucien rose from the sofa and swore. "Console myself about what?"

His cool tone didn't put Niles off. "The fact that you still want her."

Lucien felt a restlessness not present since the first revelation of Ravenna's adultery. Perhaps the duchess was under his skin more than he cared to admit.

At a discreet knock, Lucien bade a footman to enter.

"An urgent message for you, my lord, delivered by the Duke of Warrington's page."

His gut seized up tightly as he took the note from a tray. "Thank you."

A message from the duke? Or duchess, more likely. And what could possibly be urgent?

Turning it over in his hands, Lucien studied the unfamiliar wax seal with a frown. Trying to still his suddenly thudding heart, he broke the seal and unfolded the note.

I regret most deeply that my actions have hurt you. Although I doubt I can ever explain myself to your satisfaction, please know I never intended to harm you in any way.

S —

A surge of bewilderment and ire ran through Lucien's veins. What could Her Grace's ploy be now?

"Is the page awaiting a reply?" he asked the footman.

"No, my lord. He was instructed to deliver the message only."

"That will be all," Lucien said, and with a bow the footman exited.

"Damn." What was the woman hoping to accomplish? He studied the mystery from all angles, and failed to discern how this latest bit of duplicity would further her cause, whatever that was.

"What is it, old man? Is it from the duke?" Niles asked.

"The duchess."

Niles raised a brown brow. "What does she say?"

With a sharp flick of his wrist, Lucien sent the note sailing along the surface of a Thomas Hope library table. "She apologized for using me. How polite."

Wincing at Lucien's sarcasm, Niles said, "Perhaps she's genuine about that."

Lucien's cold gaze sliced to his. "And perhaps men will fly to the moon."

Niles gave an exasperated sigh. "She may truly feel she made a mistake. Give the girl some credit for trying to atone."

"Haven't you learned yet, young pup? Women only atone if it suits their purpose."

"No. I haven't found that at all." Niles rose from the sofa and changed the subject, which was obviously going nowhere. "What are your plans for the evening?"

"I'm going to White's. Care to join me?" Lucien said.

Niles shook his head. "No. I've been invited to attend a charming little rout. Why not come with me?"

Lucien paused. "Polite company holds no appeal at the moment."

"You cannot continue to avoid every social function to evade the Duchess of Warrington."

Lucien poured a glass of brandy, studiously avoiding Niles's probing gaze. "I can until I figure out what her game is." *And rid her from my thoughts.*

"Just what will you do until then?" came Niles's sardonic question.

What indeed? Take a mistress? Maybe that would stop the horrifyingly vivid dreams of Serena haunting him each night. Another woman might erase the sweet taste of her honey skin from his memory.

Perhaps, but the terrifying reality was, another woman was the last thing he wanted.

****

Alastair cast his gaze down the narrow East End alley and found it cursedly devoid of anyone who could help him. Despair permeated the air, tainted by hopelessness and violence that swirled in the night's fog. It crept beneath his clothing, seeping insidiously under his skin. His heart pounded and pumped. Staring at the two mountainous men before him, Alastair knew real fright.

"Now, gentlemen," he began nervously. "Let's talk this over. I will pay it all off."

"That's right, guv, or we'll break yer legs."

"It is simply a matter of time. Couldn't you see your way clear to extending me just a few more days?"

One of the thugs scowled. Alastair cursed the fear that made him tremble. He cowered before *no* man, damn it, especially not any the likes of these back-alley scum.

"Ye knew the terms," one of the ruffians said. "Briney told ye; five days, or we start cuttin' ye up, piece by piece. He even gave ye an extra day 'cause he's so nice."

Christ, why had he ever gone to Whitechapel's Rosemary Lane and gotten mixed up with a cent-per-center? He wished he hadn't almost as much as he wished he had a bottle of strong Irish whiskey. But he had owed that East End slum the manager called a "club," and he hadn't had any way to pay except to take a very temporary loan—one he was now having a tad of trouble repaying.

"I realize that. However, tell Briney I will be a very wealthy man soon, if he will simply be patient."

"He don't have to be patient. He just has to be paid. Pay up, guv," the man ordered. "Or else."

Alastair cleared his throat. "I cannot do that just now. But next week—"

A solid, jaw-splintering blow interrupted Alastair. Just as he recovered from the terrible burst of pain, the other man rammed his fist into Alastair's stomach, shoving the breath from his body, then followed that blow with a knee, hard and straight up, to the groin.

Alastair fell to the ground, clutching his genitals, only slightly cognizant of the puddle of urine he had fallen into, now dampening the knees of his pants.

As he tried to rise, a meaty hand grasped his hair cruelly, then propelled his head with smashing force against the wall of the brick building beside him. Pain exploded in his head. The blood trailing down his face in a small but steady stream was a secondary concern.

Alastair stumbled to his knees and tried to back away.

One man grabbed the lapel of his superfine coat and tugged him closer. At the stench of his unwashed body and black teeth, Alastair's stomach revolted, giving up what was left of his dinner. The thug jumped away in disgust.

"Ye can't run from us or Briney, guv. We'll find ye wherever ye hide."

"That's right," the other one added. "Ye've got two days to pay up, or you'll be seein' us again. We won't be so nice then," the man warned.

Alastair sagged against the cold wall with relief as he watched the two men leave the alley.

"Damn it," he muttered to himself. How could he possibly pay them back in two days? He knew very well he couldn't. But this evening had clearly demonstrated the need to put his half-formed plan in motion now.

With that in mind, he half-walked, half-crawled to his coach and ventured to Butcher Row where no sane man who valued his life would dare be, either day or night. But desperation overrode sanity, and Alastair knew two men there, both dangerous, who could be persuaded to commit any crime for a price. And Alastair felt certain he knew enough about the extent of his forthcoming inheritance to convince the old boys he meant business.

CHAPTER EIGHT

That night, Lucien saw Serena, all glorious golden hair and enticing honey skin, the instant she walked into the ballroom. Her low-cut bodice revealed more than a hint of the full breasts he still ached to touch. Her waist looked small indeed beneath a high-waisted gown the color of a ripe peach.

His head spun; his thoughts churned. Desire surged, filling him with pounding need that had gone unsatisfied since that magical night with Serena.

She mumbled something to the woman by her side, who he suspected was her turbaned companion from Vauxhall. Then she directed her eyes toward the room and scanned the crowd.

Her gaze met — and locked — with his.

He watched her lips part slightly, the expression rife with both surprise and vulnerability. An unsettling urge to fight his way across the room and kiss her senseless rushed through him. As if she could read his thoughts, her cheeks flushed like a beguiling pink bloom.

What a lovely liar she made, presenting the picture of innocence.

Lucien yearned to throttle Niles for persuading him to attend this damned rout, then curse him for insisting they stand beside the entrance to await anyone of interest.

He did neither.

He stared at Serena, reminding his runaway desire that she had used him to cuckold the elderly Warrington, had purposely given her virtue to him, a stranger, rather than her husband. That reality did not dissuade his gaze from touching her alluring curls and curves, then meeting her smoky blue eyes.

The woman he recalled Serena referring to as Melanie spoke. The duchess looked to her friend again. A flood of relief filled Lucien, along with an unsettling stab of disappointment.

His hands trembled slightly as he set his empty champagne glass aside. Again, he fixed his attention on the woman mere feet, and yet miles, away.

"The duchess is here, I see," Niles said beside him.

Lucien closed his eyes for a moment, trying to block her from his vision. "Yes."

"You all right, old man? You look sick as a cat."

Lucien nodded, wishing he were anywhere but here, wishing he didn't have to endure the sensual torture of Serena's presence all evening.

She paired up for the next set, and Lucien knew her partner ranked among the worst rakes. Eyes narrowed, he watched the rogue stand much too close, despite the fact the music had yet to begin. Feeling the rush and churn of his blood, Lucien noted Serena politely trying to put space between herself and her partner. The rake was having none of it.

Lucien gripped the handle of his cane. Maybe the duchess wanted the man. Maybe she was teasing him. He told himself to walk away, leave the party.

He stood still, watching her unblinkingly.

The rake pulled Serena yet closer, one hand lingering infuriatingly high on the side of her waist. And Warrington was nowhere in sight. The man's hand moved again, inching ever closer to the underside of her breast. Serena's eyes turned wide with anxiety as she made discreet efforts to pull free.

Lucien hadn't danced in more than five years. His surgeon had claimed that, due to the severity of his knee injury, dancing was one activity he could never indulge in again. He tossed his cane into an empty chair beside him.

Not caring how rude or shocking his behavior was, Lucien's awkward, angry strides carried him across the floor to Serena.

He tapped the rake on the shoulder. "Excuse me, but I believe Her Grace promised this dance to me."

The buck opened his mouth to refute Lucien's claim when Serena spoke instead. "I apologize, but I am afraid Lord Daneridge is right. How silly of me to forget."

At that, the rogue lifted Serena's hand to his lips. "Perhaps another time, Your Grace." He turned to Lucien with a mocking bow. "Daneridge," he acknowledged, then disappeared into the sea of silk-clad women.

Conscious of the fact people were staring, Lucien took Serena in his arms. He tried not to revel in the feel of her pliant, honey-warm body in his embrace, of her hand in his. No luck. His every sense tuned in to her, inciting a mind-robbing desire. Damn her.

A moment later, the strains of a Viennese waltz floated to his ears, taunting him. Five years ago, the waltz had been vulgar. He had never learned the dance.

For a moment, he watched other couples around him, observing the patterns of their feet, how they flowed in time to the lilting music.

Serena lifted her face to his in question. "My lord, are you all right?"

"Fine," he answered tersely.

Without further thought to the fool he would no doubt make of himself, he led Serena through steps that mimicked those around him. His knee was stiff, more so than he had expected. After only three steps, pain shot in bolts through his joint and up his thigh. He lurched more than glided, and knew he looked like the beast leading the beauty.

To his right, he heard a young girl snicker. Serena never mentioned it. In fact, she did nothing to indicate she was even aware of his less than graceful gait. For that, he was grateful.

She simply whispered, "Thank you, my lord. That man was certainly no gentleman."

"If you wanted to be pawed, that's your affair. I thought, however, you might save yourself the embarrassment from doing so in polite company."

Her mouth tightened. "I have no wish to be pawed by anyone."

"Too bad you didn't decide that six weeks ago."

She tightened a hand about his shoulder and inhaled sharply. "As soon as this set is finished, I want you to leave me be."

"I had planned on just that, sweetheart."

One, two, three; one, two, three. He struggled to concentrate on the beat of the music in the tense silence that followed, until Serena's uncertain voice interrupted him.

"Did you not receive my note, Lord Daneridge?"

"Indeed, I did, though it said precious little."

She lifted her chin. "I thought an apology would convince you I meant you no harm."

Serena looked so damned sincere. He'd swallowed this lie once before. "But you said nothing of the matter I truly wish to understand. Why did you let me bed you in the first place?"

Serena's gaze darted to a couple close by. "Can we continue this discussion elsewhere?"

His first instinct was to refuse. He shouldn't become more involved with a married woman he could not banish from his memory. But somehow, he needed to understand the whys of their explosive night together, needed to understand what circumstances had driven an ethereal virgin to his bed.

"Follow me," he said, then escorted her off the floor.

Once out of the cloying fragrances and hot air stifling the ballroom, Lucien breathed deeply. He turned to face Serena in a deserted alcove just round the corner and down the hall. In the background, the orchestra began a country reel as Lucien watched an apology move within her stunning smoky eyes.

"I *am* sorry," Serena began. "I realize I should have insisted you take me home. I knew it was improper. But...after you rescued me, I could not repay your gallant deed by leaving you intoxicated and grief-stricken."

The duchess was full of surprises. She hadn't approached him with false remorse, one of Ravenna's favorite ploys. She shed no tears designed to win his pity. Christ, Ravenna could have won awards performing her act in London's theaters, had she set her mind to it, but Serena's expression was entirely different. Nervous, but startlingly direct. What act was this?

Despite the fact she was married, Lucien wanted to touch her. Her gardenia-like scent filled his senses, reminding him of the pleasure gardens where they met, where he had first noticed her unique fragrance. It also reminded him of the hours they had shared heaven, each giving and receiving it, in his bed. He pushed the memory and the accompanying regret away.

"So you thought to repay me with your virginity?"

She folded her hands nervously before her and bowed her head. "No. You looked sad and desperately in need of someone to comfort you. I know because...I needed those things myself. I realize I should never have allowed—"

"Shhh. I did the chasing," he admitted softly. "I maneuvered you into my coach." He sighed. "Just tell me what sort of reaction you expected to provoke from your husband."

"Provoke?" she asked, puzzled. "I expected to provoke nothing. As I said, it was an impulse I simply did not...could not resist."

He paused, weighing her words for truthfulness. "How is it you're married, but had never been touched before?"

She bit her lip, chewing on it for long moments until he ached to take it between his own and soothe the enticing, abused flesh.

Finally, she blinked once, twice, then swallowed. She looked away before answering, "My...my husband and I rarely occupy the same household, on purpose, I'm afraid. We've been known to have terrible rows—"

"That doesn't account for your wedding night. Why didn't you have one?"

She swallowed again. "My husband was ill at the time, and by the time he was well, I had grown quite accustomed to...being alone."

She was breathing a little too quickly. Her eyes were too wide, and directed anywhere but at him. She was lying. Apparently, this temptress practiced her own form of evasion, albeit an artless one. What was she hiding?

"Fascinating," he drawled. "Perhaps you would like to tell me the truth now?

"Lucien?" he heard a familiar voice call. "Oh, Lucien?"

He swore softly, his brows drawing together in a scowl. "Later, you will give me the truth, Your Grace. All of it." Whirling away, he replied to the intruding voice, "Yes, Aunt Elizabeth?"

He saw her halfway down the passage. Because he was burdened by an injured knee, she moved quicker and greeted him just a foot away from Serena.

"Could you see me home? Your dear uncle is quite swept up in some card game, and my head is simply pounding."

Torn between anger and confusion, his guts shredded by Serena's startling honesty, then her deception, Lucien nodded. "Of course."

His aunt bent to the side, peering behind him. "I apologize. I had no notion you were...engaged."

"I'm finished." *For now.*

****

With a sigh of satisfaction, Cyrus leaned back in his seat, relaxing to the sway and rock of the carriage. He eyed the passing London scenery, watching as they drove out of the city toward Hampstead on the Heath. Sultry late summer air hovered all around, slowly giving way to the whisper of coolness the nights provided.

His journey promised to be a productive one. Lord Mansfield was not only a good host, but also open-minded to a sound political argument, even when the views opposed his own.

Life in general was better than ever. His career was at a pinnacle he had never hoped to reach, even in his wildest youthful imaginings. And most of all, he had a beautiful wife, who might even now be carrying a child—the child that would rid him of Alastair's impending threat to the dukedom.

Sweet Serena, he thought, shaking his head. As he had anticipated she would, she had followed the urging of her young body and heart once he had given her leave. Her choice of a lover had surprised him, however. Cyrus had imagined she would gravitate to a sensitive, romantic type, not a war-hardened soldier and marriage-cynical lord.

But Cyrus was not displeased. According to his investigator's latest report, Lord Daneridge was more than a little infatuated with Serena. That gave Cyrus cause to breathe easier, for he had no doubt Lord Daneridge would protect Serena from any threat Alastair posed after he himself cocked up his toes. He had seen to that.

Suddenly, hoofbeats and a gun blast sounded behind the coach. Cyrus peered out to see two burly men, masked and armed, galloping past his vehicle.

"Stand an' deliver," one shouted.

The two thieves had blocked the road. Realizing escape was next to impossible without armed riders, Cyrus gave the signal to stop.

Dust flying, the coach rolled to a halt. One bandit yanked the door open. Cyrus studied the young face. He looked East End hard, indifferent to such trivialities as pain and compassion.

"Get out, Yer Grace. We got business with ye."

"Now see here," his coachman Roberts said, waving a pistol of his own. "My employer will not deal with the likes of you."

In a quick blur, one highwayman raised his gun and fired. The coachman fell to the ground out of Cyrus's sight, leaving him to fear the extent of his employee's injuries.

Then Cyrus felt the coach sway as his footmen stepped off its back, no doubt creeping off in the dark to save their own pretty skins. The bandits' cries of "bloomin' cowards" confirmed his suspicion. He was alone with two highwaymen, who were both armed and unafraid.

Fear broke a sweat on Cyrus's skin. By God, they did mean business.

Calmly, so as not to give the appearance of rebellion, Cyrus stepped from the coach. "I'll come out, gentlemen. I'm assuming you would like all my valuables?"

The two men exchanged glances, as if conferring, before the one before him spoke. "Aye, all o' them."

Without a word, Cyrus gave over the watch from his waistcoat, the rings off his fingers, as well as his snuff box and all his currency, right down to the last farthing.

As the thieves counted the money, Cyrus asked, "Does that complete our transaction?"

The one before him shook his mangy head. The tight line of the man's jaw and the ruthlessness in his dilated eyes sent a tremor of dread snaking up Cyrus's spine.

"Not quite, Yer Grace," the thug said. "We was hired to kill ye."

CHAPTER NINE

Serena paced in the drawing room nearest the entrance hall. She wasn't in the mood to appreciate the soothing qualities of the rich burgundy- and ivory-hued surroundings.

Restlessly, she whirled about. Her eyes darted to the Chinese mantle clock. Sweet mercy, that hour hand was inching close to the three o'clock mark. Where could Cyrus be at this time of the morning? He'd said he would return from Hampstead no later than midnight. He was nearly three hours late, a rare occurrence for a man who prided himself on the utmost punctuality.

Please God, don't let anything have happened to him. Cyrus couldn't leave her alone, not without his comforting friendship.

Ever since she had confessed to her liaison with Lucien Clayborne, a brightness in Cyrus's eyes, absent since the early days of their marriage, had reappeared. His step seemed lighter, his mood consistently jovial—all because he was banking on the potency of one man and the fertility of his wife. And she herself was beginning to put some merit into the possibility; she was over three weeks late in her menses.

The front door crashed open, startling her from her thoughts. Heart pounding, breath held, she raced down the stairs to the entrance hall.

A specter from her nightmares swayed where he stood—Cyrus's coachman, filthy, bruised, and bloody. Gruesome splotches of blood stained his gold-trimmed uniform. His hair hung limply, wig askew. Fear and dismay etched the ravaged lines of his face.

"What's happened? Where is my husband?" she demanded, trying to force aside the feeling that Fate's hands were grasping for her throat.

"Your Grace ..."

"Where is he?" she demanded.

Panting, gasping, the coachman said, "In the coach, but—"

Serena never heard the rest. Feet flying, she darted across the entrance hall, out the open door, into the chilly night air. Terror clawed at her. Would her premonition be a gruesome reality? Vaguely, she heard the uproar of the servants rushing out behind her.

"Wait! Your Grace!" she heard the porter call.

She knew what that shout meant—felt it in the darkest, most dread-filled part of her soul, but not for an instant did she consider stopping. Cyrus was still in his coach, not alighting the minute he'd pulled to the front, as usual. That fact, accompanied by the coachman's pale, disheveled state, could only mean something dreadful, unthinkable, had happened.

Around her, the thin yellow light of the flares permeated the London fog swirling eerily before her, filling her head with the surreal visions of gray, deathly faces. The burning cloths from the flares with their oil-saturated scent exploded in her head, spurring her forward.

Not Cyrus. She had prayed for his safety. "Please don't punish him for my sins," she implored above. "Please let him be alive."

Serena never stopped her frantic dash until she reached the coach, gleaming a sinister black in the cold night. With numb, trembling fingers, she yanked the door open.

Cyrus lay inside, pale and still, his form stretched awkwardly across the seat, as if he'd been dropped that way. Shock haunted his achingly familiar, death-frozen eyes.

She backed away in horror. "No!"

Cyrus couldn't die. He wasn't ready to leave this earth. She wasn't ready for life without him.

Her desperate eyes roved his form, wanting more than anything to deny the drying crimson stains of his life's blood covering his face and once white shirt.

"Tell me he will live," she screamed to God above.

Silence.

"Tell me he will live, damn You!"

"Milady," Caffey said, gently grasping her shoulders. "I'm very sorry."

Cyrus could not die. She wouldn't let him. Life without his gentle guidance was too frightening. "Have the porter take him to his room. Lay him out on his bed. I will heal him."

"'Tis sorry I am, milady, but it's too late." Vaguely, Serena noted her maid's pale face and sorrowful eyes.

Her feet moving with their own will, Serena tried to climb into the coach. Without the aid of the steps, the waist-high vehicle became an obstacle she felt compelled to overcome. If she could just touch him, certainly she would discover this was a hoax, a cruel trick of the dark. Her arms ached, her knees stung where she scraped them. Still, her only thought was to close the distance between her and Cyrus.

She struggled into the vehicle, sinking to her knees at his feet upon the coach's floor. Through the ghostly light of the flickering flares, she saw blood covering the familiar face stemming from a shot to the forehead. Cyrus's coloring was an unnatural gray. His chest did not move.

Serena released a guttural animal sound. The hot rush of tears and a swell of nausea rushed from the flood of grief and the powerful urge to deny what her eyes told her.

Caffey's hand touched her shoulder. "Come inside, milady. It's much too late to be out."

Serena's sobbing began anew. Grief crashed through her, robbing her of all but the will to cry. What would life be like without his wisdom and patience?

"I understand, milady," Caffey whispered softly, her touch gentle. "But His Grace must be brought inside and laid out. This cold won't be doing him no good. He'll get...stiff," she finished awkwardly.

At that moment, the porter appeared. Several other of her servants hovered behind his, a few of them shaking their heads.

"Go away!" she ordered.

The servants' gazes registered pity as they ambled away—all except Caffey and the porter.

"You heard me," Serena directed to her maid.

Squaring her shoulders, Caffey lifted her chin. "This is one time, milady, when you'll be doin' as I tell ye. Now come out of that coach."

Serena resisted until Caffey grasped each of her arms and dragged her away from her husband. Immediately, the porter moved forward to remove Cyrus from the coach. The manservant labored under the heavy burden.

The vision of Cyrus lying unmoving within the porter's arms brought about the stark truth, the realization that Cyrus was genuinely no more. She turned into Caffey's waiting arms and sobbed.

Moments later, her maid urged her toward the town house. She went, her limbs moving automatically, as if inside, she, too, were lifeless. The porter followed behind with Cyrus.

Once inside, the trio encountered Cyrus's coachman again, bleeding and wheezing upon the cold marble of her entrance hall.

"Your Grace," he gasped. "Sorry...so sorry."

She nodded, not trusting her voice as she watched Caffey examine his wound. True, the coachman was injured, but he was breathing, damn it; *he* was alive. Why wasn't Cyrus?

With a mumble, the porter excused himself to the duke's chambers, still bearing Cyrus's body.

"Your Grace ..." The coachman coughed before continuing. "It happened so fast ..." He broke off into a groan as Caffey began sponging the bleeding hole in his shoulder.

"What happened, Roberts?" Serena's voice dropped to a bewildered whisper.

Pain flickered across the coachman's face. "Looked like the bridle-lay."

"A highwayman?" she questioned in horror.

"Two," he gasped. "Only I don't think they was."

"What do you mean? Why did they shoot him? Did my husband refuse to give them his valuables?"

"No, that's" — he coughed — "my point. He did what the culls demanded, but when His Grace asked if...he was free to go...one told His Grace they was *hired* to kill your husband. Then they shot 'im." The coachman gasped again under Caffey's probing fingers.

"They knew who my husband was?" Serena pressed on.

The coachman nodded weakly. "Called him Your Grace."

Serena's mind raced with possibilities. Hired to kill him? Certainly, he had political enemies. He possessed a thousand philosophical differences with easily a hundred men, but it was doubtful any of them would wish Cyrus dead. No, only one person stood to gain so much from her husband's death; only one man held him in that much contempt: Alastair.

"I'm going to have you repeat your story to a Bow Street Runner after you've rested," Serena said.

Roberts nodded once more, then fell unconscious.

The porter returned, and with Caffey's help, saw the coachman to the servant's quarters for patching.

Whirling thoughts of Alastair's ruthless plot crowded her mind as Serena wandered to the library.

Caffey entered behind her minutes later. "Let me pour ye a bit of brandy, milady. Ye need it."

Serena nearly recited her ready-made speech about sinner's drink. After all, she hadn't had a drop since her wonderful, disastrous night with Lucien. That seemed like another lifetime. She nodded and accepted the glass without protest.

Caffey saw her seated on a cream-tone Hepplewhite sofa. Serena gulped the brandy, praying for the fortitude to endure.

"Milady," she began. "What about the...arrangements for His Grace?"

"I will see to them." She paused, turning over the ramifications of the coachman's tale. "All of them."

In the lonely hours ahead, Serena would wonder where she'd found the will to push aside her grief and deal with the issues at hand. But deal with them she did, from the undertaker's arrangements, to Cyrus's solicitor, Mr. Higgins. After she directed the porter to throw straw in the street and ordered the staff into mourning, she penned a note to the agent at Warrington Castle, telling him to prepare for Cyrus's impending internment in the family vault.

Then she summoned the Bow Street Runners, and spoke with John Vickery, an experienced officer. Vickery didn't seem very hopeful that they could find the "highwaymen," despite Roberts's description, much less link the killers to Alastair. But Serena swore she would do just that—or die trying.

*

At nine o'clock that same morning, Lucien finally reached his Hanover Square town house. He felt like hell. After sleepless hours plagued by memories of Chelsea, and damn her, Serena too, he had arisen in the wee hours and dressed, opting to find solace in his club and a bottle.

Back home, Lucien discarded his hat and gloves in the entrance hall, automatically handing them over to Holford. Rubbing gritty, sleep-deprived eyes with his thumb and forefinger, he headed for the stairs, mentally counting the number of steps to his bed.

"Excuse me, my lord," Holford called. "A gentleman awaits you in your study. He arrived with an urgent summons an hour ago and asked to wait for your return."

"An urgent message?" He frowned. "From whom?"

"I believe the gentleman identified himself as the Duke of Warrington's solicitor, my lord."

Warrington's solicitor? Here? What the hell for? Lucien searched the possibilities for that answer and only one seemed plausible: The duke meant to initiate a divorce.

Foreboding ate at his gut. The last thing he wanted was public scandal all over again. But clearly, Warrington had somehow learned of the night he had made love to the duchess. His Grace must have decided to sue him for Criminal Conversation, which Lucien knew well was the first step in obtaining a divorce through England's lofty Parliament. He swore again.

From firsthand experience, Lucien was well aware how down-in-the-mire such proceedings could become. Lord Wayland had not chosen to appear at his own hearing to defend himself. The man hadn't any defense. Lucien had dug up too many witnesses. It was at that proceeding he heard in minute detail of his wife's encounters with Wayland, his one-time friend.

Gripping the ivory-handled cane in his left palm, Lucien wondered just who Warrington's witnesses would be, and how much of the night he had spent in Serena's arms would soon become public knowledge, and therefore, the *ton's* major scandalbroth.

Inhaling a deep breath, Lucien made his way to the study.

He spotted a wiry, silver-haired man perched uncomfortably on an azure-blue elbow chair. Gray superfine stretched crisply across the solicitor's tautly held shoulders and back.

"You wished to see me?" Lucien asked into the silence.

The small man turned and rose in a single, startled motion. Once recovered, he bowed his head respectfully.

Lucien cocked a cynical brow, wondering at the man's deferential manner in light of an ugly, impending divorce.

"My Lord Daneridge?"

"Yes, and you are ...?"

"Higgins. Mr. Meyer Higgins. I am...was the Duke of Warrington's solicitor."

Lucien was curious about the man's sudden change in wording, but said nothing. "What can I do for you, Mr. Higgins? My butler indicated you have a message of an urgent nature."

"Indeed." The solicitor fished through his coat pockets, his thin fingers curled with age, until he produced a letter bearing the Warrington seal. Mr. Higgins held it out. Almost reluctantly, Lucien took it, fearing the missive would open a whole Pandora's box of scandal.

When he made no move to read its contents, an alarmed Mr. Higgins said, "As I indicated earlier, this communication is of the utmost urgency. In fact, His Grace asked me to deliver this to you immediately before dealing with any of the other instructions he left regarding his estate."

"His estate?" Lucien quizzed, a chill of dread darting through him. Certainly, the Duke's estate had nothing to do with his divorce. "What do you mean?"

"I'm terribly sorry. I assumed you already knew...I mean, since he instructed me to come to you first, I assumed that you and His Grace were well acquainted." When Lucien didn't respond to the implied question, Mr. Higgins continued. "His Grace was killed by highwaymen last evening on Hampstead Heath."

Killed? There had to be some mistake. Lucien's mind whirled as shock numbed his body. "Dear God."

Mr. Higgins cleared his throat. "Yes. The coachman brought the body back to Her Grace early this morning."

Serena. Yes, what about Her Grace? Would she mourn her husband's passing? Or feel a sense of emancipation? Would those sultry blue eyes be shining with tears of sorrow or joy?

Those unanswered questions and others rolled through the confusion in his mind as he broke the duke's wax seal and read.

Lord Daneridge,

If you receive this missive, it is because I have died by means most foul. Nor am I the only target of this evil; my wife will be in terrible danger after I am gone. I tell you this because I hope, in light of your intimate acquaintance with Serena, you will consent to protect her from the violence that has ended my life and threatens to end hers also. I beg you to consider this plea. I trust no other with her welfare. Watch over her. Keep her from harm's way by any means necessary so I may rest in peace.

Cyrus, Duke of Warrington

What "evil" had Warrington written about? He could not discern how a duchess, unless traveling on a near-deserted road, could be in danger from highwaymen. And how on earth had Warrington learned of his own "intimate acquaintance" with Serena? Had she told Warrington in the hopes of provoking a response from her busy, politically involved husband? Maybe that had been her game all along.

Slowly, Lucien lifted his gaze from the letter, trying to smooth out his scowl of confusion. "I'm afraid I do not understand, Mr. Higgins. What exactly did Warrington want?"

The small solicitor cleared his throat in obvious discomfort. "I fear I cannot shed any light on the letter, my lord. His Grace did not share its contents with me, which I must admit I found highly irregular. In fact, if I may say so, I found the entire...situation highly irregular."

"Situation?"

"Yes, well, His Grace usually consulted with me in all legal matters...and occasionally a personal one or two," he boasted. "But in this, he was most secretive, and most insistent I reach you immediately upon being notified of his death."

Lucien wondered how much Mr. Higgins did or did not know about himself and the duchess. "And he left nothing else? No other clue?"

"I'm afraid not, my lord, except the wish that you attend the reading of his will."

"Why?" Lucien demanded. "I can't see a reason for my presence. I cannot possibly be mentioned."

"But you are, my lord." When Lucien opened his mouth to question the solicitor further, Mr. Higgins cut in. "I'm not at liberty to say more now. The reading will be a week hence in my offices. I shall leave the address and time with your butler."

Lucien nodded and turned to show the man out when, unexpectedly, Mr. Higgins spoke again. "You know, my lord...it's as if His Grace knew his time had come. He composed that missive and rewrote his entire will this Tuesday past."

Less than a week ago. Lucien swallowed nervously, confusion infusing every thought. What the hell was all this about?

The diminutive solicitor took his leave. Lucien nodded absently to the man, his mind in turmoil. He read Warrington's missive once more, slowly this time, hoping to discern a message he had missed the first time. Nothing. Only a jumble of unanswered questions.

A moment later came the realization that if Mr. Higgins couldn't explain the meaning of this mysterious missive, a certain duchess might well be able to.

CHAPTER TEN

Despite the fact Lucien knew Warrington was dead, the sight of straw dusting the street before the town house brought the secondhand news into the realm of stark reality.

At the door, a conspicuously red-eyed butler greeted Lucien. "I'm sorry, my lord. Her Grace is now mourning and not receiving callers."

"I am aware of Warrington's death." Lucien paused to withdraw Warrington's letter from his coat pocket. "His solicitor delivered this missive this morning from the duke. I must consult the duchess about its contents."

Discreetly, the butler's eyes drifted down to examine the broken seal. It must have satisfied him, because he opened the door further, allowing Lucien to step into the entrance hall.

"May I say who is calling?"

"Daneridge," Lucien answered impatiently.

"Right this way, Lord Daneridge. Her Grace is in the duke's study."

Gripping the handle of his cane for support, Lucien followed. They stopped before a pair of massive dark wood doors, embellished in Baroque-style carvings. The butler announced his presence with a discreet knock.

"Yes, Mannings?"

Lucien knew that soft voice. It was just a hint shy of husky. It rang with femininity. Her voice brought recollections of a soft gardenia scent, her honey skin, hair of golden fire...and the powerful combustion of her awakened passion. He swore beneath his breath, willing the surfacing memories back into the recesses of his memory, where he could again call them forth at a more appropriate time.

"Lord Daneridge to see you, Your Grace."

She paused. "Show him in, Mannings."

The butler opened one imposing door, and Lucien entered. Immediately, his eyes fixed upon the petite width of her back as she stood stiffly before the white marble fireplace. He noted she had dressed, from the cap covering her glorious golden hair to her no-nonsense slippers, in unrelieved black. Because she meant it or because it was socially expected?

Slowly, she turned. She crossed her arms over her chest. He wondered if the gesture was designed to ward off the cold or keep him away.

"My lord," she acknowledged, her voice barely above a whisper.

Lucien nodded in return. He took three steps toward her; on the fourth, she backed away.

Her skin did not appear a healthy peach tone, as it had the night he had held her. Today, she looked pale and gaunt. The change had as much to do with her grief-stricken state as with the mourning black she wore. Her blue-gray eyes, rimmed in sleepless, tear-induced red, stood out in her oval face. For an adulteress, she looked genuinely anguished.

"I'm sorry," he offered, and discovered he felt the sentiment.

She bit her lower lip mercilessly. Lucien saw her wrestling against the urge to cry.

"I heard less than an hour ago," he continued.

Still, she said nothing.

She looked out of place here. Delicate amidst the towering mahogany bookcases lined with political and historical titles, incongruously sorrowful beside the ivory and warm green of the library's decor, utterly feminine within her late husband's masculine high-ceilinged domain.

Behind her, above the fireplace, hung her gilt-framed portrait, one she obviously sat for in happier times. Her painted expression was placid, her smoky blue eyes open and friendly—so different than the guarded look she wore now. The artist had captured the curve of her mouth perfectly. Her lips whispered that she knew a secret, a pleasurable one. Lucien found himself wanting to persuade her to share it with him.

"Why did you come?" she finally asked, interrupting his runaway thoughts.

Clearing his throat, he answered, "Mr. Higgins came to see me this morning. He delivered this missive your husband wrote me last week."

Serena took the letter from his extended hand with trembling fingers. Slowly, apprehension flashing across her pale face, she unfolded it. Lucien held his breath while she read. He wondered how much of this, if any, would be a surprise to her.

As her eyes moved across the paper, she gasped. Her cheeks suffused with a becoming pink that relieved the severity of her mourning black.

She finished and refolded the missive, careful to keep her gaze directed down.

"Well?" he prompted. "What does this mean?"

She blinked rapidly, unsuccessfully fighting off a barrage of tears. The crystal drops fell down her face as she clutched the letter in her hand. "I'm so sorry. Terribly sorry. Cyrus should never ..." She trailed off in obvious mortification.

"Never what?" he asked, determined to keep his voice gentle.

She paused and turned away. Lucien watched as sobs shook her shoulders. "H-he should never have contacted you this way, never tried to force responsibility for my welfare upon you."

"But he did because he knew I seduced you, is that not right?"

Gaze averted down, Serena nodded.

Lucien stared at the nape of her neck, watched tendrils of her fair hair caress her soft skin. Her shoulders shook in grief again. His self-control snapped. Certainly she deserved a bit of sympathy on her loss. Even if she had cuckolded the man, she had clearly cared for him on some level.

He moved toward her and set aside his cane, leaning it against a gleaming mahogany desk. He remembered the searing blade of grief well, still experienced its gut-ripping pain every day. And she looked like a woman seized by that pain. He paused, puzzled by an urge to lend her comfort, despite her deception. How would she react to the physical contact? How would he?

He reached for her, lightly placing his hands on her shoulders. Beneath his palms, her shoulders lifted and stiffened, but she did not protest. Slowly, praying he would not scare her, he turned her into his arms.

He needed only half a step to close the distance between them and cautiously took it, hearing the rustle of her black crepe as he moved closer to her body. His heart thudding against the wall of his chest, feeling an awareness of her almost tangible grief, he eased his arms around her. Without a word, she accepted the embrace, the fabric of her widow's weeds swaying against his legs as she cried.

No coyness, no ploy to use the situation to instill pity; she was much different than Ravenna in that respect. Instead, she welcomed his comfort by moving further into his embrace, sliding her arms around his middle.

God, it felt good to hold her, so good he hated to admit how much. The embrace made him all too cognizant of the fact he had yearned for the perfect fit of her body against his, made him aware that one night with her hadn't been nearly enough. With her softness, her pliancy, he could almost push aside the harsh fact that she was an adulteress.

Almost, but not quite.

He shoved the thought away and soothed her cheek with the pad of his thumb. "How did he find out about us?"

She swallowed and wiped her eyes with a soft, white handkerchief, exactly like the one he kept in his pocket.

"He—he overheard us talking in the library at the Raddingtons' ball."

Lucien swore softly. "How angry was he?"

Against his chest, she shook her head. "He wasn't."

He frowned, trying to digest her answer. "What did he say?"

"Very little. In fact, he didn't tell me he knew about that night until last week."

The same time Warrington had rewritten his will. A coincidence? Probably not. From everything he had heard, the Duke of Warrington had not been the kind of man who allowed anything to happen by coincidence. "Do you know why he waited so long to tell you?

At that, she swallowed and backed out of his embrace. "He had you investigated."

"He *what*?" Lucien exploded. "What the hell for? Why didn't he just call me out?"

"Cyrus never believed in violence and did not want to duel." She shrugged. "As I said, he wasn't angry."

"Why did he send me this letter?"

She paused and turned. She began pacing, and Lucien watched the black toes of her slippers peek out from beneath a black flounce trimming the bottom of her dress. "I think you should sit down, Lord Daneridge."

Was she planning to impart bad news?

She turned her gaze upon him, clearly refusing to say anything more until he had done as she bid. Reluctantly, a mixture of suspicion and apprehension moving through his blood, he sat on an emerald brocade sofa.

Serena took a deep breath, the air lifting her shoulders before she said, "You were right earlier. Cyrus believed, though incorrectly, our liaison should make my safety your responsibility, and he had you investigated because he wanted to ascertain your suitability as a protector."

"And what was his verdict?" Lucien asked tightly.

She lowered her gaze. "He was quite satisfied, but you needn't heed it. I hardly hold you accountable. I shall see to myself."

Lucien cocked a brow in question. "Exactly what is this danger he wrote of so nebulously? I fail to see how this same highwayman could endanger your safety."

"It's nothing," she insisted, her hands moving together. "Cyrus was quite protective of me, perhaps too much so. He often imagined all manner of perils that could befall me."

Lucien didn't believe her for an instant. He knew Warrington's reputation. The man would never have written that note, would never have involved him in Serena's life, because of an imagined danger. The man, quite simply, had been too shrewd for such nonsense.

And Warrington had been murdered.

The question was, what was Serena hiding?

"How about the truth this time?" He laced his tone with hard-edged command.

She hesitated, and he continued, "Either you tell me, or I shall find out for myself. Don't think I won't."

She clenched frustrated fists. "Cyrus erred in sending you that missive. It means nothing."

Lucien bolted from the sofa, ignoring the protesting jolt from his knee. "Damn it, he sent me the note for a reason. I want to know why."

"Do not use that language with me! Whatever you think, I'm still a lady."

"I'll use any kind of language I damn well need to get you to tell me the truth." He grabbed her arm, fingers gripping tightly. "If you're truly in danger, I want to know."

"You have no right!"

"I'm making it my right."

Yanking her arm from his grasp, she held her palms forward to ward him off. "All right. The danger Cyrus wrote of is not from the highwaymen. It's from the man who hired them."

She paused, directing her gaze upward. Whether she fought off tears or asked for divine strength, Lucien wasn't sure.

Finally, she continued. "My husband had no...legitimate issue. His nephew, Alastair, the former Earl of Marsden, is his legal heir."

Lucien vaguely remembered from gossip that Marsden was a slovenly philanderer, a gambler, and a drunk. He had heard whispers that the earl's creditors were becoming impatient, even physical, in their demands.

"If you know of him at all, you know he is a disgrace to Cyrus's family," Serena added.

"I've heard something to that effect."

Serena paused. "I believe Alastair hired these highwaymen to kill my husband for his inheritance."

Lucien stood unmoving in stunned silence. Did she understand the serious nature of her accusation? Her nervous expression, accompanied by her hand-wringing, told him she did, and believed it, too, with a fear she did not want to admit aloud.

With a deep breath, she forged on. "I also have reason to believe that once Cyrus's will is read, Alastair will want me dead as well."

CHAPTER ELEVEN

Hoping for a few private moments to calm her nerves before the reading of Cyrus's will, Serena arrived at the solicitor's office in the City twenty minutes early. But when Mr. Higgins's clerk escorted Serena into the dim, candlelit office, she found the small, cluttered room already littered by Alastair's foul presence.

Behind her, the clerk carried in a small wooden chair. "Where would you like this, Your Grace?"

Serena pointed to the corner of the tiny room, the one furthest from Alastair, a scant two feet away.

Afterward, the clerk departed, closing her in with Alastair. She directed her gaze perfectly forward, neither looking at the shelves lined with deed boxes to her left, nor the cur slouching in a spread-legged position on another chair to her right.

At her cut, Alastair laughed, an obnoxious, smug chuckle that ripped through her raw grief and boiling anger. Serena sat stiffly in her appointed seat, refusing to give him the satisfaction of acknowledging his insidious presence. She consoled herself with the thought that somehow, someway, she would see him in Newgate.

"What's the matter, *Your Grace?*" Alastair taunted. "Are you offended that people will soon address me as 'Your Grace'?"

Reluctantly, she turned her frosty gaze in his direction. Keeping a tight rein on her urge to jump from her chair and label him a killer, she lifted her chin. "Nothing that concerns you interests me in the least."

She returned her stare forward and focused on Mr. Higgins's bulky desk, nearly swallowed whole by stack after stack of documents. More than anything, she wanted to scratch the victorious, self-satisfied grin off of the face Alastair had for once shaven.

"Everything that concerns me will interest you from now on. You'll be beholden to *me* for your upkeep." He paused. "Would you like to see Warrington Castle again?"

Serena clenched both fists and teeth, refusing to answer. She loved the serenity of Sussex, loved the earthy people, the quaint castle village, the majesty of the keep itself. The sadistic bastard knew it.

"I know you want to go back to that pile of stones, but I won't let you. I'll deny you admittance, you holier-than-thou bitch!"

He inched to the edge of his chair, leaning forward across the much too small space separating them, into her line of vision. When she resisted meeting his stare, he grabbed her arm. Though Serena tried to twist away, Alastair's vise-like grip ensured his hold. "Do you hear me? Warrington's doors will never be open to you again."

He jerked her closer. "I know your kind. You're nothing but a fortune-hunting slut. You prostituted yourself into marriage for his money, didn't you? Did you do your 'wifely duty' at his insistence? I'll wager you did, and that you hated every minute of bedding down with a man old enough to be your grandfather so he could get a brat on you." Alastair laughed evilly again. "But it never worked. It's all *mine* now."

He paused, the pale blue of his eyes resembling ice chips. A malicious smile turned up the corners of his thin mouth. "Unless you choose to share my bed. I could be persuaded to give over a couple of pounds for a good tumble from the Queen of Sanctimony herself." He laughed. "I would love to know just how much of your mother's hot blood you have. What do you say?"

Rage erupted inside Serena. She turned to Alastair and slapped his face with all her might, and couldn't bring herself to be horrified by her own violence. Instead, she clenched her palm, which tingled with both impact and satisfaction, into a fist. "Does that answer your question?"

Alastair recoiled, slinking back into his chair before turning his hate-filled glare upon her. "You'll regret that. You *will* share my bed, and be happy to do it, too, if you want to see Warrington Castle again."

Serena barely restrained the urge to spit in his face. "Judgment day will come before I let you touch me!"

Before Alastair could reply, Higgins's clerk opened the door. The bespectacled man cleared his throat and carried yet another chair into the room. Alastair retreated to his seat.

Lucien entered the office. Immediately, his unnerving green gaze found her. He studied her, his eyes narrowing in question, then suspicion. A moment later, he swerved his gaze to Alastair. Serena swallowed, certain Lucien would see the red imprint of her hand on the miscreant's cheek.

He faced Alastair, quiet menace dominating his stance, filling the air around him. Alastair returned his glare, his narrow face holding insulting dismissal.

Lucien continued to stare. Alastair met him, measure for measure. Tense moments dragged on. Serena fidgeted during their strained silence. She felt as if they were holding a contest of wills to see which could force the other to flinch first.

Serena held her breath, wondering what Lucien would do, praying he would not make a scene. She hardly felt relief when Alastair swore and looked away from the silent battle in apparent indifference. The fury behind his facade hardly fooled her. She made a mental note to inform Lucien about Alastair's vindictive nature.

Without a word, Lucien yanked his chair from the clerk's hands and slammed its wooden legs against the hard floor directly between her and Alastair. The resulting thump resounded ominously in the small office.

Biting her lip, she turned her gaze to Lucien's familiar face and read the animosity in the hard edge of his jaw, in the tense set of his broad shoulders beneath a Devonshire brown coat.

"Who is he and why the hell is he here?" Alastair demanded.

Mr. Higgins entered the room behind them. "Lord Daneridge is here at your uncle's request."

Alastair shot Lucien a suspicious, venomous stare, but made no other comment.

"Shall we begin?" Higgins asked, directing his question to no one in particular, making his way to the front of the room.

"Damn it, of course," Alastair said impatiently.

Serena folded her hands in her lap, trying to ignore Lucien's unwavering stare at her right, his eyes filled with silent question.

For days, she'd tried not to think about the financial aspects of Cyrus's death as they related to her. She had no doubt he would have thought to provide for her, but agonized that Warrington Castle, the largest of the entailed estates, was beyond her reach forever. And Alastair thought of it as a pile of stones. Dear God, with that attitude, she knew he would neglect it, never put money into its upkeep. He would clearly run it into the ground, and the thought filled her with impotent rage. Legally, she could do nothing.

She also wondered exactly what Cyrus had left her to warrant sending Lucien such a dire warning regarding her safety.

Mr. Higgins sat behind the cluttered desk and cleared his throat, his small mouth pinched tightly in disapproval. "Before I start, I must tell you I've summoned you to my office for this reading because His Grace requested it, despite the fact I told him it was highly irregular. And I apologize, Your Grace." he said to Serena, "but surely you know how unusual it is to have a woman present at such a time, wife or not." Serena made no answer, and Higgins continued as if he'd never expected one. "However, I will honor his request and summarize the will's contents, as it is a very lengthy document. Of course, it will be made available to you upon request.

"First, His Grace bequeaths five hundred pounds to every servant for every five years of their employment."

Alastair grunted. "Get on with the important details, man."

Brows raised, Mr. Higgins continued. "And to Waterson, my valet of thirty years, I leave an additional two thousand pounds, plus the aforementioned amount, as well as the cottage in Wales."

Alastair squirmed in his chair, a whispered curse littering the air.

Mr. Higgins cleared his throat. "To Catherine, Madeline, and Anne, my three natural daughters, I leave each twenty-five thousand pounds in trust with their mother, Maria, until their majority at twenty-one, plus an additional ten thousand pounds each for their dowry, should they choose to wed. If not, they will each receive that sum upon the occasion of their twenty-fifth birthday."

Alastair shot up out of his chair, his face a mottled red. "Over a hundred thousand pounds to his by-blows? That's bloody ridiculous!"

"My lord," Mr. Higgins directed to Alastair. "Please be seated so I may continue, and try to refrain from further such outbursts."

Alastair sat reluctantly, his hands curled up into fists.

"To my wife's grandmother, Lady Harcourt, I leave my two spaniels and the sum of five thousand pounds to see to their upkeep."

Suddenly, Mr. Higgins paused. Serena looked up from her lap and scanned the room. Alastair sat perched on the edge of his chair, his round face flushed and tense. Mr. Higgins appeared thoughtful, as if trying to choose his next words. Lucien leaned back in his chair, his casual posture doing little to hide his interest.

After several silent moments, the solicitor ventured, "This next portion of his will, His Grace rewrote just a week before his death. It's most odd, I must say."

"What is it?" Alastair demanded to know, his face a bright, unbecoming red, his eyes narrow.

Glaring at Alastair, Mr. Higgins said, "To you, he left the entailed estates of Warrington Castle, Coleshill in Berkshire, and Eltham Lodge in Kent, as well as the entailed family jewels."

"What else?" Alastair demanded. "How much money?"

Higgins ignored Alastair and turned to Serena. "Your Grace, again, I find this most odd, but your husband left all other family funds, all liquid assets, all five unentailed properties, including the London town house, and everything within each residence, exclusively to you. The value of your portion of the estate is an estimated four hundred thousand pounds."

Serena gasped and closed her eyes. Cold dread pervaded every muscle, every pore. This was the reason Cyrus had written Lucien asking him to protect her; Cyrus had known exactly how enraged — and deadly — Alastair would be upon hearing this.

As if to prove her and Cyrus correct, Alastair exploded from his chair. "*All* the money? He left his whole bloody fortune to that whore?" He whirled on Serena. "No doubt you learned from your slut of a mother how to mesmerize a man, how to squeeze his cock with your tight little—"

"That's enough." Lucien's voice sliced through the thick animosity vibrating in the stifling air. Alastair fell silent, his wild eyes blazing hate at Serena.

Alastair turned his malicious gaze to Lucien.

Higgins glared at Alastair. "Please sit. There is more."

The brute turned his attention to the solicitor. He stormed across the minuscule room to lean nose-to-nose with Mr. Higgins. "I'll contest the will. The old fool was insane." His gaze shifted to Serena, stabbed her with a hate-filled glare, then returned to the solicitor. "Or bewitched."

"Sit down," Higgins commanded. Once Alastair had reluctantly done so, the solicitor explained, "If you contest, as His Grace assumed you might, you forfeit all rights to the entailed lands. Those would instead to go charity."

"I bloody well won't forfeit anything!"

"To contest, you must," Higgins explained. "The choice is yours, my lord."

"That's no bloody choice at all," Alastair muttered, wearing a dangerous sulk.

Higgins cleared his throat, casting a disdainful glare upon Alastair before turning his attention to Serena. "Now, I must apologize in advance for this indelicacy, Your Grace, but I am required to ask if there is any possibility that you are...oh, how shall we say" — he formed a tight smile of embarrassment — "perhaps with child?"

For a moment, Serena didn't know how to respond. The possibility she was indeed pregnant existed, but she knew, as Lucien would, exactly who had fathered any babe she might be carrying. She was suddenly aware of three sets of eyes riveted on her. The weight of Lucien's stare pulled her gaze to his. Briefly, she met the hard probe of his green eyes, demanding her answer. She couldn't respond, not honestly, not here—and not before Alastair.

Knowing a prolonged stare would arouse Alastair's suspicions, her gaze skittered back to Mr. Higgins. Instantly, Lucien's casual posture vanished, replaced by an on-the-edge-of-his-chair pose that told her he would exact answers, whether she wanted to give them or not, as soon as he could orchestrate a moment alone with her. And she had no idea what she would say, when, or even *if*, she would trust him with the truth.

But the announcement of an impending heir would buy her and the Bow Street Runner time to prove Alastair's involvement in his uncle's death. It would also save Warrington and the other entailed estates from Alastair's cruel ruin and the dukedom from scandal and disgrace. It wouldn't be a lie...exactly; she wasn't certain of the truth herself yet. She would worry later about the consequences if she proved barren. She sighed. Cyrus would have wanted her to do this.

Judiciously avoiding any eye contact with Lucien, she prayed his shock wouldn't give away her ploy or reveal her sin.

Taking a calming breath, Serena announced, "I am with child."

****

With child? Yes, *his* child. Lucien curled his fingers around the arms of the wooden chair, using every ounce of his strength to restrain the turmoil within him.

Alastair's voice ripped the momentary quiet. "That's a lie!"

Was it? Mr. Higgins didn't seem to put any stock into Alastair's doubt.

"Splendid news," he vaguely heard Higgins say to Serena. "Might I ask when the babe is due?"

Serena paused, then whispered, "The middle of March."

Quickly, Lucien subtracted nine months, and swallowed a lump of incredulity. The child's conception would have been roughly eight weeks ago, in June—exactly when he had taken the duchess to his bed.

He fixed his intent gaze on Serena's delicate profile, willing her to look his way, to either confirm or deny his suspicions. She did nothing.

"And you're certain, Your Grace?" Higgins asked.

Lucien watched Serena's shoulders and chin lift regally. "I am quite certain, sir."

Mr. Higgins mouth lifted in a small smile. "His Grace would have been pleased by such news."

Serena swallowed. "Indeed. I was not sure myself until last week. I regret I could not tell him before his death."

"In light of your news, Your Grace," Higgins began, "all entailed estates and jewels will be kept under my executorship until the birth of the child and the determination of its gender."

"I will not have this!" Alastair yelled. "This...this fortune-hunting slut and her brat cannot steal what is mine!"

"I'm afraid that until we learn the child's gender, you have no other recourse. It is the law, my lord," Higgins responded, barely hiding smug satisfaction.

"Lord Daneridge," Higgins directed his speculative gaze to Lucien. "This is where you are mentioned in the duke's will."

Lucien's entire body tensed, excruciatingly suspended from an invisible string that the solicitor's next words could snap in two. Good God! He'd just learned Serena carried his child. What now?

"Indeed?" He forced a casual note into his voice.

"Yes, this is the oddest portion of the will. His Grace indicated that, should his wife be breeding and the child is male, he wished you to act as the new heir's trustee until the child's eighteenth birthday."

For long moments, no one spoke. Lucien himself was too stunned. What kind of muddled thinking had led Warrington to this provision? An instant later, Lucien realized that brilliant thinking was his answer. Warrington hadn't trusted his nephew to protect the child's interest in the family fortune, but he could trust the child's biological father. And Lucien knew he could never legally prove he had sired the child. Because Serena had been the duke's wife at the time of conception, the law assumed the babe was Warrington's spawn and heir.

Damn! Warrington had him well trapped, and from the wide-eyed expression bursting across Serena's shocked face, Lucien could see she realized it, too. He would be shut out of his own child's life except in the most impersonal ways, unless ...

No. It was an unacceptable solution. Hell, it bordered on unthinkable. So why was he thinking it?

Alastair rose. The man's silent fury and threatening gaze first fell upon Lucien, then Serena. "This isn't over yet, you whore. I won't let you take what is mine!" he vowed before storming out of Higgins's office with a slam of the door.

Mr. Higgins cleared his throat, and Lucien was vaguely aware of the little man speaking to Serena. She responded softly, and the sound of her sensual, husky voice permeated the shell of Lucien's shock.

Higgins turned his back for a moment to return Cyrus's will to its designated box; several just like it lined the room's many shelves. Lucien's gaze swerved to Serena.

He watched her swallow. She did that when she was nervous. Her hands trembled, and her breathing was altogether too shallow. Her exquisite profile bespoke tension. Her face was so taut, Lucien felt certain that if he touched her cheek, she would shatter as surely as glass.

"Look at me." He whispered the demand.

She bit her lower lip, a sign of anxiety, and Lucien felt another jolt of pure alarm that catapulted him from his numbing shock. She turned wide, smoky eyes on him in a face much too pale.

Her expression confirmed he was going to be a father again. Lucien wasn't sure whether he should be furious, elated — or scared as hell.

He opened his mouth, to say what, he wasn't sure. Then he remembered the solicitor's presence and closed it again.

Higgins spoke, drawing Serena's gaze from Lucien's. "If you have no objections, Lord Daneridge, I must confer with Her Grace about some of the remaining estate matters requiring privacy."

Lucien tapped his foot angrily against the wooden floor. He did have objections, damn it. He and *Her Grace* were long overdue for a confrontation. Now, more than ever, he needed to understand the facts behind her half-truths at the Raddingtons' ball.

His gaze pinned Serena to her chair. He watched as her nervous tongue darted out to wet her lips. At that, a bolt of desire scorched him, and the taut string in Lucien's gut snapped. He leaped from his chair with a curse. Hadn't he learned anything? His lust for Serena had lured him into this predicament in the first place.

But the fact remained, he wanted — needed — answers from her, and soon. He wanted to hear the truth come from her luscious mouth, every last damn word of it.

As he stalked past Serena's chair, he whispered in her ear, "I will call on you tomorrow morning. Without fail. Be ready."

CHAPTER TWELVE

The following morning, Lucien left the carriage parked before Grosvenor Chapel, waved away an inquiring footman, and climbed the grassy knoll. Taking the last hesitant steps, he halted at the gray stone marking Chelsea's final resting place. He stood unmoving, watching the dawning sun inch into the foggy sky and cast a murky light over his daughter's grave. Despite his searing anguish and the disbelief of the first days of her death, he had chosen this very spot for her because she had been so fond of sunrises.

Lucien knelt at the edge of the dirt-covered mound, strewn with yesterday's flowers. The familiar wave of grief crashed against his heart. He closed his eyes.

Thoughts whirling, he retrieved the old bouquet of white carnations and replaced it with a fresh one, as he did daily, this time leaving baby pink roses — their silky petals the color of Chelsea's cheeks.

A flash of her tiny crimson-covered body, helpless and crumpled beneath the team and carriage wheels of a sobbing stranger, taunted him. He should have been there to save her from the accident, instead of identifying her after the worst had happened. After it was too late.

I am with child, Serena's voice crowded into his head, demanding attention. With a savage curse, he pivoted away.

Throwing his head back, he stared up at the muted London sky. "Why?" his half-bewildered, half-accusing whisper asked of the God he had renounced on this spot just two months past. "You gave me a child once, and my neglect caused her death. Why are You giving me this chance again?"

No answer rained down from the heavens, not that he really expected one. As usual, he was on his own.

Scowling, he dropped his gaze to the cold earth. His mind filtered through treasured images of Chelsea as she had played a stranded princess in a tower, as she had carried a rag doll he had bought for her at a country fair, as she stroked the pet frog she had named Herman upon capturing it in the garden.

He was still haunted by each of those memories every day.

Now there would be another babe. How could he survive fatherhood again when Chelsea had been gone just five months?

He raked a stiff hand through his hair, wondering if he was ready for fatherhood again. What if he failed this time, too?

For a moment, everything about him was still, as quiet and motionless as the graveyard's inhabitants. Then, from out of nowhere...a gentle wisp of wind skittered through the air, ruffling his hair and the bouquet at his feet. A bird's sweet song tinkled in the air.

A sign that life would, and must, go on.

A gentle wave of tranquility suffused him. As if God had imparted the wisdom, Lucien's questions now had answers, a wealth of explanations where none had existed before.

He had to be ready for fatherhood again, God had given him no choice. Serena and the baby would need his protection. And if this birth was a test, it was also a gift. And a responsibility he would live up to with the best of his ability.

He would make damn certain he didn't fail at fatherhood twice.

Lucien rose, yet a strain of fear still resided in his heart. This child would never be his in the eyes of the law, and he would have to provide and care for the babe with the alternative means available to him — an added challenge, no doubt.

But more than anything else, the fear stemmed from the Earl of Marsden, Alastair Boyce. The man was plainly furious with his late uncle's will.

Lucien's long, fitful strides took him down the length of Chelsea's grave. Alastair had most likely had his uncle disposed of in the hopes of obtaining the Warrington fortune. So what was to stop him from targeting Serena? Not a damn thing. He had no choice but to keep his eyes on Marsden — and Serena as well.

Yet to do that, and become a real part of this new child's life, he had one option. And he didn't like it.

But that child was *his*, damn it. He wanted that babe, needed it to redeem himself in his own eyes, perhaps even make himself whole again. Not to mention that both mother and child were in danger.

He really had no other choice.

His decision made, the pain he had weathered since Serena's startling announcement lifted. For the first time in almost a month, his lips turned up in a semblance of a smile.

"Poppet," he said to Chelsea. "Daddy promises to make you proud."

A warm breeze whispered across Lucien's skin, the kind which lingered on summer days he had spent outdoors with Chelsea, slicing a ray of hope through the chilly morning air.

Fatherhood would be better the second time. He would do anything and everything to make certain of that.

****

Lucien arrived home from the graveyard. While trying to capture his whirling thoughts and process them, he slowly handed his hat, cloak, and gloves to Holford.

"My lord," the butler said somewhat loudly, making Lucien aware that Holford had probably said it two or three times to get his attention.

"What is it?"

"Lord Niles is in your library."

Lucien withdrew his watch from his waistcoat and stared at it with a frown. "At nine o'clock in the morning?"

"Indeed. He's ranting about his boredom."

Despite his grim situation, the corners of Lucien's mouth lifted into a wry smile. "Thank you."

Lucien pushed the library door open and found Niles slouched on a settee, reading the morning paper.

"That can't possibly be interesting enough to hold your attention," Lucien called across the room.

Niles's head snapped up. "It isn't. I've never known this town to be so dull. Even my mistress is tedious."

"You'll seek another soon, I'm sure."

Niles shrugged. "So where were you this morning? At the graveyard?"

"Indeed. I had a great deal of thinking to do." He paused. "Warrington's will was read yesterday."

"Ah, that's right. How is the duchess holding up?"

Lucien weighed the question before answering. "Better than I would under the circumstances, I think. I do not envy her. She is clearly grieving Warrington's demise, as odd as that seems. But she is a strong woman and will deal with her grief."

"In time, yes."

"Warrington's heir is the Earl of Marsden. Do you know him?" At Niles's grimace and nod, Lucien continued. "Serena is convinced he paid to have her husband murdered."

"Really? What do you think?"

He recalled the vivid palm print on Alastair's cheek, and Serena's aura of suppressed rage. His mind replayed Alastair's taunts and veiled threats. His guts twisted with anger. "It's very likely. He's a greedy bastard."

"Do you think he will try to kill the duchess?"

"I've no doubt. Especially now."

Intrigued, Niles raised his brows. "What do you mean? Did Warrington leave her something the Earl of Marsden wanted?"

"His entire fortune," Lucien answered. "All four hundred thousand pounds of it."

At that, Niles's eyes widened until they threatened to pop from their sockets. "And what did he leave Marsden?"

"Nothing but entailed estates, and not a farthing for their upkeep."

Niles let loose a low whistle. "Mad, was he?"

"Enraged. I sent two men to watch her house, just in case Marsden decided to try something." He shrugged. "It required no genius to see he was furious, especially after he called Serena a whore and accused her of bewitching her husband."

Shaking his head, Niles sank down on the settee again. "Did you call him out?"

"The thought occurred to me," Lucien admitted. "But it would have raised both suspicion and scandal if I had."

"True," Niles conceded.

"There another reason for Marsden's anger."

"Indeed?" From Niles's curious expression, Lucien could tell he had his friend's undivided attention. "Do tell."

Lucien hesitated before answering. Striding to his desk, he poured a glass of port and tossed it back, letting the liquid slide down his throat in one long swallow. Slamming the empty glass on the desk, he turned back to Niles, grateful for the one friend he knew would keep his secrets.

"Serena is pregnant."

Niles's jaw dropped to his chest. "And you think the child is yours?"

"I know it is. Her virginity, the timing...No other possibility exists." Holding his cane tighter, Lucien crossed the room and stopped before his friend. "Both she and the baby are *my* responsibility."

Niles nodded in agreement. "What do you mean to do now?"

Lucien's thumb tapped nervously against his cane, his jaw tight. "I've decided to marry her."

Niles's mouth fell open in shock. "Marry her? You?"

Lucien wasn't sure what kind of husband he would make. Damn it, he had no desire to be married again—ever. Ravenna had seen to that. But his desires were not the issue. His child and its mother were. Period. They clearly needed his protection.

"Yes."

"Have you asked her already?"

He shook his head. "It isn't a question. She will assent, no matter what I have to do."

****

An hour later, Serena paced the length of a Merman sofa along one of the drawing room's walls, awaiting Lucien's arrival. Where was the man? Not that she looked forward to this, or any other, confrontation. On the contrary, this meeting was one she wanted, more than anything, to have behind her.

Lying to Lucien was going to be anything but easy. He seemed not just to sense, but to know when her words were less than honest. No doubt, something in her face gave her away. But no more could she allow herself that weakness. She had already convinced Mr. Higgins and Alastair of her impending state of motherhood. Now, she also had to convince Lucien she was truly with child. An unpleasant task indeed, but the Warrington lineage and fortune, and possibly her life, depended upon her singular ability to lie until she could determine for herself if she truly was *enceinte*.

She didn't dare trust anyone, not even Lucien, with the truth behind her ploy. If she told him everything, he most likely would refuse to corroborate her scheme, since he appeared so opposed to any kind of deception.

Her idea was underhanded. Her conscience made her well aware of that fact. Deception was not something she felt at all comfortable with. Indeed, guilt already plagued her, but she had chosen her path yesterday at Mr. Higgins's office, and now she had to walk it to the end.

With a deep breath, Serena eyed her surroundings, seeking calm in the midst of the nervous tumble of her thoughts. She had chosen the most formal drawing room for this confrontation because of its size. She could direct Lucien to sit in an elbow chair across the room. Keeping the man as far away from her as physically possible was key.

The room was also intimidating. Nothing within lent it any air of intimacy, particularly not the looming religious painting above the fireplace and the marble molding hovering above the double doors. Surely Lucien would not dream of mentioning intimacies, nor starting any, here.

Lastly, the decor was neoclassical, a leftover from the late Georgian period, and Cyrus's favorite. Serena remembered the number of times she had approached him about modernizing this room, only to be turned away with a resounding no. Now she was glad. Greeting Lucien in a room so reminiscent of her husband would give her strength to keep on the course she felt sure Cyrus had intended her to follow.

At the sound of two sets of footsteps echoing in the hallway beyond, one too bold to be a servant's, Serena ceased her frantic pacing and raced across the room to one of the pale yellow brocade sofas. She seated herself on the edge just in time for the butler's knock.

Her heart pounding in her ears, she bade the servant to show Lord Daneridge in.

She met Lucien's intent green-eyed gaze the moment he crossed the threshold. He hadn't slept well, if at all; dark smudges and a conspicuous puffiness beneath his eyes told her that, though he was still more handsome than God should allow. His limp was more pronounced this morning, as if the joint pained him. The ruthless grip he exerted on his cane reminded her that, despite his injury, he still possessed tenfold her own strength.

She swallowed, praying her nervousness didn't show. Her butler quietly shut the door, sequestering them away from prying eyes and ears. Serena's anxious pulse raced at the thought.

"Good morning, my lord. Won't you sit down?" she asked, indicating the chair furthest from her, across the imperious room.

With a scowl, he accepted the seat, fitting broad shoulders stiffly against the pale yellow backing. His dark green coat eclipsed the delicate shade of the chair's upholstery.

"Would you take tea? The servants can bring us a tray in no time at all," she assured, forcing a glib note into her voice.

"No, thank you. I came here to talk about—"

"The reading of Cyrus's will, of course." When Lucien's expression turned icier, Serena rushed on. "I hope you weren't too surprised by Alastair's behavior. I've grown quite accustomed to his outbursts."

"Your late husband's nephew, nasty as he is, isn't the issue, either." The boom of his voice carried across the high-ceilinged room, and probably into the hall.

Lucien rose from his seat. His angry stride brought him to her side within moments. To Serena's shock, he sat beside her, a mere foot away. "I refuse to shout across the room at you."

She tried to scoot to the far end of the sofa. He curled his fingers about her arm to stay her.

"I came to talk about your little announcement." His gaze cornered and trapped hers, refusing to let go as he spoke again. "Are you truly with child?"

Her gaze locked with his. "Yes."

"Am I correct in assuming the child is mine?"

She hesitated, but lying to him would gain her nothing but more of his contempt. "Yes. I've been...intimate with no man but you."

Fierce satisfaction crossed his face before he blanked it. "Forgive my indelicacy," he said, though nothing in his tone sounded apologetic in the least, "but I would like to ask you a few questions so I may be as certain as you about the matter."

"Questions?" She wrung her hands. *Mercy, what would he ask? Was she equipped to give the appropriate answers?*

"How late is your monthly?" he demanded.

Serena's eyes widened in shock; her mouth dropped open. She felt the hot flush of red race up her face, heating every inch of skin with embarrassment. "How indelicate! That question is most crude and inappropriate. I will not answer it."

His grip about her wrist tightened. "The question is most appropriate, and you will damn well answer it this very moment. How late are you?"

She directed her mortified gaze to her lap. "Nearly six weeks."

His exhalation was long and controlled. "Does this sort of lapse happen frequently?"

Serena blinked several times, trying to absorb her shock. How could he ask such personal questions? And how had he come about such intimate knowledge of the workings of a woman's body?

"Answer me," he growled at her hesitation.

Impossibly, the temperature of her cheeks heated a few more degrees. "I am usually quite regular."

Serena wished the couch would swallow her up. Her face felt a hundred degrees. Unfortunately, nothing in Lucien's manner indicated he was finished questioning her.

"Any part of you more tender than normal?"

Just this morning, she had awakened with aching breasts, the likes of which she had never experienced. Lucien's gaze drifted to her chest and fixed on the swells rising above her dress. She began to tingle.

Resisting an urge to find a wrap to cover her, Serena crossed her arms over her breasts instead. "Yes."

"How about mornings? How does your stomach feel?" he quizzed, his gaze still probing.

"Not well." The nausea she woke to this morning had abated somewhat, and thankfully she hadn't lost the contents of her stomach as she had the previous morning, but even now her insides rolled and lurched.

"Queasy, are you?" he prompted.

She nodded, refusing to clarify that further.

"Other than that, how do you feel?"

She sighed, grateful the topic had shifted to something slightly less uncomfortable. At length, she replied, "Exhausted. I feel I could sleep forever and still require more sleep."

He nodded. "Do you find you're more irritable? Perhaps more prone to tears?"

How had he known that? She had cried more in the last week than in the last five years. Was it simple grief? Or some symptom, as he was alluding to? "On all counts, yes."

"Have you seen a doctor or midwife?"

She shook her head. "I didn't think I had experienced anything untoward to warrant medical examination."

Finally, he replied. "No, you haven't. Based on what you've said, I would agree that you are pregnant."

She stifled a gasp. Truly? She wanted to ask, but knew she could not. If she had displayed all the symptoms, that accounted for Caffey's pointed comments.

If Lucien's suspicion was indeed truth, God had finally answered her most fervent prayer, at a time both blessed and accursed. The Warrington lineage would be assured if the babe were a boy, but Cyrus wouldn't be with her to share in the joy, to see the fruits of his plans, boy or girl, make its way into the world. She fought back another wave of grief.

And what must Lord Daneridge think of this turn of events?

"My lord, do not fear I expect anything," Serena hastened to reassure. "You need not make an acknowledgment or settlement."

"You may not expect anything, but you need something," he stated matter-of-factly. "My protection. Marsden does not strike me as a particularly sane man."

She bit her lip. "No, but I shall look after myself. Despite Cyrus's letter, you need not involve yourself further."

Lucien leaned closer. "Do you really believe you alone can avoid the danger your husband, his coachman, and several footmen could not? If Marsden could arrange for the murder of a powerful man, certainly he would allow nothing as paltry as a grieving widow to stand between himself and a fortune."

"Alastair wouldn't be foolish enough to have me killed as well," she argued. "Such a deed would seem suspicious."

"A logical person would think so. Marsden can hardly be described as logical."

Serena looked away from the intent green of Lucien's stare, knowing he was right. Alastair would rather take the risk of having her killed than let Cyrus's fortune remain in her possession. But having Lucien as her protector...She shook her head. Such a scenario provided too many possibilities for temptation.

Trying to ignore the spark of awareness dancing across her skin, she faced him. "Perhaps Alastair is not logical, but I would not term him an imbecile. Truly, I do not think he will do anything to cast suspicion upon himself."

Lucien grabbed her arm. "Are you willing to bet your life on that? As well as the life of our unborn child?"

Put like that, her avoidance of Lucien seemed petty. His protection afforded her the best chance of staying alive. But she must resist his enigmatic charm. She owed Cyrus a proper mourning, and herself the assurance Mama's wicked propensities didn't flourish within her.

Serena rose. He rose with her.

"You are right." She sighed. "I must stay alive to avenge Cyrus's death...and raise this child." Her hands slid across her middle, cradling the life she surely harbored within.

Lucien raked his fingers through his hair. "I will protect you in every way I can."

"Thank you."

He hesitated, a taut expression masking his face. "It's not your gratitude I seek."

A note of foreboding shivered down her spine. "Then what?"

A moment of still passed. The clock in the hall tick off the tenuous seconds as his penetrating gaze held hers captive. "For you to become my wife. Today."

A first splash of shock washed over her, followed by wave after incredulous wave. "*Your wife?* Certainly you know that such an alliance anytime in the next year would be impossible, but today ..."

"Today," he reiterated implacably.

"It would be unseemly! People will whisper about me — and the baby — viciously."

"I've lived through a *divorce*. Do you think I give a damn about the ton's gossip anymore? Besides, it will blow over when the next scandal rolls around."

"But I — I hardly know you."

He scoffed cynically. "You know me well enough to have my child. Under most circumstances, that requires marriage."

"I am in mourning! I appreciate your sense of honor, to make such a sacrifice, but I hardly think — "

"Honor be damned!" He leaned too close to allow normal breathing. The arched ebony brows and angled planes of his high cheeks both bespoke anger, which his voice echoed. "It isn't honor that interests me, sweetheart. I very much care about that child. The babe will never be mine legally; I'm well aware of that, but I *will* play the part of its father. Nothing — not you, nor silly social conventions, and certainly not Marsden — will keep me from taking part in this child's life and having him or her raised as a part of my household. I'll be damned before I allow you to rob me of my own seed."

She backed away from him, digesting the fury of his speech. Few of the *ton's* gentlemen cared so fervently for their children. Since he did, denying him access to this baby would be nothing short of cruel. Yet how could she choose any other path? Vicious tongues would ensure she'd be shunned forever for marrying one man while mourning another. And to be tied for the rest of her life to a man who had every reason to hold her in contempt...It did not bear thinking.

"We must not wed. Such a union would be disastrous at best, and I cannot imagine—"

"I could arrange it, *Your Grace*," he sneered, "so you would rarely have to see me. I assure you, I'm talking about the most fashionable of marriages."

His cold voice sent ice straight to her heart. Closing her eyes, she shook her head in denial of such a terrible prospect. Though she and Cyrus had never shared passion, a wealth of affection and respect had always flowed between them.

"My lord," she began gently. "I was not objecting to you, for you can be most...pleasant when you desire. Rather it is your reasoning I question. I shall allow you to visit your son or daughter at any time you wish, under any pretense you devise." She held up supplicating hands. "I simply feel that, in light of society's disapproval and the fact we bear no love for one other, perhaps the notion of a rushed marriage is ill-conceived."

"Ill-conceived or not, I insist. Love is not necessary for marriage and never has been. If you were expecting something more romantic, I apologize. We had our evening of romance. Now we must face the result."

He pulled a piece of paper from his cream-colored waistcoat pocket and held it up for her inspection. Serena felt the blood leave her face in a rush when she realized the document was a special license for marriage.

"As you can see, I'm quite prepared and quite serious." His voice broke through the haze of her shock.

She shook her head. "I will not marry you."

His green eyes narrowed, glittering with anger. "You will. I'll expect you at my town house at eight this evening. If you do not come, I promise you will find the consequences are more unpleasant than marriage."

He released her, then stalked from the drawing room, slamming the door behind him.

CHAPTER THIRTEEN

Eight o'clock that evening brought no sign of Serena's arrival. Nor did eight-thirty.

At nine, Lucien swallowed both anger and pride, and sent the clergyman home. Niles tried to soothe him with a drink and a friendly pat on the back, but he found neither of any comfort.

Damn it, Lucien didn't want to make this situation any uglier. But their child was more important than their wishes, and regardless of Her Grace's thoughts, that boy or girl would grow up knowing the love of both mother and father. He would have the opportunity to prove he wasn't a failure as a parent. He would ensure that mother and child remained alive.

"Well, old chap, now what?" Niles questioned. "Will you give up the notion of marriage?"

Turning to his friend, Lucien retrieved a multi-colored bouquet of heather, roses and carnations he had procured for the bridal bouquet. "No. Something I say or do will bring her to my side." He tossed the flowers onto a nearby table. "I just haven't a clue what."

"Why doesn't she want to marry an old rogue like you?" Niles tried to tease.

Lucien found it anything but amusing. "She's worried about what people will say. Think of it: Her first husband not yet in his grave a month, and she weds another." He sighed. "I understand her reluctance. But damn it, I must make her understand somehow."

Niles grinned. "My friend, you just solved your own dilemma."

Lucien cocked a brow. "How so?"

"She's afraid of what people might say. So you need only threaten her with a scandal more dreadful if she doesn't fall in line with your plan."

The idea was underhanded and would make her hate him. But that wasn't his primary concern. "In what way?"

"Threaten the lady with a bigger scandal, something worse than wedding before mourning blacks should be doffed."

Such a simple solution — one that would forever mark him a manipulative bastard in her eyes. But if it kept her and their child safe and by his side, he would live with whatever opinion she held of him, no matter how low.

"You can be a real a genius, young pup." Lucien clapped Niles on the shoulder. "And I know just the scandal to threaten her with."

With a triumphant smile curving his lips, he raced to the desk for ink and paper.

****

As Lucien had predicted, his threat brought Serena round to his door at precisely eight that next evening, as his note had instructed.

Lucien awaited Serena in the comfort of his drawing room when he heard the first notes of her raised voice in the entrance hall. Moments later, Holford opened the door to admit her.

Serena swept past the butler and erupted into the room. Her smoky blue-gray eyes spitting resentment, Lucien noted with satisfaction that her gaze sought him immediately. The color in her cheeks ran high against the severe black muslin of her mourning dress.

She was beautiful. God, how he wanted to touch her.

"How *dare* you?" she questioned without preamble, each word hissed like an oath. "This," she spat, holding up Lucien's missive, "is nothing short of blackmail!"

Setting his brandy aside, Lucien rose and closed the door behind her, shutting out an inquisitive Holford. "I am well aware of that," he said in a low, soothing voice. "If you will sit, I shall explain—"

"Nothing you have to say will change my mind." Her fingers clenched into fists at her sides. "This *scheme* is the most ruthless, underhanded...How could you?"

Because he had little choice.

Lucien reached for her arms in a gesture of supplication. She jerked away. "Don't think of touching me. Not now or ever!"

Anger whirled in his blood and thoughts, but he controlled it, letting her spend her fury.

"Answer me. How could you threaten me with this? Only the most reprehensible blackguard would callously use his own child and threaten to besmirch its birth by making its parentage public, especially by planting it in the ear of gossips like Lady Jersey!"

"Serena—"

"What if gossip doesn't ruin me enough, my lord? What then? A few lines in the *Times* letting all of London know that I'm a fallen woman and our child is a bastard?"

Lucien inhaled deeply. "If that is what is required to bring you to the altar, yes."

Her eyes narrowed. "How can you expect me to ruin my late husband's good name by wedding again so quickly? Do you care so little for me that you would think nothing of making my behavior and my condition the *ton's* latest scandal?"

Lucien retrieved his drink and poured the liquid down his throat, never tasting it. "I thought I made my reasons clear yesterday. Your protection and our child's upbringing are responsibilities I take very seriously. You chose not to present yourself here last evening. I warned you of consequences if you did not." He pointed to the note in her hand. "That, Your Grace, is the consequence."

She crumpled the note up in her fist, then threw it at him. It struck his chest and fell at his feet. "You self-serving knave! I stumble once." She held up her finger. "Just once from the path of moral decency. And you insist on making certain the *ton* labels me my mother's daughter."

Her mother's daughter? He pondered the meaning of those words as he bent to retrieve the note. "I've no notion of what you speak. I merely wish to raise my child and see that you live long enough to bear it."

She laughed. "Everyone else knows Lady Abbington. I was lucky to make a match at all, much less with a duke, thanks to her indiscriminate liaisons. I've spent my entire life striving to be different, and you think nothing of destroying all that with a single whisper." Her eyes sparked with blue fury. "I wish I had never set eyes on you."

"You did set eyes on me." His voice dropped to a dangerous whisper as he curled his fingers about her arms and pulled her closer. "And much more, as I recall. No amount of regret will change that. The question is, will you make me carry through with my threat? Or will you be a docile bride when the vicar arrives?"

Her eyes widened, glaring with visible fury. "I have little choice, unless I want to be branded the same whore as my mother. But then, you planned it that way, didn't you?"

"So that's a yes. What a charming acceptance," he drawled.

"What else did you expect from such a gallant proposal?"

"Touché," he quipped. "And settlements?"

She gasped, jaw dropping. "Cyrus left his fortune to *me*, and me alone. I won't give it over to you to squander."

"I assure you, I have neither the need nor the desire for the man's money. It's yours to spend as you please, and I'll sign anything to that effect you would care to have drawn up."

"My solicitor will contact yours."

Serena was proving tougher than he ever fathomed, given the shy creature he'd first made love to. He released her arm to whirl away and paced, coming to a halt behind the sofa. Broad palms gripping the cherry-trimmed backing, he offered, "Serena, I will endeavor to be considerate. I will check with you before committing to social engagements requiring us both. I will consult you on matters of holidays and households. You may redecorate however you like. I understand you're less than happy about this match, and I am prepared to be indulgent—to a point."

The anger shimmering from her in hot waves matched the tone of her voice. "What is it you expect of me in return?"

He paced again, stopping only long enough to lift his brandy from an end table. "Three simple things. One, to be a proper mother for the child, one who takes an active interest in his or her welfare."

"That, my lord, will be easy. I've long wanted children."

Serena bowed her head as she rubbed her belly protectively. The light shone off the golden fire of her hair, shimmered off her flawless, warm-toned skin. To him, she looked part angel, and it stirred something within him to realize that he had been the first man to discover what a wanton this particular woman could be.

"Yet never had them. Why?" he fished, hoping she would divulge more of the relationship she had shared with Warrington.

"That subject is closed. What else do you require?" she asked with a stubborn tilt to her chin.

He let the matter of her first marriage drop, for now. "I will, at some point, require an heir. Certainly, anytime soon would be impossible, given your...condition. After that, however, I shall expect it."

Serena stiffened. Her pink lips, which he craved to claim, flattened in displeasure. "As long as you understand that once a boy is born, no further intimate contact will take place."

He arched a brow that questioned and mocked at once. "If that is your wish."

"It is, without question. And number three?"

"I *demand* absolute fidelity. You will not cuckold me as you did Warrington."

His words sent color flaring into her cheeks once again. "And pray tell me, will I receive that same consideration?"

"Will I be granted access to your chambers with any regularity?"

Her eyes widened at his blunt question. "Absolutely not."

"Then expect to receive no consideration on that score."

She flew across the room, stopping before his perch upon the sofa. "I hardly think that is a fair arrangement."

He shrugged. "I agree. It's tedious to leave the house for something I would rather have here with you."

One Wicked Night   Shayla Black

Shock burst across her face before her eyes narrowed.
She looked ready to slap him. "You're insufferable and
crude! I cannot fathom why I ever—"

Holford's knock interrupted them. Lucien bade the
servant to enter, and the man opened the portal for Niles to
enter. His sister, Lady Raddington, followed closely behind.

"Did we come too early, old chap?" Niles asked,
glancing back and forth between Lucien and Serena.

Lucien rose to greet his guests. He and Niles shared a
hearty handshake. "Not at all." He briefly kissed Anne's
hand. "Good evening, my lady."

Niles's sister raised her gaze, piercing Lucien with her
censure. "Are you certain this is wise?"

Her question brought forth the painful reality. If Serena
had never wed Warrington, Lucien might have desired to
court Serena, woo her, win her. And under different
circumstances, she might have welcomed his suit.

But maybes and might-have-beens were irrelevant. The
only relevant fact was that he would soon wed an adulteress
who carried his child.

He looked across the room to Serena. Her eyes showed a
mixture of anger and the desperation of a hunted animal. He
suppressed an urge to shelter her in his arms, tell her he
would never be the ogre she imagined. Raking a hand
through his hair, he sighed. He had always been a fool for a
pretty face.

A moment later, Holford ushered in the clergyman.

****

The jovial old vicar smiled at Lucien, then his eyes
alighted on Serena, and the smile widened. "I hope you are
feeling better, my dear. It's dreadful to postpone such a
happy occasion for an illness."

Serena's gaze flew to Lucien. His stare dared her to
refute his story. And she wanted to, the Lord knew. But she
curbed her anger. To display it here, before virtual strangers,
would be to stoop to Lucien's vulgar level. Instead, she
murmured to the white-bearded man, "A shame indeed."

"Shall we begin?" With a smile and a merry wink, he added, "Your groom is eager."

Nausea and resentment swirled within her. A hasty marriage would only make her slightly less scandalous than allowing the *ton* to know she had conceived Lucien's child during her marriage to Cyrus. Either way, she was certain to be the center of gossip. Her indiscretion would undoubtedly dredge up Mama's past. Comparisons between mother and daughter would be made. And her own child would be denounced before he or she was even born.

She glared at Lucien. "He indicated his impatience."

"Bodes well, an eager groom," the old man said. "I was eager, and Tessie and I have been married nigh on thirty years."

But Tessie probably had not been forced to the altar. Serena glared at Lucien again.

The vicar spread out the kneeling mats he had brought with him, then motioned for both Lucien and Serena to join him before the fireplace.

He opened his prayer book, then paused. "Ah, I do hate to be indelicate, my dear," he directed to her, "but are you planning to wear...that?"

Serena looked down onto the severity of her plain black bodice. A wedding in funeral garb? In this case, it seemed appropriate. Resolutely, she nodded.

In her peripheral vision, Serena saw Lucien whip his gaze to her face. At his furious glare, she raised her chin defiantly. "I will not change. I'm in mourning."

Lucien looked away and swore beneath his breath.

"Begin," he snapped at the vicar.

With a puzzled shrug, the old man flipped open *The Book of Common Prayer* and read. Serena barely heard his words.

How had her life come to this? Fighting tears, she vividly recalled the brilliant spring morning she and Cyrus had exchanged vows. Innocence and hope had filled her heart, so much different from the heart-churning dread and despondency she felt now. With this marriage, she would pay for one night of searing ecstasy with the rest of her days. Lucien had seen to that.

A moment later, Lucien nudged her ribs with his elbow. Startled, she looked first to him, then the clergyman. Clearly, both expected an answer.

"I apologize," she said. "Could you repeat the question?"

The old man smiled. "What's your name, my dear?"

She answered, and the clergyman resumed the ritual. "Wilt thou, Serena Mary Elizabeth Boyce, have this man to thy wedded husband, to live together after God's ordinance in the holy state of matrimony? Wilt thou obey him, and serve him, love, honor, and keep him in sickness and in health, and, forsaking all others, keep thee only unto him, so long as ye both shall live?"

She tried not to notice that Lucien looked excessively masculine with his broad shoulders stretched tightly into a coat of midnight blue. Or remember the way he'd commanded her body and her pleasure with every single touch. She tore her gaze away.

"Do I have a choice?" she whispered.

Lucien gripped her arm, exerting a light, but nonetheless demanding, pressure. "No."

Eyes closed, fighting tears, Serena replied, "I will."

And silently pledged to hate Lucien for the rest of her days.

"No need to be nervous," the vicar soothed, then turned to Lucien and repeated the vow.

"I will." His strong voice echoed in the room.

Though she knew it was dangerous, Serena slid her gaze in his direction again and met his stare. Those brilliant emerald eyes mesmerized her, held her heartbeat captive, making it pound harder with his fierce, yet knowing expression.

Something in the tense set of his face called to her, something needy. He roused unwanted, excessively clear remembrances of their night together. He slid his thumb to her wrist, which began a little dance on the sensitive, blue-veined skin inside. When her pulse raced even faster under the pad of his thumb, he sent her a slow, seductive smile.

The impact of that expression trapped her breath in her lungs. It looked far too much like the one he had flashed during their greatest intimacies—as he rolled down her stockings, stretched his magnificent, naked length beside her, and eventually filled the female part of her body with the most male part of his. Flushing, Serena jerked her gaze away.

The clergyman laid the ring on the book and blessed it, then instructed Lucien to place the ring on her finger. Under the holy man's curious eye, Lucien took her hand and did so.

As the vicar began to recite scripture, Serena looked down to discover this was no ordinary golden band. Instead, it was encrusted with small diamonds in three rows that encircled the length and width of the ring.

When he released her, she automatically touched the band, her fingertips moving across the smooth, shimmering surface in awe. She turned to him, her face silently questioning his reasons for such an elaborate symbol of their marriage. For all that she and Cyrus had been content, he had never gifted her with any but simplest of wedding rings. A part of her proclaimed Lucien's ring worldly, a sinful display of wealth. Her other half could only acknowledge its beauty. Was it a family piece or had he bought it with her in mind?

The old man pronounced, "Those whom God hath joined together, let no man put asunder."

Lucien led her to a writing desk. On it lay the registry. From the corner of her eye, she saw him lift the quill, before he placed it directly into her hand.

"Sign, dear," the watchful vicar prompted with a smile.

Serena hesitated. Signing this document would make their marriage legal, official...binding. Then she felt the pressure of Lucien's hand at the small of her back as he whispered, "Sign it now."

With both the clergyman and Lucien looking on, she did. And choked back her tears.

She had come here tonight expecting to talk Lucien out
of this outrageous wedding. Instead, she found herself with
a new husband. What could she have done to prevent it? He
had devised the perfect threat. And the certainty she was
indeed with child was strong now. This morning, and again
this afternoon, she had lost what little food she had put into
her stomach.

Lucien took the quill from her numb fingers and signed
the registry himself. The vicar added his scrawl before Lord
Niles and Lady Raddington witnessed the document.

The clergyman gave Lucien his compliments, then
bowed over Serena's hand before departing.

Holford closed the door behind the reverend, leaving
Serena alone with her new husband, Lord Niles, and his
sister. She collapsed into a chair in the far corner of the
room, away from Lucien. She wished desperately she could
drift into peaceful slumber and forget this mess. Better yet,
she wanted to wake up and discover this mock marriage
was no more than a sleep-induced nightmare.

"Let's celebrate!" Lord Niles suggested, spurring Serena
from her preoccupation.

Lucien and Niles lifted glasses of brandy in toasts to
wedded bliss, partaking of the bridal cake one of the
servants had ushered in moments ago. She was married now
to a sinful ogre of a man, bound to a man who drank,
cursed—and seduced like the devil. Serena's stomach
churned. She declined her piece of cake.

To her surprise, Lady Raddington declined her slice as
well and trod across the room to sit beside her. "Are you
well, Lady Daneridge?"

That name! It sounded so foreign. So telling. But it was
hers now, for the rest of her life. "I shall be well soon."

The slightly older Lady Raddington smiled in sympathy.
"You need to rest. You look quite pale."

Serena found herself returning a weak smile. "Not
surprising, for that is how I feel."

"Relax. I shall fetch you a glass of wine."

Lady Raddington rose before Serena could protest the
liquor. She needed it; anything to take the edge off this harsh
reality, if only for a moment or two.

A moment later, Lady Raddington returned with some sherry. Serena sipped, not wanting to consider how low her morals had slipped. One sunny June day she had been a married lady of chaste virtue and upstanding morals. On that rainy night, she had become a wanton adulteress who consumed both alcohol and passion. She had slipped into her mother's skin. What could a glass of sinner's drink hurt after her plethora of sins?

"Do not frown. Happiness may yet come your way," Lady Raddington offered.

At those words, Serena lifted her gaze to Lucien. She found his stare riveted on her, all too captivating. The hunger in his green eyes reminded her of the hot desire that had spilled between them during their night together. He was remembering, too.

Drawing in a shaky breath, she turned away. "Thank you for your concern."

Lady Raddington took her hand in a gesture of comfort. "Of course. Let me know if I can do anything else to help."

Serena watched as Lucien set aside his glass and started across the room to her. She held her breath when, moments later, he wrapped hot fingers around her arm and lifted her from her chair.

"You can do something," she whispered to Lady Raddington in return. "Pray for me."

Lucien bid their guests a good night and escorted her from the withdrawing room, down the hall, toward his bedroom. In the hallway, she jerked out of his hold.

"Where are you taking me?" she demanded.

With a scowl, he pulled her before one of the doors. "To your chamber. You looked ready to nod off in that chair."

"I will not sleep here," she insisted. "I will not *live* here! I have a house of my own."

He halted before her, set aside his cane and grabbed her arms. "You will live here. Despite the fact you dislike it, we are now husband and wife."

"I may be your wife, but I am not your servant, and I will live where I please. And I please to live in my house!"

His brows drew together in a furious frown. The grasp on her arms tightened. "You are my wife now, and *my* wife lives under *my* roof with *me*."

"Like the first one?"

As soon as the jibe was out, Serena stepped back from the palpable anger he radiated.

"Simple military intelligence training instructs an officer that he cannot protect a target of violence from afar. You will stay here. You may send for your things come morning."

Alastair. She had forgotten about his threats in the midst of Lucien's. She swallowed, supposing her new husband was right. He could hardly protect her from down the street and round the corner.

"Very well, but know it's only the possibility of Alastair's evil intent that keeps me here."

His eyes narrowed. "I don't give a damn why you stay as long as you do," he retorted.

"Stop swearing," she hissed. "It's obscene."

He ignored her. "If you want, redecorate the chamber. I never bothered to do so after my ex-wife left." His eyes narrowed with anger. "It's vulgar. She was fond of red. Then again, you may like it."

With that, he found his cane, pivoted away, and disappeared into his own rooms.

CHAPTER FOURTEEN

Red indeed, Serena mused once inside the boudoir that
had been Ravenna Clayborne's domain. A sea of scarlet
glared around her, papering every wall, covering the floor,
draping the sumptuous bed. The color was unrelieved
throughout the room, except for a pattern of black woven
into an occasional cushion and the gold trimmings on the
carpet. Porcelain knick-knacks, red glass jars, and a gilt-
handled brush and mirror set rested undisturbed on a
dressing table, as if their mistress had been gone moments
instead of over a year.

Serena wandered around the room, taking in the garish
decor, only semi-conscious of the fact her mouth hung wide
open. What kind of a woman wanted her bedroom to appear
so...carnal? A complete wanton. The kind of woman who left
a handsome, exciting husband for one of his best friends.

And Lucien thought she would like this? She dropped
her forehead to her palm tiredly. He must think her very
much like his ex-wife. In truth, she didn't understand
Ravenna any more than Lucien did.

The room said everything about his ex-wife, and nothing
at all. Certainly, it shouted her taste for the dramatic, as
evidenced by the bed's blood-red velvet coverlet and the
four gilt posts surrounding it. But who had Ravenna
Clayborne been? What had motivated her to leave Lucien?

Turning in a slow circle, Serena saw a red dressing
screen painted with gold and black dragons, Chinese
fashion, and the fabric-draped door to a dressing closet.
Curiously, she opened the door—and stood rooted in shock.

Sunken into the floor lay a round tub of red tile. The rim
consisted of a series of hand-painted tiles depicting men and
women, utterly naked, intimately entwined in various
positions.

Gasping, Serena backed away, scalded by the sight, and
slammed the door behind her.

Then she saw the painting.

Immediately to her left hung a portrait of Ravenna *a lá* Venus, signed by the artist, Vigee Le Brun. Ravenna had been captured partially reclining on red silk, holding a wine goblet. The nearly transparent Grecian drape she wore outlined her curves and threatened to bare her breasts. The look in her dark eyes could only be termed lazy satiation. Black hair, loose and tousled, framed her face and clung to her sides. The end of one strand lay above the mound of her femininity, as if pointing there to draw the viewer's gaze.

This woman was a beautiful temptress, a sensual creature of abandon. Serena didn't wonder why men, including Lucien, were driven to possess such a wild soul. Cyrus had explained such male fantasies to her. Then, as now, they left her feeling inadequate, for she could never tempt men to sin as the ivory-skinned, ruby-lipped Ravenna obviously had. Not that she wanted to possess such an ability. She favored Christian morals to wallowing in secular pleasures of the flesh.

A vision of Lucien, his face dark with stubble, flushed with intent as he had thrust inside her flashed into her mind, mocking her morals. Had Lucien made love to Ravenna with that same slow purpose or with mindless, driving desire? And why did the memory of Lucien's hands on her body incite a hot, sinful burn?

"Good evenin', me lady," a cheery voice called from the doorway, startling Serena from her guilty thoughts.

A flush crept up her cheeks as Serena bade the woman to enter.

"Me name's Mildred," the plump fortyish woman offered, bobbing a curtsy. "His lordship sent me to care fer ye, since yer without yer own maid tonight."

Serena nodded, and before she could even take a breath, the servant continued, "I see yer lookin' at the first Lady Daneridge's likeness."

"Yes. It's...unique."

"Is that why yer blushin'?" Mildred teased, then leaned forward in a conspiratorial whisper. "I served the first Lady Daneridge while she lived here. She was a wild one."

Serena stared at the likeness of her husband's former wife, inferiority bleeding through her again. "She was beautiful."

"Aye, no mistaking that. Every man who saw her wanted her. And she wanted them, too. The young, handsome ones, anyway."

Serena had the urge to ask Mildred a hundred questions about Lucien's marriage to Ravenna and what had gone awry, but she quelled it. Encouraging such gossip was irresponsible. And knowing the extent of Lucien's feelings for Ravenna would only disturb her.

At Serena's bidding, Mildred helped her out of her dress. "There are a few of the first Lady Daneridge's dressing gowns here, if you be wantin' to wear one until ye can send fer your own."

She thought nothing of Ravenna's could surprise her further, but was astonished when Mildred held up a nightgown in transparent red gossamer, another in black silk, and yet a third in an exotic green satin, embroidered with black flowers.

Had Ravenna worn one or all of these for Lucien and seduced her husband? Had he pulled the garments from Ravenna's body in his haste to make love to her? Serena tried not to care about what Lucien and Ravenna had done together while married, but as she stared at those erotic gowns, the questions haunted her.

"I'll sleep in my chemise."

Mildred gave her an approving smile. "I agree. These're naught but Satan's tempters."

Serena said nothing as the maid braided her hair. Afterward, Mildred pushed her toward the bed. "Ye best lie down. Ye look plum ragged." Serena thought to protest, but the maid said, "Don't ye worry. I'll see to ye. Bring ye chocolate in the mornin' and send fer yer clothes, I will."

Serena slipped beneath the red but mercifully clean sheets. A fluffy pillow cushioned her head, and sleep began to creep up on her. "I'll wish to see someone about redecorating tomorrow. And I would like that portrait removed immediately."

The maid nodded. "I'll fetch some of the menservants to take the heavy thing down."

Serena sighed tiredly. She did not want to leave the comfort of the downy bed. Yet for the male servants to enter, she would have to do so, as well as dress again and seek another room—one where she might run into Lucien. She reconsidered.

"In the morning will do."

"I'll see that it's done as soon as you're dressed. Ring fer me if ye need anything." She paused and frowned. "Also, his lordship asked me to say he's gone out fer the evening."

With that, Mildred departed.

Out? Serena wondered what Lucien could be doing away from home on their wedding night. Attending some rout or ball? Though that was possible, her mind evoked an image of her husband of less than two hours embracing another woman, seeking the pleasure she had denied him, as he had warned he would.

She shut her eyes, trying to shut out the disturbing vision. She did not care who Lucien saw or sinned with. If he chose to secure his place in hell, that was his affair.

But the tears she had to fight off made a liar of her.

****

Lucien inhaled deeply of the brisk, biting air before throwing open the door to his town house. The porter, roused from his predawn slumber, rushed to greet Lucien.

"My lord," the servant said.

Lucien paused, trying to make his inebriated brain communicate to his mouth. "Is my wife still abed?"

The porter nodded. "I believe so, my lord."

Lucien handed over his cloak and gloves, then hurried to the stairs. Serena. He wanted to assure himself she was still alive and had not run off in some silly display of temper. She was his wife, the mother of his unborn child, and his responsibility now—one he planned to take very seriously.

After their flash of a wedding, Lucien had gone to think, to sort out this new twist in his life. He had finally come to some conclusions after collecting Niles and driving them to a favorite pub. Once there, he proceeded to consume a bottle and a half of port and turn away three women of questionable virtue.

He did not imagine his little wife would like his decisions.

Once inside his room, Lucien eased open the door between his chamber and Serena's and slipped inside the domain he had not entered for two years. He crossed the floor, using the gray morning light to guide him.

Lucien halted at the side of the bed. She lay on her back with her hair braided primly. The coil, as thick as his wrist, rested on her pillow. The weak morning sun highlighted the white-gold strands, so different from Ravenna's ebony.

He curled tense fingers into a fist. True, his new wife did not seem to want him any more than the last one had. She had only wanted him when cuckolding Warrington. Nor should he want her. After all, he had suffered no further desire after discovering Ravenna's true nature. He could not explain why, knowing Serena's adulterous tendencies, he had been unable to think of little else but divesting Serena of her clothes and burying himself deep inside her.

The whys of his desire hardly mattered. England's laws gave him the right to exercise his husbandly privileges. After much thought, he saw no reason to pursue any other avenue. They were wed until death, and he intended this marriage to last that long. He would not endure another divorce, nor would Serena become tangled in another adulterous scandal.

He planned to make absolutely certain of that.

Still, she looked like an angel, even lying amidst the red satin linens. His eyes traveled over the short, gathered sleeves of her lace-trimmed undergarment, the delicacy of her rounded cheek, the honey of her skin. The desire she always roused soared to a driving urge to bare her, mount her, pleasure her. And he would. Soon.

Unconsciously, his eyes wandered up a red wall to Ravenna's portrait a lá Venus. No doubt, she was among the most beautiful, carnal creatures God had ever created. During her come-out, some had called her the Devil's Daughter. Her silky raven hair, fair skin, and opulent red mouth had added to an image enhanced by entrancing dark eyes that seemed to peer into a man's soul and read his darkest sexual desires.

From the moment he had set eyes on Ravenna Stansworth in his Aunt Elizabeth's drawing room, Lucien had been driven to possess her. And he had, for a short time. But Ravenna had resented the fact her parents had chosen him as her husband simply because he had been the wealthiest of her suitors.

He could hear Ravenna now, lamenting to anyone who would listen that she had been forced to marry a cripple. And she had never enjoyed sex, until she had realized she could have it with other men — younger and unscarred. Pretty boys who hadn't fought a bloody war against Napoleon on the Continent.

He turned away from the portrait and the memories it evoked. Instead, he focused on his current wife.

Marriage would be different this time. Before, shock, fury, and pride had kept him from intervening in Ravenna's liaisons. Not with this one. He had learned the depth of deceit of which women were capable. Experience had prepared him to defend his right. The trick was to keep Serena too sated to seek another.

Lucien vowed she would know satisfaction again and again in his bed — every damn morning and night, if need be — to keep her from another's arms.

Starting this night.

He spun toward the door adjoining their rooms, ready for sleep. Serena's voice stopped him short.

"What are you doing here?"

Her trembling tone held both fright and uncertainty. Slowly, he turned to face her once more, and found her sitting upright in Ravenna's brothel-red bed, looking strangely out of place. She clutched the covers to her chin like a child who had suffered a nightmare. Against his will, something within him softened.

"Nothing," he assured. "I wanted to see if you were well."

Through the golden rays of weak morning sun, he watched her face cloud with suspicion. "Or that I had not fled, more to the point." Her voice was edged with sarcasm. "Now that you've seen I'm indeed *well*, I want you out of this room."

Her insistence he leave lit the match to his short fuse. "It is my right to be here, dear *wife*." He stepped closer. "Why do you want me gone so badly? Are you afraid I will jump into your bed and seduce you again?"

Her pink-cheeked face reflected guilty surprise as she pulled the covers up higher. "I have no notion what you would do, nor do I want to know. I simply want you to leave."

"Liar," he accused softly. "That is exactly what you fear."

He stepped closer. She inched back in the bed, hanging on to the covers as if her very life were at stake. He wondered if she was really afraid of him or of her own response. The question planted a devilish idea in his head

Lucien stalked closer still then inched onto the mattress, watching her back away, wide-eyed.

He reached for her, pulling her beneath him in the damp heat of the September morn. Her breath came in shallow gasps. Long moments passed. He did nothing more than stare. He wished to God he could read her thoughts.

Her tongue peeked out to wet her lips in a gesture that betrayed her nervousness. He swallowed, watching her with hungry eyes, craving the taste of her lips. Desire spiraled within him, swelling and impatient. Her body, stiff but warm beneath him, was a heady aphrodisiac. The feel of her came coupled with potent recollections of his most explosive night in memory.

She was *his*, legally and physically. His to taste and drink of, to touch and arouse and satisfy. He smiled.

With the feel of her beneath him, her sultry gardenia scent driving him, Lucien bent his head and seized her lips.

At the first brush, she hesitated, neither pushing him away nor responding in kind. Lucien prepared himself for her refusal. Faintly, he heard her shallow breathing over the roar of his heart. But she made no protest.

He drank from her lips again. A small whimper sounded from the back of her throat. Triumph spiked through him as he kissed her again. She molded her lips softly beneath his, opening slowly, almost shyly. He dipped into her mouth, savored her taste. Her mouth turned warm and yielding and responsive.

Pleasure erupted. His cock turned hard, demanding. Needing more of her, Lucien cupped her face in his palms and cradled her cheeks. She answered with a gasp, then thrilled him by circling her arms about his neck.

Trying to hold back a groan, he parted her lips even more. She responded, opened, allowing him to deepen the kiss. Her tongue rose to swirl about his with the sensuality of a gypsy girl's body dancing by firelight. His consciousness receded as the rhythm of their kiss escalated to something needy and urgent.

Lucien fitted one hand beneath her hips, elated to find her pliant as he molded her to his aching arousal. He closed his eyes, the feel of her soft flesh rippling through him with a tidal wave of sheer pleasure. A groan tore from his chest as he threw his head back in need.

His other hand rose to envelop one of her full breasts. He'd dreamed of touching them again, his thumb sliding across an erect nipple. His palm gloried in the feel of her flesh in his hands, tingling with ecstasy.

She panted small, short breaths against his lips.

"Damn it, how badly I want you." Lucien dipped his head to take her lips again.

Serena turned away. "No. I cannot."

She bucked beneath him. He held her easily, wondering what had caused her abrupt, violent reaction.

"Get...off...me!" she spat while struggling, her arms pushing at his shoulders and chest, her legs taking a lower aim.

"What the hell—"

"Happened?" she finished his question for him. "I shall tell you what happened. Exactly what I feared would if I let you in my chamber. Out!"

"This is my right," he growled. "I'm your—"

"We agreed to certain terms of marriage before we exchanged vows," she interrupted. "You had your fun last night with strong drink and, most likely, light-skirts, as well. I expect you to keep your end of the bargain and not seek further amusement here." She gave him a final shove before she jerked the blankets between them again like a barrier. "Until I've recovered from this birth, you will not step foot in here again."

Suppressing the urge to seduce her and prove her wrong, Lucien rose. "I'll step more than a foot in here, Serena. I'll claim every inch of you. You delude yourself to think otherwise."

"You promised!"

"I changed my mind." His smile was chilly. "This morning, however, I will take my leave for sleep. Tonight, expect me."

With that, he turned and entered his own chamber, closing the adjoining door behind him. He smiled wolfishly when, seconds later, he heard Serena lock the door from her side.

****

Completely disregarding the decorum she had been taught since childhood, Serena rushed between the iron fencing and through the Ionic columns buttressing her grandmother's St. James Square residence. She raised her fist and pounded on the door, instead of gently knocking, as a lady should.

The bewildered butler answered, his elderly arm drawing back the portal so slowly, Serena thought she would scream with impatience. She held her tongue.

"Good morning, Your Grace. I shall inform her ladyship you've arrived."

Cyrus's two spaniels, now entrusted into her grandmother's care, swarmed at her feet, barking in greeting. Serena nearly succumbed to tears at their familiar sounds.

"No need for that formality," Serena's grandmother called from the top of the stairs. "I hoped you would come round. I should like to ask you about a bit in this morning's *Times*."

Serena frowned in impatience. "Grandy, I've no time for the newspaper this morning. I must speak with you immediately."

Her grandmother nodded, then led her to the morning room. Grandy had barely closed the doors behind them when she said, "Did you come here to tell me you've married Lord Daneridge?"

Serena eyes widened with shock. "How did you know?"

"The *Times*." Her grandmother sat, meticulously adjusting the folds of her gray morning dress. "Serena, I know you realize you've done a terribly scandalous thing. The damage ..." She threw up her wrinkled hands with a sigh. "I know you had a grand passion for the man—"

"Wait. The announcement of our marriage is in the *Times*?"

Her grandmother handed her the morning's edition with a nod. The pit of dread in Serena's stomach grew to a gaping hole.

Folded to the correct page and before her in black and white glared the announcement that she and Lord Daneridge had married yesterday evening at his house by special license.

How dare that man! A scandal like this would ruin her forever, and he hadn't even consulted her.

"Is it true?" Grandy prompted.

"Unfortunately, yes. That is why I came." Her voice cracked.

Grandy's lined face softened. "Tell me what happened."

Serena did, giving her grandmother a brief account of her pregnancy, Lucien's threats, and Alastair's sinister shadow. Through it all, Grandy said nothing, merely nodding at the appropriate times and trying to suppress a smile at Serena's announcement of impending motherhood.

When Serena finished her tale, Grandy replied, "You're married and the announcement is out. Nothing will change that. What you need to consider now is the best way to live with the situation."

"Live with it?" Serena exclaimed. "When what I would really like to do is kill the arrogant knave?"

"Of course you would like to kill him upon occasion. He is a man, after all, and as such, is subject to notions you would surely like to strangle him for." She patted Serena's hand. "That aside, he is your husband now, and he is a young man, who will most likely live for some years, as will you. You must ask yourself what you plan to make of this marriage."

"A civilized separation as soon as possible," Serena snapped.

Grandy shook her head. "You mustn't be so headstrong as to waste your youth on pride. It will hardly keep you warm, as a man's love will."

Serena sighed. "Grandy, do you hear me? I despise him! He tricked me. He manipulated me. Thanks to him, everyone will think me just like Mama. Why would I want his love?"

"He had his own reasons for forcing the issue." She shrugged. "Even if he did not, you must realize that an unhappy marriage will most likely lead to an unhappy life." She smiled in self-deprecation. "Believe me, I know."

When Serena would have argued, Grandy raised her hands. "A good marriage consists of love, respect, and trust, all of which take time to develop. You found those with Warrington eventually. Yet you haven't been married to Clayborne one whole day and you already condemn the match as a dismal failure."

"But—"

"Of course," her grandmother interrupted, "in this situation, it would appear dismal. However, your future is up to you. You may try to foster those sentiments in your relationship to feed your own happiness, or live with the results if you do not."

Serena threw up her hands in incredulity. "Love a man who trapped me into a scandalous marriage with selfish disregard for my reputation? Respect a man capable of such perfidy? Trust a cur that most likely spent our wedding night partaking of strong drink and loose women?"

At that, Grandy chuckled. "No doubt your refusal to share a marriage bed rankled his pride." A moment later, the smile faded, replaced by gentle understanding. "Each of you will need the ability to compromise and forgive to have a happy marriage." Her grandmother's gaze probed, pinning her uncomfortably against the broad sofa. "Serena, someone must make the first step toward reconciliation. If he will not apologize, and men rarely will," she offered sagely, "try to forgive him, then find a way to prevent him from straying again, if that is what you fear."

Serena set her jaw and glared defiantly at her grandmother. "I do not care who he spends his nights with as long as he does not darken my door."

Grandy grinned. "Yes, you do. Since you came here for my advice, I shall give it to you. Either you must forgive him and accept him as your husband or plan to live the rest of your life with a polite enemy. I cannot make that decision for you, but I can say I think he will make you an excellent husband. Perhaps, with a man like him to keep you warm at night, you will have no further need for Hannah More's preachy tomes."

Serena felt the anger still serrating her insides, seething within her lungs. Forgive him? Make amends? Accept him into her bed and heart? Never.

"As for the scandal," Grandy continued, "perhaps I have a few strings to my bow yet. I shall call upon Lady Bessborough on the morrow and see what we can devise to bring things round," she added. "We'll simply have to see what can be done. In the meantime, go home to your husband and think about what I've said."

****

The carriage ride home from her grandmother's residence seemed excruciatingly long. Serena's anger had risen to fever-high proportions and escalated with each block because she couldn't vent her anger on the cause of her fury. Oh, but when she caught up with Lucien, he would feel every bit of that rage for that mortifying announcement he had given to the *Times*. Forgive him, indeed. That advice was preposterous!

With considerable foot-stomping, Serena marched into the entrance hall of Lucien's town house. "Where is Lord Daneridge?"

"I believe *your husband* is in his study, my lady," Holford answered, putting subtle emphasis on the word that defined her relationship with Lucien.

That she ignored. Up the stairs she raced, intent on force-feeding him a healthy dose of her anger.

When she reached the appointed door, she threw it open without the lightest of knocks.

"You selfish, unscrupulous — "

"There you are!" he interrupted her tirade, whirling to face her. His eyes narrowed with anger of his own. "Where the hell have you been? I have sent the entire household into a frenzy searching for you. I have pages all over town trying to find you."

He set his cane aside and reached for her shoulders. She tried to jerk from his hold. He held tighter. "Not even your maid knew where to find you. Why didn't you take her, at least? Do you want Marsden to kill you?"

"Of course not. I simply wanted to speak to my grandmother privately."

"Do not ever disappear like that again!" He shook her, his anger and worry clearly defined in his scowl. "You had me worried. I had no idea where you had gone. I feared Marsden had captured you."

For a long moment, Serena stood ensconced in his grip and couldn't move, her mind whirling. He had worried about her. Or just about his babe? The concern on his face seemed directed at her and touched something within she very much wanted to ignore.

After a moment of stunned silence, she lifted her eyes to him. Worry and relief radiated from him. Her heart turned over in her chest. Why did she find him so fascinating?

She shook her head to clear it. "As I said, I went to see my grandmother, Lady Harcourt, to tell her of our marriage. Of course she wasn't surprised that we had wed, thanks to you. Why not let all of London know that the former Duchess of Warrington married far too soon after the Duke's death? Why not make certain she is shunned by the *ton*, just like her mother, for the rest of her life?" Her voice rose to a shout that would have mortified her a mere month ago. "Why not start whispers about a man on the other side of the grave and ruin his reputation as one of the most respected members of the Lords?"

His grip on her shoulders softened. "Serena, I thought making the announcement now, as the season is ending, would be wise. The worst of the gossip will pass before the little season."

Serena's temper heated another degree. "A scandal like this may never die down! And of course, my grandmother was quite shocked by *my* behavior."

He dropped his hands from her shoulders and retrieved his cane. "I will send a note to Lady Harcourt at once explaining that we married at my insistence."

"You need not bother," Serena spat. "I have explained everything to her."

"Everything?"

"To the last detail. She already knew that I had been foolish enough to spend a night in your bed."

Lucien's jaw tensed. Clearly, she'd infuriated him. "The announcement has been printed; it cannot be retracted now. I regret any inconvenience it caused you."

He had apologized, something her grandmother would think rare indeed. That he had said it with all sincerity and taken the "first step" toward reconciliation simply made her angrier. She didn't want reconciliation; she wanted her old life back. She had no wish to live a stone's throw from a tempting sinner who would inevitably drag her further into the mire of his iniquity.

Serena lifted her chin in defiance. "I have been thinking since you invaded my room this morning, Lord Daneridge, and I've decided to take the risk of residing in my own house." She glared at Lucien, daring him to challenge her. "Maybe that will stem the gossip."

He shook his head. "Leaving will only fuel it. And until Marsden's threat is neutralized, you will not only live here, you will not leave this house without protection. I plan to make myself available for whatever outings you may schedule, but if for some reason I cannot accompany you, two former soldiers who served under me on the Continent will follow you. I've dressed them as footmen and armed them to protect you."

"How dare you order me about like a child!"

He pulled her against him. "I dare because our wedding vows gave me that right. You agreed to this protection. I plan on ensuring your safety. Damn it, you *will* cooperate with me."

"Take your hand off me!" she grated between clenched teeth.

"Give me your word," he demanded, his grip still tight.

Oh, how she would love to toss a defiant "no" in his face, fight him to the last breath. But common sense prevailed. Mr. Vickery of the Bow Street Runners had sent round a note only yesterday morning explaining that he had no new developments in her case. Alastair was still running loose, greatly in debt. Only she stood between Alastair and a fortune. To stay alive, she and the babe needed Lucien's protection. Any woman with half a mind would know safety existed in numbers, particularly if one of those had been trained as a soldier.

After a resentful sigh, she conceded, "I will cooperate, but I will not like it or you. Now take your hands off me."

"Gladly," he growled, smile menacing. "At least until tonight."

CHAPTER FIFTEEN

That night Serena took her solitary dinner on a tray in her room. She had finished with the decorator an hour ago, and felt satisfied that all visible traces of Ravenna Clayborne would be erased within a week.

Still, it galled her to reside in a room so reminiscent of Lucien's first wife. But being here alone was entirely preferable to supping with her infuriating but sexy husband—the man who had sworn to invade her bed tonight.

Looking at the food on her plate, she swept it about with her fork. Why had Cyrus wanted her to wed Clayborne after his demise? She could never ask her late husband now, but she resented his schemes. And him. He had left her a widow, without clues, without reasons, and had all but given her to an autocratic bully who desired her body, yet thought her little better than a common doxy.

While Lucien had infuriated her by making her the talk of the town, he also had the disquieting ability to disintegrate her resistance with a single kiss. What the devil was she going to do?

Serena considered explaining that Cyrus had asked her to take a lover in the hopes of conceiving, but her late husband had been embarrassed by his impotency, and she couldn't desecrate his memory. In life, he had wanted his ailment kept secret. She still respected that wish in death. Besides, Lucien might well hate her more for the truth than the lies she'd led him to believe.

What baffled her most was that, despite Lucien's low opinion of her morals, she couldn't resist his touch. This morning when he had sneaked into her bed, she'd meant to call him every kind of a beast and send him packing. Then he had kissed her, thoroughly, slowly. The touch of his persuasive lips, the gentle rasp of his morning beard against her cheek, had melted her resolve and reason. Equally humiliating, she feared if not for his words, which had brought her to her senses, she would have surrendered to his passionate persuasion again. Would she be able to resist him tonight?

With that thought, her dwindling appetite for food dissolved.

She pushed her tray away and paced to the window. Parting velvet drapes an offending shade of red, Serena looked out to the square below. Fog hung in the night air like a dense gray blanket, exacerbating the summertime humidity sweltering about her. Carriages moved to and fro on the streets, even at this late hour. Serena wished she could take one and go away — and never have to deal with Alastair or Lucien again.

An instant later, she spotted a man across the street, his dark clothing that of the lower orders, his squat body half-hidden by a tree. Though she could not see his face, she felt as if he was looking at her, staring, studying. Unnerved, she dropped the drape and spun away.

A knock sounded on the door connecting her room with Lucien's, announcing that he had come for his pound of flesh.

"Go away," she demanded.

"Serena, open the door."

"No." She curled her fists into balls to steady her trembling. "I know what you've come for."

"Then do not force me to indulge in the melodrama of breaking the door down."

Serena hesitated. She had little doubt Lucien could carry out his threat. The ancient lock would prove no match for his strength.

With a long sigh, she turned the key and opened the door. "I am letting you in to keep this door upright between us, not as a sign of acquiescence."

Lucien raised a cynical brow, but made no comment as he swept into her room, dressed in black breeches that fit too well for her sanity and a loose white shirt.

She gaped at his tall figure. The sight of his broad-shouldered body unleashed a tidal wave of sinful memories she had been trying to bury since that long ago morning she had awakened in his bed. Her knees went weak. The pristine shirt emphasized his sleek raven hair. His green eyes smoldered as they returned her stare. Flushing guiltily, she turned away.

He reached for her, his arms encircling her waist as he pulled her closer. "Thinking naughty thoughts?"

Heat. Pleasure. Danger. He aroused all three. She swallowed hard.

"Do not be ridiculous." Her denial came out a breathy rasp as she wrenched from his touch. From the two steps separating them, she felt the weight of his disquieting gaze upon her with the intimacy of a touch. Her heart began to pound when she realized she had not dissuaded him from pursuing her in the least.

"Ridiculous, Lady Daneridge?" he asked smoothly. "Not when your stare indicated you had very improper thoughts indeed."

"Not in this century. And definitely not about you!"

He snatched her chin between his thumb and forefinger. "What coy little game is this? It will be my pleasure to play the conqueror, if that's what you seek."

The thought made her knees weak. "Stop manhandling me and leave me alone."

His eyes glittered green fire as he bent closer. "Why don't I quite believe you?"

The words, whispered against her mouth, sent a flurry of tingles down her spine. His lips were so near. His nearness and all-male scent stabbed an ache low in her belly. Dear God, if his mouth met hers, touched, caressed, and devoured her lips, she feared that she would surrender the fight—and her body—to him.

Gathering her strength, she turned her face away.

With a whispered oath and slow, calculated movements, Lucien released her. "Serena, we will consummate this marriage."

"The only way you will have me tonight is by force," she said, hoping she could resist whatever wicked ploy he had planned. She refused to consider the repercussions if she could not. "We both know if that is your wish, I cannot stop you."

"You are my wife. If I choose to consummate our marriage, that is my right."

"Yes," her voice trembled. "But not our agreement."

"To hell with our agreement."

"No, my lord. To hell with you!"

Serena pivoted away and felt the withdrawal of his nearness too acutely for comfort. Dear God, she was crazy to want him when they had nothing more in common than an unborn child and electrifying lust. He was divorced, he drank, he cursed. His kind of man had never appealed to her. So why did Lucien?

"Very well, then," he said to her back. "I see you need some time, so I'll leave for the night. I expect you will have reconciled yourself to our marriage within the week. Do I make myself clear?"

She nodded, resisting the urge to inquire about his plans for the evening.

"I've stationed a footman outside to keep watch." His tone was purely informational. "Another will guard the entrances."

It occurred to Serena to tell Lucien of the man she had spotted outside her window, but realized he was probably one of her husband's guards.

Serena knew it bordered on the irrational, but for all Lucien's ungentlemanly ways, she would feel much safer with him here. She faced him again. "Will...will you be back soon?"

"Not before morning." His eyes drilled into hers. She read his challenge, his hunger. He waited. A heartbeat passed, then two. She made no reply.

With a curse, Lucien swung away and left.

Throughout the long evening, Serena wondered what her husband was doing. Attending an opera? Had he gone to Drury Lane to see a play? She wanted to believe that, but another image, one of a scantily clad woman well versed in the art of love welcoming Lucien in her bed, as she herself did not, haunted Serena.

For comfort, she unpacked several books, naturally gravitating to Mrs. More's *Christian Thoughts*. However, she found her own thoughts revolved around things much more carnal than Christian. And when a gold and black mantle clock chimed one in the morning, Serena took up a vigil by the window to await her husband's return.

At two-thirty, with burning, heavy eyes, she gave up and surrendered to sleep, certain Lucien had again found pleasure in another woman's arms—and hating the stab of jealousy she felt at the thought.

****

Lucien glanced over his shoulder at the riffraff on the street before he followed Niles down the cellar steps and into The Beggar's Club.

Inside, the room was raunchy, smoky, loud. One serving girl, her short skirt exposing her ankles and much of her calves, passed as they seated themselves at a table.

Winking, she said, "I'll be right with ye, me fine lords." Then she sauntered away, juggling several glasses of beer and a bottle of gin.

"Do you think Cripplegate is here?" Niles whispered across the table.

Lucien, with his back to the wall, made a quick survey of the place. "I don't see him, but we will ask."

"Do you really think he'll know anything?"

"If Alastair Boyce hired someone to murder his uncle here, as that cent-per-center suggested, the Earl of Barrymore will know about it. This is his establishment, and he rules it with an iron fist, I'm told."

Niles did little to hide his grimace. "And a lovely place it is. I always enjoy eating with utensils chained to the table. And what are these holes?"

Lucien grinned. "In the table? The one in front of you is about to become your plate."

Niles's expression became a full, open-mouthed stare. "Damnation, old man. What kind of place have you dragged me to?"

"The absolute worst hell hole in the East End," Lucien answered, his tone low.

A momentary hush fell over the crowd, and a thin, hunch-backed man entered the room. He settled himself in a chair at the front, his small eyes ferreting out the people within.

"The Earl of Barrymore?" Niles asked.

"Yes, that's Cripplegate himself. The whole family is frightful, but he's the worst."

A moment later, the dark-haired serving girl sashayed beside them, her curls swinging freely against a trim back, and took their orders. She left and returned shortly with their drinks.

She leaned down to Lucien, letting him see the tops of her breasts and the hint of pink areola just below the edge of her coarse bodice. "Anything else I can get ye, guv?"

He returned her suggestive smile with one of his own as he slipped a silver crown into her palm. "I would like one thing."

At his silky, suggestive voice, she deposited the coin in a pocket in the folds of her skirt and moved closer, her merry dark eyes twinkling. "Anything, guv. Ye name it."

"There's more coin where that came from if you can get me a word with the earl. Can you do that, love?"

She swallowed nervously. "I can try."

As she walked away, Niles whistled. "What a beautiful creature. And willing, too."

"Willing to give you a pox, I vow," Lucien retorted.

His thoughts drifted back to Serena in the silence that followed. He had handled her badly this evening, intimating he had a mistress he planned to bed until dawn, when he had no paramour and didn't want one. Knowing his wife, she would only try to resist him more now, if for no other reason than her damnable pride.

Turning his attention to the serving girl, Lucien watched as she approached the Earl of Barrymore. Wringing her hands, she spoke. Moments later, the earl raised his eyes and found Lucien across the room, who gave a slight nod in return. Cripplegate spoke to the serving girl.

She whirled away a moment later, and with a bright smile, approached the table. "He'll see ye, guv. In his office."

Lucien pressed another crown into her palm. "Thank you."

She deposited that in her pocket as well. "Thank ye, guv. If I can be doin' anything else for ye...I mean, I'd be pleased to spend an evenin' with a handsome gent like yerself."

Lucien hesitated. She was a pretty girl; the invitation was clear. His body craved release, having been without it since the night he had rescued and made love to Serena. He was within his rights to seek physical solace elsewhere, since his wife had denied him her bed. But something within him, something he didn't want to examine too closely, rejected the idea.

"Thank you, but not tonight."

With that Lucien rose, bidding Niles to stay put. He noticed the Earl of Barrymore had left the room, and followed the girl's directions back to Cripplegate's retreat.

The door to the surprisingly well-appointed room stood open. Lucien entered, eyes fixed on the round-shouldered man behind the desk.

Blowing a thin stream of cigar smoke, the man asked, "Who are you and what do you want?"

Lucien leaned against his cane for support, then answered, "I'm the Marquess of Daneridge, and I've come to ask you about another lord I'm told frequents your pub."

The older man shrugged, then gestured to Lucien to shut the door behind him. After doing so, Cripplegate bade him to sit.

As Lucien came to rest in a burgundy leather chair, the Earl of Barrymore quite surprisingly asked, "What is the cane for? Temporary use?"

The question puzzled Lucien, but decided to play the man's game to see where it led. "No, it's permanent. A shattered kneecap. A little gift from Napoleon's men."

Cripplegate's thin lips actually lifted in a small smile. "Good. The world has too many perfect people. Now what do you want to know?"

Lucien wasn't sure how or why, but he felt as if his injury had helped him to pass some odd test. "I'm given to understand that the Earl of Marsden is a frequent visitor here."

Barrymore's face screwed up into a grimace of disgust. "Yes, and the little bastard owes me money."

Lucien held his breath, praying he was on the right track. If he could just get enough evidence together to hang Alastair in court, he could keep Serena safe. "Do you know his uncle, the Duke of Warrington, died recently in an unfortunate highway robbery?"

The older man emitted a cynical grunt. "Unfortunate, yes. Warrington was a political whirlwind. A simple robbery, doubtful, as you well know, Daneridge."

Lucien didn't pause even a moment to revel in his good fortune. "Did he hire someone to do the job while here? Someone you know, perhaps?"

"No," Barrymore answered, bursting Lucien's bubble of hope. "I did hear him discuss the idea, but where he found the cull and the coin, I don't know."

Damn it! He had been so sure...Now what? "Can you think of anywhere else I can inquire?"

Cripplegate's small eyes narrowed. "That weasel Marsden owes me four hundred pounds. Will you pay it if I pass on information?"

Lucien wondered what the man was thinking, planning, but decided to answer. "Gladly."

Cripplegate nodded. "Good. Come back in a week. I should know something by then."

Lucien nodded and rose. Full of both victory and defeat, he exited the room.

****

The next afternoon, Niles appeared on Lucien's doorstep, his urgent knock demanding the butler's immediate attention. Lucien rushed down at the news of Lord Niles's agitated arrival.

"Hello, pup," Lucien greeted Niles upon entering his study. "Is something amiss? Holford said you looked out of sorts."

Niles stood, his usual teasing face completely devoid of a smile. "Have you been out today, Clayborne?"

Baffled by the question, Lucien said, "I—no, other than my morning trip to the graveyard."

"Damn," Niles muttered, fishing something from the pocket of his red and gold embroidered waistcoat. "I assume then you haven't seen this?"

He handed a piece of paper over to Lucien. Wearing a scowl, Lucien took it.

At first glance, he saw nothing more than a common cartoonist's satire of a member of the *ton*. During his divorce, he had been the subject of several, along with Ravenna and her lover, Lord Wayland. But upon closer inspection, he saw what had disturbed Niles so: Serena was the object of this cruel lampoon.

The artist's drawing depicted both himself and the former duchess being wed upon Warrington's very grave, with the old duke in his coffin wearing a scandalized expression.

Lucien swore. "Are these out?"

Niles nodded. "All over town. It's too late to buy up the circulation."

A silent pause fell between the two. Lucien wondered what he could do to stop the ridiculing cartoon from spreading further into the city's environs.

Suddenly, a female scream pierced their quiet. Lucien scrambled out the door to investigate, with Niles close behind. Both men raced to the entrance hall, Lucien trying to determine the source of the sound.

Again, the high-pitched tone of distress resounded, and Lucien realized with some confusion the cry for help was coming from outside, in his own courtyard. Tightening his grip on his cane, Lucien strode for the door and yanked it open.

Immediately, he encountered a small mob hurling stones and insults at a black-clad figure huddled on the cold ground. As he watched, another rock hit the form. He heard another distinctly female cry.

"Ye bleedin' 'ore," one man called out. "Yer not fit to lick me boots."

"Aye," another sounded ominously. "I wouldn't take ye to me bed even if ye offered to spread yer legs fer me. Sluts the likes of ye sicken me, spittin' on a dead man's grave!"

The mob rushed forward, rocks in hand. Lucien surged ahead to meet the indignant crowd. To his shock, the figure on the ground took on a familiar shape as he approached.

"Serena!" he shouted. Fear pumped through his blood upon recognition. Ignoring the sharp needles of pain in his leg, he raced toward her, with Niles close behind.

"Leave me be!" she called to the mob, struggling to rise to her feet.

"Ye hussy!" a woman yelled, brandishing another rock—and one of the cartoons. "I wouldn't have ye marry me dog, much less a marquess."

Lucien reached Serena's side before the mob did. With Niles's assistance, he lifted her to her feet.

He pulled her stiff, trembling form into his embrace, her eyes spitting anger and fear. He held her to his chest, feeling her fright in the thump-thump of her heart. His urge to protect her surged to white-hot anger.

He growled to the crowd, "This is private property and you are trespassing. Get off and leave my wife alone."

Fully expecting the indignant mob to swell and surge forward with their rocks and their dirty mouths and stone them all, Lucien was puzzled when Serena's attackers did no more than mutter a few more angry oaths before disbanding. Niles chased them down the walk and into the street, stopping some to ask questions.

A moment later, Serena pulled herself from Lucien's embrace, her eyes silently damning. He examined her face, noting she had been hit in the cheek. The spot of blood marred that honey perfection. Another trickle of blood wound its way to her golden brow where a second rock had found her forehead. He cursed beneath his breath.

He pulled out a handkerchief and dabbed the wounds. "Are you hurt?"

Tears pooled in her eyes as she pushed him away. "Hurt, no. I am humiliated!"

Lucien absorbed her anger. Whatever her sins, Serena hardly deserved to be treated like a common whore. Rage shook his fingers as he finished wiping away the blood on her face.

She grabbed the handkerchief from him. "Don't touch me."

Lucien stared at her in surprise. Her jaw clenched in rigid lines; her face seethed. Damn. She blamed the incident on him.

"I plan to do much more than that," he reminded.

"Not in public."

"No," he conceded. "I would prefer that we be quite alone."

Her face flushed a beguiling shade of pink. "I'm going inside."

"Good idea." He waved at Niles to join them when ready.

Once seated in his study, Lucien poured her a glass of wine. She drank it quickly, without question, silently telling Lucien how disturbing the incident had been for her.

He sat beside her. "What were you doing outside?"

Avoiding his gaze, she touched a hand to her hair, its golden strands falling from the confines of her pins. "I had gone out to stroll in the park—"

"Alone?" he prompted, incredulity blazing inside him.

She winced. "I usually take Caffey with me, but this morning I wanted to be...alone."

"*This* morning?" he growled. "You do this every morning?"

She blinked in apparent confusion. "Yes. I always have."

"Are you daft?" he questioned. "Marsden wants to kill you. Do you want to make that feat easy for him?"

She frowned, then sighed. "Sorry. I thought I would be safe so close to your house. But it's as if the mob was waiting for me. One...one man hit me with a rock. I ran and fell. I tried to get up. They hit me again." She looked up then, tears shimmering from her eyes, and a new rage struck him. "That cartoon was awful. And the hideous things they said to me ..."

"This is why you must stay here, *inside*, for the time being. It's the only place you're safe."

She rose and paced across the room. "Do you see what you've done to me with this mockery of a marriage?"

"Oh, no," he retorted. "I am *not* the one who died and left you a bloody fortune."

She tossed her shoulders back, as if ready for battle. "But none of this would be happening had you not seduced me."

He laughed, the sound bitter even to his own ears. "No, none of this would be happening had you bothered to tell me you were married the night I fucked you."

Serena gasped. Her eyes narrowed, as if she wanted to slice into him with her sharp tongue, but Niles entered.

"You are vulgar," she hissed at Lucien before she presented him the stiff line of her back and fled the room.

Niles tiptoed into the study with a low whistle. "She's none too happy, I see. Is she hurt?"

"No." He loosed a long sigh, rubbing aching temples with his fingertips. "Serena is angry and embarrassed. And she blames me."

"She shouldn't," Niles answered. "I stopped one of the thugs, and for a little coin he was willing to tell me that a 'fancy gent' paid to have this incident staged."

Lucien's eyes widened. Was this the break he needed to put Alastair away? "Really? Do they know his name? Have a description?"

"Unfortunately, no one saw his benefactor personally. But it has to be Marsden."

"Of course," Lucien answered. "But how can we prove it? The word of East End riffraff pointing the finger at an unnamed 'fancy gent' won't do."

Niles nodded. "The man also confessed they were instructed to stone your wife. To death."

Shock rippled through Lucien's already tumultuous emotions. "Christ, that's crazy!"

"It's bizarre but ingenious. And I would say that well describes the earl, my friend," Niles answered. "Mob violence is a common, blameless crime. They cannot hang an entire crowd—and you can never prove he ordered it."

Lucien voiced his agreement with an angry oath and decided to step up his efforts to lock Alastair in Newgate forever.

CHAPTER SIXTEEN

"Lady Harcourt is here to see you and Lady Daneridge, my lord," Holford announced.

Lucien glanced up from his glass of brandy and cast his gaze to the mantle clock. Eight p.m. Two hours above the time for an intimate to call. He found the observation less than reassuring.

"You may tell her my wife is sleeping, and we will call tomorrow."

"He will tell me no such thing," a slender, silver-haired woman asserted from the portal, dressed in a bright slash of blue. "Seeing a gentleman alone was scandalous in my day, too, but in light of the fact I am twice your age, I hardly think anyone will be appalled if we converse alone."

He suppressed a smile from the saucy older woman. "Please, come in."

"Indeed." She drew herself up to her full five feet.

Lucien cleared his throat to conceal a laugh and gestured to the sofa directly across from his chair.

"Tea?" he offered. "Or wine, perhaps?"

She peered into his glass on the table between them, then raised a brow in challenge. "A brandy would be lovely."

Lucien bit back a reminder that ladies did not drink strong spirits and rose to fetch her a glassful. Clearly, she was much less inhibited than her granddaughter. Moments later, he set the snifter before her and sat. "As I said, Serena is asleep."

"That's just as well, young man. I spoke with her two days since, just after you were married. I should like to speak with you now."

The smile slid off his face as he settled back against his chair, bracing himself for confrontation. "About our marriage, I presume?"

She nodded crisply. "If you'll allow an old woman to meddle, could you not have waited three or four months, at least, before shoving the poor girl to the altar? A few weeks is hardly discreet."

Direct and to the point. Lucien tossed back his own swallow of brandy. "Even one day alone in her house could have been too long since Marsden is trying to kill her."

"He is tiresome, I agree. However, Serena could have hired someone to protect her until a more sufficient mourning period had passed."

Since the lady preferred direct discussion, Lucien decided to respond in kind. He set his snifter aside and leaned forward. "Not to be indelicate, but your granddaughter is carrying my child. I was not willing to take any risks with her life or the babe's. I should think you wouldn't be, either."

Serena's grandmother sighed. "Serena *is* special to me, and I have long waited to hold her child close. But you have made Serena the talk of society, and that does not set well with her. Too reminiscent of her mother's scandalous days."

A reference to her mother again. What the hell did it mean? Not that her mother's doings would have made any difference in his decision to marry. Still, the knowledge might provide insight. "Serena mentioned the woman, but I'm afraid I cannot recall her."

Lady Harcourt brushed an imaginary speck of dust from her dress with a white-gloved hand. "My daughter, quite frankly, was spoiled. I granted Abigail too much freedom, I suppose. She demanded to be the center of attention, and would do anything to attract notice." She sighed, grimace tight. "When Abby was a child, the penchant was merely annoying. As she grew and married, it became an embarrassment."

Lucien frowned. "Forgive me, but how did flirting earn such a scandalous place in everyone's eye?"

Serena's grandmother cleared her throat. "She did much more than flirt, and she did so with every man who turned his head in her direction."

He could see how Abigail's cuckolded husband might be shocked, but the *ton*? "My lady, the behavior you have described hardly makes your daughter different than many of London's 'well-bred' ladies."

She fingered the lace at her sleeve. "But most of London's well-bred ladies make a pretense of keeping their indiscretions a secret."

A clearer picture developed for Lucien. A woman who loved a man's attention. A woman who would stop at nothing to catch the notice of the gentleman she desired, and everyone around her.

A woman much like Ravenna.

He drummed his fingers against the arm of the sofa. "And based on her mother's doings, Serena would prefer to keep her sins to herself?"

The older woman shook her silver head. "You misunderstand. Serena spent her most of her life in Sussex with her aunt, living in religious study. Quite contrary to her mother, she has no sins to hide. She never wanted any."

He absorbed the information with a skeptical ear. "I hate to be crass, but it isn't as if Serena accomplished the second immaculate conception."

"Exactly! She horrified herself with her own behavior and has spent every moment since trying to repent and praying to avoid ugly gossip. Your untimely marriage has made her the very subject of scandalbroth. And the ugly whispers suggest that she must certainly be her mother's daughter, in all respects."

He retrieved his glass. "Sometimes the truth is ugly."

The woman squared her shoulders and tossed him a pointed glare. "Serena is very unlike Abigail, I assure you.

"Not from my vantage point."

"Do you deny you were the first man to touch her?"

Lucien looked away, certain the woman was about to impart some piece of feminine logic designed to baffle men. "No, but—"

"She has hardly had the time or inclination for a lover since," the woman said.

"That says nothing of her future, and based on my knowledge of your granddaughter's ways— "

"But you do not base your 'knowledge' on my granddaughter at all," she argued. "You, Lord Daneridge, are reflecting on your ex-wife's ways, are you not?"

Lucien felt his stomach clench. "Ravenna has no bearing on this discussion."

"Except to cloud your opinion," she contradicted. "In truth, Serena spent three years in marriage to Warrington before she encountered you. That hardly makes her a light-skirt."

"Nor does it make her pure. But as long as we are discussing Warrington, why did the man never bed Serena? Had he no interest?"

Shock flared across the older woman's face, displayed by wide eyes and paling skin. She rose hastily. "If Serena has not told you herself, I should hardly be the one to impart such information."

Dismayed by the woman's retreat, Lucien stood. "Wait. Perhaps if I understood—"

"I have meddled far too much already, I suspect. I merely came today to ask that you keep her from the *ton's* notice as much as possible until the scandal of your marriage has dwindled. Such would set her mind greatly at ease."

With that, the diminutive woman was gone. Lucien sank down to the sofa once more, frowning. Everyone, it seemed, knew the truth behind Serena's marriage to Warrington but him. Bloody hell.

And this bit about judging his current wife by the previous one's behavior...perhaps so. But no matter how nicely Lady Harcourt phrased it, her granddaughter *had* committed adultery. It was possible that Serena had inherited more of her mother's blood than Lady Harcourt wanted to admit.

True, Serena seemed to dislike the gossip swirling about her, but the woman also possessed the capacity for explosive passion beneath that proper surface. He vowed to experience her sensuality again, the erotic curl of her fingers against his skin, the aphrodisiac of her moans, before someone else did.

He took another swallow of brandy, admitting that he was not willing to share his wife with another man. Not this time. If Serena needed fulfillment, then by damned, he would be the man to give it to her. Today, if possible.

And if he had to seduce her again, so be it.

****

An hour later, Serena closed the study door softly behind her and crossed the room. She felt rested, but no more refreshed. Silently, she seated herself on a settee to await a dinner she did not really want, but resolved to eat for the baby's sake. Her mind wandered back to her violent humiliation of the other morning, caused by her three-day marriage.

Her social stigma was Lucien's fault. If he had not forced this marriage, she would still be at Grosvenor Square in proper mourning. As her pregnancy progressed, people would have commented how sad it was that Cyrus had died before the birth of his child. She would have been an object of sympathy, not vicious gossip. Now, thanks to Lucien, the *ton* would only wonder at her child's parentage once they discovered she had conceived.

So why couldn't she stop thinking about him? About his smile, the power of his presence, his touch ...

Chastising herself, Serena dropped her gaze to a Chinese marble-topped table before her. On it sat a chessboard, its pieces also made of marble in majestic black and white. She fingered the rook, remembering fondly her matches with Cyrus.

She missed his logical mind and his understanding. No doubt if he were here, she could explain all her troubles to him. He would present her with some perfectly rational course of action.

She grasped the rook in her palm and clutched it to her chest. But then if he were here, she would not be married to Lucien and suffering the *ton's* wagging tongues—and her own irrational desire to touch the man who had ruined her reputation.

"Do you play?"

Serena gasped at the unexpected voice and turned to find Lucien standing in the open doorway, resplendent in a dark green coat. Why did the man always have to look as handsome as a fallen angel? "I did not hear you come in."

"My apologies. Do you enjoy the game?" He nodded toward the chessboard.

Serena set the rook aside. "Yes, I used to play often."

"Who with? Warrington?"

Serena dropped her gaze to the board to avoid the disconcerting curiosity of Lucien's stare. Could he read her mind? "Yes."

"Who usually won?"

Hearing the smile in his voice, Serena once again brought her gaze to her husband's face. The upturned corners of his mouth matched his tone. She felt herself smile just a bit in return. "Cyrus always won. The man was a genius. I never stood a chance."

"You never won? Not even once?" he baited.

"Once," she answered, feeling her smile widen. "But Cyrus was unusually foxed, for which I scolded him, but I do not suppose it truly counts as a victory on my part."

"Nonsense. A victory is a victory. If he inflicted such a liability upon himself, it was no fault of yours." He crossed the room and sat in the chair opposite her sofa. "How do you match up with others?"

"Quite well," she replied. "I don't believe anyone else has ever beaten me."

"Well," he said in mock seriousness, "we'll have to remedy that."

She cocked her head, meeting the teasing light in his eyes. "That sounds conspicuously like a challenge."

"It is. That is, unless you're afraid of me?"

Chin lifted, she replied, "Indeed not."

"Do you prefer the white or black?"

"You take black. I'll be generous and let you have the first move."

He nodded, his smile conveying amusement, then positioned his knight before the pawn covering his bishop.

Serena frowned and shifted the pawn before her king out one space, endangering his knight with her bishop.

Lucien pursed his lips together in thought. She found her gaze drawn to his mouth. Full and firm, his lips brought back a score of memories of their night of passion. His kiss and the rasp of his tongue against her breasts; she remembered each in vivid detail, despite the fact she had tried repeatedly to exorcize them. Now, as before, the mere sight of him, coupled with those powerful memories, started a coil of heat and need in the pit of her stomach.

Flushed with both guilt and desire, Serena looked away while Lucien spent several minutes debating his next move. But her gaze wandered back to him, this time to his long fingers stroking the square firmness of his clean-shaven chin in thought. He'd focused intently on her, too. His concentration brought forth another flood of memories centered on his caresses, of his hands pleasuring her body, both outside and deep within.

"Serena?" he called, jarring her from her runaway thoughts.

She jerked her gaze up to his, and realizing her cheeks had flushed. She prayed he could not guess her thoughts.

"It's your move." He looked at her knowingly, his tone holding lazy seduction.

Serena swallowed, feeling the same disconcerting connection to him she had experienced the night they met. The inexplicable need to touch him followed quickly.

"What are you thinking, sweetheart?" His tone was soft, allusive.

Her breathing shallowed. Maybe the man was a mind reader. Or did he simply know the effect his stare, his voice, had on her?

"Naturally I was considering my next move," she lied, knowing the morals she had once prized were slipping more each day.

The corners of his mouth lifted suggestively. "Naturally. What else would you be thinking?"

"Indeed," she said, forcing a light tone into her voice.

She broke their stare and glanced down at the board between them. He had moved his knight out of her bishop's path. Without thought, she moved her bishop back within striking distance of his knight.

She watched his fingers curve around the pawn in front of his queen, wondering if they would feel as arousing, as soft, as they had before. Chastising herself for such lascivious thoughts, especially on a Sunday, she took his knight without considering why he hadn't moved it from harm's way.

With a killing grin, he slid his bishop across the board to capture hers. "Will you surrender now?"

Her gaze flew to his. His eyes were a captivating green, deep and mischievous, challenging and erotic. She took a deep breath to steady her pulse. "Of course not. It's only a momentary setback."

He grasped his queen, holding her in the palm of his hand. His thumb caressed the length of her body. "I'll give you fair warning: When I've set my sights on something, I do not give up until it is mine. Completely."

The hot look speared her with desire. Contemplating his touch had gotten her bishop captured in the first place.

"I shall take a chance."

The next twenty minutes passed in silence. Yet this quiet was charged with an energy she couldn't explain, but found increasingly familiar in his presence. Though she made her required moves, too often her eyes and thoughts strayed from the game at hand to Lucien. And he knew it. She could tell by the smoldering smiles and stares he sent her way.

Serena slid her queen across the board, paying little attention to where she put it. She studied her husband instead, taking in broad shoulders, inky raven hair, the strength of his jaw, the glitter of his green eyes. Air suddenly seemed scarce.

He reached for his bishop and glided it diagonally across the board. With a confident tap, he positioned the piece before her king, two diagonal spaces away.

"Check," he uttered softly into the silence.

Serena lifted her gaze to his, surprised by his assertion— yet not. She sensed that, as with the chess pieces, he was closing in on her, breaking apart her defenses, sliding beneath them to capture what he desired.

He watched her with a hypnotic stare. His knowing look told her he knew the effect he had upon her. In alarm, Serena bit her lip, stifling the urge to reach across the table and touch him. The heat in his eyes flared to new, intense heights. The most secret part of her moistened in response.

Serena swallowed nervously, knowing she should look away and assess the danger to her king. But Lucien's stare drew her in and in, refusing to release her.

"Mate." His voice dropped another octave, sending shivers across her skin.

Mate? With him? Now? She began trembling. She could no longer deny that she wanted him far more than was wise. Worse, he knew it. Where on earth was she going to find the strength to resist?

She should leave the room immediately, call him a rogue and turn away. Instead, her gaze remained rooted to his. Her breath turned fast, shallow. Her pounding heart roared in her ears.

Serena swallowed—hard. Did he have any idea what those wicked green eyes did to her?

"Mate?" she choked out.

He inched his broad torso forward, closing the distance between them over the board. "Yes."

His gaze zeroed in on her mouth. Her lips parted; her breathing accelerated. He reached for her arms, fingers wrapping around her, toppling game pieces as he pulled her closer.

Without thought, she leaned forward. Their lips met in a rush. That kiss ended. He began another. She didn't protest. Instead, she reveled in the press of lips to lips, the togetherness. With each additional kiss, she realized how much she had missed this...missed him.

Hunger set in: dark, vibrating, thought-robbing. When his tongue touched the seam of her lips, surging more pent-up desire through her, she gladly opened her mouth beneath his gentle prodding.

She wasn't sorry.

He tasted like coffee with rich cream. He smelled like bay rum and male musk combined. He felt more perfect than heaven.

She wanted him—and could not push him away when he skirted the edge of the table and eased onto the sofa beside her.

Breaths tangled. One kiss mingled into the next. Serena clutched his shoulders as his mouth worked its magic.

He pushed her back against the cushions. She went willingly, shivering at the feel of his lips exploring her throat. She should stop him—and herself. Lucien and his provocative charm had caused her fall from social grace. The fire between them did not need this kind of feeding. But the razor edge of desire sliced her logic to ribbons.

"My God," he breathed against her skin. "How can you make me want you so completely, so quickly?"

A thrill shot through her body, some burst of feminine confidence too heady to ignore. Before she could respond — or think — she felt his hand against the back of her knee.

Higher he climbed, the feathery touch of fingers sending sparks straight up her thighs, to the wet, secret place in between. Lucien studied her with an expression akin to wonder in his green eyes. Dying firelight cast its light, illuminating his features with a golden glow. Her nerves teemed with tingles, her skin sensitive to his slightest breath.

She felt so gloriously alive, so wonderfully whole and aware as he pressed his lips to hers again. The winter of her senses gave way to spring, to a bloom of sensations swirling though her body. Inhaling raggedly, she drew in his scent, something as mysterious and intoxicating as midnight.

Serena clung to Lucien as he smoothed his fingers up the outside of her thigh with a touch softer than velvet, then slid his way across her hip. She gasped. Her most secret flesh burned with heat, with impatience for his touch. Perspiration beaded between her breasts as he inched his hand closer...so close.

He claimed her mouth once more. She melted against him, into him, until his palm finally covered her sex.

Serena moaned. Above her, Lucien tensed before his caresses dipped lower, his fingers plowing straight into the heat of her clenching channel.

Lightly, he stroked the sensitive nub, his touch infuriatingly slow. A demand that he do something to ease this ache swelled along with her need. He captured her mouth again, trapping her words inside.

His tongue swirled, played, teased hers, engaging her in a game of advances and retreats. She followed where he led, feeling as if the center of her being were ablaze.

He pressed his fingers inside her a moment later. A shower of pinpoint heat shot through her. She arched upward, bringing their bodies closer. His fingers nudged and fondled — and drove her halfway to insanity.

"Lucien," she said between pants.

"I know," he murmured, his own breath no less steady. "I know."

After a moment's adjusting, Lucien opened his breeches. He lifted her skirt as he touched his lips to hers, then positioned himself between her thighs.

Her gaze clung to his face. The impassioned intensity clear in his blazing eyes, the determined set of his mouth, echoed the feelings thundering inside her. She floated on a tingling sea of sensation as she parted her legs, opening herself to him in offering.

"I've wanted you," he admitted. "So much ..."

God help her. She had wanted him, too, even more today than the day before. More now than five minutes ago.

"Lucien," she murmured, not knowing what else to say.

"Shhh. Hold on to me." He pressed her deeper into the sofa, settling more of his weight on her, in the cradle of her thighs.

A discreet knock sounded on the door. "Your dinner is ready, my lady," Holford announced from the other side.

Startled, Serena shoved at Lucien, then leapt away like a guilty child. Through the haze of desire, she stared at him, blinking, confused. Dear Lord, what had she been doing? Giving herself to a man who had made her the biggest scandal in London, who cared only for her body and the child she carried. A man who believed her no better than her mother.

Right now, she felt no better.

"His timing leaves a lot to be desired," Lucien muttered and reached for her again.

She found her way to her feet and retreated from his outstretched hand.

"Serena," he entreated.

"My lady?" Holford inquired through the door.

"Come back later," Lucien barked to the servant.

A certainty that Holford must know what they had been about spawned embarrassment. "I'm opening the door."

Lucien tried to block her path. "Sweetheart, please. Come with me. Nothing should prevent us from the pleasure of being man and wife."

He caressed her arm, her shoulder. When jolt of pleasure wound up her arm and spread inside her, she jerked away. "Pleasure? I am the talk of every drawing room in the city. Because of you. Because of this farce of a marriage. Do you have any idea how terrible it feels to be spoken of so viciously?"

"Your grandmother told me about your mother."

She lifted her chin. "You think I'm no better. That with a few kisses and pretty words, my blood will give me away and I will fall into your bed. Is that not right?"

He paused, as if weighing his words carefully. "I did not know your mother."

"Well, my lord, you do not know me, either. And it will be a cold day indeed before I give myself to a man who thinks me a whore and cares not whether the whole world concurs."

With that, she darted to the far side of the room and threw the doors open.

"Serena," Lucien called after her.

She drew in a deep breath and swept out of the room. "Damn it, Serena!"

Halfway down the hall, she turned back to find her husband standing in the doorway. "This isn't over. You will share my bed."

****

The next day, Serena awoke to a voice calling, "Me lady? Me lady?" Roused from her sleep, she recognized the intruder as Mildred.

"Come in," she answered groggily.

The maid entered, and Serena sat up in bed, frowning at the bright sunlight streaming through garish red drapes. "What time is it?" she asked, bewildered by the sun's brightness.

"Just about eight, me lady. Ye were sleepin' so well when Caffey and I came to get ye at six, we couldn't wake ye."

Serena pried open her gritty eyes and bit back a reply that she probably had not fallen asleep until six.

In the wee hours of the morning, she had come to a conclusion about her new marriage, one she planned on making perfectly clear as soon as she could find her rogue of a husband.

With a tired groan, she rose. Mildred helped her dress, explaining that Caffey had gone to Grosvenor Square to supervise the remainder of Serena's packing. As the maid buttoned up the back of her dress, she said, "Are ye feelin' well today? Yer cheek is healin' right quickly."

Serena tried to smile at Mildred's mothering ways.

"We're all glad — the staff — ye married his lordship," she said. "The house needs a mistress, and Lord Daneridge is much too kind to be without a good wife."

Kind was not the word she would have used to describe Lucien Clayborne at the moment. He had forced this marriage at the sacrifice of her good name. Yes, presumably to protect her, but certainly he had other means to keep her safe. Then after nearly seducing her last evening, he had gone out — all night.

She had watched him leave the house in full evening black at ten. For a few hours, she read, pretending she did not care what whore he spent his night with. At three, she took up a place by her window to await his return. At dawn, she had retired to her bed, furious that he had the audacity to spend the night out, probably cavorting with loose-moraled women.

Why did that bother her? It wasn't as if she loved him, or had any intention of succumbing to his seduction again herself. Still, the fact he had set out to tempt her and nearly succeeded hurt. That she had wanted him enough to surrender hurt even more.

Was she becoming more like Mama each day? That question had haunted her sleepless hours almost as much as the vision of Lucien in another woman's bed.

"There. Ye look right as rain," Mildred declared after carefully applying a bit of rice powder to the small bruises on her cheek and forehead.

Serena thanked the woman and went downstairs. She skipped the offer of a hearty breakfast, intent on finding her husband. If she was going to live under Lucien's roof until Alastair could be stopped, they obviously needed to review some of the previously established rules.

She just hoped her own resistance could hold out if Lucien proved uncooperative. And what of his nights? He would undoubtedly continue to spend them out on the town, as he had said he would if she disinclined to share his bed. She found it hard to decide which was worse, giving in to his enticement or knowing some other woman would.

She descended the stairs and sought Holford. "Where, pray tell, is my husband?"

A grim expression entered his eyes. "At St. George's graveyard, my lady, where he goes every morning at this time."

Serena recalled that he had been grieving someone when they met, but had never learned whom. At the time, she had assumed he had lost a parent, sibling, or friend.

"Who does he visit there, Holford?"

The old man's rheumy eyes widened with shock. "My lady, you do not know?"

Serena sent the man an embarrassed grimace. "No, and apparently I should."

Holford raised silvery brows "Indeed." He hesitated, then said, "Follow me."

Without another word, he led her up one flight of stairs, then another. Down a dark hall they walked, her curiosity intensifying with each step.

Finally, he paused before a locked door. Producing the key, Holford said, "I had no notion his lordship had not informed you about Lady Chelsea."

Lady Chelsea? Another woman? Serena absorbed that apparent fact with a pang of jealousy she despised.

Knowing she was frowning beneath Holford's assessment, Serena tried to smooth her expression out, but the astute butler discerned its cause. "His daughter, my lady. She would have been five in October."

Everything within Serena went cold.
Oh, God.

He mourned not a woman, but *his* child. Squeezing her eyes shut as she imagined his pain, she whispered, "When?"

Holford cleared his throat, but his voice still sounded hoarse. "About five months ago."

He opened the door before them. Its hinges squeaked, hinting the portal had not been used in some time.

"Most of Lady Chelsea's things remain as they were on the night she died."

The butler stepped aside and Serena entered the bedroom. It was obviously that of a child. Toys were scattered in every corner; a variety of dolls lay strewn across the bed. Serena touched the soft, faded clothes of one. The tears in its cloth skin said the toy had been the little girl's favorite.

Venturing farther into the room, Serena spied drawings obviously done by a child's hand. One was of a large-petaled flower, the next a green blob with "Herman the frog" written below it in big, clumsy lettering. The last was a dark-haired stick figure titled "Daddy." She lifted the paper, cringing at the crinkle of paper in the silence.

"Chelsea was a laughing child, my lady. Everyone adored her," Holford explained.

Serena laid the drawings down, feeling the unmistakable sting of tears in her eyes for Lucien's profound loss.

His motive for forcing her to wed snapped into place with absolute clarity: He had lost one child and could not bear to lose the one she carried as well. And she, wrapped up in shame at her wanton behavior and the *ton's* wagging tongues, had never thought to ask why the babe she carried was so important to him. She had fought their marriage, railed at his insistence, and given him the sharp edge of her tongue at every turn.

And he was certainly still mourning the little girl's loss.

Serena's gaze traveled the room once more, struck by a sense of loss, of grief.

A moment later, a smudge on one window drew her attention, for the panes were usually spotless. She wandered closer until she could discern a small, sticky hand print.

Seeing the object of her attention, Holford said, "Lady Chelsea left that on the day she died. She had been eating candy that afternoon. After she died, his lordship left strict orders that it was not to be wiped away."

Another wave of grief assailed her, and she clutched the skirts of her own mourning black dress, pressing her lips together, feeling tears burn the back of her eyes.

Poor Lucien. Mercy, what he must have lived through, she could only begin to imagine. True, she had lost Cyrus, but with each day she was able to feel more and more as if she had lost a good friend and could hope he resided in the home of the Lord. But to lose a child, a little one he had seen in napkins, then walking shoes. One he had heard speak for the first time, one he had lived with and loved. The pain must be overwhelming.

Suddenly, Serena wished she could replace for Lucien all that he had lost. Though she could not give Chelsea back, she could give him the life growing inside her and her compassion.

Turning Holford's way, she touched his shoulder. "Thank you for showing this to me."

Holford beamed. "Always glad to be of assistance, my lady."

Serena nodded. "When my husband returns, would you tell him I await him in his study?"

The butler smiled in understanding. "I would be delighted."

CHAPTER SEVENTEEN

An hour later, Lucien's arrival put an end to Serena's nervous pacing. He entered his study, dressed to the nines, as always. But his usually robust complexion was pale, the light in his green eyes stark and dim. The smidgen of mud on one Hessian boot brought the reality of a little girl's cold grave to Serena all over again. With her heart in her throat, she approached him as he stood in the threshold.

"You wanted to see me?" He emphasized no word over another, his question an emotionless formality.

She nodded nervously and swallowed. The simple meeting she had devised an hour ago now seemed a hopeless tangle of sympathy, regret, and another nameless ache underscored by the heavy pounding of her heart.

Perhaps he didn't want her understanding; maybe he wanted nothing more from their marriage than her body and an heir. It wasn't impossible that his heart was involved with another woman, one he might have been with these few nights past. Though that prospect hurt, she realized they could not continue this hellish existence of living as enemies for the rest of their days.

Lucien stood before her, staring. She cleared away the tight lump in her throat with a discreet cough. "Perhaps you could shut the door, and we could sit for a bit?"

He scowled, his brows clashing together over suspicious eyes. "Is this about yesterday evening?"

Blast him for bringing that up, she thought, folding her hands in her lap. "I would like to talk about...our marriage."

With a curt nod, he shut the door, then seated himself on the sofa. "You have my attention, but don't think to ask me for an annulment. I've no intention of giving you one."

"That isn't why I wished to see you," Serena placated him as she sank into a Chippendale elbow chair. "Actually, I...I wanted to tell you that I understand now why you were so insistent upon this marriage, and I am very sorry for your pain."

He said nothing for long, excruciating moments. His face remained a blank mask as he drummed his fingers slowly on the table beside him. Serena feared she had made a dreadful mistake, that he didn't care for her sympathy at all.

Unable to bear the unresponsive silence, she rose from her chair. "I've nothing more to say. Good-bye."

She scurried to the door, thankful Lucien could not see the embarrassment in her flushed cheeks. She had been a fool to think her feelings mattered to him one way or another. Clearly, they did not.

"Come back," he commanded quietly.

Hesitantly, Serena turned to face him.

"Come here and sit down."

Serena scanned his face as she sat cautiously, hoping to read something of his thoughts, but Lucien gave away nothing. She deposited herself on the edge of the chair, breath held.

"I apologize if I seem suspicious, but it was only a few mornings ago you could not bear my presence in your bedroom. After that, you accused me of ruining your life with this, how did you put it?" His voice turned acidic. "Ah, yes, this 'mockery of a marriage.' Yesterday, we almost consummated our union, until you pushed me away and ran. Now you want to give me comfort. What, pray tell, brought about this change in sentiment?"

Serena chewed on her bottom lip, her gaze locking with his. Lucien's direct stare was closed and challenging at once. Gathering her courage, Serena reached across the space separating them to touch his shoulder. She sighed with relief when he did not withdraw.

"Holford told me about Chelsea," she said quietly.

He drew in a hard breath and jerked away with a curse. Serena felt Lucien's hurt in the air between them. He slammed his eyes shut. A pained frown crossed his features as his hands curled into white-knuckled fists. "Damn it to hell and back."

Serena leaned close. "Her loss must hurt terribly."

Lucien nodded, wanting to say more, but the words tangled in his throat. The harsh sting of tears clawed their way to his eyes. Swallowing the unmanly emotions, he sat stiffly.

Serena moved closer, her palm gliding between taut shoulders. Her gentle, comforting touch penetrated his coat, seeping under his skin to diffuse warmth throughout his chilled body. She reached toward him hesitantly with her free hand and curled her fingers around his own. Lucien closed his eyes as an aching warmth burst from his frozen heart and raced through his body. She squeezed his hand reassuringly.

Somehow, the fact Serena had committed adultery ceased to matter when she touched him so gently. She offered understanding and the comfort of her soft touch. She stayed beside him, warm, gentle—his wife.

Lucien allowed himself to revel in the contact, the sense of togetherness. No anger or acrimony lay between them. No deceptions, no betrayal. Instead, he felt an understanding borne of mutual loss, he for Chelsea, and she, no doubt, for Warrington.

Lucien leaned closer, until the hand that touched his shoulder crossed his back. He raised his palm to her cheek, bringing his face within inches of hers. "Her death hurts. I never knew I could hurt this badly."

A tear rolled down her cheek. "How did you ever bear it?"

"Hour by hour. Losing her was so damned painful. One moment she was here, playing, laughing...Then she was gone."

He took a deep breath. "I am sorry you found out from Holford. I wanted to tell you myself, but we haven't been on the closest conversational terms."

"I understand. It must be difficult to speak of."

"You have no idea." He shot to his feet with a grunt. "I'm the reason she's dead."

The raspy confession came out before he could stop himself, and maybe for the best. She should know the truth since she carried his child. Too bad his admission would slam the final nail in the dismal coffin of their marriage.

"That cannot be," she protested. "You clearly loved her. I cannot conceive that you did any such thing."

Lucien looked back to find shock and doubt on her lovely face. Odd, she had more faith in him than he had in himself. Then again, she did not know him all that well.

"It's true," he insisted. "The night she died, she begged me to search for Ravenna with her." He cast his gaze to the floor. "I refused. Then I left."

"Leaving for an evening can hardly be construed as killing the child."

He loosed a short, cynical grunt. "While I was gone, Chelsea apparently decided she would find Ravenna for me. She thought it would make me happy." He hesitated, rubbing a hand across his tired face. "She sneaked past her sleeping nanny and wandered outside. A passing carriage struck her."

Serena hesitated, then crossed the room to his side. "You mustn't think her accident was your fault. How could you have known she would leave the house?"

She reached for his hand, gripping it with her own. In passion, her touch was explosive, consuming; in this gentle sympathy, she was a healing balm for his soul.

A pity he wasn't worthy of such compassion.

He shrugged, breaking their contact. "I should have suspected the little imp would sneak out and stay with her instead. She had already lost one parent. What the bloody hell was I thinking, leaving her without the other."

"You could hardly confine yourself to this house every moment. This is not your fault." She captured his hands once again.

He smiled faintly, sadly. "Niles shares your sentiment. I am trying to believe it, as well." Lucien paused, deciding her gentle understanding deserved some in turn. "I realize our hasty marriage has caused you pain. For that, I am deeply sorry. You must be feeling grief, too." He peered into the golden face that haunted his sleepless nights. "Do you miss Warrington?"

Pressing her lips together, Serena nodded. "I shall always miss Cyrus. He was my best friend."

"But not your lover," he countered. "You cared for him, and he for you. So why did he never make love to you?"

- 196 -

She dropped her gaze to her lap. An agonizing moment of suspense later, she said, "The reason is in the past. I would prefer to leave it there."

Though her answer was hardly what he had hoped for, Lucien nodded. He had been foolish to hope he could trade one confession for another. Confidences weren't privy to any bartering system. Still, why did it bother him that she remained so closed? Unsatisfied curiosity. A wish to understand what had driven her into his arms, so he could prevent her from seeking another, he supposed. Still, some foolish part of him had hoped for more. That at least they could talk without arguing. That they could make some sort of civil marriage.

Maybe she didn't share his wishes.

****

As loath as Lucien was to leave Serena that night, he knew Cripplegate was expecting him. He hoped the earl had been able to find something, anything, in the way of hard evidence that would point the accusing finger at Alastair.

After ensuring that an armed man was stationed at every door of his home, Lucien climbed in his coach, giving his driver his destination.

He leaned back in the seat and considered his conversation with Serena earlier. Her understanding of Chelsea's death lightened his mood. Certainly, she had surprised him. He hoped they weren't destined to quarrel for the rest of their days. Perhaps, in time, they could come to some mutually agreeable marital arrangement. If not happy, at least civil. Anything had to be better than the last few days.

Yet one thought haunted him: Why did she insist on keeping the details of her first marriage such a secret? He couldn't fathom why it had never been consummated. Had the duke preferred men? No. Though he hardly listened to the *ton's* wagging tongues, Lucien knew he would have heard if Warrington's tastes had leaned that way. And if such had been the case, the man would not have been such a respected member of the Lords. Besides, after a little digging, Lucien had learned that the man had sired three daughters.

Lucien considered the puzzle from another angle. Perhaps Warrington had been impotent. But no, Warrington had illegitimate children, the youngest still very much in the schoolroom. So what had their problem been? The mystery behind Serena's first marriage confounded Lucien.

Should he simply let her keep her secret? Perhaps the nature of Serena's relationship with Warrington was none of his affair. But something in him felt driven to dissect it and understand why Serena had sought a lover.

He could not allow it to happen again.

Upon arriving at the Beggars Club, Lucien seated himself at a table and watched the goings-on around him. The crowd assembled tonight was a motley one, including all walks of life from sailors to smithies with one goal in common: to sink well into their cups.

Across the room, the same dark-haired barmaid who had served him before swiveled her hips, her skirts swishing about trim calves, to dodge the groping hand of a customer. She made her way to his table, then asked, "Hello, guv. What can I get fer ye?"

He smiled ruefully. "Another word with the earl. I believe he's expecting me."

With a nod, the girl threaded her way to the far side of the room and disappeared into Cripplegate's sitting room. A moment later, she returned. "Aye, he's waitin' fer ye. Go on in."

Lucien slipped a crown into her palm, then crossed the dirty, crowded floor to the privacy of Cripplegate's domain.

After Lucien closed the door behind him, the Earl of Barrymore bade him to sit. Not a moment passed before the hunch-backed man asked, "Did you bring the four hundred pounds Marsden owes me?"

Lucien fished in his waistcoat pocket and produced a roll of bills. Silently, he tossed it across the massive desk separating him from Cripplegate.

The older man's smile was feral as he pocketed the money. "Splendid."

"Now," Lucien paused, leaning forward expectantly, "what do you know?"

The earl laughed. "You'll like this. Marsden hired two dirty culls named Jim Rollins and Dicky McCoy. For enough money, they'll do anything. Perhaps if you paid them handsomely, they would be willing to testify about Warrington's death."

Lucien could not hold back his smile of victory. He had the greedy bastard cornered. Once he talked to Rollins and McCoy, he'd likely have real proof of Alastair's guilt that could end the cur's threats on Serena's life. "Do you know where I can find them?"

Cripplegate took a swill of brandy from a half-full glass on the corner of his desk. Lucien waited impatiently for the old man to swallow and speak, and he was sure the earl knew it.

"Visit a flash house on Butcher Row; it's close to the docks. Trouble frequents the place, and so do our friends."

At that, Lucien stood. "Thank you."

Cripplegate waved him away rudely. "I have my money and Marsden's cock is under the hatchet. It's an even exchange."

Lucien then left the tavern and instructed his driver to take him to Butcher Row.

Settling himself against the seat, Lucien contemplated his impending victory. If he could threaten — or bribe — Rollins and McCoy into telling all they knew about Warrington's murder, combined with the word of the late duke's coachman, it might be enough to send Alastair to Newgate.

Closing his eyes, Lucien wished more than anything for a speedy end to this mess. If not for Alastair, Serena would be safe. And he could be at home with her, proving to her that she belonged in his bed and his life.

Through the coach's window, Lucien watched the East End streets in passing. The surrounding buildings were small and worn. Through the night fog, their dark facades hovered on the edge of the narrow streets, as if waiting to spring forward and capture unsuspecting travelers in their crime-ridden clutches. Evidence of poverty and vice lay all around him, from the children selling flowers, candles, and evening newspapers, to the prostitutes, both young and old, hawking their bodies on nearly every corner.

As they rounded a bend, Lucien saw the outline of an inert body, a man, just off the road. He frowned, wondering if the chap was merely drunk or dead.

A moment later, the coach stopped. The driver dismounted and opened the door. "Begging your pardon, my lord, but are you sure this is where you want to be?"

Lucien looked out the window again. One hut across the street exploded with activity. Young boys carried bottles to and fro, while a graying man sat atop the stairs watching everyone with shrewd little eyes. A thoroughly dissolute woman clung to his shoulders. "Unfortunately, yes."

"A body is likely to get killed here, my lord. Are you sure you want to get out? Mayhap I can fetch something for you?"

Lucien shoved the carriage door open a little wider. "Thank you, but no. I can handle myself."

Lucien alighted onto the filthy street, trying to ignore the odor of raw sewage. Other than the noises across the way, the air around him was quiet...still. The eerie sound of his own boot heels crunching into the dirt below rang in his ears.

Withdrawing a pistol he had tucked into his greatcoat, Lucien approached the shanty cautiously. The bottle-carrying boys carting gin, no doubt, took little notice of him. The greasy-haired man and his woman atop the stairs, however, eyed him with interest.

Clutching the gun in his palm, Lucien made him way toward the ragtag pair.

The unshaven man peered curiously at Lucien. "Be ye wantin' to buy a bottle, rent a room or a boy fer the night?"

Lucien smothered an oath of distaste and stepped away from the smell of the man's unwashed body. "No. I'm looking for a pair of fellows said to spend time here, Rollins and McCoy."

He eyed Lucien shrewdly. "What's it worth to ye?"

With impatience and disgust, Lucien tossed a couple of crowns in the man's direction.

The haggard blonde at his side lunged toward the shining silver coins. The man slapped her away. "Get lost, ye bleedin' whore. Go inside."

With a mutinous glare, the woman flounced away and stomped into the house, slamming the door behind her.

"You do know them, don't you?" Lucien demanded.

"Aye, I know 'em."

Through clenched teeth, Lucien asked, "Are they here, by chance?"

At that, the man's expression became perplexed. "Can't rightly say they are. Haven't seen 'em in over a week."

Lucien swore loudly.

"Now that I think about it, seems they disappeared 'bout the time that Redbreast started showin' his miserable face round here."

"A Bow Street Runner?" Lucien prompted, his interest once again peaked.

The man nodded. "Name's Vickery, he said. 'e's been lookin' for Rollins and McCoy, too."

"Did he say why?" Lucien quizzed.

The old man shrugged. "Somethin' about the murder of a duke. And he's been askin' a lot of blokes round here questions about a titled gent named Marsden."

CHAPTER EIGHTEEN

The grandfather clock struck two in the morning as Lucien entered the town house. Wordlessly, he removed his greatcoat and gloves, then thrust them at the porter. He glanced up the darkened stairs before mounting them two at a time, ignoring the twinge in his knee.

Striding between the pair of guards outside Serena's bedroom, he opened the door, then eased it closed, the soft click of the latch barely audible.

Her chamber was almost dark, the curtains drawn against all but the thinnest stream of moonlight. Immediately, he saw she had replaced Ravenna's brothel red bed with a mahogany half-tester. Gone was his ex-wife's portrait. In its stead hung a placid landscape in pastels. The red curtains and accessories had been removed in favor of innocent white and lace.

Innocent? A questionable prospect, just as questionable as the possibility the Bow Street Runner was mere coincidence.

Lucien tread across the room and watched his wife sleep, her honey features illuminated by the moon's glow, her golden plait resting against the curve of her white-gowned back. He perched on the edge of her bed, fighting down his rising lust, and gently shook her shoulder.

She stirred, fixing her groggy gaze on him. "Lucien, what are you doing here? Is something wrong?"

Closing the space between them, he asked evenly, "Did you hire a Runner named Vickery?"

"What?" Serena's voice was faint with sleep.

"A Bow Street Runner," he repeated. "Did you hire him?"

Blinking, Serena nodded. "Yes. Why do you ask?"

He groaned. "I thought you would do me the courtesy of telling me you had hired a man. I've journeyed to the East End several times, trying to put Marsden in Newgate to protect you. Why didn't you see fit to tell me about Vickery?"

"I...I," she stammered, seeming to search for the right words. Shaking her head, she finally answered, "In all truth, it slipped my mind. I hired the man the day after Cyrus was murdered. We wed so quickly after his death. And with Alastair's evil deeds, it never occurred to me."

He raked a hand through his hair. "I've been to the slums, talking with dangerous cutthroats and criminals, digging for something that will prove Marsden's guilt. Yet it never occurred to you to tell me you had someone else doing that very thing?"

She grimaced. "I did not imagine you would want to know. Besides, I had no clue you were searching for evidence. It's not as if you told me anything, either."

His fingers curled around her upper arms, bringing her closer. He realized she had a point even as the warmth of her soft flesh burned him through her nightrail. Damn it, he shouldn't notice her as a woman. Not now.

"A Bow Street Runner is nothing to take lightly," he pointed out. "We could have been working together. Perhaps we could have succeeded as a team by now." He paused, then gave a voice to the anxious demon within. "Is there other information you want to share? Anything else you're hiding?"

"I've hidden nothing," she insisted. "I did not intentionally deceive you. I never have."

"Oh?" Lucien questioned, brow arched. "No woman ever sets out to deliberately deceive a man, does she? Every woman I know leads me to believe she's experienced and allows me to bed her, when in fact, she's a married virgin."

Serena struggled in his grasp. "I apologize if you inferred I had been with a man before, and as I said once, I did not realize my marital status was of such interest to you."

"Why the hell would you think I would want the responsibility of deflowering another man's wife?"

He shook her, bringing her face within inches of his. She exhaled fast and shallow. Her breath fell sweet and enticing on his face. The scent of gardenias teased his nose. Feeling an unwanted rise of desire, he swore. "You hardly followed me into this house that night for a friendly spot of tea. You knew what was going to happen between us."

"Perhaps, but—"

"And your protests seemed very token." Memory flashed him a vision of her in his carriage, head thrown back and gasping, while his fingers worked inside her. "You were not wearing your wedding ring."

Her eyes flared wide in defense. "That thief had just stolen it!"

Lucien tilted his head, staring at her through the chill of his eyes. "Fine, but can you explain the rest? Why you failed to mention your innocence, why you sneaked off like a coward before first light? In my mind, it all shouts deception."

He paused, allowing the thick silence to intimidate her. She was nervous; he felt it, smelled it, as a new rush of memories assaulted him. "I asked you at Rundall and Bridge if you had considered the possibility of pregnancy before you came to my bed, to which you replied you had considered everything. I told you I would have left you untouched if you had simply informed me you were an innocent. You said, 'Exactly.'" He frowned. "You came that night looking for a lover, didn't you?"

Eyes wild, Serena struggled like a madwoman for release. Lucien held tight. "Answer me."

She squirmed in his hard grasp. "I told you before, it simply happened. I did not plan it."

"But you wanted a man, didn't you? You went to Vauxhall that night looking for one. Isn't that right?"

Immediately, she stilled in his arms. Then she shook her head in quick denial. "No. I did not want to go."

"Why did you?"

She hesitated, licking dry lips with her pink tongue. In fascination, he watched, feeling a stirring of arousal he didn't want to feel.

The charged pause hummed on, stretching taut. Myriad expressions crossed her face.

"Why?" he barked again.

Finally, resignation overtook her expression. She swallowed nervously. "I was looking for a lover...or at least, I was supposed to be looking for one." She drew in a shaky breath. "Cyrus wanted me to find a lover to get me...with child."

An icy wave of incredulity rushed through his body. In outrage, he stood. "No. No man of sound mind like Warrington would want, much less *condone,* his wife's infidelities. I cannot believe he wanted another's man's brat running about his house, claiming to be his son."

"He had no choice," she implored. "Cyrus knew Alastair would destroy everything he and his ancestors had spent their lives building. His nephew is disturbed."

Lucien scowled. "So he sent you into another man's arms? Damn unlikely. Why didn't he get an heir on you himself? Hell, why did he never try?"

At that, Serena shrank back, shaking her head from side to side. "Stop. Please ..."

"I think I deserve the truth. Did Warrington prefer men?"

Serena gasped. "Of course not! How can you suggest—"

"Because you will not tell me the truth." He inched closer, closing in on her. "Why didn't he bed you himself?" When she hesitated, he grabbed her arms again. "Why?"

During the ensuing silence, Lucien held his breath, wishing he could wring the answer out of her pretty little hide. His thoughts raced as he tried to deduce the secret she guarded so diligently. He came up empty.

"He...he could not make love," she whispered brokenly, so softly Lucien wasn't certain he had heard her correctly.

"Could not?" he questioned suspiciously. "He was impotent? Is that what you're saying?"

Biting her lip, Serena silently nodded.

"How, then, did he sire three daughters by his mistress?"

Face tight, pained, Serena lowered her gaze. "It happened long before we wed. I'm told his youngest daughter is thirteen."

Lucien stood, amazement rippling through him. Impotent? He paced, realizing her explanation answered many of his questions. But to send her into a stranger's arms? He turned to face her. "He wanted you to spend your nights in another man's bed and bear him a bastard?"

"Yes," she croaked, clutching the blankets in her fists. "He felt he had no choice. And it's not as if the *ton,* or even the child, would have ever known the truth."

Suddenly, the devious plan took better shape in Lucien's mind. A fury as strong as steel, as hot as the fires of hell, roared through him.

He shook her, then pulled her to her feet. "Nor, I imagine, would the child's true father ever have learned of the babe. Am I right? That's why you fled my bedroom with such haste."

"Yes," she answered, then protested, "No! I was terrified. I was confused. I was...ashamed of my behavior."

She hesitated, seeming to grasp for words, probably fabricating a story, as Ravenna had done after he discovered one of her rendezvous. He released her. "You've no need to explain, I understand perfectly. You needed a faceless, nameless man to be your stud," he growled. "You wanted some unsuspecting *fool* to impregnate you, and you chose me."

"That is not true," she protested.

He had to give her credit; she was almost convincing. Far better than Ravenna.

"Why me?" he demanded. She opened her mouth, and Lucien held up a hand to stay her reply. "Never mind. I know. I was the consummate unsuspecting fool. Hell, I was a grieving drunk. The perfect target!"

He strode away. Presenting her with his taut back and shoulders, he spat a litany of curses. Seconds later, he heard her faint footsteps traveling in his direction. She touched a hand to his shoulder.

Fire leapt to life within him. "Damn you. Go away."

"It was never like that," she vowed in that husky voice that never failed to make him hard. Christ! He had hoped somehow that she was different. Why did he always have a stiff cock for lovely liars?

Furious with her, and his body's response, he whirled to face her. "Then how was it? Can you honestly say that conceiving my child *never* crossed your mind that night?"

She paused before lifting her reluctant gaze to him. "It did," she whispered, then quickly added, "but that is not why—"

"No? Then why did you allow me, a total stranger, to bed you? Are you going to keep telling me the same lie, that you wanted me?"

She held up supplicating hands. "I did! I did not go to Vauxhall that night looking for some...some stud. I merely wanted Cyrus to believe that I meant to play along with his plan, but I couldn't. I never had any intention of taking a lover because I believed in my heart it was wrong."

"That's good, sweetheart. Blame a dead man for your sins. Obviously, he's in no position to refute you."

"Truly, I would not lie about something this important," she implored. "And I did not believe you would care about my marital status. Most men would not."

Her beautiful face was so open, her blue eyes so contrite and earnest, Lucien wanted to believe her.

Believe her after this deception? Lucien didn't see how he could ever again.

Ravenna had betrayed him by sharing her body with other men. And he had hated her for slurring the Daneridge title, for giving to others what should have been his alone. But Serena held a kingdom all her own in the realm of betrayal. To rob a man of his own flesh and blood, and what was more, never tell him of his child, was unforgivable.

"Goddamn you!" he cursed, then whirled away, stalking toward the door adjoining their rooms.

From behind, she grabbed his sleeve. "Stop! I swear to you I've told the truth. I did not tell you sooner because Cyrus was so ashamed of his...condition. He disliked being anything less than perfect. As he saw it, this made him not only imperfect, but not a real man."

"So he sent you after this?" he spat, grabbing her hand and pressing it against his stiff arousal.

With a gasp, Serena tore her hand away. Shock flashed in her smoky blue eyes as she retreated a step.

Eyes narrowing, Lucien strode after her. He curled his hand around her neck, then pulled her face to his.

His words brushed her trembling mouth. "I understand now. You only wanted me when you wanted to *use* me, could only bear my touch when you were told to. All this week you've been putting me off, turning me away, and I thought you merely wanted a gentle seduction." He snaked his other arm around her waist, molding her against him. "Obviously, I couldn't have been more wrong."

Serena tried to wriggle from his hold, rubbing instead against his aching shaft. Dozens of tingles tore through his belly and streamed down his legs, blurring his anger, blending it with blazing desire.

"You do that well, sweetheart." His voice was soft, deadly. "Did Warrington teach you that move before he sent you out to find me?"

Serena tried to twist from his grasp. "Let go!"

He shook his head, his smile thinning into a hard line. "I think not. You see, I understand now that the way to get you back in my bed is not to seduce or cajole. Oh, no," he murmured, his voice harsh. "You respond better to orders and commands."

"What are you talking about?" Her voice rose in disbelief. "Lucien—"

"Warrington told you to spread your enchanting white thighs, and you did. I am your husband now. You're going to do the same for me."

Shaking her head wildly, she implored, "I did not come to your bed because of Cyrus's request. I swear!"

He ignored her denials. "Get ready, sweetheart. In less than five minutes, I'm going to be inside you."

"No!" she protested, her eyes wide with horror. "We agreed to wait."

Her husky voice rang in his ears, ran through his surging blood to merge with the fury and lust already pounding inside his body. Fire and ice described him perfectly. He was hot; he was cold. He despised her; he wanted her. Now.

"To hell with waiting."

His mouth captured hers in a savage kiss. She struggled, her bare feet kicking his shins. She pushed at his chest, her nails digging into the muscle of his shoulders.

His lips never left hers as he cupped her bottom, his desperate hands kneading, pressing her against the granite of his arousal. Against his mouth, she opened hers to protest.

Lucien took advantage of her parted lips by sliding inside to taste her. Her flavor slammed across his senses as he pressed deeper, capturing her kiss with ruthless determination.

Oh, God. She was warm and sweet, exactly as he remembered, only better. He held her tighter, pressing her breasts into his chest, reveling in the heat. He was dizzy with her scent. It wafted through his senses and into his head, muddling reason.

A moment later, her hands relaxed against his chest. She ceased scratching and pushing. She parted her lips further at his urgings. He was lost.

Lucien lifted his head. He stared down into her delicate face, her startled eyes, her flushed cheeks, her lips swollen from *his* kiss. A dangerous need to possess her, claim her, raged through him. He lowered his mouth to hers once more. After a moment of hesitation, she met him with sweet abandon.

He continued his quest, his tongue seeking out the deepest recesses of her mouth. Suddenly, her fingers curled around his shoulders and squeezed, as if she struggled with some inner demon. He gave no quarter.

He delved inside her mouth even more and groaned with the feel of her lips and her body against his, straining against his cock. He was so hard it hurt.

With his hands cupping her backside, he bent until each palm grasped a thigh, fingers curling toward the soft folds of her sex. He lifted her off the ground, then wrapped her legs about his hips.

She gasped. "Lucien—"

He cut her off with another wild kiss.

As his body throbbed with passion, with life, blood roared through his veins, obliterating logic and restraint. Holding Serena against him, Lucien felt the wet silk of her cleft through his shirt, against his belly. Again, the urge to take her here, now, pounded him.

He sank to the carpet on his knees, holding her against him.

Serena clutched his shoulders to prevent tumbling to the floor. He leaned forward, towering over her, until her back landed on the carpet with a muffled thud. An instant later he covered her body with his own, the cradle of her thighs surrounding his hips.

His mouth ravaged hers once more before he nuzzled her neck. He slid further down her body, finding one nipple beneath the linen of her nightrail. His lips took it, his tongue moistened it, his teeth stiffened it. She cried out.

Surrender, he thought in primitive triumph. He had never wanted a woman more, never felt as if he would burst the instant he buried himself in her tight sheath. This woman was his wife, and she was damn well going to act like it.

His blood raced as he curled his fingers around the edges of her nightrail, close to her neck. Her breathing came fast, hard. Their gazes connected for a suspended second. He gave her a long moment to push him away. She stared back, her face full of breathless acceptance.

He ripped her gown down the length of her torso.

Every inch of her lay naked, exposed to his hungry gaze. The scent of gardenias and the musk of female flesh filled his nostrils, heightening his desire to an excruciating peak. He kissed her neck, his tongue exploring the soft skin there. At her gasp, he cupped one hand about her breast, larger in pregnancy, his thumb hardening the nipple for his pleasure. His other hand delved into the soft curls between her slender thighs, coaxing, arousing, rubbing the tiny bud of her desire. In savage satisfaction, he felt it stiffen between questing fingers.

"Spread your legs wider, Serena," he heard himself say in a husky, demanding rasp. He lowered trembling fingers to the fastenings of his breeches. In several jerks, he opened his pants, then pushed them about his hips. His manhood sprang free. He pressed against the moist curls between her thighs. "Open for me."

"We should not do this," she panted, her voice thick.

"We already are," he challenged, feeling as if he would explode any moment. "Can you say no?"

She swallowed, eyes wide and dilated as she whispered, "I-I ..."

With his knees, he pushed her legs further apart. "Damn it, Serena, you have too much passion to keep it locked inside, away from me. Share it. Let me give some back to you."

Before she could respond, he lowered his hand to her entrance. With a gentle push, her body accepted two of his fingers. At his invasion, he heard her breath catch, felt her body tremble beneath him. He caressed her little bud with this thumb. Around his fingers, her flesh was slick and hot and ready.

He lifted his head to gauge her expression. Her languid, now heavy-lidded gaze stared back, cheeks flushed with desire.

"You want me," he asserted, feeling the proof around his fingers, seeing it in her smoky eyes. "As much as I want you. Whether it makes any damned sense or not."

"I should not do this," she repeated, her voice trembling.

He moved his fingertips, teasing her slick inner walls, his thumb still working that sensitive knot of flesh. Her breath caught on a gasp, her legs tightening around his body, keeping him a willing prisoner.

His insides beat with elemental desire. "Shouldn't do what, receive pleasure? Have the satisfaction your body is screaming for?" He laved her nipple with his tongue, feeling a surge of triumph when she grabbed his head and pressed him closer. "With your husband, you should."

He wrapped his arms around her sides, his palms slipping beneath her to cup her buttocks. He tilted her pelvis up. Her breathing quickened. He guided the engorged tip of his cock to her wet entrance and paused. Serena closed her eyes and brought her legs up about his hips. His body throbbed with life, with power and need.

With one solid push, he thrust deep within her. The walls of her oh-so-tight sheath closed around him, permeating him with liquid fire, ratcheting his desire up another degree higher. He heard Serena's cry ringing in his ears, felt her fingers digging into his shoulders.

Quickly, he withdrew, then plunged into her again. Then again. He groaned, driving into her with mindless need, feeling her legs raise higher to wrap around his waist. He took one of her nipples between his teeth, then pushed inside her again.

No doubt, she was a beautiful liar, but his beautiful liar. She was meant to be in his bed, to house and harbor him within her heat, to surround him with her fire.

He rocked her in a wild rhythm, lifting her hips from the carpet beneath with each thrust. She moaned, her nails digging into his back. He felt the sharp jabs of pain, smelled the scent of her arousal in the air between them. He drove into her once more, burying himself to the hilt. Faster, harder, higher, he moved within her, filling her with every inch of him.

"Lucien," she whispered in one hard breath. Then another. "I...I need..."

"I know." He plunged into her moist femininity, straining to take more, give her more. "I can feel you. I'm going to give you what you need. Now!"

"Lucien!" she cried. "Oh, mercy...Oh, God!"

During her long, hoarse cry, he filled her with deep, savage thrusts. He felt her pulsate violently around him. Gnashing his teeth, he tried to stave off the climax enveloping him. But he could not. And no longer wanted to.

Spasms of pleasure ripped through his body. A blinding release shattered through him as he moved within her, spilling his energy, his lust—a part of his soul.

Slowly, he halted. His senses took in their perspiration-slick skin, the cadence of her heavy breaths, and his own. He felt dizzy, spent.

A part of his dazed mind realized the implications of what had occurred: They had consummated their marriage, sealed their union. He resisted the illogical part of him that celebrated that fact. Maybe tonight would set the pattern, as he had so often hoped, for the nights to come. But should it, given the fact his desire for her was stronger than his resistance?

"Damn it," he cursed and pushed himself away. He had lost complete control. Serena's body, her touch, her female essence, drove him beyond logic, beyond thought.

He should have walked away before this happened, had even meant to. Taking her to his bed had always been his plan, but he had wanted to do so calmly, with purpose, on his terms and in his time. Succumbing to this mind-shattering need, reeling with the fervor of his ascent into earthly heaven, served no purpose but to give her power over him.

Nor could he ignore the fact she'd lied to him and planned to steal his child. But one simple touch, her fingers on his arm, set off shock waves of desire in his veins. Had she recoiled from him? Screamed in protest? No, she had accepted his touch, then ignited in his arms.

He wanted to blame his loss of control on his anger and lengthy abstinence. Those combined with her sultry scent, her lush body, and the sensuality she hid beneath her daily facade. But he could not; the blame was his alone. He had let his arousal guide his actions. He had lost control, like a fool.

Still shaking from the intensity of his climax, Lucien rose to his feet and fastened his breeches. He tore off his cravat, then readjusted his coat on his shoulders.

Serena rolled to her side, away from him, wrapping the rent edges of her nightrail around her like a protective blanket as she curled into a ball and wept.

He told himself not to be concerned about the lovely deceiver. In plotting to conceive and never share the news with him, it became clear that she had never considered his feelings about *his* child. The fact she had not shared her little plot with him sooner told him she still didn't give a damn.

And probably never would.

Pain ripped through him as he stared at her shaking back. Some logical crevice of his mind recognized that Serena's betrayal felt different. Ravenna's had angered and humiliated him. Serena's perfidy hurt much worse, like a red, festering wound, infected further by a sense of loss and hopelessness.

He closed his eyes and drew in a deep breath. Had Serena bewitched him in some way Ravenna never had? That was the only logical answer, but hardly a comforting one.

"Damn it," he cursed, his voice cracking.

Lucien crossed the floor to the door adjoining their rooms and opened it. Still Serena said nothing. He watched her back, heaving with sobs, and swore. He had to get away—now. Before he gave into the growing urge to comfort her, soothe her, then take her gently within the white cloud of her bed.

Gripping the door's handle for support, Lucien crossed through the portal, into his room. He slammed the door between them.

Then he locked it.

****

Serena attempted to sleep, the soft mattress beneath her no lure to the night's slumber. Through the door adjoining her room to Lucien's, she could hear the impatient, odd rhythm of his pacing. Did thoughts of their heaven-hellish lovemaking keep him awake, as they did her?

She could no longer hide from the fact a parallel existed between her mother's wanton behavior and her own. No matter how pure a life she had led until meeting Lucien, how good her intentions, she had failed. She succumbed to pleasures of the flesh, like Mama. In spite of Mama.

She lowered her head to her hands. Then there was her confession of Cyrus's plot, which had been nothing short of a disaster. To most, using a man to father another's heir would mean little. Many men, even Cyrus, had fathered children out of wedlock. But to a man who had suffered a child's death, like Lucien, the plan no doubt ranked as an unthinkable deception.

His anger, his disappointment in her, could not be ignored. She knew Lucien would continue to protect her from Alastair's evil intentions. She was, after all, the mother of his unborn child...and now the person he despised most.

His feelings toward her should not matter. They shared a name, and soon, a child. Nothing more. So why did his sentiments signify? His nights out, most likely spent in the arms of some mistress, should not bother her. Nor should the fact that he must think her a light-skirt after the way she had succumbed to his touch tonight.

But her heart caught, clenched when she thought of Lucien. His feelings did matter. What he did, who he spent his time with—all of that made a difference. He was in her life now; he was her future. But her feelings extended quite beyond that. Lucien made her feel.

Tonight, seeing the fury and scorn in his eyes, hearing him lock the door between them—it all hurt. Because she had hurt him.

Why? She did not love him or anything so foolish. Yet she had the irrational urge to stop fighting with him, to make everything right between them. To give in to his touch again.

****

Alastair flew out of the hack the minute it stopped on Butcher Row. Drawing the folds of his cloak around him to stave off the night's chill, he stalked toward the flash house ahead.

As usual, Dirty Ed sat atop the stairs, bottle in hand. His whore Wanda sat beside him. They both smelled of unwashed bodies and gin.

"Where are Rollins and McCoy?" Alastair demanded.

The ruddy-faced man took a swill of gin, then said, "Ain't here."

Snatching the bottle from Dirty Ed's hand, Alastair smashed it against the railing. The shattering of glass filled the silence left after Wanda's gasp and Dirty Ed's curse.

With a predatory snarl, Alastair lunged forward, grabbing Ed's neck in one hand, and held the jagged edges of the bottle next to his cheek with the other. Ed stuttered nervously as he watched the shards of glass glitter dangerously in the moonlight.

"Are those two worth the pain of having your face carved like a piece of meat?"

Dirty Ed gave a small shake of his head, his pallor white.

"Good. Now where are they?"

"Inside," he croaked. As Alastair headed for the East End hut's door, Ed called, "They just came here to sleep a bit, is all."

Alastair never answered.

"Dirty, bleedin' cur," he heard Ed mutter.

Alastair grinned and proceeded inside. He paused, letting his eyes adjust to the dim lighting of a single candle. He saw the torn sofa and the table missing a leg; he smelled the stale odor of alcohol and vomit. Stalking from the door he had entered, he found Rollins and McCoy stretched out on the floor, asleep in the squalor of vermin-filled blankets.

Refusing to touch their covers, Alastair instead kicked Rollins in the ribs. The man raised his head, his dark, greasy hair falling into his drink-reddened face.

"Guv," he said in surprise. "What be ye doin' here?"

"I might ask the same of you."

"Dicky and I needed a quick bottle o' gin and some sleep. We was just going to stop for a sip and nap, and be off, honest. No one was going to find us."

Alastair's eyes narrowed. "Have you talked to a man named Clayborne? He's the Marquess of Daneridge."

Rollins sat up, rubbing red, dilated eyes. "No. We ain't talked to no one. We kept quiet, just like ye told us."

"That's not what I hear," Alastair rebutted. "In fact, it's my understanding you've been bragging about finishing off a wealthy duke."

"That's a lie!" Rollins tipped his bottle upward and swallowed nervously. "I...I think Wanda out there might've heard Dickey and me talkin', but by the saints, I didn't tell no one."

"And McCoy? Who has he been telling?" Alastair asked, his tone almost conversational.

Rollins glanced nervously at his sleeping companion. "You know Dickey. I think the bleedin' fool told his brother. But no one else," he assured hastily.

Alastair smiled politely. "Unfortunately, Dickey's brother likes to talk. What a shame for both of you," he said.

From his boot, Alastair withdrew a knife.

****

In the solitude of his study, Lucien spread out the *Times* before him. He attempted to read it, as he did each morning. Today, concentration was impossible.

Serena filled his thoughts. The way she clung to him last night, groaned his name. Her scent haunted him with remembrances of her soft skin and trembling response.

Damn it, how could a woman who had planned to steal his child affect him so?

With resolve, he turned his mind away from his deceiving wife. He shouldn't waste his thoughts on a woman who'd plotted to rob him of another chance at fatherhood. Yet knowing her dirty secret didn't diminish his desire for her. If anything, the memory of her tight sex clenching around him in ardor as she accepted each and every one of his furious thrusts only made him want her more deeply than ever.

He doubted indulging that desire would be a sound notion. Tasting her again wouldn't eradicate his ache for her. He knew that. If anything, he would only fall deeper under her spell.

He had to avoid that at all costs—until he could find a way to enjoy fucking her without completely losing his head. And eventually, his heart.

Lucien withdrew his pocket watch and noted it was well past nine in the morning. Serena was usually up and dressed by this hour. Was she ill? Had she left him?

Lucien hesitated, then rose from the sofa. He would check on her. Briefly, of course. She was his responsibility, after all. And although he had posted new guards at her door since this morning's wee hours, the added precaution would not be remiss.

Before he could leave the room, Holford knocked, and Lucien bade him to enter.

The old servant stepped into the room. The stark black of his coat made his chalky, lined face look whiter than snow.

"What's amiss, Holford?" Lucien asked in concern.

"You have a...guest, my lord."

"At this hour?" He frowned. "Show Niles in."

The man paused, his Adam's apple bobbing down in his fleshy throat. "I'm afraid it isn't Lord Niles."

Lucien wasn't sure whether he should laugh or frown at his butler's reluctance. "Could you be more specific, perhaps?"

Holford nodded, his eyes saucer-wide. Chills spread across Lucien's skin.

"My lord, the former Lady Clayborne is here to see you."

CHAPTER NINETEEN

Ravenna here? That wasn't possible. She lived in Italy with his former friend, Lord Wayland.

A moment later, she appeared beside Holford, as if to prove the impossible real. The quirk of her jet brow matched her mocking, ruby-lipped smile. "Hello, Lucien. You look surprised to see me."

Holford shut the study door, leaving them alone.

Lucien closed his gaping mouth, and eyed his ex-wife with rising anger. As always, Ravenna looked earthy and ethereal at once, the combination of knowing ebony eyes and angelic cream-smooth skin creating the illusion. She was dressed to perfection in a rose-colored muslin that enhanced her beauty and the carefully applied rogue on her cheeks.

She was as beautiful now as she had been at the end of their marriage, perhaps more so. Age had helped her to grow into the curves of her body and the elegant angles of her face. She looked perfectly comfortable displaying most of her soft bosom at this carly hour.

Once, the mere sight of her had incited lust, a need to bed her until they were both satiated and exhausted. He felt none of that desire now.

What the hell did she want?

"Ravenna," he greeted shortly.

Her smile turned kittenish. Lucien knew better than to trust it. "I shall have to work on your greeting. It was hardly warm, darling."

"It wasn't intended to be." He eyed her suspiciously. "Why are you here?"

With a husky laugh, she sashayed toward him. Lucien stiffened when she brushed her hand—and her breast—against his arm. Without invitation, she seated herself on the sofa, then patted the cushion beside her, gesturing for Lucien to sit. He remained standing.

Her cupid-bow mouth drooped into a familiar pout. "Why am I here? What an awful question. I've missed you. The very least you could do is tell me that you've missed me, too."

"I haven't, nor have you missed me," he ground out, fingers wrapped tightly about his cane. "Why the hell did you come here?"

Her pretty pout hardened into a petulant scowl. "You're being very unpleasant, Lucien."

"That's how I regard your visit, Ravenna."

With a gasp, she stood, the insult spurring anger that flared pink into her cheeks. "You cannot mean that. I am your wife!"

"You *were* my wife," he corrected. "We're divorced now, at your insistence, if you'll recall."

She waved an impatient hand. "A mere legality. Besides, I was a foolish child then." She wrapped imploring hands around his lapels, pressing her well-curved body against his chest in a way that had once driven him insane with want. "I realize what a dreadful mistake I made, darling, and I've come home."

Tightening his hard fingers around her wrists, he removed her grasp on his coat. "I am not your darling, and this is no longer your home. Our divorce is not a mere legality; it is parliamentary law."

Batting long, black lashes, she said softly, "But I've confessed how dreadfully wrong I was to leave you and I am sorry—"

"Isn't it a little late for apologies?" He tapped an impatient toe on the carpet stretched beneath his feet.

Lucien watched her jaw tighten, and suppressed a smile of satisfaction.

Ravenna cleared her throat, then pasted on an engaging, but tight smile. "I'm trying to say I love you. I know I hurt you terribly with my frightfully bad behavior, but I *am* different now. And ready to be the best wife ever."

Lucien tried to rein his surprise behind a tight expression. "Somebody else's wife perhaps, but not mine."

He extricated himself from her embrace and paced to his desk. Seating himself behind the massive mahogany piece, he watched her race across the room to stand directly before him—just as he had suspected she would. Her hands clenched nervously in the folds of her skirt. Whatever she wanted, she wanted it badly. The corners of his mouth turned up in a chilly smile.

"The only thing you ever liked about me, Ravenna, was my money," he said, his tone insultingly conversational. "I assume that's what brings you here now. How much do you need?"

She actually looked offended. Lucien silently commended her theatrical ability.

"What a vulgar thing to say! I did not come all the way from Italy for money. I came for you. I want us to marry again."

Lucien propped his cane against his desk, then crossed his arms across his chest. "That, Ravenna, is impossible."

She sidled around the desk and touched his arm, rubbing her thumb against his tensed muscle beneath. Her voice was a low, erotic whisper. "Nothing is impossible, darling."

Her presence annoyed him. Her insinuation incensed him. He flung himself out of his chair, stalking past her, withdrawing from her touch. "Marrying again is." He paused, turning to face her. Whatever walls stood between him and Serena, he thanked her for making this sweet, vengeful moment possible. "I've remarried."

Ravenna's black eyes flashed with fury. "What? You love me! I won't believe anything so preposterous."

"I suggest you believe it. It's the truth."

She hesitated. Lucien could see from her pursed lips and clenched fists that she was struggling to control her unruly temper. A moment later, she lifted her face to his, allowing him full view of much of the contents in her bodice. "If being with you means sharing a relationship of a...secretive nature, I don't mind. I just want you back, darling." She dropped her voice to a low note as she reached for him. "We can still enjoy each other, can we not?"

"We'll deal much better together if you stop feeding me lies." His voice thrummed with fury. "Now, if you do not seek money, what do you want? I know damn well it isn't me."

Once again, she sat, raising her tiny, round chin angrily. "No, we'll deal much better if you stop this boorish behavior. Why do you insist that I don't want you?"

He laughed harshly, surprised by her audacity. "You hated me from the instant I offered for you. You left me for Wayland." He grabbed her arm, his voice rising. "I am the despised cripple you hated to call your lord. I am the cuckolded husband you begged for a divorce. I know you, Ravenna, far too well to believe you're here because you care for me." With that, he released her arm, then lowered his voice to a strictly polite level. "Why aren't you in Italy? Where is my devoted friend Wayland?"

With all the dramatics of a stage actress, Ravenna buried her face in her hands and began to sob.

He held in a sigh. "Save your tears for someone who believes them."

Sniffling, she lifted her head to regard him with wounded eyes. "How can you be so cruel?" Withdrawing a handkerchief from her glove, she wiped delicately at her eyes. "If you must know, James left me to marry a wealthy Italian countess."

"For the money?" he asked.

"Perhaps." Her voice was small, confused. To Lucien, she sounded genuine—for the first time in his recollection. "He wanted to leave me, and the countess made doing so easy."

"Where's the baby, Ravenna?"

Her dark eyes misted, haunted by soft shadows. "He was born dead, and...James blamed me."

During the ensuing silence, Lucien felt a connection with his ex-wife that had never existed during their five year union. He understood her grief and guilt all too well, and offered softly, "I am sorry. It is hell, I know. It must make losing Chelsea even more difficult."

Ravenna gasped, clasping her hands against her chest like a child herself. "You're right. Oh, I've missed her so! Where's my darling girl? Please let me see her."

Alarm raced up his spine. "Didn't you receive my letter?"

Her perfect-oval face lit up in a smile. "You sent me a letter?" Her voice sounded breathy. She flung herself against his chest. "I knew you cared!"

Lucien grabbed her shoulders and wrenched her away. "It was no love letter, damn it!" Taking a deep breath, Lucien continued in a soft tone. "I wrote you about Chelsea." He heard his voice crack and struggled to keep it intact. "She ..." He cursed, raking stiff fingers through his hair. "She died in April."

Ravenna's jaw plummeted, then snapped shut. "Wh-what?"

"I'm sorry you found out like this. It happened suddenly ..."

"No!" Ravenna gasped, her face melting into disbelief. "Oh God, what happened? Did she become ill?"

Lucien crossed the floor to pour himself a brandy. The sounds of glass upon glass and trickling liquid broke the heavy silence. "A carriage hit her a few blocks from here."

He tossed the liquor back in a single swallow, trying to drown his guilt.

"Hit her? She was walking in the street?" Ravenna demanded, her voice incredulous. "Who was with her?"

Lucien cast his guilty gaze to the carpet. "She escaped her nursemaid."

Ravenna frowned in confusion. "How did she get out?"

Lucien dipped his head. "I cannot say for sure."

"Where were you?"

Fingers squeezing the brandy glass, Lucien admitted, "Not here...and not alone."

Ravenna's mouth dropped open in fury before she flew across the room and slapped him. He took her assault in silence. "You bastard! This is *your* fault. How could you attend to your lust instead of your daughter?"

"I know the fault lies with me, Ravenna," he uttered quietly in the face of her anger. "I am quite aware I should have properly cared for her." He clasped her wrist in his grip. "But then, you should have been home, too. Before I left, Chelsea vowed to go out and find you."

Glittering affront entered Ravenna's dark eyes as she shook her head and began backing away. "You're feeding me that vile falsehood to force your guilt on me. I won't let you!"

"Keep your voice down. The servants will gossip enough as it is, and I do not want you waking my wife," he said, knowing his words would infuriate her further—and perversely, he was glad.

With a gasp, she ran toward him on slippered feet, all pretense of adoration shattered permanently by her ugly snarl. She raised her palm to strike his face again.

He caught her wrist without effort, smiling at her dramatics. "Once was quite enough, thank you."

She shook her head wildly, her glossy dark hair falling from its pins to tangle about her shoulders. "No. I could kill you and it wouldn't be enough. I hate you!"

After a long, seething glare, Ravenna jerked her wrist from Lucien's grasp and stormed from the room.

****

Serena stayed in her room the day following her passionate encounter on the floor with Lucien. Her husband neither came to her nor inquired after her—he only kept those damned silent guards at her door, ever-alert to the possibility of danger. His lack of attention hurt, more than she wanted to admit.

She paced, feeling trapped, behind the same door for too long. But facing Lucien would be more difficult. Mercy, how could she look at the familiar planes of his face, hard in anger, so soft in tenderness, and not remember their lovemaking? Not want him again?

She had but to close her eyes and envision every detail of his muscled chest, broad shoulders, and long, hard legs. Her remembrances also included a sharp recollection of the texture and tang of his skin, the soft rasp of his body hair...the strength of his manhood within her. Looking upon him across a room or table—without each of these thoughts showing—would be impossible.

She just couldn't face him.

Her behavior was cowardly, she knew. Cyrus wouldn't have hesitated to tell her so, were he here. Logically, she realized she could not spend the rest of her days in this ridiculous self-confinement, but she was like a caterpillar — not quite ready to emerge from her cocoon.

Caffey knocked and the guards admitted her after Serena's call. "Here, milady. Chocolate and fresh-baked bread with strawberry preserves. Yer notes and whatnot are on the side."

Serena looked down at the pitiful number of notes and invitation cards and frowned. Only three. When she had first arrived in London, she had been bombarded with both. Everyone had wished the duchess to attend their soiree or masque. She had been invited to waltzing parties, card parties, and weekend jaunts. More had arrived each day than she could decline in a week, much less attend.

Now, after the scandal of her hasty marriage four days ago, only three people sought her attention. Not that she enjoyed mingling with the *ton*, but such blatant exclusion hurt. Only a middle-class matron politely requested another donation for an orphanage. Her grandmother asked if Serena felt up to an outing at Lackington's Bookstore in Finsbury Square tomorrow afternoon.

Most devastating, her grandmother's note also stated she had planned a dinner party to launch the newlyweds.

Serena covered her face with her hands and cried. She couldn't even face her husband in their own home. The possibility of surviving Lucien's disturbing presence as well as the sharp tongues of the *ton* was nil.

Lucien entered her bedroom a moment later without even the most cursory of knocks a moment later. She knew it by the odd rhythm of his cane-assisted footsteps and the sudden stillness in the air. With a resolute breath, she wiped her tears away.

In a quiet, authoritative tone, he dismissed Caffey. The maid bobbed a curtsy and shut the door behind her.

"Serena?" His voice was soft, bringing forth an emotion-jumbled rush of memories: Lucien removing her stockings tenderly the night they met, sharing his sorrow over Chelsea's death.

"Serena, why are you crying?"

His rushed whisper pierced her heart. He sounded so concerned...almost caring.

"Are you hurt?" he asked.

Unable to tell him the truth, that she hurt inside, her pride and heart both wounded and uncertain, she shook her head. "Here," she said, thrusting her grandmother's note at him. "It's a dinner invitation."

He gave it a perfunctory skim. "If you're feeling up to it, we will go. She has influential friends who can help smooth things over."

Stiffly, she nodded, dreading the function. "I shall send word for her to expect us."

He stepped back, putting distance between them. Serena ached to reach out and touch him, to soothe the emotions behind his troubled expression.

"I talked to your man Vickery this morning. We're working together now. We compared notes. We both learned that Alastair hired a pair of bad characters named Rollins and McCoy to kill Warrington."

Serena, heart wildly beating with hope, leaned toward Lucien. She clasped his hand in joy, exclaiming, "That's wonderful! Did you find them? What did they say? Do you think they can convince anyone of Alastair's guilt?"

Lucien stared, brow furrowed, at their joined hands. A moment later he withdrew his. "Not anymore. Vickery informed me someone slit Rollins' and McCoy's throats two days ago. And supposedly—" he said, a cynical note creeping into his voice, "—no one saw or heard anything."

Serena's hopes died in a swift crash. "What can we do now?"

Lucien shrugged. "Without proof, we can only wait until Marsden makes his next move. Hopefully, we will catch him *before* he tries to harm you and the baby again."

She nodded, her body shaking with disbelief, confusion, awareness, and despair. Cyrus was gone, his killers dead as well, and with them, their best chance of proving Alastair's guilt.

And she'd made a mess of their marriage.

"Lucien, a-about last night ..."

"We have nothing to say." His voice held all the passion of a deep winter chill. "You got what you wanted, as did I. It means nothing."

Serena drew in a deep breath and fought the fresh tears stinging the back of her eyes. Nothing. That was all their lovemaking meant to him. He viewed her as the whore who happened to be his wife. A whore like her mother. And maybe she was.

She closed her eyes. In the end, despite her efforts otherwise, she had turned out no better. Lucien had illustrated that fact with ridiculous ease. She wanted to hate him for it. Yet the fault lay entirely with her for wanting him, for giving in to his compelling seduction. That she cared for him only seemed a more cruel irony.

She redirected the subject. "I referred to Cyrus and his plan for me to take a lover. I never meant—"

"You made your motives for falling into my bed quite clear. You'll give birth to the evidence of that in another six months."

She flinched. "I didn't intend to follow through with Cyrus's plan, I swear."

"Ah. After one kiss, you simply could not resist?"

His question and tight smile mocked her, as if he fully expected her to answer him affirmatively to cover her guilt.

"Not exactly," she replied instead.

"So you took a bit more persuading? You decided perhaps that giving your virginity to me, a total stranger, would be a splendid idea when I had my fingers inside your wet little sex?"

Serena felt hot color creep up her face again, but refused to be intimidated. "Yes and no. Your touch was like nothing I had ever known. I had nothing to compare it with. You overwhelmed me."

"An excellent strategy, sweetheart. Build up a man's ego about his sexual prowess, so he will believe anything. Is that it?" His glacial green eyes mocked her words.

"Blast you, no! You won't listen to me." Frustrated hands curled into fists. "It was not the way you touched me that made me want you. It was the way you seemed to need me. I know Chelsea's death had left you grief-stricken and lonely. And I was lonely, too." Tears pooled in the corner of her eyes, and she looked at her husband's tall, implacable form through a blurry, watery world. "I looked at you and saw a kindred spirit. Yes, you were handsome and persuasive. Your touch did set me aflame, though I tried very hard not to betray Cyrus." She trembled. "I just could not bring myself to turn away from you."

"Stop it," he growled. "Not another word."

"Lucien—"

"I will not have this discussion! I am a gullible fool when it comes to magnificent faces. I do not need any more reminders of that fact. Our marriage is reminder enough."

Serena looked away from his damning expression. "If you despise me so much, have our marriage annulled."

"We consummated it, if you'll recall." He fingered the cuffs of his coat stiffly. "Besides, there's still our child and your safety to consider. There will be no annulment."

A long silence followed. During the awful quiet, Serena interpreted the meaning between his words: His damnable sense of responsibility, not emotions, held him to her. What civility or understanding they might have had together, before her bungled confession, ceased to be relevant.

She wished she could cry again. Maybe if he could feel the real wet salt of her tears he would believe...But even as she thought it, Serena refused to make her feelings so transparent. Her fear of his contempt was too great.

His sudden sigh drew her gaze back up. He raked his fingers through tousled black hair. Serena repressed an urge to smooth a stray lock back from his forehead.

"I also came to tell you something else, before the servants' gossip reaches you."

Serena frowned, not liking his tone or his words. "What gossip?"

"It's about Ravenna," he answered, fist clenching around the handle of his carved cane. "She came to see me this morning."

Disbelief burst within Serena, then multiplied twenty-fold. "Here? What did she want?"

His mouth tightened into that grim, hard line Serena remembered from the argument prior to their lovemaking last night. Warning signals blared in her head.

"She tried to convince me she wanted to be my wife again. I declined naturally, being otherwise occupied," he said acidly.

Fear and doubt exploded inside Serena. Did Lucien resent the fact they were married now that Ravenna was back? Perhaps he still yearned for the provocative beauty in the portrait that had once hung here and wished for his freedom, despite the woman's past behavior.

A sense of defeat settled over her as she watched her husband walk away without so much as a goodbye.

****

Lucien stared at the amber liquid as he swirled it in his glass late that night. The Irish whiskey stopped its circular flux when he ceased his movements.

Lying on his bed, he propped the glass against his bare abdomen. His gaze drifted to the door. Her door.

He could open it and take her. He could press his mouth to her trembling pink one. He could fondle her, arouse her, lift her nightrail and bury himself inside her. Hell, it was supposed to be his husbandly right.

The portal between them remained closed, and after the explosive way she affected him the night before, he would keep it as a barrier between them for many excruciating nights to come. He refused to lose his head to a deceiving woman again, much less his heart.

But he was hard and aching with the thought of her beneath him, wrapping her legs around him. The memory of his uncontrollable arousal and devastating release fueled his desire. Blood coursed violently through him at the thought of having Serena again in his bed.

He had to get control of himself. Now. Yes, her touch, her body, could take him to the precipice of heaven, but he would not storm her door. He needed distance—lots of it—between them. Perhaps avoidance would drive her from his thoughts. Maybe long nights without her touch, without the temptation of her presence, would allow him to think straight again.

If not, he feared falling further into the well of obsession for his lovely, deceptive wife. And that would not do.

With that thought, he tossed back his glassful of whiskey—his fifth in twenty minutes.

Christ, why did he still want her so much? He could hardly think of anything but Serena.

You're a fool, he thought in self-contempt. When he had been married to Ravenna, she had maintained a terrible hold over his lust—until he had learned of her betrayal.

That was not the case with Serena. He burned for her even in the face of her deceptions. Even as he wanted to hate her.

He couldn't run from the truth anymore. He desired his wife beyond explanation, in his bed, by his side. Why wouldn't she leave his head? He swore softly. God, what a tangle.

With shaking hands, he reached for the decanter from the bedside table and poured another glass of liquor. Within seconds it, too, was gone. He glanced at his bedside clock, which read nearly three in the morning. Six drinks in twenty-two minutes.

No amount of alcohol he poured into his system would erase the truth. Despite Serena's deception, his desire for her would not disappear as conveniently as his lust for Ravenna had.

Damn, he hated her. God, he wanted her.

What the hell did it mean?

He thrust his empty glass aside and rose from his bed.

In his mind, he saw Serena's pale, tear-streaked cheeks as he had seen them earlier this morning, tearing though his heart. Her words rang in his head, *"You were grief-stricken and lonely. I was lonely, too...I could not turn away."*

He paced. She had been so smug toward Alastair, so damned self-assured at the solicitor's office when she had announced her pregnancy. Serena had taken his seed, used him to ensure Warrington's fortune did not fall into Alastair's hands, twisting his emotions all the while.

She had only insisted she was innocent of premeditated seduction to placate him. Her reasons for doing so were unclear, however. Still, the cynic inside him suspected she had a cause; she just had not revealed it yet.

He buried his forehead in his palm with a tired sigh. What if her tearful words had been truth? Perhaps she had made love with him the first time out of sheer desire and need. Was that even possible?

Lucien reached for his glass and poured another drink. Niles had been telling him for years that he made hasty decisions, often based on less than complete information. Had he judged Serena at the snap of a finger, without really listening to her pleas? Maybe his hard-headed temperament had prevented him from considering that in her passionless marriage, she might well have been lonely.

No. Last night, she had made her intentions to conceive perfectly clear. And he was a fool to care for her beyond the fact she carried his child and bore his name.

Confused, Lucien grabbed his glass; he swallowed his seventh drink in half an hour. The familiar warmth curled in his belly, but still, he experienced no numbing relief from his thoughts.

What now? He couldn't bear living with Serena through an eternity cloaked in anger and accusations. Even if she had plotted to rob him of his child, retribution would serve no purpose. As he had told her earlier, they were married for better, for worse...forever.

A twisted part of him rejoiced in that fact.

He sighed. Regardless of his feelings, falling into the trap of attempting to build a happy marriage again was not an option. Such fruitless efforts were too painful. He must keep his distance. Serena possessed a power to hurt him that Ravenna never had. The realization was frightening.

But shouldn't marriage be more than cold silences and hot passions, if for no other sake than the child's?

He glanced again at her door, squelched once more the urge to walk through it and claim her. She wanted a celibate marriage, at least until the birth of their child. That had been their agreement before their marriage, an agreement he had violated. Another big mistake, one which kept her in his thoughts. A mistake he would not repeat until he had his passions under iron control. Until having her in his bed meant nothing more to him than blessed release.

He ignored the voice in the back of his head that said he would be waiting forever.

****

"Mornin', milady," Caffey said, bringing in a tray. "Here's your chocolate. Do ye think ye can keep it down?"

Yawning, Serena swung her legs over the side of the bed and rose. "Yes, I've been feeling better the last few days."

Caffey nodded. "I returned your husband's cloak to him."

"What cloak?" Serena asked, puzzled.

She grinned slyly. "The one ye brought home after spendin' the night in his arms. Told me he had been lookin' for it, too."

Serena blushed. "Caffey, you're incorrigible. Are you happy now that you've solved the mystery?"

"Aye. Are ye happy bein' married to him, milady? He's a handsome devil, no doubt."

"He is a handsome devil and a suitable husband. I hope that is all you wish to know."

"Hmm," Caffey retorted, mouth pouting into a frown.

A multitude of visions all rose to Serena's mind, of Lucien laughing, grieving, aroused. With effort, she pushed them away. She understood his motivations for their marriage now. But that hardly made their marriage a reality beyond mere legality. Despite that fact, she wanted him again, fiercely, in every way a woman wants a man. Clearly, she had not escaped her mother's blood to experience such urges.

Worse, Lucien didn't seem to want or even miss her. She doubted he ever lay in bed in the next room and desired her while she ached for him.

Foolish, useless, hedonistic thoughts.

He thought every word she uttered was a lie. He had taken her body and walked away without a backward glance. To him, she was nothing more than the mother of his unborn child, legally his wife. Never his love. And for the protection of her fragile heart and self-respect, she would not share Lucien's bed until after the birth of this child, no matter how he seduced or tempted her with his charm and smiles.

Easier said than done. Their lovemaking two nights ago had been magical. Cataclysmic. The steely warmth of Lucien's body atop hers, his mouth persuading her with sweet kisses that brought back a rush of memories and a thrill of pure desire...All of that seemed near impossible to ignore.

She would have to find a way to accomplish the impossible.

"Will ye be wantin' a bath?" Caffey asked.

"Yes." As Caffey turned to arrange for the water, Serena asked, "Did you bring any calling cards from my house?"

"Yes, milady. I'll bring 'em up directly with whatever letters that prig Holford has for ye."

As she sat in the bath minutes later, Caffey returned with calling cards from her grandmother and Lady Bessborough indicating they would come round in a few days to discuss her reintroduction to the *ton*, following the "scandal." Next, she picked up a missive from Mr. Vickery of the Runners indicating he finally had a lead he was investigating. The final missive was secured with wax, but bore no seal, nor any distinguishing marks. Curious, she tore it open and in unfamiliar handwriting read:

I have information regarding your late husband's death. If you wish to hear it, meet me in the summer house on Lord Daneridge's town house grounds at four this afternoon. But please come alone. Should anyone else know of this, it could mean my death as well.

Warm water lapped around the sudden chill of Serena's skin. Someone had information? Maybe this would sew up Mr. Vickery's case; maybe she would see Alastair in Newgate soon.

Elation filled her. God had finally answered her prayers in this matter, and justice would to be served.

Or maybe this was a trap. But Alastair was her only threat, and surely he wasn't bold enough to try to end her life on Lucien's property again. It would look too suspicious.

That dismissed, Serena considered giving the missive over to Mr. Vickery, then tossed the idea aside. Whoever had written the note obviously felt his life was in grave danger; she couldn't repay that by revealing him and placing him in further jeopardy.

After Caffey dressed her, Serena tucked the note away within her reticule and went about her day. But neither reading nor needlepoint held her attention. She kept considering the note, wondering what its author knew or had seen.

The last hour dragged by as if Father Time had declared a holiday. She paced in the library, discarding first a volume of Lord Byron's *Childe Harold's Pilgrimage,* roundly deciding that an example of indulgence to earthy pleasures was not what she needed. She shied away from the usually comfortable *Christian Thoughts,* knowing Mrs. More's moral teachings would engender guilty feelings about her carnal yearnings. Instead, she paced and watched the clock.

At ten minutes of four, she told her guards she intended to lie down, then sneaked to the kitchens, past a curious Holford, and slipped out the back. Walking beyond the scrap of a vegetable garden, Serena soon came upon the summer house.

It looked wholly unlike any summer house she had ever seen. Up close proved the structure even gaudier than distance promised. Walls of gold and red, surrounded by floor-to-ceiling windows, came together to form angles and Eastern-flavored onion domes. The structure looked somewhat like a miniature of the Prince's Pavilion at Brighton, though not as lavish, but certainly as hedonistic. Serena knew instantly Ravenna had ordered its construction.

Most of the windows had been boarded shut, and Serena surmised the door had also been nailed closed. But today, someone had opened the boarded door and left it ajar.

Writing off a sudden, ominous feeling to unwarranted fear, Serena resolutely focused on her mission. With a gentle push, she nudged the door open a fraction more. "Hello?" she called.

Inside the nearly-empty structure, her voice echoed. She made a quick scan of the room, looking for the note's author, but saw only cushioned benches and deserted, dust-laden tables strewn haphazardly throughout.

Cautiously, Serena stepped farther inside. "Hello?" she called again. "Is anyone here?"

A moment later, Serena felt, more than heard, a presence behind her. A muffled footstep confirmed it an instant later.

As she whirled to face the sound and its source, she heard a whoosh, then felt pain explode at the back of her head. Frantically, she tried to retain consciousness, tried to turn to her attacker.

She sank to her knees instead, her world turning black. Then nothing...

CHAPTER TWENTY

Lucien stared at his account books, adding a column of figures for the third time. He came to a third different sum.

With a sigh of frustration, he stood and crossed the room to pour tea the maid had brought earlier. After Lucien seated himself once more, he sipped the brew, finally acknowledging his thoughts were not on his finances, but on his wife.

Thrusting the tea cup onto its saucer, Lucien wondered what it was about Serena that fired him to such desire. Why did she saturate his every thought? He was not certain why, but he wanted her. Not just her body. Heaven help him, in the days he'd been avoiding her, he had missed her company, even her scent.

His fashionably convenient marriage was becoming more inconvenient and consuming by the moment. More disturbing, his will to avoid her and his struggle to regard her as a stranger who carried his unborn child slipped more each day.

"My lord!" Holford shouted, barging into Lucien's office. The door slammed into a paneled wall. "My lord, come quickly!"

Lucien rose, grabbing his cane. The utter horror on Holford's old face sent a chill through him. "What's happened?"

"The summer house. It's on fire," he exclaimed in a rush. "And I fear her ladyship may be in it!"

Serena.

Lucien didn't pause to examine the cold fear clawing at him as he cast aside his cane. He rushed past Holford and fled down the hall, through the commotion of the kitchen, then tore the door open and bolted outside, praying she was nowhere near the summer house.

Panic ate at his insides, dissipating the jolts of pain smashing their way up his leg.

She had to be alive.

Outside, a rising cloud of black smoke and orange flames assaulted his senses as did the acrid stench of charred wood. It was indeed the summer house, the atrocity Ravenna had insisted on building for her parties and trysts. Lucien had never hated it more than he did in that moment. Around him, servants stood in a line, each passing buckets of water from one person to the next, the final man futilely tossing it on the roaring fire.

Lucien sprinted to the door. He grabbed the handle, only to yank his hand back a moment later when the scalding metal scorched him. Cursing, he tore off his coat, then wrapped his palm around the latch.

He yanked and tugged, his efforts aided by the stable master, but to no avail. The door remained resolutely closed. A horrifying instant later, he noticed a jagged stick of wood wedged in the threshold.

God damn you, Alastair. I will kill you!

Grasping the wooden stick with bare hands, Lucien barely felt the splinters digging their way into his skin. He tugged on the wood. The stick broke, leaving its arrow-slender tip stuck in the door's frame.

He envisioned Serena trapped within, pounding on the inside of that locked door. The vision sent more panic tearing through his veins.

Flinging his coat aside, he ran to the side of the house and spied a window that had not been boarded up after Ravenna's departure. Thankful for the oversight, he kicked the glass in.

He ducked through the opening, only to be brought to his knees by smoke thicker than London fog at its worst. He could see nothing before him as he crawled deeper into the orange-flamed inferno.

"Serena!" He heard no response. "Answer me!"

Lucien took a deep breath, then realized his mistake as the dense smoke invaded his lungs. His body protested, racked with coughs. Could Serena breathe...or had she ceased to do so?

"Serena!" he yelled. "Whimper or cough. Anything. Tell me where you are."

Again, cloying, smoky silence prevailed. Fear screamed across his skin, in his veins. He crawled further ahead, noticing the visibility improved closer to the floor. As he moved across the wooden surface, heat pelted him from every direction, the thick, unbreathable air ravaging his lungs.

He shouted her name again. And received no answer.

On hands and knees, Lucien made his way forward, close to the front door. He willed away the dizziness, the black closing in at the edges of his vision.

A few feet away from the door, he encountered a foreign object. Squinting to see through the smoke, he saw a soot-smudged hand. Not just any hand—Serena's hand, wearing his diamond wedding ring.

With a joyous cry, he reached for her, curling his fingers around her arm, then her waist, glad just to touch her, to feel the warmth of her body. But she didn't respond at all. Straining with effort, he pulled her dead weight into his arms and stood, tugging Serena up beside him.

Smoke curling its way down his lungs insidiously, Lucien ducked his head, then darted toward the smashed window.

He stumbled over the leg of a chair and tumbled to the hard floor. His injured knee ached from the jarring contact as he skidded across the ground, Serena landing on her side above him. She laid limp and lifeless, just beyond his grasp.

Grunting, he hauled himself to his feet and lifted her again. Ahead, he could see the afternoon sunlight beaming through the open window, penetrating the smoke. Like a ship's captain on a foggy night, he ran, following the beacon to safe harbor.

Finally, he stepped through the window frame. A jagged edge of glass sliced his arm. Grimacing, he held Serena tighter, angling her legs away from harm.

Beyond the confines of the blazing walls, Lucien deposited Serena gently on the grass. Her usually honey skin looked a macabre mixture of bloodless white and sooty black. Her mourning dress, torn and smudged, displayed a lace collar nearly as dark as the muslin of her bodice. With shaking hands, he smoothed the blackened hair away from her face. He encountered dampness and jerked away to find his fingers wet with Serena's blood.

Panic serrated his insides like a knife, slashing at his composure. Trying to force panic aside, he bowed his head to her face, listening for any trace she still breathed...still lived.

Servants rushed to his side, staring at their fallen mistress. He shut out the noise and turmoil.

A moment later, he felt a whisper-light but nevertheless existent rush of air from Serena's open mouth to his cheek.

With a warm shower of relief, he scooped her up again and carried her into the house. "Holford," he yelled in the entrance hall. "Send one of the stable lads after Doctor Thompson. Now!"

Clutching Serena in his arms, Lucien struggled up the stairs, cursing his limp with each step. Vaguely, he heard Mildred and Caffey behind him, talking in frightened whispers of herbal medicines.

At the top of the landing, he swerved toward his bedroom, then rested Serena's inert form on his bed, the one in which he had first made love to her. He refused to believe she would die on this bed, too.

"Damn it, live," he whispered to her unresponsive face. "You cannot die on me, not now."

Caffey rushed forward to remove to help him remove Serena's soiled clothing, while Mildred sponged her face and arms of soot. Lucien's apprehensive gaze never left his wife's face. He pushed back the bitter fear that he would lose Serena to the specter of death, as he had lost Chelsea.

Damn it, he couldn't let her die. He must beat death at its own game. Then, he vowed to spend his every waking moment by her side; post a hundred guards in the house, whatever required to ensure her safety.

If Serena died, Lucien vowed Alastair would pay the ultimate price—slowly, painfully, at his hands.

****

Doctor Thompson arrived after the longest hour of waiting Lucien had ever endured. He refused to leave the room during Serena's examination. Instead, he stayed close, hovering near Serena from a nearby Sheraton chair.

"Will she live?" he asked, fingers locked together.

The doctor paused in his examination, his gray mutton whiskers moving as he frowned. "I cannot rightly say yet. The damage to her lungs may be extensive."

Lucien grabbed the doctor's sleeve. "What does that mean?"

Thompson shrugged. "It means I cannot speculate on her condition now."

With curse, Lucien sank back in his chair and watched the doctor stem the flow of blood at the back of Serena's head. "Have you any notion how the bleeding started?"

Thompson nodded. "She's been struck, I believe. A knot of swelling surrounds the wound."

He vowed then to see Alastair swinging from Tyburn.

Lucien swallowed as another thought, one forgotten in his panic, returned. "Doctor, my wife is with child. If she lives, will she miscarry?"

Thompson whirled about, brows raised in surprise. Lucien delivered him a hard stare. The doctor wiped away the questions looming in his expression. "Again, it is far too early to tell, my lord. But an injury of this nature may be harmful to the babe, indeed."

On second thought, he'd have Alastair drawn and quartered.

The doctor put away his bottles and equipment, then turned to Lucien. "I can do nothing more now. If her condition takes a turn for the worse, call upon me. In the meantime, I suggest plenty of bed rest. I've left a bottle of laudanum here to ensure just that. If she awakens and requests food, keep her on a lowering diet—you know, fruit, soups, fish, no animal meats. Keep her away from coffee, tea and alcohol. Such heating foods after a shock like this can be damaging to the body."

Nodding distantly, Lucien heard the doctor leave, but his gaze lingered on Serena's sleeping form. Even in repose she coughed, and with each of the spasms that ripped through her chest, Lucien feared further injury would overtake her.

Gripping his hands around the arms of his chair, he stared at the ethereal beauty of her fine-boned face, delicate shoulders, and graceful, long-fingered hands.

He might lose her. Forever.

For reasons he didn't want to examine too closely, he found himself thinking that if she died, a piece of him would wither away and die with her. He recognized that awakening part of him as the ability to care. And it scared the hell out of him.

****

For the next three days, Lucien barely left Serena's side. She remained tucked in his bed, two armed guards standing diligently in the hallway. If Lucien slept at all, he did so in her bedroom, with the door between them open—and the fervent, increasingly desperate hope that she would wake.

The day following the fire, Caffey had found the anonymous note that led Serena to the fire. Damn, how he wished she had trusted him enough to tell him of the missive. But he'd been so angry about her deception, that she doubtless felt he would not care or could not be trusted.

If she lived, she would never feel that uncertainty again, he vowed. They would reside in civility, without acrimony for a past that could not be altered. Lucien doubted he would ever be able to trust her completely, nor had he any intent to give her his heart, but they would no longer be wedded enemies.

On day four, he sent for Doctor Thompson, who, after another examination, proclaimed that Serena would indeed live. He also declared that her "delicate condition" was not in jeopardy. But, as for when Lady Daneridge would awaken...he could not comment.

On the fifth day, Lucien woke in the Sheraton chair by Serena's bedside. A quick glance confirmed no change had occurred overnight, and he began to wonder if she would ever awaken. For the first time since Chelsea's death, Lucien sank to the carpet on his knees and prayed.

As if divinely inspired, as if God had truly been listening to his prayers for once, Serena moaned and rolled toward him. Lucien sprang up from the floor and hovered over her. He clutched her salved and bandaged hand between his.

Pushing her hair from her cheeks, he said, "Serena, wake up. Open your eyes."

An instant later, her brown lashes lifted to reveal her blue eyes, sleepy and confused.

"Where am I?" she croaked, her voice hoarse.

Relief crashed through him as he stroked her hand. "In my bedroom. How do you feel?"

She frowned. "As if I've been beaten."

Lucien stroked his palm across her forehead. "Breathe in and tell me how your lungs feel."

She did so and a coughing spell seized her. Once recovered, she answered, "Burned. It hurts."

"But you can breathe fairly well. That is a good sign." He rubbed his thumb along her forearm.

The skin beneath his touch was the only part of her that wasn't filled with pain. "What happened?"

"Tell me the last thing you remember," he said.

Caffey delivering calling cards while she was in her bath. Lady Bessborough and her grandmother were supposed to call and— "A note," she blurted, her voice gaining strength. "I received a note instructing me to go to the summer house if I wanted to know more about Cyrus's death."

Lucien's eyes narrowed with suspicion. "Who signed it?"

Serena thought for a moment, then shook her head. "No one. It was anonymous."

"And you chose not to tell me about it?" His expression went tight with anger.

She coughed again, then cleared her throat. "I...The note said to go alone. Its writer said he feared for his life. I felt certain that if I told you, you would demand to go." She paused. "Where did you come by those cuts on your face?"

He stared at her. Serena noticed the exhaustion and anxiety etched around his eyes and mouth, along with a puzzling collection of cuts, scrapes and bruises.

"Sweetheart, do you remember the fire?" he asked.

She didn't recall anything of the sort. With his various scratches and contusions, he looked as if he had been caught in it. Had she? Confused, she shook her head.

"What do you last remember?" he prompted.

She hesitated. "I went to the summer house. The door was ajar." She coughed. "I went inside to look for the person who had written the note, but didn't see anyone about." Her eyes widened with remembrance as she said, "Then I heard something behind me and I tried to turn, but...my head hurt. Back here." She lifted her fingers to her wound, wincing when she touched it.

Quickly, Lucien pulled her hand back into his. "Alastair or one of his henchmen hit you, then locked you in the summer house while you were unconscious. They set the building on fire."

Serena gasped, then succumbed to another coughing fit. Once recovered, she asked, "How did I get out?"

She fixed her gaze on his familiar, now battered features. Again she noted the small cuts slashed across one cheek, visible even through several days' growth of beard. A glance down told her his hands were bruised, covered with small scabs and painful-looking blisters. Reality dawned. "You saved me?"

"Holford thought you might be inside."

Her mouth fell open. "You went into a burning building on the chance I might be there?" Bewilderment tinged her voice. "Why?"

Lucien glanced away, leaving Serena to realize he would not expound on the event or his heroics, but the fact that he'd risked himself to save her flooded her with warmth. But she dropped the subject for now. "You're sure Alastair set the building aflame?"

"Who else would do this?"

She nodded. "He's serious about killing me."

Grimly, Lucien nodded. "Until he is caught, I want you to spend your mornings, afternoons, and evenings with me. If I cannot be with you, someone will watch over you. I promised you protection before we wed. I intend to make certain you get it."

She stared anxiously into his implacable face. "Do you think Alastair would dare to come into the house?"

"At this point, I think Alastair would dare almost anything. He's already had the audacity to torch a building on my grounds, with you in it. Nothing stops him from gaining entrance but the guards I've placed at each door and the protection of my presence. And I will protect you, with my life, if necessary."

She didn't disagree with his caution, but spending every day and evening with her handsome husband would take its toll on her resistance. If she wasn't careful, she would end up in his bed all too soon. Yet with her life and the babe's in danger, she had no choice but to agree to his plan.

"Of course," she whispered. "Thank you."

"I will catch him," Lucien vowed. "Niles and I will continue to search for clues...someone who knows something. Though Alastair's hired killers are dead, it's only a matter of time before I find enough evidence to prove his crimes."

He was still willing to risk his life to prove Alastair's guilt and save her skin? Maybe he had been searching for clues during his evenings out, instead of bedding another woman, as she had assumed. Maybe he truly did care about her.

Lucien Clayborne was becoming more of an enigma each day.

Grandy's voice sounded in Serena's head, reminding her that a good marriage consists of respect, the ability to forgive, trust, and love. Did she hold those emotions for her husband?

She respected him, she realized an instant later. He was intelligent and brave. He no longer appeared to be a manipulative cad, as she had told Grandy. Her discovery of Chelsea's death gave her an understanding of his reasons for forcing this hasty marriage — and the ability to forgive him.

But trust? That was harder to give. Perhaps he had not been dallying with other women. God, how she wanted to believe that was true, yet the hope he had been playing detective during all his nights out on the town seemed far-fetched. Besides, how many men would have remained chaste when an angry wife refused them and easy comfort awaited elsewhere?

She tried to conjure up what Cyrus would advise, but found his memory was dimming each day, replaced by images and feelings Lucien inspired. Did she care for the husband she had sworn so recently to despise?

Yes, and perhaps admitting to herself that she harbored feelings for Lucien wasn't so terrible or dangerous. After all, he was her child's father. So long as he never learned that a sinful part of her yearned for his fiery touch. He need never know she missed his handsome face when he was gone. Or were her feelings more?

Had she, by chance, committed the most foolish sin of all and fallen in love with him?

****

Three days later, Lucien entered Serena's bedroom with flowers in hand after a perfunctory knock. "How do you feel?"

Serena glanced up from her morning chocolate. Her heartbeat accelerated at the sight of Lucien's smile, at his dimples prominent above the firm angle of his jaw.

"I am well now." She smiled shyly in return.

His eyes were the color of summer grass. His powerful shoulders, branded in her memory, fit the seams of his soft gray coat to perfection. The waistcoat surrounding his broad torso and lean waist was a deep, exotic blue trimmed in opulent gold thread. Black pants hugged narrow hips and long, muscled legs.

She feared the catch in her heart had more to do with her emotions than the desire he roused within her.

He sat on the edge of the bed. She couldn't ignore the small thrill at his nearness, yet he made no move to touch her.

Dropping her gaze to her lap nervously, Serena tried to slow her rapidly beating heart. The base side of her wondered if he longed to repeat their lovemaking once she had healed completely. She could no longer deny that she wanted to relive the splendor of their ecstasy, yearned to become his wife again in every way.

Yet another part recalled her confession and Lucien's resulting contempt.

"Here," he said, handing her the bouquet. "I brought these for you."

She put her nose to the flowers. Her senses lit upon smelling a familiar scent. "Gardenias. My favorite."

"Their smell reminds me of you."

That anything at all reminded Lucien of her astounded Serena. But something as beautiful as a tiny white gardenia?

Inhaling a shaky breath, she took in the sultry scent of the flower once more. It swam inside her head, making her dizzy with a longing she wanted desperately to ignore.

She clutched the bouquet closer to her chest. "Thank you. They are lovely."

"You're welcome."

He rose from the bed and stepped away. "Your grandmother called on you yesterday while you slept." He paused, appearing to choose his next words. "We had an interesting talk."

"What about?" Serena bit her lip. There was absolutely no telling what Grandy had said, how many secrets she had revealed. "What did she tell you?"

"That she has waited a long time for great-grandchildren from you."

"Oh, yes. And she never tried to hide her impatience. I do not understand, really; Catherine gave her a second great-grandson in May."

Lucien nodded. "She said so, but I think she's particularly anxious for your confinement because you hold a special place in her heart."

With a shrug, Serena said, "I suppose you're right."

"She also said that you possess a voracious appetite for strawberries. Is that true?"

Feeling color crawl up her cheeks, Serena answered, "Yes."

"You'll enjoy breakfast then. Mildred?" he called.

The older maid entered a few moments later bearing a tray—and a platter full of strawberries and bowl of cream.

"Here ye are, me lady." Mildred set the tray in her lap, then left on Lucien's dismissal.

Serena turned her puzzled expression to Lucien. "How? Where.... Strawberries are so rare. How did you find these?"

He waved her question away. "A trivial detail. Come on. Eat up. You need your strength, and the baby needs nourishment."

Serena realized that was the first time he'd mentioned her pregnancy beyond the confines of an argument. Looking up to him, she asked hesitantly, "Are you happy...about the child?"

His warm gaze caressed her. "Yes. I will not lie and tell you I'm completely happy with the circumstances. To the law, the child will always be Warrington's. But we know the truth, and someday, I think the babe should know, too." He nodded in her direction. "And what of you? Are you happy about the babe?" he countered. "I know you have long wanted children, but will you be content to have mine?"

"Children are a gift from God. I shall be happy to bear any babe God sees fit to give me."

"That is not what I asked, Serena, and you know it."

After a hesitant pause, she admitted. "I am pleased. No matter what you think, I have no doubt you were a good father to Chelsea, and will be to this babe, too."

Lucien drew his brows furrow into a painful frown. "Time will tell."

Tentatively, she reached for his hand. "You're strong and protective, and you care so much for this babe already, you cannot be anything but the best of fathers."

As his fathomless gaze delved into hers, he rested his other hand against the almost indiscernible curve of her abdomen. "I hope you're right."

A long pause ensued. Serena hardly knew what to say without shattering the tender moment she so wanted to cling to her heart. In the last week she'd seen such a gentle side of her husband, a side she would never have dreamed existed the evening they had exchanged vows.

She hung her hope on the possibility that the future of their marriage wasn't as bleak as she had once thought.

****

Seated at her dressing table, Serena looked up from the letter she penned to her sister, Catherine, to find Lucien striding into her bedroom. A quiver of longing passed through her before she looked away, pretending concentration on her correspondence. But his image stayed with her, the dark sweep of his hair, the green flash of his eyes, the breadth of his hard shoulders.

"Shouldn't you be resting?" he asked with a scowl. "I will wake you for dinner in an hour."

She frowned. "I have been resting faithfully for days now. I feel much improved."

As if to prove her wrong, her cough asserted itself. She hacked noisily into his disapproving silence.

"Yes, you sound much improved," he drawled.

"I am," she insisted. "Besides, I received a letter from my sister yesterday. Catherine and her family wish to visit next month. Would you mind very much?"

He shrugged. "If a visit from your sister would cheer you, then by all means, tell her to stay with us as long as she wishes."

"Thank you," she murmured, stealing another glance. "It's been an age since I've seen Catherine and her children."

"Your color is better," he conceded. "I suspect you'll be up to a visit by then."

Serena smiled her appreciation and studied her husband beneath lowered lashes. In the week following the fire, Lucien had been an attentive husband and caretaker. His tenderness and easy consideration for her feelings and health surprised her almost as much as it warmed her.

Lucien's tender care had forced Serena to admit that her feelings for him ran deep. Not in the way she'd had feelings for Cyrus. Her emotions for her current husband hardly resembled any gentle consistency of sentiment. Instead, her love felt like a tempest, something too volatile to ignore, too large to outrun, too tangible to deny.

She feared more and more of late that she loved him.

Not that he loved her in return. She would be foolish to hope so. Lucien hardly acted like a man caring for a cherished wife. Yet he was much more than distantly accommodating.

Surprisingly, he had not mentioned their lovemaking, nor behaved as if he wanted to resume relations. Serena knew she should be pleased. After all, she'd wanted a chaste marriage until the birth of their baby.

But she could hardly deny that his current disinterest disappointed her.

Beyond logic, she desired him in her bed, despite the fear that such feelings made her no different than her mother. Since realizing her love, her traitorous body trembled for his touch every time he came near.

Turning back to her letter, Serena penned her signature. Across the room, she heard Lucien's slow approach. As she folded and sealed the missive, her hands shook.

"I will send that for you tomorrow, if you like," he said.

Serena glanced up to find Lucien only inches away. Her heart leapt at his closeness. She ached for his kiss. "That would be splendid. Thank you."

He inclined his head in response. "Rest. I shall see you at dinner."

Disappointment pierced her when he turned away. His presence had been the only cheer in her otherwise dull day. She did not want to spend the next hour without him. She didn't want to spend another moment without him, in fact.

"Wait," she called to his retreating back. "If anything, I'm sick with boredom. Don't go."

Lucien cocked a brow at her in question.

"Perhaps you could read to me. Or we could play chess."

"Chess?" he questioned.

His tone reminded her of their last chess match, when she'd almost let him make love to her on the sofa. Judging from the speculation stirring in his stare, he remembered, too. Heat crawled its way across her face.

"Where did we leave off?" Lucien baited. He could no more forget the game pieces strewn all over the carpet and her skirts about her thighs than he could forget breathe.

Her expression widened at his question. That soft, pink mouth and the stain on her cheeks hinted at her titillation.

He groaned. Why was she trying to tempt him so? Perhaps she sought to obliterate his anger at her deceit by using his own lust. Yes, the cynic in him said. A woman would try that.

Lucien tore his eyes away from Serena and the nightrail that hinted of beckoning curves beneath. He clenched his fists, restraining the urge to tumble Serena onto the white cloud of her soft mattress and unleash his repressed desire.

Damn. He wanted her, but if she truly sought to manipulate him, he must turn his back on her and occupy his mind elsewhere until he could control the roiling emotions that plagued him.

Oh, but he wanted to stay. Risking a glance at his wife, the remembrance of their gentle times together these past days was almost his undoing. He eyed the golden tumble of her hair down her back, against the soft white linen of her gown. With a silent curse, he stifled the urge to run his hands through the strands, then lay her back until she looked deliciously loved.

He drew in a deep breath. *Control*, he reminded himself.

Yet he could find none. He even enjoyed caring for Serena in a way he'd never expected, despite the fact their constant proximity only fueled his desire. Sleep had become a monumental task with an open door between them as he listened for her even breathing and an occasional cough. Concentration had grown pointless with her perfume lingering in the air.

He no longer attempted to delude himself into believing he could be near her without wanting her, that they could be merely civil spouses. The last week had proved that fact completely.

He had to regain control of himself, his thoughts. He had to leave.

"I've no time for games," he snapped. "Give me your letter, and I'll be off."

She handed the missive to him, and he took it. Her stare lingered on him, and he could not make himself move away.

She touched his hand with gentle fingers. Lucien fought back an urge to drag her into his arms, twine his hands in her hair and kiss her senseless, then confess that he cared for her much too much.

"Thank you for your care and concern," she whispered. "And for saving my life. You've been a model of consideration this past week. Mildred and Caffey assure me my recovery would have progressed more slowly, if at all, without your attention."

Lucien nodded without comment. The texture of her warm skin wrapped around him, bringing with it the essence of her touch, her scent. A connection leapt to life between them. The sweet seduction of that familiar spark rocked him.

His heart swelled with a nameless emotion, engulfing him, enthralling him—before he reminded himself that she had the ability to break his heart—a power he'd never given anyone, not even Ravenna.

While caring for Serena, he'd enjoyed her much too much, spent almost carefree days with her engaged in little more than reading and idle conversation. It would all cease today. He could not afford the kind of emotion she created in him, especially when he was not certain he could now—or ever—trust her.

Lucien withdrew his touch. "Not at all. Merely seeing after what is mine."

Before he could turn away, he saw disappointment burst across Serena's face. It would be mad to tell her that she mattered to him. But nothing could stop the urge to hold her.

With a curse, Lucien strode out the door and walked until he found solace in the descending London twilight. As he called for his coach, he vowed to spend the evening, indeed the whole night out—anywhere far, far away from the temptation of his wife.

****

The next day, Serena decided an outing with her
grandmother might bring her spirits round. She penned a
note to Lady Harcourt to meet her at Lackington's at two
that afternoon.

Lucien's abrupt departure last night had hurt. She lay
awake until the morning's wee hours, waiting for his return,
praying he continued to seek clues to Cyrus' murder, not
another woman's arms.

Yet he did not come home, leading her to wonder if the
activity he engaged in was much more carnal, satisfying.

When she had inquired as to his whereabouts this
morning, Holford told her he knew nothing.

Her imagination still tortured her with visions of what
he had done last night, who he had been with.

Pain sliced though. He seemed to want her so little now.
Given his cool caring recently, she certainly couldn't find the
courage to tell him she now craved his touch, not without
giving her heart away. And sharing herself with no
emotional reciprocation would cost her too much peace of
mind.

The carriage stopped, and reluctantly Serena alighted to
a delightfully sunny September afternoon, feeling
conspicuous flanked by former soldiers dressed in finery.
The two armed servants escorted her to the door, and
thankfully, stayed there when she entered the bookstore.

Several women bordered the semi-circular counter. A
young, bespectacled man working behind it politely
answered questions.

At Serena's entrance, several women turned their heads
toward her. Serena recognized Lady Griffin and Lady
Calverton staring and conversing in heated whispers.

She nodded in silent greeting. Lady Calverton sniffed in
disapproval. Both women turned away. To her right, several
young girls tittered and directed coy glances at her.

Wishing the floor would open up and swallow her
whole, shame and all, Serena moved forward. Hot flags of
embarrassment surfaced in her cheeks.

She lifted her chin and strode to the corner of the room.
Turning her back on the other patrons, she pretended
interest in a volume of Chaucer, vowing she would not give
these biddies the satisfaction of seeing her tears.

"Lady Daneridge?" a soft inquisitive voice rang from behind.

"Yes?" Serena replied, turning to face the woman.

She froze in shock. Before her stood the most stunning vision of femininity—and her worst nightmare.

"Ravenna," she breathed, as the blood drained from her face.

CHAPTER TWENTY-ONE

The gaudy portrait *a la* Venus had not done justice to the beauty of Lucien's former wife. Glossy dark curls swirled about her delicate face, accentuating its small-boned structure. Skin creamier than fresh milk and more flawless than Hermes porcelain acted as a backdrop for long ebony lashes.

Dear Lord, how could she ever compete with Lucien's memories of marriage to this delicate deity?

Though Serena rarely compared her looks to others, for a tiny instant, she would have given her fortune to possess even a quarter of Ravenna's ethereal beauty.

Envy was a sin, and Lord knew she'd been guilty of too many transgressions recently. But recognizing that fact did not change her feelings. She shifted under the woman's scrutiny.

Ravenna's dark eyes gleamed with unshed tears, her expression compatible with the perfect propriety of her Celestial blue dress. "I suppose he told you about me."

Serena nodded and demanded, "What do you want?"

Ravenna glanced about. Serena followed her gaze and noted several of the ladies lurking around the book shop inched closer.

Wearing a polite smile, Ravenna said, "Perhaps we can sit in the corner and talk privately?"

Serena crossed her arms over her chest. "I cannot imagine that we have anything to discuss."

The other woman's voice dropped to a whisper. "Please, it's about Lucien. I feel terribly guilty ..." She caught her breath as if holding back a sob. "I know what we share is wrong. He is your husband now, but when he came to me, I must confess, I simply could not turn him away."

Serena's blood ran cold. "What are you saying?"

Ravenna cast her gaze down to her feet and whispered, "Must I confess my sins aloud? Lucien is a very sensual man with more than his share of male urges. I made such a foolish mistake in leaving him, that when he came to me for...comfort, I could not help but welcome him with open arms."

"Comfort?" she whispered numbly. Lucien had turned to his former wife for sexual satisfaction? When? He had not left her side in almost two weeks.

Except for last night.

While she had been feeling guilt for her sensual sins, had Lucien been out committing his own with Ravenna?

Serena had a vague awareness, as if in a dream, of the bookstore's other patrons whispering in hushed tones. She drew in a deep breath and forced herself to shut them out.

Ravenna's eyes widened, her expression contrite. "Oh, I feared our liaison would hurt you. But I could not keep my guilty secret and live with myself. I had so hoped you would understand that I have always loved Lucien, and when he told me he cared for me still, I'm afraid our passions carried us away."

Her husband, the man who had married her solely for his unborn child, still loved his ex-wife? That would explain his behavior of late, particularly his lack of interest in sharing her bed. And why wouldn't he be disinterested? Ravenna was a sensual goddess, a beauty she wondered how any man could resist. Apparently not even the man Ravenna had treated horribly and humiliated in the *ton's* eyes could stay away.

If Lucien desired the woman despite the past, Serena knew the pain would be hers to suffer, since she cared for him, no matter how much she had tried not to.

Around them, several women sniffed and looked away as they passed. No doubt, she would be the object of more gossip for weeks to come. But even that prospect wasn't as terrible as the possibility that Lucien still loved Ravenna.

Serena forced her gaze back to the dark-haired beauty before her. Why would he be involved with a woman he once divorced, one who humiliated him? Unless the heat of his passion for Ravenna burned away his logic.

"I do not believe you," she challenged, praying for the sake of her sanity and her future, the woman was lying.

Ravenna smiled sadly, as if expressing sympathy to a wounded puppy. "If you choose not to, I understand."

"Serena?" a familiar voice said. "Am I interrupting something?"

Startled, Serena jerked her stunned gaze about. "Grandy."

"Are you well, Serena?" She frowned. "You look pale."

Serena shook herself mentally, trying to clear the tangled mess of her thoughts.

"Yes, I—" Serena began.

"Lady Harcourt," Ravenna greeted. "How good to see you."

A narrow-eyed expression confirmed Grandy was suspicious. "What did you say to upset my granddaughter?"

"Nothing but the truth." She smiled and patted Serena's arm. "I apologize. I had no idea I was keeping you from an engagement. Excuse me."

With that, Ravenna departed. Numbly, Serena watched the skirt of her blue dress sway in rhythm as she sashayed from the bookstore.

Serena looked down at her own dour black dress. Ravenna looked as colorful as a peacock when compared with the plain crow she must resemble. It pained her to admit that she had little trouble understanding why Lucien might have turned to a lovely like Ravenna for gratification.

But the suspicion hurt, not to mention infuriated her. How dare he, after making her the subject of the hottest scandal in London, further humiliate and toy with her? People now ignored her or snickered when she passed, treating her much as Mama had been. And he'd made her love him. When she caught up with the knave, she would not give him the satisfaction of telling him that his dalliance affected her in the least.

But, oh, would he pay with a lifetime of frostbite.

"You look whiter than snow," Grandy exclaimed. "What did she say?"

Hot tears rushed to Serena's eyes. She raised her gaze to the ceiling, struggling to control of her feelings of anger and betrayal—and mortification. Heaven help her, this latest on-dit would give London's chatty ladies something to chew on for weeks. If she cried in public, the gossip about her would never die.

"Not now," she whispered to Grandy. "I must leave."

The older woman responded to the panicked tone. "You cannot mean to believe anything that woman said."

"I know not what to believe."

As she marched outside, Serena set her gaze forward resolutely, ignoring the biddies patronizing Lackington's. Grandy, at her side, held her head at an equally proud angle.

Once the cool wind outdoors struck Serena's face, she felt sheer relief at escaping the confines of the bookstore and the prying eyes of its customers.

During her solitary carriage ride home, Serena tried to envision telling Lucien about her conversation with Ravenna. If he denied everything, would she believe him? Trusting the adulteress who had experienced life by Lucien's side seemed no more foolish than listening to her own doubting heart. But what if he admitted to bedding Ravenna last night? She closed her eyes, wondering if the pain would kill her.

Once home, she sought the sanctuary of her own chamber, the one that had belonged to the previous Lady Clayborne. Though she had removed all visible traces of Ravenna, she still felt as if the woman were here, taunting her.

Sprawled across her bed, Serena surrendered to the tears clawing at her throat. In her mind, she pictured Lucien branding an ardent kiss on Ravenna's red mouth. Did he feel a passion for his former wife that she simply could not rouse in him?

He seemed to want her, at least when they had last made love that fateful morning on her bedroom floor. But since then, he had not come near. And since her recovery from the fire, he had barely looked at her, except to be certain of her health.

Had she lost him to Ravenna before she ever really had him?

****

"This will be a success," Grandy declared as Serena and Lucien joined the scattered assembly of people and colors in her drawing room. "The timing could not be better! All anyone can talk about is that awful book *Glenarvon*," she murmured. "It's quite obvious Caro Lamb wrote it."

"So I've heard," Serena whispered, feeling the curious stares of the other members of the *ton*.

"Can you not see?" Grandy said. "They're so busy talking about her scandal, they've quite put yours aside." Her grandmother leaned closer and confided, "Of course, Harriet is worried about her daughter, but Caro has survived so many scandals already. She will weather this as well, I'm certain."

"Where is Lady Bessborough?" Serena asked, looking past the swirl of pastel bodices and dark coats for her familiar face.

Grandy peered through the small gathering, then shrugged. "Harriet is probably off charming some lovely gentleman, knowing her. Now do smile and try to enjoy yourself, and tell that handsome husband of yours he must do the same."

With that, Grandy turned away to greet her newest guests. Serena followed her grandmother's advice and pasted on a smile she hoped looked less false than it felt. Taking a fortifying breath, she turned to Lucien.

Dressed in impeccable evening black, he looked somber, distant...untouchable. The drawing room's lighting shone across half of his angular face, almost making him appear a stranger. A stranger she loved who did not return her sentiments. Yearning and despair tangled thickly in her stomach.

"Smile," she instructed, her voice trembling. "Otherwise people will think all isn't well between us."

His green eyes held a maddening aloofness. "We would not want to prove them right, I suppose."

Serena flinched at his resigned tone. "Please, it's just one evening. Grandy has gone to so much trouble to see us straight again."

He nodded. "And I will play her charade."

Assuming a false smile that matched her own, Lucien placed his hand at the small of her back and guided her forward. His touch brought forth a rush of longing. Yet lingering doubts about Ravenna's claims remained. Though Lucien had not ventured far from her last night, she could not push aside the ache his ex-wife's words caused.

Grandy had done well in assembling the guest list. Certainly, no one present could make any pretenses to perfect behavior. Not Lady Bessborough, who had borne children other than her husband's. Serena also spotted the Countess of Bentmoor, who had been caught in her footman's bed, draped on a velvet settee. A few feet away the Earl of Waltingham, a man who had housed his wife and mistress, along with all their accompanying children under the same roof, chatted gaily with a Whig crony in the corner.

She, no longer living in the shadow of her mother's reputation but standing right beside it, was no better.

Ironically, these people were considered good *ton*. Their opinions and invitations were highly sought, and anyone who received their favors could be assured of social success.

She smiled politely as they passed through the crowd, nodding and exchanging pleasantries. Though reserved, their fellow guests were polite. For that, Serena thanked God. Perhaps Grandy was right; maybe the party would be a success indeed.

A close crony of Cyrus', Lord Davenport, stopped Serena and Lucien some moments later.

"My lady." The older man gave her a courtly bow, then kissed her hand. "You are a vision, as always."

"Thank you, Lord Davenport. How nice to see you again," she greeted in return.

"Nice?" the thin, graying man repeated with a faux pout. "I had hoped for more than that."

Lucien's hand at the crook of her waist tensed. Serena flashed him a questioning glance, but not a single thought showed on her husband's face. He couldn't possibly be jealous.

Turning back, she forced a laugh for Lord Davenport's effusive charm. "You've always had a sweet way of turning a phrase, my lord."

"In truth, I meant it, but then again, I realize I'm not the handsome devil your new husband is. Lord Daneridge," Davenport held out his hand. After a moment's pause, Lucien nodded and shook Davenport's hand.

"Quite an awkward position you two are in," Davenport said, "but I wish you the best. You have my backing."

Finally, Lucien relaxed his hold on her. "Thank you, Lord Davenport. It means a great deal to my wife."

The older man waved away the thanks. Twisting the ends of his moustache, the older man replied, "No thanks needed. Warrington was a good friend, and I know his primary concern was for his wife's happiness. If she's happy now, he would approve."

A pregnant pause followed. An aching lump coiled in her stomach and rose to her throat. No, she was not happy. She loved Lucien, despite trying to resist her feelings and wanton nature, while he might well harbor feelings for his ex-wife.

Swallowing surfacing tears, Serena forced a smile. "I have never been happier."

He returned her flat smile with a teasing one of his own. "Splendid. Hope to see more of you two soon. Say at a dinner my wife and I are hosting Wednesday next?"

"We would be delighted, Lord Davenport," Lucien answered when Serena could not find her voice.

"Perfect. See you there," he said, then turned to greet another acquaintance.

A long silence ensued between Serena and Lucien. Finally, he said, "I think your position with the *ton* is all but ensured."

She sent him a shaky answering nod. "With time."

"Too bad you had to lie to get Davenport's endorsement," he said, his voice grim.

Speechless, Serena watched Lucien turn away and cross the room to chat with Niles, who had just arrived.

During the next hour, she kept her gaze on her husband as he made pleasantries with several of society's matrons, charmed a group of young ladies in their first season, and debated politics with two of Cyrus' old cronies. Not once did he look her way.

Would he go to Ravenna tonight?

Serena tried to bury her hurt, pretend her torment didn't exist, all the while struggling desperately not to reveal what a dismal failure she made of the task. The *ton* always pounced on the marital unhappiness of others. Coupled with the fact she and Lucien were the scandalous newlyweds, all had to appear well. The only alternative was permanent social disaster. The time to release her emotions would come later, alone.

She spoke with Lady Bessborough and Grandy for twenty minutes. Lady Davenport paused to wish her well in her new role as the Marchioness of Daneridge. The Countess of Bentmoor engaged her in several minutes of gossip about the Caro Lamb-Lord Byron scandal.

"What a tempting tidbit," the Countess aahed. "Do you suppose Lord Byron is truly having an intimate liaison with his half-sister, as Caro claims?"

Serena simply shrugged, trying to hold her smile in place.

Just before dinner, the Earl of Rathburn whispered behind her, "You're looking lovely, my lady. Marriage agrees with you?"

Serena spun to face him. Dashing, blond-maned, and broad shouldered, Lord Rathburn looked dazzling in his evening black. He smiled, displaying dizzying charm and a row of white teeth.

She returned his smile. "It's wonderful to see you again. How are you?"

"Quite well. I was sorry to hear of Warrington's death. He was a brilliant man."

Hands trembling, Serena nodded. "Thank you. Cyrus always enjoyed debating with you at White's and Parliament."

"I enjoyed it as well." Silence ensued. He glanced at her empty hands and said, "You don't have any sherry. I shall see that you get some, if you like?"

Hoping the alcohol would calm her nerves, she pushed her misgivings aside. "A sip of sherry might be just the thing."

Rathburn gestured to a nearby servant, who brought her a glass of the amber liquid. Serena turned to accept it—and found Lucien talking with Grandy. He said something and flashed the older woman a grin, complete with dimples. Serena forced back a new barrage of tears. She hadn't seen Lucien smile in weeks.

Did he smile with Ravenna?

A fit of coughs racked Rathburn suddenly. He bent over, fist covering his mouth.

"Are you well?" she asked in concern.

Still coughing, he gasped, "Outside. Fresh air."

She nodded. "Let's step out onto the balcony. I find it a bit stuffy in here."

Catching Rathburn's arm, she lent him subtle support as they exited the dimly lit drawing room.

Once outside, he recovered from his ailment quickly. A ray of light spilled from the drawing room and lit up the warm tones of Rathburn's gaze. "It is refreshing to see you about again."

"I confess, milling about the *ton* is not among my favorite activities. Cyrus wasn't fond of it either, so I'm afraid we allowed ourselves to rusticate in Sussex more often than not."

"You're back now, and I have high hopes this season will be one I shan't forget soon."

Serena offered her companion a smile. "I am certain you'll find ways to amuse yourself."

A moment later, Rathburn patted her hand, and with it, brought her closer. "I plan to."

A glance at Rathburn did not indicate whether he was indeed flirting with her, as she suspected. In past meetings, he had been the model of gentlemanly behavior, deferential in all respects. She could hardly picture him differently.

"You must smile more," Rathburn insisted.

Serena felt the caress of his thumb on her hand. She held her smile in place, while she considered subtle ways to escape his over-familiar touch that wouldn't raise eyebrows.

"Forgive my boldness, but if Lord Daneridge is so foolish as to ignore you," Rathburn continued, "then he cannot see the treasure he has. I shall happily consider it my good fortune."

Serena affected a laughed and stepped away. Rathburn clutched her fingers and followed into a corner of the garden. "You have quite the honeyed tongue, my lord."

"Only because you are the most beautiful woman here."

Serena shook her head and glanced about for help. "Nonsense. The *ton's* loveliest ladies are in attendance."

"These are the same jaded birds I see everywhere. You, my dear, are fresh and exciting." He moved closer and draped his arm about her waist. "I have a quaint house, a cottage really, in St. John's Wood. I would be most honored if you would consent to visit me there."

"You're suggesting I become your mistress?" she asked sharply.

"I would like to spend time with you, and yes, make love to you." Rathburn brought her closer, his blue eyes delving into hers. "I would enjoy giving you the attention you deserve. I confess that I have long fancied you."

Serena jerked from his hold. "Lord Rathburn, I—"

He pressed his lips to hers in a rush of breath and night wind. His mouth felt cool and capable. She steeled herself against the tidal wave of desire that always came with a handsome man's kiss, a throwback of her mother's lustful blood.

Strangely, only embarrassment and discomfort stirred for the man who held her.

As Rathburn's hands slid down her arms, to her waist, Serena felt frozen in time, rooted by revelation. His lips swept and brushed over hers again. The handsome earl's kiss not only left her unmoved, but stirred no more than a shrieking feeling of wrongness. She did not yearn for his touch, as she did Lucien's, or ache to know fulfillment at his hands.

Did the fact her cravings followed her heart prove her different than Mama?

At his groan, Serena pushed her companion away with a gentle shove. "Please, release me."

Rathburn answered with a puzzled frown. "I see plainly that Lord Daneridge is...neglecting you. I dare you to tell me otherwise."

"Even if he were, infidelity would only make matters worse," Serena declared, backing away from the earl.

Rathburn cleared his throat. "All right. I apologize if I've made you uncomfortable. Should you, however, change your mind—"

"I will not." Conviction rang in her shaking voice. "I refuse to dishonor my husband or myself in such a fashion."

Rathburn stepped away. "Should you change your mind, you know where to find me."

Eyes narrowed, she advanced on him. "If you thought to test the gossip which says I have my mother's appetites, tell those who spread such ugly lies that I shall have no man but my husband. Now excuse me."

Clutching her reticule, Serena turned away from Rathburn, toward the door, only to stop.

Lucien stood in the doorway, draped in murky shadows. Serena saw him immediately, a mere five steps away, silent, watching.

Her eyes widened. Color left her cheeks as Serena clutched her reticule tighter in her gloved hands.

Lucien stared hard at his wife through the grainy light. She looked terrified. He had never wanted to kiss her more.

He'd followed her out into the gardens because he loved her, despite his reservations, regardless of what she had plotted with Warrington. But for his future, for his sanity, he'd had to know if she, like Ravenna, would be swayed by another man's pretty face and words.

Now, euphoria enveloped him. Based on Serena's impassioned refusal of Rathburn, she believed in fidelity. Maybe that meant he could trust her with his heart.

But what had driven her to his bed the first time? Maybe she had succumbed to the loneliness and need she insisted she'd felt. If that were the case, he would happily bestow upon Serena the ardent attention his body craved to give her tonight—and every night—without fear he was doomed to relive his past.

Lucien started toward Serena, yearning to hold his wife and shout his joy to the heavens. He did neither, knowing such actions would incite further gossip. He vowed to make up for the missed opportunity later.

Instead, he adopted a polite expression and proffered his arm. "I came to see you inside. We're going in to dinner."

Serena glanced from his face to his outstretched arm with wide eyes and placed trembling fingers on his forearm. "Th-thank you."

"You're welcome, sweetheart." He leaned forward to place a gentle kiss on her lips, reveling in her sultry scent and a tender flood of feeling.

Then he turned to Rathburn. "My wife is indeed a treasure to me. If you give me cause to prove how highly I value her, I promise you will regret it beyond words."

Lucien heard Serena gasp at his side as he led her away. Perhaps he had misjudged her from the start, measured her against Ravenna. If so, maybe their marriage was just beginning.

****

At the unexpected knock on her door, Ravenna rushed to the portal. Lucien! He had come to accept her offer to share her bed, and when he did, she would simply explain she had a small financial problem. Certainly, she hadn't chosen to stay in this second-rate Drury Lane lodging house for her pleasure.

Hand grasping the latch, Ravenna hesitated. Lucien was no doubt furious that she had approached his pale excuse for a wife at Lackington's, and from the horror on the chit's face, Ravenna would bet her last shilling that Lucien and his new wife were no longer on intimate terms.

Ravenna giggled. She was more than willing to fill that void—for ample monetary support, of course.

"Hello, darling," she said, drawing the portal back.

Her welcoming smile wilted when she encountered an unfamiliar man standing in the spot Lucien should have occupied.

"Who are you?" she demanded.

The blond man, no older than his early thirties, smiled. His thin features were craggy, holding a ruthless sort of handsomeness. His eyes glittered with ambition, with danger.

"You must be Ravenna Clayborne." The stranger stepped inside uninvited, his eyes traveling her body.

Reading attraction in his eyes, she answered, "Yes. I'm afraid I have not had the pleasure."

"In good time, dear lady."

His grin assured the pleasure would extend much beyond his acquaintance. Ravenna took note again of his interest and sent him a saucy smile.

The stranger's eyes left her for a moment to wander about her rented room. Disappointment stabbed Ravenna, and she stepped in front of him once more. His mouth curved in a knowing grin.

"Do you like these rooms?" he asked.

Ravenna frowned. "Why do you ask? Who are you, anyway?"

The stranger didn't answer right away. He paused, scanned her face, then raised his hand to her cheek. "I can make you wealthy again. You would like that, I'll wager."

Ravenna's eyes widened with hope, then narrowed with suspicion. "How? I will not sell myself like a common street trollop."

"Nor would I ask you to, dear lady. You're much, much too beautiful for that," he murmured, stroking her cheek. "Actually, I had something more like a favor in mind. A little assistance in a small matter."

"What type of assistance?" she asked, nearly salivating at the thought of money.

"It's a complicated matter, but suffice it to say that, should you successfully...distract your ex-husband for—" he shrugged, "—an hour or so, I will give you ten thousand pounds."

Ravenna gasped. "Ten thousand. Really? And I only have to bed down with the cripple once?"

The man curled his hand around her shoulder, his thumb caressing her arm. He smiled as he answered, "Only once."

"How did you know Lord Daneridge is my former husband?"

"I have sources."

Eyes narrowed, Ravenna stepped away. "How did you know where to find me?"

"I have a man watching his house. After you visited your former husband on Tuesday, he followed you here."

"Why?"

"Must you ask so many questions?" His voice was silky. "You either agree to help me or you don't. Which is it?"

Ravenna retreated another step. "I shall have to know more before I..."

The stranger flashed a dangerous smile that stopped her words and dampened her knickers. "Let us say his wife may not find herself in the best of health soon."

Glee spread through Ravenna's body, and a feline smile swept across her face. "You plan to kill her?"

"The bitch controls a fortune that belongs to me." The stranger stepped closer, neither confirming nor denying her suspicion.

Ravenna retreated. He advanced; she withdrew.

Several steps later, Ravenna found herself trapped against the wall, the stranger's palms anchored on either side of her head, caging her. He leaned closer. After two months without a man's touch, she welcomed a new lover and felt her pulse quicken.

"Do I have your help?" he asked, pressing the length of his body—and hard arousal— against her, drawing her breast above the neckline of her gown for his fingers' pleasure.

Ravenna threw her head back and moaned, melting into the stranger.

"Shall I take that as a yes?"

"Yes," she gasped.

He pulled back and drew a calling card from his vest pocket. Dropping his calling card on a nearby table, he laughed. "When you've arranged an appointment with your ex-husband, send a note up to me with the date and time."

Without awaiting her reply, he took the swollen bud of her breast into his mouth. Aroused by his masterful touch, Ravenna moaned her assent.

The man unfastened his breeches. Ravenna's eyes lowered to his swollen member, watching greedily as he stroked its length between thick fingers.

"You want this, don't you?" he taunted.

Ravenna turned away from his smug expression. "I am no trollop."

The stranger grinned as he pulled her face back toward him. "Yes, you are. You," he said, raising her skirt and petticoats to her waist, "are a juicy little whore who likes a hard man between your thighs. Admit it."

His fingers probed her femininity. Ravenna inhaled sharply as his fingers found their mark.

"That is not true," she gasped.

"Of course it is. And I'm about to prove it."

With that, the stranger lifted Ravenna by her bared thighs, and fitting her back against the wall, drew her down on his shaft. Clutching his shoulders, she released a ragged moan.

"Damn you," she cursed breathlessly. "Who are you?"

Pumping inside Ravenna, he panted, "Alastair Boyce. I think we're going to get on very well."

CHAPTER TWENTY-TWO

Serena left her chamber the next morning and lingered at the top of the stairs. A part of her consciousness registered a guard falling into place directly behind her, an ever-present reminder of Alastair's sinister plot. But she refused to dwell on that this morning.

She drew in an anxious breath. She needed to find Lucien and discuss Rathburn's advances with him, ask about his silence afterward. Had he interpreted the event as she had, a revelation? Or had he believed she'd invited the attention? Or did he even care, given the fact he had Ravenna again?

She had pondered the event most of the long, sleepless night. Her refusal of Rathburn had shown her that not every male affected her as Lucien did. Upon further reflection, she realized that her desire for Lucien stemmed from love and had grown as her feelings for him had. And the fact her sensual cravings followed her heart, not her mood, proved her different than Mama.

Vastly.

Love had taught her that to share her emotions, soul and body with her husband was as God intended. She should feel no shame in making love with Lucien. Being with him in every way, as often as joy and desire brought them together, would foster the happiness Cyrus had wanted for her.

But only if he cared for her in return.

If she told him that she would open her door and her arms to him, what would he say? She feared he would refuse her because his heart belonged to Ravenna. She would have to confront him on that score, no matter how much the truth hurt.

Shaking away the thought, she descended the stairs, fingers trembling on the rail. At the bottom, she spotted Holford, his stance stiff as always.

"Good morning, my lady."

"Good morning." Serena drew in a deep breath. "Is my husband here or with Mr. Vickery again?"

"I'm not certain where he is, my lady. I believe he said something about another appointment before he left. Shall I tell him to see you when he returns?"

"No," she said, disappointed. "No. Don't bother. I shall see him later."

"As you wish, my lady. Speaking of Mr. Vickery," he said, holding up a small missive, "this urgent message arrived a moment ago for you. The delivery boy indicated Mr. Vickery sent it."

Holford handed her the plain note. Serena tore it open to find a hastily-crafted scrawl in slightly smudged ink.

My lady,

I have discovered a possible accomplice in your late husband's murder. He has been shot and may not live long. We need your assistance during his questioning to confirm some pertinent facts about Warrington. Come immediately to Tothill Fields. Along Whitehall Road, small cottages are scattered. Enter the one with two candles burning in the front window. Your husband is with me.

Yours,
John Vickery

An accomplice? Elation mixed with suspicion. She had nearly died the last time she had received a note. However, the coward had not signed the last one. And if she hesitated in following the note's instructions, she might well lose the only real clue available—and might never put Cyrus' ghost to rest.

"Quickly, Holford. This is an emergency, indeed. I shall need a carriage brought round. And don't worry for my safety; I will take two men and Caffey with me for protection."

"Of course, my lady. What shall I say to his lordship when he returns?"

Serena handed the note back to Holford. "It appears my husband is with Mr. Vickery at Tothill Fields. I shall meet him there."

"Very good, then," he answered as she called for Caffey and summoned another guard.

In moments, she sprinted out the door. She would help prove Alastair's guilt in Cyrus' murder, and she would not let her last link with hope die before she could learn the truth.

****

Lucien knocked on Ravenna's Drury lane door, dreading the appointment. He understood her grief for Chelsea, and knew his guilt had led him to answer the second and more desperate of her messages. But he wanted to be home, with Serena, watching her, protecting her. Trying to discern exactly what lay between them.

Watching her refusal of Rathburn had given him hope that Serena and his ex-wife differed in many ways, but most of all in their motivations for seeking a lover. Ravenna had taken lovers for spite, for entertainment. Serena had done so out of loneliness and a wish to end her childless existence.

As soon as he finished here, Lucien vowed to be sure she never felt lonely again. He wanted to give her his trust. He yearned to fill her life with laughter and children.

And love.

She deserved nothing less than his heart, and hoped to hell she would let him close to hers.

Ravenna opened the door, wearing a sultry, welcoming smile.

Lucien frowned, eyeing his scantily-clad ex-wife warily. "I received your messages. You wish to discuss Chelsea?"

Toying with the ties at the neck of her thin red gown, Ravenna stepped back, inviting him to enter. She shut the door behind him, then leaned against it. "Our last conversation ended badly, darling. I wanted to apologize...personally."

Ravenna disentangled the ties of her gown. The garment fell down her arm, revealing one creamy shoulder—and a full, rouge-nippled breast.

Swearing, he closed his eyes.

She stroked his arm. He yanked away from her touch. "Darling, don't you understand? I was dreadfully wrong to blame you for Chelsea's death. It was not your fault."

He snapped his gaze to her, expression cool. "Indeed?"

"Of course. Had you been home that night, you hardly would have heard her leave. She was a clever little thing. And the nursemaid we hired was the best. I made certain of that myself."

Lucien shot her a cynical glance. He doubted Ravenna had given the matter much consideration, or even believed her own words. She was hardly the reflective type.

Yet he could not refute her. There was truth to her claim for once, despite the fact she had said it to win his favor. Had guilt prevented him from acknowledging those facts before?

"Perhaps you are right," he said slowly.

"Of course I am. I'm so very glad you've realized that!"

"As am I."

Ravenna's coy smile fell. "You know, I hated the fact she loved you more than me. You always had a way of making her smile that I did not." She paused. "Maybe that is why I wanted another child, one that was not yours. One that no one could take from me."

Lucien scowled. "I never intended to make you feel less than a mother. I would share Chelsea today, if she were here."

"You simply shared a bond with her that I did not."

Lucien drank in the truth of her words. That connection he had formed with his daughter had only added to his sense of responsibility and guilt. Remembering this lifted his burden.

"Thank you," he said quietly. "Your words mean more to me than a 'personal apology,' so cover yourself."

"But I insist," she assured — then bared her other breast. Its nipple was also rouged a deep red. "It's the only way I know to tell you how sorry I am and give you everything you asked for during our marriage."

She sidled closer; Lucien retreated a step from her smooth, scented flesh.

"Ravenna, stop this silly game. I am no longer interested."

"Don't be ridiculous." She laughed. "That pale little willow you call wife can never give you what I can."

"True. She is capable of giving love."

Ravenna laughed. "Love is an illusion, darling, nothing more than a powerful case of lust. I thought you must have realized that by now."

"No," he insisted, churning with the intensity of his emotions. "Love is real and strong. I have come to learn that it is about trust and respect and empathy. Things we never shared."

Her lips tipped up in a sly smile. "Well, after my little chat with her, I doubt you're sharing much."

"You spoke to Serena?"

She nodded, her smile widening to that of a naughty kitten.

A cord of fear vibrated within him. "When? What did you say to her?"

Ravenna cocked her head to one side. "A few days ago at Lackington's I...suggested that perhaps you and I share more than a past. She looked quite devastated."

Lucien stared at his half-undressed ex-wife, a combination of incredulity and confusion sweeping him. Serena had not mentioned it, not confronted him. Yet only last night she had turned Rathburn away.

"You told her we were involved in some liaison?"

Nonchalantly, she shrugged but sent him a saucy grin, now all minx.

"Damn you!" he cursed, grabbing her arm. "Stay away from Serena. Do you hear me?"

She shrugged. "Oh, all right. Pity you never had much sense of humor."

Easy capitulation had never been Ravenna's style. Lucien glared at her as, with a lazily raised brow, she turned away.

He rested his elbow on the mantle beside him and watched her through narrowed eyes. A scrap of paper fell to the floor at his feet. He bent to retrieve it, noting the paper was in fact a calling card. He scanned the name on the front. A cold chill ran through his blood.

Alastair.

His eyes shot to Ravenna's half-clad form. She stood still, her back facing him. He charged toward her. Two strides later, he saw the purplish-red mark on her neck, lying conspicuously below the mass of dark curls piled on her head—the kind of love bite a man leaves behind with the suction of his mouth.

In a haze of roaring fury and chilling fear, he lunged for her and grabbed her arms. "Is Alastair Boyce your lover?"

"Are you jealous?"

"Don't play games with me. Is he?" he barked.

She stared up at him, blinking long lashes over innocent eyes. "Lucien, I would never—"

"Don't lie!" he shouted. "Are you helping him?"

"Helping him? I'm certain I have no notion what you mean."

His mind raced beyond her lies, to the possibilities. When he had reached a hideous but logical conclusion, every muscle within him tightened in dread and horror. He swallowed a lump of cold, living fear. "That's what this is about, this seduction. It has nothing to do with an apology."

"Whatever are you saying?" she asked too sweetly.

From her guarded expression, he knew he was right. "I do not know what Marsden promised you for your role in this scheme, and I don't give a damn. But if he hurts Serena, I swear I will hunt you down and see you hang next to him."

Terror gnawing on his insides, heart slamming against his chest, Lucien dashed out, despite Ravenna's clinging protests, and fled for home.

He found Serena gone and an apparently forged note his only link to finding her.

****

Serena instructed her coachman to travel south of Westminster, onto Whitehall Road, and urged him to drive faster. At a seeming snail's pace, she watched civilization give way to the occasional inn or cottage perched on the mean little road. Night descended, turning the open, uninhabited fields about them into dark, shapeless voids. Serena shivered.

"I'm not likin' this, milady," Caffey said. "Not many folks live out here. Why can't the fellow come to ye?"

Serena shifted in her seat, hoping her maid's fears were unwarranted. "Because the man I am to speak to is dying."

"Somethin' about this ain't right," she maintained. "I've a sense fer these things, ye know."

"Stop," Serena instructed. "You're making me nervous. Besides, Lucien is there."

Just before the southward crook of the Thames, the carriage slowed in front of an isolated cottage with two candles in the window. She drew in a deep breath. This was it. Given Vickery's note, justice might soon be hers. Cyrus could rest in peace. Then perhaps she and Lucien could work at their marriage, expand the magic they had discovered their first night together. Maybe, in time, he would forget Ravenna.

Without waiting for assistance, Serena scrambled from the vehicle to the green grass beneath her and ran toward the cottage. Caffey followed suit, with the armed footmen close behind.

Through the closing darkness, shots rang out. The sound came from her right and sliced past her. As she shrank back, one of the guards sprinted to her side and lowered her to the ground before covering her with his hard, unfamiliar body. Serena knew her first taste of fear. Was Lucien here? Had he been harmed?

Or had she simply walked into Alastair's trap?

An instant later, two more shots rent the silence. The footman standing behind her crumpled to the grass. From somewhere behind her, Caffey screamed as four men swarmed forward from the surrounding desolation.

The guard lying atop Serena twisted around and shot one of the intruders, only to gasp in pain a moment later, apparently shot by another armed villain. Serena heard her protector's groan of agony, felt his heavy breathing...then nothing.

Caffey's second scream rang in Serena's ears again as she tried to wiggle out from beneath the dead guard's weight. She sprang to her feet, running blindly from the attackers. Behind her, two more shots sounded. Serena tried to shelter her head with her arms.

Without warning, a heavy pair of arms tackled her from behind. Serena tumbled to the grass on her knees. The man spun her about and flung her onto her back. She gasped for air as the man bound her hands with rough hemp.

As the ruffian jerked her to her feet, she gasped, "What are you doing to me?"

"Just what I'm paid to do, me fine lady." He yanked on the rope, pressing her shoulders back in their sockets.

"You're hurting me," she protested.

He laughed. "You'll hurt a whole lot more 'afore the gent what paid me gets through with ye, I'll wager."

Alastair! Serena shivered with fear and struggled to rein in rising panic. She had to find a way to escape, before Alastair killed her.

With a push of the rope at her wrists, her captor shoved her toward the cottage. As they neared, Serena saw her driver lying on the ground, a red stain on his chest. Another attacker had Caffey pinned beneath him. The man tied her maid's hands, then stared beneath her skirt with a rapacious grin.

"Leave her be!" Serena shouted.

"Shut yer mouth, ye bitch," her captor grated out, grabbing her hair with his filthy fingers. "Yer next, right after `is lordship finishes with ye. Now move!"

As he pushed her forward, she struggled for freedom. Her impotency to help Caffey in the face of her screams twisted at Serena's heart.

A solitary laugh from the cottage sliced through the commotion. Serena whipped her gaze up at the sound.

Alastair.

Her stomach flared with hot fear and hotter fury at the sight of him, chains in one hand, a knife in the other.

"Tell that fiend to let my maid go!" Serena demanded. "She has nothing to do with this."

He paused to glance at Caffey and her captors. The maid screamed once again as one man grabbed her breast with a laugh that made Serena's stomach turn. Beside him, the other men knelt and held Caffey down.

"They're just having a little sport." Alastair stepped toward her, coiling the chains in his hand. "Were I you, I would worry for myself at the moment. What I have planned for you will be much more degrading."

Again, Serena struggled in her captor's grasp. The brute pushed her toward the cottage. She fell to her knees at Alastair's feet. Cyrus's nephew dragged her upright, holding her against his wiry body. Serena felt his breath on her face, saw the glint of cruel satisfaction in his eyes. Her stomach roiled in riot.

Alastair wrapped the chain about her waist. Its heavy, cold weight settled about her like an albatross.

"Can we take the wench and hide?" one of the men asked.

"Yes," Alastair answered. "But for God's sake, keep her screams down."

"Ain't no cottage fer two miles."

"As loud as she is, they can likely hear her," Alastair snapped. "And don't stray far, in case I've need of you."

Alastair turned to her with a chilly smile. "If you're thinking that Lord Daneridge will save you, don't. I assure you, Ravenna is keeping him well occupied."

Despair plunged her stomach to her knees. He and Ravenna were still lovers. Serena knew a feeling so hopeless and dismal, for despite her feelings, Lucien's heart was still entangled with the woman once termed the devil's daughter. Her husband's solicitous behavior at Grandy's party had probably been nothing more than a ploy to prevent another man from claiming his property, and she could never hope to win his affections.

Even if she survived this night by some miracle, she was doomed to marriage with a man who would never love her.

But she was going to die. Fear and pain would be her last emotions. A shout lodged in the back of her throat, begging release, at the realization that the child she had created with Lucien would die with her.

Alastair laughed. "Ravenna is such an accommodating bed mate. I am surprised he stayed away from her this long. But I have no doubt she'll seduce him with ease."

"Seduce him? Aren't they already conducting a liaison?"

He shot her an ugly smirk. "Ravenna has no need to bed a man she considers a cripple when she has so many other options." His thin lips twitched in amusement. "Of course, she promised to make this exception a favor to me."

"But she told me that Lucien has been spending time in her bed already," Serena said.

"I've kept her too busy for that recently. Besides, she only offered her...companionship to your husband since she's in need of funds. She seemed surprised that he turned her away."

Serena allowed herself a moment of joy, despite the danger. Ravenna had lied to her just for spite. Elation cut through her fear for a moment, followed by hope. Now she could only hope Lucien would not succumb to his ex-wife's seduction today. Maybe then he would find her.

"You know," Alastair said, "I shall be most interested to see which of Clayborne's wives is the better whore."

Serena struggled against him. "Don't touch me!"

"I'll do that, and much, much more."

Alastair yanked on the chain around her and dragged her inside the cabin, slamming the door behind him. When he turned to face her once more, his dark eyes were alight with lust and vengeance.

Feral anticipation crossed his face as he advanced toward her. Serena wanted to scream, but her instincts told her a display of fear would only incite him further.

"Now, you little slut, I'm going to find out why old Uncle Cyrus thought bedding you was worth a fortune. He was certainly eager to give up his last shilling after a tumble between your legs. What is it you have down there?" he asked, his hand fondling its way down her breast, past her waist, to grope the juncture of her thighs. Serena twisted away. Alastair brought her closer with the imprisoning chain. "Do you have a wet, golden treasure? Is that it?

"You are repulsive."

With a short, sharp yank, Alastair dragged her closer still. "Well, *Aunt* Serena, because of you, I've been subject to humiliations you haven't the experience to fathom. Tonight, you will gain that experience. I will humble you until you beg me for mercy."

"You shall burn in hell for this!"

His smile was flat and evil. "I already have. Now it's your turn."

Alastair shoved Serena to the crude dirt floor, dragging her down with the aid of the chain. With a cry, she fell on her shoulder and hip with a thump. Lying atop her, Alastair used his weight to force her to her back.

"When did you start letting Clayborne bed you? Before old Uncle Cyrus died? Is that Clayborne's bastard in your belly?"

"No." Her voice trembled.

"You lying bitch." He struck her across the cheek.

With a gasp, more of anger than pain, Serena kicked out at him, her feet connecting with his stomach. He grunted.

"You will regret that," he swore.

He raised his knife above her. Serena screamed, fearing Alastair planned to end her life now. A hundred regrets rose to her mind, crowded by her chilling fright, the strongest that she should have told Lucien how much she loved him.

"A pity I didn't slice you open at Vauxhall before Clayborne saved your pretty hide," Alastair jeered.

Incredulity and icy anger permeated her every pore. "That was you?" At his grin, she snapped, "You bastard."

"No, Uncle Cyrus only treated me like one," Alastair returned. "That was one reason I had the old man killed; I hated him. And you're next, but not yet. You owe me too much for a quick, merciful end. I want you to beg me for death first."

"I will never beg you for anything. I despise you."

"The feeling, my bit of muslin, is mutual."

To her horror, Alastair reached beneath her skirt, insinuating the blade of his knife under the top of her bodice. With an evil laugh and several thrusts upward of the knife, the fabric of her bodice gave way in a ragged fray downward. Serena struggled until Alastair swept the knife up to her throat. The blade pricked her skin. Serena had no doubt each wound was intentional, meant to teach her to lie still or invite death.

Trembling, Serena lay beneath Alastair, hearing his harsh breathing. With a mad glare, he cut away the short, full sleeves of her dress, then tossed the garment away. Next, he severed the waist-ties of her petticoats before turning her over to make short work of her corset strings. Clad only in her chemise, Serena snapped her eyes shut. A moment later, she heard the hiss of Alastair's blade again, this time slicing through the thin lawn material.

A moment later, she felt a rush of cold air against her bare breasts and abdomen. She cried out in horror, feeling Alastair's eyes crawl over her exposed flesh. He laughed at her discomfort.

With the dagger at her throat, Serena could not struggle while Alastair unfastened his trousers.

"Finally, I get some of this tight, wet flesh Uncle Cyrus threw away his fortune for and Clayborne guards with his life." He reached for her feminine folds. Serena clamped her legs together, denying him.

"Get off me!" she demanded, panting in fear and fury.

"Shut up and spread your legs! And I warn you," he took her face between cruel fingers, "you had better be good."

Alastair tried to force her legs apart. Serena remained stiff, resisting, but felt the blade at her neck inching forward, pricking her skin.

A gunshot sounded outside. Alastair paused and cursed.

The door burst open, swinging back on its hinges to slam against the wall. Serena gasped as Alastair jerked his gaze around to the intruder.

Lucien stood in the doorway, his broad shoulders dominating the portal. He pointed a gun at Alastair's head.

"Get off my wife."

His voice was level and deadly. Even in her shaken state, Serena didn't miss the barely-leashed rage in his command.

Slowly, Alastair rose to his feet.

"I should shoot you now," Lucien said, eyes narrowed with hate. "I should pull the trigger and watch you die."

Alastair's smile was rife with challenge. "You won't. You're hardly the kind to shoot a man unable to defend himself."

"That's not it at all. I simply want to see you die a humiliating public death." Glancing at Serena, he asked, "Did he hurt you, sweetheart?"

"No," she breathed. "But Caffey.... Those men took her—"

"Vickery's got her. She's safe."

Glaring at Alastair, Lucien said, "Sweetheart, wrap yourself in one of those blankets and come here."

She fetched a blanket from the pallet in the corner. After wrapping it about her body, she crossed the room to Lucien's side, restraining an urge to hurtle herself in his arms. "Thank God, you came."

"Thank God, you're alive." He risked a glance at her. His eyes were as dark as the sea—and held infinite relief. His brief glance reassured her.

"My, how touching," Alastair mocked. "You appear quite the couple in love."

Serena risked another glance at her husband. His gaze touched her again, filled with an outpouring of emotion she had never seen. Tears welled in her eyes as she met his.

In that second, Alastair charged forward. He collided with Lucien, pounding her husband against the wall. The gun fell from Lucien's grasp and landed on the dirt with a sickening thud.

As the men grappled, Serena knelt and grabbed the cold weapon. She aimed at Alastair, but hesitated. She had never fired a gun, and the combatants moved so quickly—against the wall, across the room, to the floor.

As if her worst fears had become real, Serena saw the blade of Alastair's knife gleam in the candlelight as he held it above Lucien's heaving, unprotected chest.

"Lucien!" she screamed.

He only grunted as he grappled to push Alastair away.

Blind to all but her fear, her fury, Serena aimed and pulled the trigger.

The gun exploded, kicking back in her hands. The sound made a deafening reverberation in the small cottage. Then came a gasp. She opened her eyes to find Alastair slumping to the ground, the white of his shirt front rapidly turning crimson. Slack-jawed and wide-eyed, he looked stunned as he fell. Within seconds, the absolute still formed an eerie silence.

"Oh, God," she whispered, her voice trembling.

Lucien knelt before Alastair and tested his pulse. He sighed and rose. "He's dead."

"I killed him."

"He deserved to die for what he did to Warrington and you."

She nodded slowly, taking in Lucien's words, and drew in a deep breath. Killing him might be a sin, but..."You're right. I'm not sorry."

He crossed the room to gather her in his arms. Tears stinging her eyes, Serena flung herself against his chest, reveling in his size and strength, so representative of the security he gave her.

His relief was visible. "I worried about you, what he could do to you. I thought I had lost you."

"His note said you were here. I feared he had killed you already."

Vickery stepped inside the crude cabin then, then glanced at the body. "Is Marsden dead?"

Slowly, Lucien lifted his head from her shoulder and nodded.

"Are you all right, Lady Daneridge?"

Serena turned to the Runner. "Yes, thank you."

"Good. My lord, I've rounded up the other culls. I'll take them and Marsden's body to the Magistrate. I'm certain they'll send someone round later for a statement."

"Fine. Thank you for your help, Vickery."

He waved Lucien's thanks away. "Only doing my job."

With that, Vickery turned away. Lucien wrapped his arm about Serena's waist, clutching the quilt to her, and led her through the darkness to his waiting carriage. Tenderly, he tucked her inside, then settled himself beside her.

The door had barely closed before Serena threw her arms around him. He felt as strong and solid as the Rock of Gibraltar. She clung to him; he stroked her hair, her back, and the hideous memories of Alastair and his threats were gradually replaced by the here and now of Lucien's soft touch.

Neither moved for the span of a heartbeat, as if doing so would end the purity and reverence of the moment. The scent of dirt mingled with the smell of impending rain in the air. The clippity-clop of the horses' hooves provided a steady backdrop to their even breathing.

Serena eased away finally, bringing her face inches from his. His green gaze slid over hers, distinctly concerned and laced with tenderness. He was her husband, she his wife. No one, least of all Alastair, could come between them now. And nothing, not the unfounded fear that her mother's blood had tainted her, nor mistrust, would keep them apart.

She wanted Lucien in every way, in every facet of her life. The broad shoulders and inky hair were hers to touch every day. His smile, his grief, his joy and his emotions were hers to tap into, if she had the courage.

Serena pressed her lips to his. He welcomed her kiss with his own, a gentle affirmation of life and breath. He held her closer, sliding his arm about her.

Serena clutched his face, holding his mouth to hers as if he were her lifeline. He didn't let her go.

The coach stopped. The door opened, and Lucien stepped down. With an ironic smile, he turned and extended his hand to her. "Come inside the house, sweetheart. It will be heaven. I promise."

His words sent her memory careening back to their first night together, when he'd made love to her tenderly and they had conceived the child she carried. She yearned to experience the joy and fire of his touch now.

As she did that first night, Serena touched his fingers, then placed her trembling hand in his.

Inside, she gathered the blanket about her ankles and led Lucien up the stairs, past the shocked servants, to his room. Shaking with both uncertainty and desire, she closed the door behind them.

With a puzzled frown, he said, "Sweetheart, wouldn't you..."

Lucien fell silent as Serena unwrapped the blanket and let it drop to the floor, exposing her nakedness.

"Oh, dear God," he breathed as he took one step toward her, then another. As he reached her, Lucien drew her into his arms. The confusion on his face said what he did not.

"Touch me," she whispered. "Make love to me."

He held her close against him and exhaled raggedly into her ear. "Are you certain?"

"Please." She kissed her way up the strong column of his neck, nipping at his jaw.

With a shiver, Lucien wrapped his arms about her. I can think of nothing I want more."

As one, they made their way to the bed, a tangle of arms and lips, to experience the ecstasy of their union. Lucien's touch and gaze cherished her with each caress. Serena, in turn, displayed the depth of her love with her welcome as he entered her, and with every frantic, possessive thrust, they soared closer to the peak of pleasure. Serena found a satisfaction greater than ever before because it came without guilt or worry, stemmed purely from love.

Afterward, they lay entwined, silence cocooning them from the outside world.

Serena finally spoke as the shadows of dawn began streaking through the curtains. "Thank you for coming to my rescue. I wouldn't be here, if not for you and your refusal of Ravenna's charms."

Lucien leaned on his elbow to gaze down into her eyes. "She holds no charm for me now. Do not ever think she has the power to come between us. Despite what she told you, I would never hurt you like that. I want you. Only you." He grinned. "I'll be happy to prove that again, if you like."

She smiled in return. Sobering again, her gaze sought his familiar green eyes. "I should not have doubted you."

"Just as I never should have believed you were anything like her." He took her hand, entwining their fingers. "Sweetheart, we both made mistakes, but God has given us a second chance, and we won't make those mistakes again. Next time, instead of letting fear or pride take over, we'll talk to each other. Agreed?"

She nodded, then paused, searching for the right words. "Lucien, I swear I made love with you the first time because I could not resist you. I still can't, and I won't ever try again. But I never went to your bed because Cyrus wanted me to."

"I know. You are nothing like Ravenna, and just like a fool, I treated you as if you are, always believing the worst." A low, self-deprecating laugh later, he said, "I'm nowhere near perfect, sweetheart. I'll have to work on trust. But I do trust you."

Serena smiled tremulously. "I love you." As Lucien's eyes widened, she quickly added, "I—I don't expect you to return the sentiment. I know I've been difficult, and that I wasn't a model wife in my refusal to share your bed, but if you'll give me the chance—"

"You don't need any such chance," Lucien interrupted, squeezing her tighter. Then cupping her face with his hands, he locked her gaze to his. "Do you know how many times I wished I could hear those words from you? A thousand at least." With a soft brush of his fingers, he smoothed strands of her hair from her face. "I'm so fortunate to have you. You have given me a richer life, and God willing, another child soon." He touched his mouth to hers, then whispered, "I love you, too."

They kissed, Lucien's lips moving over hers softly, with a reverence that both elevated and humbled Serena at once. When it ended, she snuggled tighter into his embrace, then asked, "Would you be happy with a little girl?"

Lucien smiled tenderly, his thumbs caressing her cheeks. I would be the happiest man alive."

"I think it's going to be a girl," Serena confessed, hands gliding over her slightly rounded abdomen. "I just feel it."

Lucien's hands followed hers, memorizing her ripening contours. "Then we'll raise her with love and give her a herd of brothers and sisters to play with."

"Do you promise?" she asked.

He smiled, then kissed her forehead tenderly. "Sweetheart, I will settle for nothing less."

The End

Read on for an exciting peek at THE LADY AND THE DRAGON

A Runaway Heiress
Lady Christina Delafield was as bold as she was beautiful. When her overbearing grandfather threatened to tame her in a Swiss finishing school, Christina stowed away on the first ship leaving London harbor, determined to make her own way in life. But the mysterious captain of the Dragon's Lair was a seductive reason to relinquish her independence–and embrace desire.

A Gentleman Pirate
Drexell Cain had lived for four years as the merciless Black Dragon, the scourge of the seas. Bent on rescuing his brother from the British Navy, Drex would do anything to return him to his wife and son in Louisiana–even kidnap the Lord Admiral's granddaughter for ransom. A lovely blonde stowaway was an unexpected complication, until he discovered her real identity–and her passionate claim on his lonely heart.

Chapter One
1813

"What do you mean, blackmailing Manchester is out of the question? The old bastard doesn't have a single vice?" Drexell Cain demanded, fists clenched as he leaned across the warped surface of the pub's battered table.

Within the seedy inn's common room, raucous laughter exploded and drunken singing abounded. The smell of old liquor lingered. His friend, Gregory Bryce, Viscount Monroe, dressed in a fine coat of Devonshire brown, looked as out of place rubbing elbows with the dockside scum as the Prince Regent would.

Greg shook his head. "Not one sin, my friend."

"Damn!" Drex pounded a fist into the table. "I'd hoped he was following Melville's lead and using the Admiralty's money to speculate for his own profit."

"Why should he? Manchester is nearly as wealthy as the Admiralty's treasury."

"The old bugger can't be perfect," Drex insisted. "Isn't he sampling the goods in any bedroom but his own? What about gambling debts?" He raked a tense hand through his hair. "Did you check at White's and Watier's?"

"I've come as close to the man as I can without moving in like some spinster aunt. He doesn't indulge in tête-à-têtes or drink. He even runs with the tediously dull crowd at Boodle's."

"Sounds like a damned saint." Drex swore.

"Indeed, our Lord of the Admiralty appears the utmost in devoted family men. He is deeply involved in his granddaughter's life and attends services at Mayfair Chapel every Sunday."

"No man is without at least one weakness. He must have a flaw of some sort..." Drex pressed on, his voice urgent.

"I found nothing, nor did the detective we hired," Greg insisted. "Drex, you must try to free Ryan in other ways or you will get yourself killed. How do you know he is still alive? It's been four years. The conditions in the Royal Navy—"

"Are deplorable. I know." Drex grimaced. "But damn it, Ryan is my twin, my only family and my responsibility."

"He chose a life at sea."

"He didn't choose life in the Royal Navy," Drex bit out. "True, he wouldn't be at the whim of the Admiralty if he hadn't run off to seek adventure. I fully intend to make Ryan see that he has obligations, a wife and son who need him. I won't make excuses for him, but he deserves his freedom."

Greg sighed. "Very well. What other brilliant suggestions do you have? Blackmail is out of the question."

Drex swallowed a lump of anger and thumped his fingers against the table. "What about the signet ring I showed you? Were you able to find out who my scoundrel of a father is?"

Greg nodded, then paused. "The Earl of Ashmont."

"He sounds like a man of consequence, then." Even if he only used his position to impregnate his upstairs maid and cast her into the squalor of London's streets. But Ryan's plight insisted he ignore the fury and resentment pounding in Drex's veins. "Perhaps he can work with Manchester's office to—"

"Drex, he is not well. He's spent the last twenty years holed up in his country house in Devonshire and does not have the political connections needed. But I spoke with him—"

"He knows someone who can help?"

"Damnation, Drex, no. I am telling you that he has been searching for you and Ryan for fifteen years. He knew nothing about you until he received your mother's diary by post shortly before she died."

Drex spotted a man with a ragged beard on his mean face staring intently two tables down and lowered his voice. "You told him my name, my identity?"

"No, of course not. But the man wants you in his life."

Drex suppressed a surge of icy rage. "I've had no use for him in twenty-eight years. If he can't help me with Ryan's release, I have no use for him now."

"If that is truly your sentiment, the only other suggestion I have is diplomacy. Perhaps it will prove fruitful if you try again."

"Like hell." Drex gripped his mug of ale in white-knuckled fingers. "President Madison spares little concern for Ryan and the other Americans the Royal Navy has impressed. He's more intent on creating peace, even if it's false. Besides, the British Admiralty simply thinks they've reclaimed their own."

Greg winced. "Technically, Drex, you and Ryan are their own, being London born. The Admiralty doesn't care how long you've lived in America. To them, you're English citizens."

Drex took a sip of flat ale. "Another reason Madison's administration was reluctant to get involved."

"Indeed, but what other options do you have?" Greg leaned in, his voice dropping. "You haven't found Ryan by traipsing the seas in the guise of the Black Dragon, as you'd hoped."

Drex nodded gravely before adopting a rueful grin. "But more than a few of His Majesty's ships have met a watery grave. A sunken warship is one that can't impress more Americans."

Greg raised a pale brow. "With that outlook, it's no wonder you have a huge bounty on your head. God, for five thousand pounds, I might be tempted to turn you in myself." Greg laughed. "Then again, if you were caught and hung, Chantal would murder me for allowing that to happen."

With a hollow laugh overshadowed by drunken revelry, Drex scanned the crowded room absently, trying to erase the guilt that stung from his failure. He hadn't returned Ryan to his wife, Chantal, as he'd promised. Closing his eyes, Drex rubbed his aching forehead, mentally scrutinizing other solutions. Surrender was unthinkable, defeat unacceptable. He would find Ryan, alive, and force his brother to learn responsibility. Or he'd die trying.

Shaking the dismal thought away, he glanced across the poorly-lit tavern. A burly hunk of a man slid his beefy arm around a serving wench. The slender girl swatted him and danced away. Watching the two, an outrageous idea jolted Drex.

He tossed it around, examining it from every angle. It was easy, almost flawless—and too good to pass up.

"What is his granddaughter's name?" he asked suddenly.

Greg swallowed from his cup, prolonging Drex's suspense. "Lady Christina Delafield."

"What do you know of her?" Drex prompted impatiently.

Greg grinned. "Manchester may control the Admiralty with an iron fist, but that hoyden has proven unruly since her nursery days. Impulsive through and through. Haughty as only a woman born to extreme privilege can be. A beauty, yes, but her grandparents, who have raised the chit, can scarcely control her. Why do you ask?"

Through the smoky air, Drex leaned closer, his voice dropping to a whisper. "Because if I can't hold a scandal over his head, I can hold his granddaughter hostage. When he releases my brother, I'll let the girl go."

"Have you gone mad?" Greg's brown eyes grew impossibly wide. "You cannot mean to add abduction to your crimes. You're wanted for espionage, thievery, illegal trade, and if they catch you, you can tack on treason, too. Perhaps it's time to quit."

"Quit? Not yet. This is my last chance to make the Admiralty meet my demands. All I have to do is exploit Manchester's weakness, his granddaughter." Sitting back, Drex sipped his ale. "After that, I'll gladly retire the Black Dragon and leave my criminal life."

"That is absurd!" Greg insisted, tossing his hands up in emphasis. "You cannot kidnap the girl."

Drex smiled, his grin deceptively pleasant. "Of course I can...with your help."

"Oh, no." Greg shook his head adamantly. "Absolutely not. You saved my life once, and though we've been friends for ten years, I am not willing to dig myself a grave for you. I've already arranged for you to meet an arms dealer and secured papers for you to dock here in London. Nor did I mind spying on Manchester, but I won't assist you in anything this devious. You'll ruin her for polite society and any sort of marriage."

"If I don't, and Ryan is still alive, he will die and Rory will grow up without a father, as Ryan and I did. I can't break my promise to Chantal." Dragging in a deep breath, Drex reached for his mug and offered, "Look, I'll make it easy for you. You know her, right?"

"Yes, through Manchester, of course. And were she to disappear, she could—"

"I'll make certain she can't point the finger at you," Drex assured. "Can you think of a social event where you plan to see her?"

"Manchester has decided to cut her season short, which can only mean she has done something beyond the pale, and will send her to a ladies' school in Switzerland."

"A ladies' school?"

Greg smiled. "I told you, she is quite a hellion. Circumspect is the last word anyone would use to describe her behavior."

Drex clenched his fists anxiously. "When does she leave?"

"Next week."

"Does Manchester have any upcoming social engagements she might attend?"

Greg paused. "Tomorrow night. His political crony, Lord Hartford, will host a ball. But—"

"Perfect. Tomorrow night it is."

"Drex, no. You will undoubtedly scare the poor girl. Lady Christina is high-spirited, I grant you, but far too sheltered for your—"

"I promise, I'll be gentle." Drex smiled mischievously.

Greg snorted in disbelief. "And I'm Henry the Eighth."

"I won't touch the girl."

"That is irrelevant. Everyone will believe you did."

"Lady Christina and whichever husband Manchester chooses for her will know the truth."

A long sigh signaled Greg's defeat. "I let you talk me into the most outrageous things." He turned and shouted, "Another ale!"

****

The short, gruff man tossed a scowl over his shoulder. "When did ye say you made this appointment with the cap'n?"

"Several days ago," Christina answered, calling on the acting skills she'd last used two nights past when she made her bow on the London stage. Beneath her cloak, she adjusted the tight collar of her carriage dress and pulled on the bishop sleeves clutching her wrists.

"And it's personal, ye say?" the man prompted, frowning.

"Quite."

He shrugged. "Watch yer step," he advised from the dark bowels of the companionway. "It's hard to see these here footholds when the sun's goin' down."

Christina held in a sigh of frustration. Clearly, this man did not understand the urgency of her situation. In his defense, no one had ever threatened him with Swiss finishing school, where girls literally disappeared from polite society for years. She shuddered. He, a free-roaming sailor, had never been denied the opportunity to experience life. And she would not allow her grandparents to prevent her from experiencing hers. Aunt Mary awaited in the Bahamas and had offered to teach Christina all about her business.

The odd little man glanced over his shoulder. Anxiously, she gestured for him to go ahead. "Go on. I'm following."

He trudged on, mumbling incoherently.

She continued to trail the narrow-backed man down the cramped companionway, her nose wrinkling from the stench of the Thames that permeated the ship's damp wood.

As she'd paid a lad working the docks to discover, this ship was the only one leaving for Grand Bahama. She'd hidden since last night in a longboat beneath a greasy tarp slathered in animal fat and vowed to sail with this tub. Although Grandfather would probably never think to search for her among London's seedy docks aboard a merchant ship bound for the Bahamas, she knew better than to underestimate him by waiting for a more optimal means of escape.

Christina's shipboard guide halted at the end of a hallway, bringing her out of her reverie and back to the present. He knocked on the door before him.

"Who is it?" a deep voice, sharp with impatience, barked from behind the closed door.

His tone pierced Christina with a needle of doubt. Would he refuse her? Pulling the collar of her cloak up to cover cold ears, she lifted her chin. She couldn't let him turn her away. Her future depended on convincing the captain to accept her as a passenger. Otherwise, years of a cold Swiss castle's walls awaited. All because she'd spent a few trifling hours acting on a London stage!

"Cap'n, it's me, Hancock."

"I figured as much. What is it?"

"There's a woman here. Says she's got business with ye."

"If I'd wanted a woman's business, I would have had one last night."

Christina gasped. The man had intimated she was a—

"Not that type of woman, Cap'n." Hancock cleared his throat. "A lady."

"That variety of female I have no use for," he said in a hard-edged tone. "Get her ashore now. We sail within the hour."

His words plummeted to the bottom of her stomach, along with her heart. She had to persuade him, had to stay on board. If she failed, her grandfather would ensure she surrendered her freedom indefinitely and never saw Aunt Mary again.

Hancock nodded. "Aye, aye, Cap'n."

He faced her, his back pushed against the door, as if looking to add mettle to his spine. His puffy, wind-worn face clearly bore reluctance. "Ye heard the cap'n, miss."

Reining in her panic, Christina stole a glance at the warped wooden door. He didn't have time for her? Well, she'd insist that he make time.

A plan forming, Christina nodded tragically, eyes cast downward. "I understand."

Hancock frowned suspiciously.

Ignoring that, Christina stepped aside. "Please, lead the way. It's so dark, I shall certainly trip without your help."

Hancock shrugged, then took the lead. "Follow me."

She smiled before he turned to the ladder-like stairs.

Hancock stepped forward; Christina drew in a quick breath and whirled to face the captain's door, white-gloved fingers clutching her valise. She clasped the cold latch and lifted. The door opened with a quiet click. She dashed inside.

The captain's naked back, golden and muscle-hardened, filled her vision. She stifled a gasp at the snarling black and green dragon tattoo dominating one shoulder blade. Its open mouth breathed fire across the width of his back, to his other shoulder. The curling tail wound around a powerful biceps.

She couldn't move, could not tear her eyes away. A tattoo? Dear God, what kind of a barbarian would have that arrogant monster permanently embedded into his flesh?

One without the worries or scruples of a gentleman.

Uncertainty assailed her. This man was the antithesis of all she'd known, spawned from an opposite end of the Earth. She knew nothing about his less-than-civilized world. Would she survive long enough to see Aunt Mary in Grand Bahama? Trembling, she shoved the dismal thought aside and glanced about his cabin.

An exotic, Oriental aura dominated the space, which looked half the size of her dressing room. A burning taper filled the room with a pungent musk. Her shocked gaze fixed on the dramatic austerity of the black decor, relieved only by the pale wooden walls. An ebony and emerald silk coverlet on his bunk boasted the same scaled symbol of fire and power as his shoulder.

He reached for his shirt and pulled it on, concealing the intimidating dragon from her view. She swallowed in relief.

Feet planted apart, broad shoulders filling his black shirt, he tucked the cotton garment into skin-tight, biscuit-colored breeches. "I told you I didn't want to see you."

Startled by his acknowledgment, she stammered, "But I must speak with you. Please. Five minutes."

He whirled to face her. The sight rooted her in place.

A scrap of black silk stretched along the upper part of his square face, from brows to the bridge of his nose. She shivered. Only one type of man wore a mask: the dangerous kind.

The sight of his hard, bearded jaw arrested her next. A wall of power surged toward her as he stepped closer. Christina could not decide if she should attribute the feeling to the foreboding impression he made with black shirt, black mask, black beard, black eyes...or the displeasure thundering across the hard angles of his face. Then again, perhaps the sleek ebony length of his hair grazing his mammoth shoulders and the golden ring dangling from his left ear roused her unease. Either way, he was no one to trifle with; he'd made that abundantly clear without a word.

"W—why do you wear the...mask?" she stammered. "Oh, my... You hide your identity."

"Hmm. Perceptive." His low quip cut and didn't invite further conversation. But she could not give up and return home. Life in Switzerland was much more abhorrent. And cold.

Hancock burst through the door. "Cap'n, I'm sorry. The vixen tricked me." He turned to her, his look less than friendly. "Come on. The cap'n wants ye gone."

A crooked smile curved the captain's mouth as he waved the man away. Christina did not find his expression comforting.

"No need," he assured, his gaze shifting to regard her. "I'll handle her. Dismissed."

The little man glanced from her to the captain, then back again, smiling now. "Aye."

Hancock closed the door behind them, leaving them alone. In the ensuing silence of the small cabin, the captain scanned her with a thorough gaze.

She crossed protective arms across her chest and buried her apprehension. "I came to make you a proposition, Captain."

"A proposition?" His already suggestive tone dropped to a purr that set her instincts on full alarm. He leaned his hip indolently against the small cherry-wood desk bolted into the cabin's wooden floor. "Well, now you do have my attention."

Christina gasped. The cur actually had the nerve to smile! She trembled, and he grinned like a well-fed cat.

They stood on opposite ends of the minuscule cabin—three steps from each other. The captain pushed away from the desk; his stride ate up one of the precious steps separating them. With her back at the door, Christina had nowhere to retreat.

She struggled for her next breath. The scents of salt, incense and man filled her nose. She forced herself to hold his stare, even as a tingling awareness of the captain rose inside her.

"I am talking about a business proposal," she corrected. "And I will thank you to stop leering at me."

An infuriatingly insolent grin lifted the corners of his mouth. "Don't thank me; it won't happen."

He stepped closer. Closer still—only a breath away, a breath nearly shared. His gaze Dear Lord, was he going to touch her?

touched her face. The massive breadth of his chest rose a mere inch from hers. His presence swirled around her like a gust of hot wind. She found her gaze trapped deep in the intensity of his dark eyes.

"If you don't wish to be leered at, don't wander where you aren't welcome." His breath fanned across her cheek as he lifted a hand toward her.

About The Author

Shayla Black (aka Shelley Bradley) is the NEW YORK TIMES bestselling author of over 30 sizzling contemporary, erotic, paranormal, and historical romances for multiple print and electronic publishers. She lives in Texas with her husband, munchkin, and one very spoiled cat. In her "free" time, she enjoys reality TV, reading and listening to an eclectic blend of music.

Shayla has won or placed in over a dozen writing contests, including Passionate Ink's Passionate Plume, Colorado Romance Writers Award of Excellence, and the National Reader's Choice Awards. Romantic Times has awarded her Top Picks, a KISS Hero Award and a nomination for Best Erotic Romance.

A writing risk-taker, Shayla enjoys tackling writing challenges with every book.

Steamy historical romances coming soon from Shayla Black
writing as Shelley Bradley:
STRICTLY SEDUCTION
STRICTLY FORBIDDEN

The Brothers in Arms series
HIS LADY BRIDE
HIS STOLEN BRIDE
HIS REBEL BRIDE

Available now:
THE LADY AND THE DRAGON

Made in the USA
Lexington, KY
16 September 2011